Praise

'Another warm-hearted and superbly researched historical romance from an author whose popularity is rapidly growing'
— *Bolton Evening News*

'Judith writes with warmth and affection for her Black Country setting and soap-opera characters, but her great gift is her readability'
— *Sunday Independent, Plymouth*

'Believable characters combined with well-crafted writing ensure the continued success of this established author'
— *Telegraph & Argus, Bradford*

'A well-researched novel . . . packed full of quirks of character which intrigue the reader to read avidly to the end'
— *Evening News, Worcester*

Also by the same author

The Stallion Man
Sisters and Brothers
To Everything a Season
Birds in a Gilded Cage
The Imagination of the Heart
Tiger Lilies
Mirabelle
Minerva Lane

Pride of Place

Judith Glover

CORONET BOOKS
Hodder and Stoughton

First published in Great Britain in 1995
by Hodder and Stoughton
A division of Hodder Headline PLC

A Coronet paperback

10 9 8 7 6 5 4 3 2 1

A CIP catalogue record for this title is available
from the British Library

ISBN 0 340 66598 X

Typeset by Palimpsest Book Production Limited,
Polmont, Stirlingshire
Printed and bound in Great Britain by
Cox and Wyman Ltd, Reading, Berkshire

Hodder and Stoughton
A division of Hodder Headline PLC
338 Euston Road
London NW1 3BH

Pride of Place

Larret Fitzgerald had eyes for only one woman that
evening of the party celebrating his engagement. Not
Sybil Parrish his fiancée, her cheeks already flushed from
drinking too much champagne and her high, little-girl
laugh full of edgy excitement; no, not Sybil. It was her
half-sister Vanessa whom he watched, and wanted.

Occasionally Vanessa would glance across the smoke-
wreathed, crowded room in his direction, and smile
that wonderful sweet smile of hers, so innocent, so
unconsciously seductive; and then she would look away
again as though, after all, she hadn't really noticed him
enough to wonder why their eyes kept meeting.

In this, however, Larret had been wrong. Ever since
arriving an hour ago at the Victoria Hotel, where a
private suite had been taken for the evening's celebration,
Vanessa Antrobus had been aware of the handsome young
architect's attention, and it embarrassed her. She liked
Larret Fitzgerald – what she knew of him – and was
genuinely pleased that her half-sister Sybil had made
such a catch; but just now she would prefer that he paid
more regard to his fiancée, and rather less to herself, even
though it was flattering in an awkward sort of way to be
stared at with quite such admiration.

Larret had a habit of staring like that, Vanessa had
noticed. She secretly thought him a bit of a lady-killer,

though her husband Roland Antrobus dismissed him as just a male flirt in love with his own Irish charm. Roland could be quite scathing about people – spiteful, almost – but in this Vanessa was inclined to agree with him, that Larret Fitzgerald *was* a flirt.

She glanced back over her shoulder. Between the shifting, animated faces of the other guests she could see Larret and Sybil together, arms lovingly entwined, talking to another couple; but even as she watched, his glance moved beyond them to seek her out again, and self-consciously she found herself wondering suddenly what sort of lover he would be.

'Darling, I really think you should go and be polite to the Parrishes.' Her husband's voice, raised above the syncopated rhythm of the jazz trio, brought her back. 'We can't ignore them the entire evening, you know.'

'I suppose not. I'll go across in just a while.' She reached up to brush a speck of something from the black satin lapel of Roland's dinner jacket, the chandelier lights catching the fire of an antique rose-cut diamond on her left hand. Roland had bought her that ring on their own engagement two years ago in 1925; now it was partnered by the plain gold wedding band he'd placed upon her finger twelve months later.

'In any case, I waved hello to them as we came in,' she added as excuse. 'Mother won't think it rude of me that I didn't join them straight away. They wouldn't expect it, not this evening, not when they've got Sybil to fuss over.'

As she spoke Vanessa glanced automatically towards a middle-aged couple seated inside the arch of a window alcove. Even from this distance she could see the nervousness in her mother's face from the strain of trying to humour the bald-headed man beside her, Vanessa's stepfather, Ernest Parrish, and the peevish sourness of Mr Parrish's expression fixed in permanent irritation.

'Actually, I *will* go and have a word with Mother,' Vanessa went on suddenly, finishing off the cocktail she'd been drinking. 'I'll catch her while she's unoccupied – will you come?'

'Not at the moment,' Roland answered. 'A little later, perhaps.'

He took his wife's empty glass and put it down, watching as she made her way between the noisy groups of guests, her small neat head with its shining bobbed helmet of hair held so gracefully erect on the slender stem of her neck. He still found himself astonished that he'd made such an extraordinarily beautiful acquisition when he married her, even though the union had caused raised eyebrows and some snide remarks from those who'd had him marked down at almost forty as a confirmed bachelor. Now they were all too busy telling him what a remarkably lucky beggar he was. If they did but know . . .

Vanessa saw her mother's faded, pretty features break into a look of relief as she approached the alcove table.

'Hello, Mother dear.' She bent to kiss the air beside the offered cheek, her face just brushing the dry, soft skin. 'Good evening, Father.' A polite smile for Ernest Parrish, who returned it with a nod through the blue cloud of his cigarette smoke. 'How are you both?'

'Your mother's complaining of a headache from this dratted music,' said Mr Parrish tersely.

'Oh, no, not really, Ernest, I only remarked it seemed a weeny bit loud—' Mrs Parrish hastened to appease him, looking at him quickly in her timid, fearful way. 'I'm sure

3

it's very nice, very modern. It's what Sybil wanted for her party.'

Mr Parrish drew on his cigarette. 'And how are things with you these days, my girl?' he asked Vanessa. 'A pity you can't visit your mother more often to let her know how you are. She worries, you know.'

'Yes. I'm sorry. It's a matter of finding the time.' Not strictly true, but then it wouldn't be polite to tell the truth, that she visited the house at Tettenhall Green so seldom because she hated the memories the place contained.

'Our Sybil's as bad,' Mr Parrish went on, his thin mouth tightening under the waxed moustache. 'We've hardly heard a word from her since she took herself off to work at that gown-shop in Birmingham. Too busy swanning around, I suppose, like you.'

Vanessa let the criticism pass. She had long ago trained herself not to respond to her stepfather's barbs, and since leaving home almost four years ago when she was eighteen, she had matured enough not to let his dislike hurt her as it had all through her childhood. There were some things she couldn't bring herself to forgive him for – destroying all the evidence of her own father's existence so that she'd never seen so much as a photograph, for instance – but it was easier to understand now why he had always resented her presence, why he'd always pushed her into the background in favour of his own child, her half-sister Sybil.

'Sybil's looking very glamorous this evening, isn't she,' she said, and at once Mr Parrish's expression softened a little. 'She and Larret are so well-matched.'

'Yes, they make a handsome young pair.' His eyes sought out his daughter, now engaged in an energetic Charleston, the boyish figure in its bugle-beaded frock

4

and bandeau claiming everyone's applauding attention. 'Marriage will do her good, quieten her down a bit,' he added, leaning forward to stub out his cigarette.

'Oh, how nice, here's Mr Fitzgerald coming to join us—' Mrs Parrish brightened nervously, touching a hand to her hair as she caught the young man just making his way towards their table.

Vanessa glanced round.

'If you'll excuse me, I'd better go back and find Roland again,' she said rather too quickly, 'you don't mind, do you, Mother? Only it's awkward for him, not knowing anyone here.'

'I hope your husband will condescend to come and speak to us before the end of the evening,' said Ernest Parrish as she was turning to move away. 'You'd best remind him of his manners, I think. He's an invited guest, after all, and it's me that's paying for his entertainment.'

Vanessa felt indignation stain her cheeks. She exchanged a look with her mother. Then, mastering herself, she responded, 'Of course,' and left it at that; but her stepfather's boorishness had stung her. As she went past Larret Fitzgerald she gave the young man no more than the briefest of smiles, leaving him staring after her in disconcertion.

Later, towards eleven o'clock when she and Roland had made their farewells and left the party, Vanessa said suddenly and rather vehemently as she was getting into the car, 'I wish we didn't live in Wolverhampton. I wish we lived a hundred miles away.'

Her husband didn't answer. He had found the whole evening a strain, having to mix with a crowd of young and slightly drunken people, none of whom he knew or wished to know, having to endure their inanely artificial chatter; worse, having to make himself polite to that wretchedly unlikeable little man Ernest Parrish.

He put the Morris Cowley into gear and started away, the acetylene headlamps cutting a wedge of yellow light through the darkness of the sidestreet. In Queen Square there was still a number of people about, coming from the pubs to catch a last trolley-bus home; but once beyond Chapel Ash and into Compton Road the only signs of life were the illuminated windows of houses behind high laurel hedges, and the occasional figure strolling along the pavement with a dog.

Compton Road was one of the better-class areas of Wolverhampton. At its top end was the Grammar School where Roland Antrobus had been educated, and at the other, running into countryside, the handsome private residence of Compton Hall. The Antrobus's house lay somewhere in between and was a fairly substantial Victorian villa in the Gothic style which had earlier belonged to Roland's parents, now both deceased. He had been their only child, born late in the marriage, and had inherited not only the house but a substantial income from his father's prudent investments on the Stock Market.

Without the obligation to work for a living, Roland Antrobus had been in the happy position of choosing to indulge his interest in the Arts, and after military service during the Great War he had opened a gallery in premises in the town centre, exhibiting works by Midland painters, potters and sculptors. He was a man with an eye for proficiency and promise; he appreciated talent where he saw it. Consequently he had succeeded by the age of thirty-seven in building for himself and his gallery a reputation second to none in the area.

Turning the Morris Cowley into the gravelled drive of 'Mayville', Roland brought the car to a stop in front of the coach-house doors and switched off the engine.

'Thank God to be home!' he said with some feeling. 'I'm afraid I found this evening a most thoroughly tiresome experience. I'm sorry.'

'I have to admit, so did I,' Vanessa agreed. 'And there's Sybil's wedding still to look forward to – though we *do* have six months' respite.'

Roland groaned. Getting out, he walked round to open the passenger door, putting a hand under her elbow to help her from the car. The sound of their arrival had been heard within the house, for one of the maids was already at the front door.

'Thank you, Iris.' Vanessa gave her a smile as she went up the porch steps and past the neatly-uniformed girl into the hall. 'You needn't wait up any longer – oh, unless you want anything, do you, darling?' she added quickly, turning to Roland who was following behind.

'No, no, you can go to bed now, Iris. I'll see to the locking up myself.'

'Yes, sir. Thank you, sir.' The housemaid dipped a curtsy, and after taking their outdoor clothes, left them to go into the drawing room where a fire was still burning cheerfully against the dampness of the February night.

'Can I get you a nightcap?' Roland went over and poured himself a generous measure of whisky from one of the crystal decanters on a satinwood console-table. 'A small brandy, or something?'

'A brandy would be lovely, thank you, darling.'

Vanessa threw herself gratefully down in one of the

deep armchairs beside the fire and pushed off her shoes, curling her toes like a child against the warmth of the flames. The pale amber glow of the electric wall-lights gave a sheen to her flawless skin, and gilded the smooth silky fairness of her hair. There could be no doubt why Roland Antrobus had married her. He was a man who enjoyed the possession of beautiful things; and to all who saw her Vanessa *was* strikingly beautiful, the epitome of the 1920s ideal with her long, slender, graceful limbs, and slim, small-breasted figure which lent itself so perfectly to the tubular curve-less fashions of the day.

'Thank you, darling,' she said again, reaching to take the glass her husband handed her.

He went and seated himself opposite.

'By the way, I forgot to mention – I've found a new tenant for the flat,' he remarked after a moment, referring to the second-floor apartment above the Antrobus Gallery.

'Anyone I know?' Vanessa took a sip of brandy. She had particular reason to be interested, since the flat held such romantic memories: for almost eighteen months after packing her bags and leaving her stepfather's house, she had rented the place from Roland – at that time her landlord – and so began an acquaintance which later had ripened into love and the lifetime's commitment of marriage.

'No, I don't think you'll know the chap,' he answered. 'His name's Michael Wright. Matter of fact, he's teaching at the School of Art and Design. Only started there last term. I may be able to sell one or two of the etchings he's brought in for me to look at – they're very good, very spare and clean, rather in the style of Charles Meryon.'

Vanessa smothered a small yawn with her hand. 'I

thought Charles Meryon only did architectural subjects.'

'That's right. He did. Clever girl for remembering.' Roland was pleased by his young wife's intelligent observation. 'Meryon's reputation rests on a small number of plates he did of the streets and churches of Paris—' He launched into a dissertation which, despite her interest, Vanessa felt a little too tired to follow; then concluded, 'This fellow who's coming into the flat is doing a series on Wolverhampton architecture – not churches so much, but commercial buildings, the Grand Theatre, the Market Hall, that sort of thing.'

Vanessa yawned again. The brandy combined with the lateness of the hour and the warmth from the fire was starting to make her feel sleepy.

'What's your opinion of Larret Fitzgerald?' she heard herself enquire suddenly. The question startled her. What on earth brought Larret into her mind just then? 'As an architect, I mean,' she added awkwardly.

'I don't know that I have an opinion.' Roland looked faintly non-plussed. 'I've never seen any of his work. Why do you ask, darling?'

'Oh . . . just mild interest, since we were speaking of architecture.' She passed the subject off.

'I will tell you one thing—' Finishing his whisky, her husband got from his chair. 'I can't see him and Sybil making a go of things. In fact it wouldn't surprise me if that engagement weren't to be called off. Save us having to attend the ghastly wedding, at any rate.'

'Why should it be called off? Sybil adores him!'

'Sybil's an emotional mayfly. An *immature* emotional mayfly. And Mr Fitzgerald simply happens to be the latest handsome novelty.'

9

'Now, darling, that's not fair—' Bending to pick up her discarded shoes, Vanessa rose in turn and handed him her glass. 'They've known one another for at least a year. And I don't think my stepfather would have consented to the engagement if he suspected Larret was just another of Sybil's pashes.'

'Sybil can twist your stepfather round one scarlet-painted finger,' said Roland unpleasantly, going and putting their empty glasses on the decanter tray. 'If Daddy's little sweetie wants a thing badly enough, Daddy's little sweetie *has* to have it. A frock or a fiancé, what's the difference. Anyway, why are we discussing Sybil—'

Suddenly irritable, he took up the poker and began prodding at the coals, making the fire safe before adjusting the guard.

Tactfully, Vanessa let the matter drop. 'Look at the time – I think I'll be off to bed now. Will you be long?'

'I might have another whisky before I lock up. Don't stay awake for me.' Straightening, Roland kissed her lightly on the forehead. 'Night, darling. Sleep tight.'

It was a charade they went through at the end of every evening, this 'will you be long' and 'don't stay awake' and 'sleep tight'. Vanessa occasionally wondered why they bothered to keep it up. It would be easier and more honest simply to wish one another good-night and go to separate beds, in separate rooms; except Roland insisted they must share the same double bed for the sake of appearances – no, not appearances, so much as for the sake of *pride*. As long as he and Vanessa still slept together they could both go on pretending there was nothing amiss with a marriage which after twelve months of loving intimacy had yet to be consummated.

When one was young and very inexperienced in affairs of life, as Vanessa was, twelve months was a long time to spend with one other person. She was growing accustomed now to the rather unusual relationship shared with her husband. She loved him very much, very dearly. These days it no longer troubled her quite so much that he demanded nothing of her in the way of sexual intimacy.

At first, naturally, the fact that she didn't seem able to arouse him properly had used to upset her, used to make her feel terribly guilty of failing him somehow, even though the failure was his and not her own. Before she'd married Roland, Vanessa had been proud of her virginity; but to be somebody's wife and *still* a virgin struck her as being a matter almost for shame, as though she were not a 'real' woman.

She could have sought medical advice, but that would have been to admit her own inadequacy. She was very naive about sexual congress. Her only tuition had been the sniggering secrets whispered by more knowledgeable schoolchums, and later, the occasional half-embarrassed references made by women friends. She had longed to ask questions, discover the answers, satisfy her aching curiosity; but no one talked much about sex. It simply wasn't considered the done thing, not by 'nice' girls.

And so she continued in ignorance, knowing there must be more to the intimate side of marriage than merely kisses and closeness and sleeping in the same bed together; yet not knowing *what*, and being too inhibited to ask. It was not the ideal all-consuming passionate relationship of which she used to dream, but it held kindness, and loving affection, and security, and with that Vanessa learned to be content.

The large Art Deco-decorated bedroom felt chilly after

the warmth downstairs. She undressed quickly, laying her clothes over the back of a chair for one of the housemaids to hang away in the morning. From choice, she didn't have a personal maid; young Iris normally saw to her wardrobe.

Once ready for bed, she climbed between the sheets and lay for a while thinking back over this evening, waiting for the blessed unconsciousness of sleep to claim her. Her hand touched her breast under the silk of the pyjamas Roland liked her to wear. She thought about Larret Fitzgerald for a second, then turned onto her side and shut him from her mind.

2

The Welsh county of Pembrokeshire had always held a particular attraction for the English – so much so that the county was known as 'little England beyond Wales'. Its Welshness had become diluted. In its dramatic coastal scenery, its patchwork landscape, its sturdy little villages, there was more than a look of Devon or of Cornwall; and even its accent held something of the soft West Country burr.

Pembrokeshire people were an interesting mixture, an amalgam of Norman–French and Norse as well as English and Celt, enriched in centuries past by the hotter blood of Mediterranean mariners. It was a mixture which produced poets and dreamers and lovers.

Vanessa's father, Owen James, had been a Pembroke man. His home was the small fishing village of Amroth, along the coast from Tenby, where the Jameses had been settled for generations. In the 1890s Vanessa's grandmother had opened a boarding-house, and among the families who came each year to spend their fortnight's holiday was one from Wolverhampton, with a young unmarried daughter named Florence.

Owen James and Florence fell in love. For three idyllic summers the good-looking Welshman courted the lovely fair-haired English girl, stealing her away for rides through the high-hedged lanes, or walking with her on the sands at sunset. When the holidays were over and Florence had returned to Wolverhampton, her lover kept alive their tender romance with his poetry – not clumsy bumpkin doggerel, but lyrics of disturbing mystic imagery. Young Owen James had talent. Though a fisherman by occupation, at the age of twenty-three he'd already published a volume of his verse, and on the strength of that single collection, promised to be one of the most gifted poets of his generation.

Alas, Florence's father was opposed to their betrothal. She was already 'intended' by the family for another man, her second cousin Ernest Parrish. Ernest was a solicitor, very respectable. Ernest was sound and solid, no nonsense there. Ernest had his own house, a nice neat property at Tettenhall Green, just waiting for a little wife to make it home.

Florence didn't want her cousin Ernest Parrish. He was as dull as ditchwater, and small-minded with it. She wanted Owen James, Owen's passion and romance and laughter, and she didn't care a hoot where they lived, palace or pigsty, as long as they could be together. Let Ernest keep his nice neat property and his solid, respectable life. Florence's heart had been stolen away by a poet, a handsome young man with the sea in his eyes and the wind in his hair; she had fallen in love with the sound of his voice, with his gift to change words into music so glorious it conjured the stars from the sky.

Compared to all this, cousin Ernest had nothing to offer.

In the spring of 1904, Florence and Owen eloped. They were married by special licence, and set up home in a harbourside cottage at Tenby, where their life together was one of blissfully contented domesticity. In September

14

the following year, their daughter Vanessa was born, and in an effort at reconciliation with her parents Florence took the baby back to Wolverhampton.

Had she been an unmarried mother bringing home her bastard child, the reception could hardly have been frostier. Only Ernest Parrish, surprisingly, had a civil word to say to her; though like the rest of the family, he treated her elopement as something only slightly short of kidnap, and her marriage as an act of gross seduction.

She stayed a week, no more, hating their narrowness, their enmity for Owen, and took her baby back to Wales determined she would never again return to Wolverhampton.

Fate, unfortunately, had other plans for Florence.

Her husband – popularised by admiring critics as the Fisher Poet – was working aboard a smack with the Tenby fleet. On a freezing, squally, winter's day in the New Year of 1906, the boats encountered foul weather in the open seas beyond Carmarthen Bay, and with their decks awash and a force nine gale battering them about, they'd turned and made a run of it for home. Conditions were atrocious. Caught broadside on by icy waves that thundered down in wind-whipped sheets of water, one of the smacks capsized. Despite the efforts of their mates, not a single member of the crew survived.

It was days before the sea gave up its drowned, young men to be mourned for the waste of their lives and their talent; and none more than the Fisher Poet.

Florence always said in later years that her own life ended there in the sand and weed and seawrack – the life of the girl who'd been Owen James's wife, who had lain in his strong safe arms and shared the precious gift of his golden love. When he had died, Florence's heart died too, and all there was left was an empty, hollow shell.

Yet she still had Owen's legacy, his child; and although she could perhaps have stayed in Tenby, in the end she'd swallowed her bitterness and for Vanessa's sake went home to Wolverhampton. It was a decision Florence afterwards regretted, but at the time her state of mind was so disturbed, so numbed by the savage agony of grief, that it was a natural reaction to turn to her own family.

Their way of dealing with the situation was to behave as though her marriage to Owen James had never existed. A pity there was a child; but since its presence could not be ignored, it must be tolerated. After a decent interval of time, cousin Ernest asked Florence to become his wife, making it clear that his proposal was an act of charity for which she should be duly grateful. He could have looked elsewhere, he pointed out, but family loyalty constrained him to whitewash over what had gone before, and ignore those errors for which Florence, badly influenced, could not be truly held responsible. She had been foolish; and she'd suffered for it. Ernest was satisfied she would not be so imprudent as to refuse the rehabilitation to decent society which he offered.

Florence did not refuse. She was a widow with a little child to think of, a child for whom she wanted security, a home, an education. There was a price to pay, of course. Ernest Parrish was adamant that his predecessor must be expunged entirely from their lives, permitting not a letter, not a photograph, not a single treasured memento to be kept. He even went so far as to insist Vanessa's name be altered to his own – and contact with the James relations severed.

There was one thing the child's new stepfather could

not order, though: he could not change her blood, nor take from her the gift she had inherited. Once she'd learned to read and write, that gift began to manifest itself in the excellent reports she had from school for English composition; and try as he might with his sarcasm and his sneers to belittle her efforts, Mr Parrish could not stop Vanessa winning prizes for her poems, nor deny her the scholarship which she won at the age of eleven to the High School for Girls, in Wolverhampton.

He took no pride in her achievements. He was a narrow-minded, unimaginative man who regarded his young stepdaughter as a cuckoo in the nest, the unfortunate fruit of his wife's infatuation for another man. He did not treat her cruelly or neglectfully; yet even so, cruelty and neglect Vanessa suffered at his hands in that he gave her neither kindness nor affection.

Perhaps it was this emotional starvation, this lack of a paternal bonding in her childhood, which later would be reflected in her choice of a man so many years her senior as husband.

A Saturday afternoon about three weeks after Sybil Parrish's engagement party, Vanessa was coming down the steps of the central lending library in Wolverhampton when someone called out her name. She paused, looking round. On the opposite pavement Sybil was standing with Larret Fitzgerald.

It was Larret's voice, not Sybil's, she'd heard calling. When she gave a hesitant wave in response, he caught his fiancée by the arm and came dodging between the traffic to cross over, holding on to his brown felt trilby hat with his other hand.

'Hello, Vanessa!' he greeted her warmly. 'Sybil and I are just off to Lyons for tea. Care to join us?'

She glanced at her wristwatch. Roland was expecting her home before five o'clock.

'Oh, don't let us put you out at all,' followed Sybil, plainly put out herself by Larret's behaviour. He might at least have asked *her* if she'd mind, said her tone. 'We don't want to hold you up if you're going somewhere.'

'Actually, I was just on my way to catch the bus,' Vanessa answered awkwardly. 'But it's all right – it doesn't leave until twenty-five past four.'

She tucked her library books beneath her arm, hoping her embarrassment wasn't too obvious from her manner. She'd seen nothing at all of Larret since the party – nor Sybil, come to that – but the young man had been in her thoughts quite a lot in a girlishly romantic sort of way, and meeting him today so unexpectedly had thrown her into a state of some confusion.

'Right, that's settled then. Come on—' He held out an elbow for her to take, his dark blue Irish eyes smiling down at her; and with Sybil at one side and Vanessa, self-consciously, at the other, the three set off through the crowds of Saturday shoppers up Dudley Street towards Queen Square.

Sybil and her fiancé had been to a matinée at the Agricultural Hall Cinema on Snow Hill to see Rudolph Valentino in *The Son of the Sheikh*. It was the last film Valentino had made before his sudden death the previous year at the pinnacle of public adoration, and a couple of ladies sitting in their row, said Larret, were so overcome by the end of the picture they'd both had a fit of hysterics and fainted.

He seemed to find it amusing.

18

'You wouldn't do that sort of thing, would you, Vanessa,' he asked her in Lyons' restaurant while they were waiting for a 'nippy' to come and take their order. 'I'd say you were a girl too much in control of her emotions to throw a scene like that.'

'You think so?' She glanced round the busy tables, wishing he didn't have to stare at her so much, not wanting him to notice her discomfort.

'Oh, Vanessa never shows emotion, do you, darling,' said Sybil nastily, patting into place the kiss curl peeping below the brim of her smart cloche hat and inspecting the result in her handbag mirror. She had very pretty features, with a pert nose and full, sulky lips painted a vivid red like her heroine Clara Bow, the 'It' Girl, whom she liked to think she resembled.

She put the mirror away. 'Vanessa's an absolute iceberg, everyone knows that.'

'Icebergs fascinate me,' said Larret, still looking at Vanessa. His leg brushed hers beneath the table, 'They're such teasing things. Teasing . . . and yet dangerous, wouldn't you say, the way they only show a little of themselves.'

Vanessa was gratefully saved from an answer by the arrival of their waitress; and after they had ordered, she turned the conversation to Sybil, enquiring about her half-sister's job as a junior sales assistant in Rosenshine's Gown Shop at Moseley in Birmingham.

'Oh, that. I've chucked it in,' said Sybil offhandedly. 'I told Mr Rosenshine I couldn't possibly work full-time after I was married, and he said he didn't want me going in part-time unless I could manage it Fridays and Saturdays.'

'And that wouldn't suit?'

19

Sybil looked insulted. 'Fridays and Saturdays? No thank you! Weekends will be the only time I'll have to share with Larry,' she said, giving Larret the casual name by which his acquaintances knew him.

'But you're not getting married till August. What's made you decide to give up your job this early – you've found something else?'

'No. And I'm not looking. In any case, Daddy didn't like me living so far away, you know he didn't. He was always going on about it. I only moved out to Moseley because Larry was there.'

Sybil's eyes went to her fiancé in a little cat-like glance of possessive affection. She and Larret had met in Birmingham at some dance party or other, and after a lot of argument at home, she'd left Wolverhampton to get a job and lodgings nearer to him. It was typically Sybil to behave in such a headstrong manner. But then, her father Ernest Parrish had made her like that with over-indulgence. From infancy she'd had everything which her half-sister Vanessa was denied, and she had grown up selfish and spoiled, demanding whatever she wanted – and getting it, usually.

'So you're living back home again now?' Vanessa asked, with a quick smile of thanks to the waitress re-appearing with their order. 'I didn't know.'

'Well, you wouldn't, would you.' Sybil picked up the teapot and poured. Then, changing the subject, she said, 'We've decided where we're going to spend our honeymoon, haven't we, Larry. We thought the French Riviera might be fun—'

'No, darling, *you* thought the Riviera might be fun,' Larret corrected, lighting himself a cigarette.

'All right, I did.' She passed a cup to Vanessa. 'But

in the end we both liked Paris better. *Madly* romantic, and not half as expensive, considering we'll spend most of the time anyway in bed.'

There was a pause.

'Roland and I went to Paris,' said Vanessa, recalling the slightly disappointing week of her own honeymoon there last spring. 'Not that we saw much of anything, either, since we virtually lived at the Louvre Museum.'

'God, how stuffy. But then, Roland *is* pretty stuffy, isn't he.' Sybil treated her to a sarcastically pitying look. 'Always droning on about boring old pictures and things. I don't know how you can stand it, being married to someone like that.'

'Actually, Sybil, I *enjoy* being married to Roland,' Vanessa answered quietly. Used as she was to her half-sister's bitchiness, even so, it embarrassed her in front of Larret.

'Everybody to their own taste, I suppose.' Sybil handed her fiancé his cup and helped herself to a cigarette from the packet he'd left on the table. 'Though I'm glad *I* don't have to live with him.'

'And he's probably terribly glad he doesn't have to live with *you*, my darling,' Larret told her, reaching to give her a light. 'Mr Antrobus is a gentleman of discernment. He wouldn't have married your sister otherwise.'

The way he said that, only half-humorously, put Sybil in one of her sulky little huffs, and she gave an exaggerated shrug and looked away, blowing the smoke from her mouth.

Vanessa glanced at the restaurant wall-clock.

'Sorry, but I'm afraid I really will have to dash now,' she said, leaving her cup barely touched. 'I don't want to miss my bus home. Thanks so much for the tea –

21

awfully nice to see you both. Perhaps we'll do it again some time?' She pulled on her gloves and got up.

'You're forgetting your books—' Larret reached under the table where she'd put them. As he straightened he looked at the titles, flicking quickly through the one on top, which happened to be W.B. Yeats's *The Wild Swans at Coole*. 'I say, what's this – you enjoy reading poetry?'

Vanessa took the books from him. 'My father was a poet,' she said, 'perhaps it's in the blood.' Then to Sybil, 'Give my best love to Mother, won't you. Tell her I'll try and visit soon.'

She left the restaurant, just in time to catch her bus from the stop in Queen Square; and all the way home she sat thinking of Larret Fitzgerald. In spite of the favouritism always shown to Sybil, Vanessa had never envied her half-sister anything, not the praise, the affection, the toys, the prettier clothes; but she *did* envy her a little now for having a man like Larret engaged to marry her.

The first time she'd met him, she had found him attractive – much more attractive than Roland. Oh, not that Roland was *ugly*. On the contrary, he was really rather distinguished in an aristocratically English sort of way, even if his hair *was* thinning and his waistline a fraction over-generous . . . but of course, Roland had the height to carry that off.

No, Larret's attractiveness lay in his sexuality, the seductiveness of his eyes, the unspoken intimate flattery of his smile. He could be speaking about the weather, and yet be saying something else entirely, just by the way he looked.

She stared at her reflection outlined in the window of the trolley-bus, remembering how their legs had brushed not quite by accident in Lyons restaurant, how his fingertips had touched her wrist when he gave her her books. This ought to stop, you know, she told herself. You're being a silly fool, Vanessa. Don't you see that you're playing his game, feeding his vanity? For God's sake, what can he give you?

When she got home, Roland was waiting. She began to tell him of her afternoon, but he hardly listened to her. He'd had some news which seemed to please him greatly, about a photographic collection he was hoping to exhibit at the Gallery. The collection was the work of a young German woman whom he'd met in London last year.

Vanessa vaguely recalled how enthusiastic her husband had been at the time about this Fräulein von Losch – in fact she had teased him a little for appearing more taken with the artist herself than with her pictures. So it never occurred to her to wonder now why he should be so unusually excited about handling the exhibition. She had other thoughts to preoccupy her.

3

As a child growing up in her stepfather's house at Tettenhall Green, Vanessa had always cherished ambitions to be a poet like her natural father Owen James. By the time she'd reached her teens, however, her sights had been re-set on becoming a writer; and after completing her education at the High School for Girls in 1922, she took a secretarial course in shorthand and typing and applied for a job on a local newspaper, the *Weekly Advertiser*, as a junior reporter.

To begin with, she'd been given the routine coverage of parish council meetings, juvenile court cases, funerals and the like, cutting her teeth as a news writer on 'fillers'. Later, after she'd gained several months' experience and proved her ability, the editor promoted her to 'human interest' stories, which permitted her greater freedom of presentation and style.

Vanessa loved the work. Even though nothing like as glamorously exciting as films and fiction had led her to imagine, nevertheless she found it of enormous interest and reward. For the first time in her young life she felt she was drawing closer to her unknown father, doing something which built a bridge between them both. Often she had the strangest intuition that Owen, wherever he was, knew what she was doing, and was with her; and she wanted so much to do

well, to make him proud, to live up to the talent he'd
bequeathed her.

A close friend at this period was Dulcie Fox, who wrote
women's features for the *Advertiser*. Dulcie was a tall,
willowy brunette in her mid-twenties, still unattached and
likely to remain so, since her career came first and her
private life a long way second. While Vanessa was still at
the *Advertiser* Dulcie had moved onwards and upwards to
Wolverhampton's daily newspaper, the *Express & Star*,
and the women's feature page was taken over by another
brunette, fun-loving and flirty, named Kay Murray, who
also became a good friend.

Marriage to Roland Antrobus in 1926 had spelled the
end of Vanessa's employment on the paper. It was
something she regretted very much, but she'd accepted
that her new role as wife, and mistress of 'Mayville',
would be incompatible with the irregular working hours
of a reporter. Roland was happy, however, for her to
continue writing on a freelance basis, and so for the
past six months Vanessa had been contributing feature
articles to various Midland magazines and newspapers.

For the first time since childhood, she had also started
writing poetry again; though not for publication. Her
poems were something very personal and private, a
way of releasing herself emotionally, of exorcising her
imagination of its febrile dreams. She showed them to no
one but kept them carefully hidden – not because she was
ashamed of them, but because they might perhaps betray
too much tension and longing.

The *Express & Star* had accepted a number of
Vanessa's features; in fact it was Dulcie Fox who'd
suggested, in view of her connection with the Antrobus
Gallery, that she might consider writing a series for them

on local artists. This had led to a second series, about literary figures such as Sir Henry Newbolt, Jerome K. Jerome, and David Christie Murray, natives of the Wolverhampton area.

'You know, I'm surprised you haven't written anything about your own father,' Dulcie commented, the day Vanessa dropped her final article into the newspaper's offices in Queen Street. 'Don't I remember you once telling me he was a poet?'

'Yes, that's right. The Fisher Poet.' Vanessa hitched her knee-length skirt to perch on a corner of Dulcie's desk, there being nowhere else to sit in the cramped little office. 'He wasn't a local man, though. He was Welsh.'

'So what was his connection with Wolverhampton?' Dulcie asked through a cloud of Sobranie cigarette smoke.

'None at all, as far as I can gather. I don't know much about him, to be truthful. He died when I was very small. I couldn't even tell you what he looked like.'

'But there must be family photographs you've seen.'

Vanessa shook her head.

'What, none at all?'

'If there ever were any, my mother never kept them.'

Dulcie examined her in a quizzical manner. 'She loved him, though?'

'Oh, yes, she loved him . . . very much. It was my stepfather, you see. He didn't wish to be reminded of her first marriage, so he forced her to get rid of everything.'

'*Everything*?'

Vanessa glanced away towards the rain-smeared window. 'Yes. Everything. The lot. You don't know my stepfather, Dulcie. He's a very thorough sort of man, to put it charitably. From what my mother's said, he was set

27

on destroying all the evidence of her previous life as Mrs Owen James. That name was absolutely taboo. I never heard it mentioned by him. It was like . . . growing up with a ghost.'

'I think I smell a story,' said Dulcie, tapping her cigarette on an overflowing ashtray and sitting a little straighter in her chair. 'Tell me, darling, have you ever tried to trace your father's background – I mean, tried to *discover* him, find out all the facts, that kind of thing? There must be surviving relatives on his side of the family. You could do us a piece about it?'

'I wouldn't know what to write,' Vanessa responded. 'As I said, apart from what Mother's told me over the years, I know nothing at all about my father. There may well be relatives in Wales . . . but my stepfather severed all connection. He even changed my name from James to Parrish.'

Dulcie made a face. Taking a pencil she pulled a notepad towards her and wrote down the name Owen James. 'What did you say was the *nom de plume* your father used?'

'The Fisher Poet. He earned his living as a fisherman with the Tenby fleet.'

Dulcie noted that and underlined it. Through the frosted glass behind her, people were passing backwards and forwards in constant movement, preparing the *Express & Star* for its first edition of the day. A non-stop clatter of typewriters and ringing of phone bells filled the air, and occasionally an open door brought the warm, oily smell of type-setting machines from the compositors' room.

'What year did he die, do you know?' she continued.

'Yes, it was . . . 1906. I was four months old.'

'Four months? Oh, well, that's even better! No, I mean,

28

it adds just a nice little touch of sentiment, losing your father so very young. How did he—'

'He was drowned at sea.' Vanessa anticipated the question. As a reporter on the *Advertiser* she'd had to ask many such questions herself in pursuit of a story. 'He was only twenty-five. He and my mother had been married less than two years. Sad, really. Especially after they'd had to elope because my grandfather refused them his permission. It caused no end of a furore, I can tell you.'

Dulcie's sophisticated features sharpened with interest. She covered several lines of the notepad in shorthand symbols before putting her next question. 'Your mother's family are Wolverhampton people?'

'Yes, Tettenhall Green.'

'Well, there you are, Vanessa – there's your local interest. It will make a *super* article for our women's page! It's got all the right ingredients, drama, romance, tragedy—'

'But I'm not going to write it,' Vanessa said firmly. 'I'm sorry . . . you must understand, I have my mother's feelings to consider.'

'Of course, and I'd expect you to ask her first, darling. It's not the paper's policy to publish sensitive material without permission.'

'*No*, Dulcie. I'm afraid the women's page will have to forgo this particular story, so you can tear up your notes. It's too near home – my stepfather would make life totally unbearable if it ever appeared. He's spent all these years trying to eradicate the past, heaven knows what price my mother would have to suffer if the *Express & Star* publicised the whole affair in banner headlines!'

Professional disappointment was expressed in a shrug of Dulcie's elegantly-clothed shoulders. She stubbed out her cigarette, and immediately fitted another into the long ivory holder she affected.

'A pity. Still, let's not waste it. You could always disguise the bare bones and turn them into something else, you know. There's enough plot there for an absolutely gripping romance if you decided to try your hand at writing a novel, for instance.'

For a moment Vanessa was taken aback by the idea of turning her parents' love story into fiction.

'Oh, you'd be surprised how many authors do it – I mean, fillet the family history,' Dulcie went on, noticing her startled reaction. 'Anyway, my dear, it's a thought, something you might like to consider now marriage has relieved you of the obligation to slave away at a living—'

Just at this point the telephone on the desk started ringing, and Dulcie interrupted herself to answer it. There was a brief exchange of conversation.

'Sorry—' she said, hanging up, 'I've got to dash. I'm needed in subs to look at tomorrow's lay-out.' She rose from her chair. 'Thanks awfully for dropping by with this—' indicating the manila folder containing Vanessa's final article on literary celebrities. 'And think over my little suggestion, darling. It would be a sin to leave such a marvellous plot collecting dust.'

Perhaps Dulcie was right. Perhaps it *would* be a sin for the Fisher Poet's story to remain neglected and virtually forgotten by the world. But it deserved better than being served up as a lightweight romantic novel.

Over the next few days Vanessa gave the subject a

good deal of consideration, and the more she thought about it the more attracted she became by the idea of tracing her father's background and history as a voyage of personal discovery. It was something which had been vaguely in her mind for a long time; but the silence on the subject of her mother's first marriage had been so absolute throughout her childhood that it had conditioned her not to dwell upon her father – rather in the way she'd been taught not to touch the fire, or to speak to strangers.

But would her mother co-operate, she wondered? All these years, Florence Parrish had set a guard upon herself and built a wall around the past, only occasionally – when Vanessa begged her – speaking of Owen James, and then reluctantly. 'It's best if we don't mention him, it will only anger your stepfather.' How many times Vanessa had heard that!

Rather than cause upset, perhaps she ought to ask her questions elsewhere; yes – search out her father's family in Pembrokeshire, and combine the quest with a holiday with Roland. It was time they took a holiday together. Since their honeymoon last spring they'd hardly been away, just a couple of weekends; and the hours Roland devoted to the Gallery, he could well do with a rest and change of scenery.

When she proposed this to him one evening at dinner the following week, however, he appeared curiously resistant. Not about tracing her father's relatives, which he thought would be a capital idea, but about accompanying Vanessa on her 'jaunt'. It really wasn't necessary for him to go as well, he argued; he'd only be kicking his heels and getting bored, and she knew how he *detested* the sea.

31

What about the art galleries and auction rooms, she countered. Wouldn't it be interesting to visit those?

No, not really. He'd much prefer to stay in Wolverhampton and get on with the job of preparing for this German exhibition planned for June.

Greatly disappointed, Vanessa decided to postpone things till the autumn, when Roland's commitments were more flexible. In the meantime, she would begin to plan the research of her father's poetry. She knew there had been a collection, *The Sapphire Shell*, published in 1902, and the county reference library at Pembroke seemed the place to start enquiries.

Before she could settle to this, however, she received a visit from Sybil Parrish.

Sybil so rarely came to 'Mayville' that Vanessa was surprised to get a telephone call one Monday to say her half-sister wanted to see her and was coming over straight away that morning. Sybil had sounded very tense; and when she arrived at half past eleven Vanessa could see how clearly upset and angry she still was.

'I was in Birmingham with Larry yesterday,' Sybil began without preamble, ignoring Vanessa's greeting as the maid showed her into the drawing room and closed the door. 'We were supposed to be going somewhere for tea, but we didn't. He took me for a walk instead.'

She flung herself down in an armchair and crossed her legs, and then immediately uncrossed them, an action which betrayed her irritation. Bitterly she went on, 'I expect you can guess what he wanted to tell me. Well, I hope you're damn' well satisfied.'

'I'd be satisfied if I knew what you were talking about!' Vanessa said, astonished. 'What on earth has got into you, Sybil?'

'My God, you can ask me that! All this time you've been acting as though you hadn't got a clue what was going on. OK, now you can stop pretending to be so bloody innocent.' Sybil fumbled in her handbag for cigarettes.

'Innocent about what? What am I accused of doing?' The two half-sisters had never got on well, so arguments between them weren't unusual, but Vanessa was at a loss to understand what had provoked this confrontation. 'Why don't you just *say* what I'm supposed to have done?'

'You bitch, you *know* what you've done!'

Starting to get annoyed now, Vanessa went across to the opposite chair and sat down. 'It would help if you weren't so abusive. There's really no need for it.'

'Oh, isn't there.' Sybil flicked her cigarette lighter. The cigarette between her lips trembled as she lit it. 'Larry informed me yesterday our engagement's off. Yes, off. Finished. Over. He doesn't want to marry me.' She stared at her half-sister. 'He doesn't want to marry me,' she repeated a little hysterically, 'and it's all because of you. He's jilted me because of *you.*'

Vanessa felt the blood rush to her face. 'For God's sake, Sybil . . . what are you saying?'

'I haven't got a fiancé any more. The engagement's off.'

'But – I had nothing to do with that!'

'Oh no?'

'*No!*'

An ugly sneer distorted Sybil's pretty features. She drew on her cigarette, then said through the smoke, 'I suppose you'll tell me next you don't know Larry's in love with you.'

For a moment, Vanessa thought she had misheard.

'Oh, don't look so bloody stupefied,' Sybil went on viciously. 'He as good as admitted the fact. He's been in love with you for months. You know how that makes me feel? The man I want to marry, throwing me over because of my *sister*?'

'What utter silly nonsense!' The other tried to sound angry but her mind was in turmoil. Larret Fitzgerald – in love with *her*? She couldn't, wouldn't believe it. 'He's making it up, you know what he's like. He's playing some idiotic joke.'

'It's no joke, not to me, not unless you think asking for his ring back is screamingly funny.' Sybil glared round. 'God, I need a drink.'

'We both do.' Vanessa got up and went through the drawing room arch to the black-lacquered Japanese cabinet where spirits were kept. The shock of the bombshell Sybil had just delivered affected her so much she was shaking. 'What . . . what would you like?'

'A very large gin.' Her half-sister pulled off the felt cloche hat she was wearing still and threw it aside. Her bobbed hair – a redder shade of blonde than Vanessa's – looked untidy, as though she hadn't bothered to brush it before coming out. 'Forget the ice, I'll just have tonic water.'

Vanessa poured herself a brandy and brought the glasses through.

Sybil didn't say thank you. 'What I want to know,' she started instead after several greedy, almost desperate gulps, 'is why the hell Larry agreed to our engagement in the first place. I mean, I feel such a bloody *fool*. He

34

said he thought he could burn you out of his system—'
She took another gulp, and drew hard on her cigarette.
'But he didn't have to get engaged to do that, did he.'

'Sybil—' Vanessa didn't know what to think, what
to say; the situation was so – *bizarre*. 'Sybil, please
believe me, I knew nothing at all about your fiancé's
feelings.'

'You're lying. You encouraged them.'

'I didn't!'

'You deliberately set out to take him away from me,
just to get even. All my life you've hated me – oh, yes
you have. Whatever I've had you've always wanted for
yourself. You couldn't bear to see me happy, could you.'
Sybil's voice began to thicken with tears. She swallowed
the rest of the gin. 'You had to do your best to spoil it,
you nasty, spiteful bitch.'

'I didn't set out to take Larret from you – I swear it!'
Vanessa said heatedly. 'None of this makes sense. For
God's sake, what good would it do him – I'm a married
woman.'

'I hate you,' her half-sister answered distractedly,
stubbing out her cigarette. 'He's all the world to me,
you know he is. Everything was wonderful between us
until . . . until . . .'

Vanessa put her brandy aside. 'Do you want any more
to drink?'

There was a vehement nod.

'You'd better have a taxi home, in that case. I'll
telephone for one.'

She poured a smaller measure of gin, then went out
into the hall. When she returned from making the call,
Sybil was smoking another cigarette and looked as though
she'd been crying.

35

'Sybil . . . listen. I know there's always been bad blood between us,' Vanessa said, now better in control of herself. 'If you don't want to believe me, nothing I can say or do will make you. I think Larret has behaved abominably, and I'm sorry he's hurt you – but I am not the cause of it.'

'He says you are. He says he can't get you out of his mind.'

'He's probably said that about a dozen other women. You know the sort of reputation he had! I even heard a rumour he's been engaged to marry before—'

'That wasn't true! *She* wanted to marry, and when Larry wouldn't she tried to make him by telling everybody he'd proposed to her.'

'I suppose you've told Mother what's happened?' Vanessa said after a pause.

Sybil wiped the back of her hand across her cheek. 'I've told Daddy as well. He's bloody furious about it.'

'I'm not surprised.' It had been a very expensive engagement party, and Mr Parrish had footed the bill out of his own pocket.

'He's furious with you, as well,' Sybil went on, the effects of the gin fuelling her vindictiveness. 'He wanted to know why that husband of yours couldn't keep you in better control. A fine marriage that's turned out to be, he said—'

'My marriage happens to be none of Father's business,' Vanessa interrupted, her feelings beginning to rise again.

'Maybe not, but from now on I'm going to make it *my* business.'

Sybil threw her cigarette into the fireplace and stood

up to face her half-sister. 'You've ruined my engagement. All right, Vanessa – I'm going to make you bloody well pay for that, just you see. I'm going to do my best to ruin your precious marriage to Roland Antrobus.'

4

Vanessa didn't believe Sybil's threat for one minute. The girl had been terribly emotional, and in that state was liable to say anything as a way of lashing out and giving hurt for the pain she herself had been caused.

Even so, Vanessa wondered whether she oughtn't to speak to Roland about it. All evening she'd been tossing the argument backwards and forwards in her mind, alternating between anger and irritation that Larret Fitzgerald should have used her as an excuse to extricate himself from his engagement, and guilty self-blame for her own naivety. She had been such a silly little fool, mooning about Larret the way she had, begrudging Sybil his attention, envying her their intimate relationship.

It wasn't until she and Roland had retired to bed, however, that Vanessa decided she really did need to talk about the situation. Her husband seemed very restless and was having trouble getting off to sleep.

'Would you mind if I read for a while, darling?' he asked eventually. 'Or will it disturb you?'

'No . . . actually, I'm not all that sleepy either.' She turned over on her back as the soft pink light of the bedside lamp came on. After a couple of moments she said awkwardly, 'Sybil called to see me today.'

'Really? She must have wanted something.' Roland reached over to the table for his spectacles.

'She wanted my blood, as it happened. I wasn't certain whether I should tell you . . .'

'Is it anything important or just another of your sister's silly dramas?' He didn't sound terribly interested, more concerned with finding the page in his book.

'No, this *is* important, darling. It's about Larret Fitzgerald. Are you listening?'

'Uh-uh.'

'He's – well, he's called off his engagement to Sybil.'

'Has he, by God!' Roland let out a bark of cynical laughter. 'What did I say to you – I knew it wouldn't last above five minutes.' It pleased him he'd been proved so correct. 'The fellow's an absolute cad. I suppose he got cold feet, is that the excuse?'

'Not according to Sybil. Actually, it's all rather embarrassing . . .' Vanessa sat up against the satin pillows, not sure quite how to phrase her half-sister's accusation. 'You see, she's claiming the whole thing is *my* doing. She thinks I've been deliberately using my wiles on Larret to lure him away from her.'

Roland took off his spectacles. 'She's *what*? She seriously believes that?'

'So she says. And that's not all of it, either. She went on to tell me the reason he jilted her is because he's fallen in love – in love with me, I mean.'

'Oh, but how preposterous! The fellow's hardly set eyes on you more than a dozen times.' Suddenly there was sharp annoyance in Roland's tone. 'Wretched girl, coming here with statements like that!'

'She was frightfully upset—'

'I don't care what she was.' He threw his book aside on the bed. 'She has absolutely no right to involve you in her grubby little problems. I can see what's happened –

she wants to find a scapegoat to take the blame, someone who'll save her face for her. Larret Fitzgerald in love with you, indeed – ridiculous rubbish! It's the kind of thing Sybil *would* invent.'

'I'm glad you don't believe her, darling.' Vanessa shifted to rest her head against her husband's shoulder and give his arm a hug. It had been on the tip of her tongue to say that of the two of them she considered Larret more at fault, using emotional infidelity as a lever to prise himself free of his commitment; but on second thoughts, instead she went on, 'It's all very childish, I know, but she went away threatening to get her own back for what I'm supposed to have done.'

'Ignore her.' Roland kissed his wife's soft, smooth hair. 'In a month it'll all have blown over and Sybil will be busily consoling herself with some other young wastrel.'

'But she talked about harming our marriage.'

'For God's sake, darling – *nothing* can harm our marriage. It's sheer jealousy and resentment, talk like that, something she can scratch her little claws on. I happen to love you far too much to allow anything as trite as Sybil's broken heart to come between us.'

Vanessa put her arm round his waist and hugged him tighter. '*Do* you love me, Roland – really and truly?' she asked, prompted suddenly by the need to have his assurance. 'I feel . . . oh, I don't know, I feel so inadequate sometimes. I suppose that's why her threat hurt, because I'm vulnerable . . . because I blame myself for failing you by not being a proper wife.'

'You silly girl.' He kissed her hair again, smelling its clean, freshwashed fragrance. 'Shouldn't it be *me* who's judge of how good a wife you are?'

'I didn't say good. I said proper. There is a difference.'

This time Roland didn't answer. They were slipping towards the start of a conversation held dozens of times in the past, when Vanessa had tried to make him confess what it was that seemed to hold him back from the loving closeness of complete physical intimacy.

She began unbuttoning his pyjama jacket, wanting to have the touch of his nakedness; but almost at once he pushed her hand away.

'What is it, my darling?' she asked a little desperately. 'What's wrong with me, why can I never arouse you?'

'It's late. We ought to think about sleep.'

'But you said you weren't tired, and I don't want to sleep. I want you to hold me . . . Roland, please, *please* . . . hold me for just a while, won't you?'

She cuddled closer, burrowing her head against his chest, refusing to be rejected; and after a moment he put an arm round her, gently, like a brother or a father, without passion.

Vanessa stroked the velvet-white skin of his shoulder, undoing the rest of the buttons and pushing his jacket aside. A small pulse of excitement began to beat within her, increasing as she touched him, circling her fingertips round the hairless, smooth chest and then running them lightly up and down, up and down, until she'd reached the cord of his pyjama trousers. Roland didn't move, not even when she unfastened the cord and slipped her hand inside.

'Don't I give you any pleasure at all, my darling?' she asked him eventually. 'Doesn't what I'm doing now excite you?'

He put his hand down and took hers, holding it there against him.

'Is this what you like?' she asked again.

'No . . . but it comforts me.'

She was silent, trying to understand; then she raised her face to look at him and said, 'I wish I knew what was wrong, why I'm always such a failure. If only you'd show me what you want me to do, Roland – whatever it was, if it meant we could make love properly I'd do it.'

He looked away. 'Poor darling, you must get very frustrated. I'm sorry.'

He sounded so indifferent that Vanessa felt a stab of anger that he wouldn't explain, wouldn't give her any chance to learn. She pulled her hand from his and rolled over. Why did it always have to be like this, she wondered. Roland had made love to other women in the past – he'd admitted it – so the fault *must* be hers.

As though he'd read her thoughts, her husband said as he switched off the bedside lamp, 'Blame it on whatever you like, Vanessa. It isn't your fault if I can't put on a performance . . . please try to understand that.'

For a man who was supposed to be so much in love with his fiancée's sister that he'd broken off his engagement, Larret Fitzgerald remained curiously elusive. Vanessa neither heard from him nor saw him; and despite her embarrassment over the way he'd behaved, she couldn't help but feel disappointed that he'd apparently chosen to remove himself entirely from her life.

She was under no false illusions about his character. He *was* a cad, as Roland had said. But he was also a charmer, and this made his caddishness something of a greater attraction to a young woman as impressionable as Vanessa.

She learned some weeks later from her mother that

Sybil had been suicidal because of the broken engagement. Mr Parrish had found the girl with his open razor in the bathroom, fortunately too drunk to do herself damage; and another time, she'd been brought home by a neighbour who'd noticed her behaving oddly down by the canal. The doctor thought Sybil was suffering from nervous hysteria, and had prescribed a holiday; so at the end of April Mr Parrish was taking the family away to Skegness.

Vanessa saw Mrs Parrish again the week after they were back. Because she so disliked visiting the house at Tettenhall Green, daughter and mother usually met each other twice a month in town to do an afternoon's shopping together. On this occasion Mrs Parrish reported that Sybil seemed a bit brighter and was talking of getting herself a job in the ladies' fashions department at Beatties in Victoria Street.

And what about Larret Fitzgerald, Vanessa enquired, deliberately off-hand – had anything more been heard from him? Apparently not; and just as well, said Mrs Parrish, after the nasty cruel way he'd treated their Sybil. Mr Parrish had carried on no end about it.

Vanessa changed the subject.

The exhibition of German art photography was opening at the Antrobus Gallery this coming weekend, she told her mother. The collection was entirely the work of one young woman, Luise von Losch, from Berlin. It had already received a lot of critical attention in London, and Roland was throwing a cocktail party on Saturday evening as a publicity launch – there'd be several newspaper reporters, including her friends Kay Murray from the *Advertiser* and Dulcie Fox from the *Express & Star*, and people from the art world, all the usual crowd.

From what Roland had mentioned about her, Fräulein von Losch sounded an interesting character. In fact, said Vanessa, she was rather looking forward to meeting her.

It had been one of those lovely June days declaring summer had really arrived at last, and the open windows of the Gallery let in the warmth of the evening streets to mingle with the fragrance of white roses. The theme for tonight's party was one of black and white, to reflect the starkness of the mounted photographs: black evening dress and tie, white cocktail frocks, white flowers, black satin wall drapes. The effect was dramatic, very *Art Décoratif.*

Vanessa had chosen to wear a hip-waisted georgette frock sewn with milky bugle-beads which shimmered as the lights caught them, and round her forehead a matching bandeau to which she'd fastened a single white silk gardenia. There had been compliments and admiring looks for her until Luise von Losch arrived, whereupon everyone's startled attention had switched at once to this extraordinary young German woman in black bow tie and tails.

On any other female, masculine attire would have looked bizarre; but not on Fräulein von Losch. She was thin to the point of emaciation, with a figure like a boy's and wore the tailored evening dress with such casual panache that she appeared quite the most striking creature Vanessa had ever seen. She had a fine-boned, ivory-pale face with high cheekbones which accentuated her narrow eyes, and her hair, so blonde that it was almost platinum, had been twisted up on top of her head like a coronet. To add emphasis to her individuality, she was wearing a blood-red carnation in her jacket lapel, a solitary splash of vibrant colour against the black and white uniformity of everyone else.

The entire room was mesmerised by her; and none more so than Roland Antrobus, who seemed quite unable to tear himself away from her side for even a minute.

Intrigued to meet their guest, Vanessa had to steel herself to patience while the Press conducted its interviews, and used the time to take a second, more leisurely look round the exhibition. Few of the photographs had been posed. Most depicted Berlin street life in all its raw, cruel, crude, matter-of-fact aspects – children on darkened stairways; an old man weeping at a window; two girls together on a deserted dance floor; blowsy women standing outside nightclubs; drunkenness, death, hopelessness – each image suggested a terrible sense of betrayal. Vanessa found they made her feel uncomfortable.

'But that is what they are meant to do,' Luise von Losch told her after the two of them had been introduced a little later. 'If my photographs do not make you uncomfortable, they have failed to make you respond to the wretchedness of human life.' She spoke English well, though with a strong guttural accent. 'You wonder why I do not take happy pictures? It is because happiness is a disguise, a smiling mask, that does not let you see behind its eyes.'

'What about beauty?' Vanessa asked. 'What about dignity? Why do you choose to concentrate so often on people's misfortune?'

'But is there not beauty and dignity in misfortune also? Look, and you will find it in these faces—' the elegant young German indicated the mounted images around her. 'Hunger has its own terrible loveliness, and grief its own pride. For me, sadness is beauty. There is nothing more ugly than the face that says "I am content with life".'

'Luise, another cocktail?' Roland came up to interrupt, having noticed her empty glass while he'd been talking to another of the guests. His eyes were all over her face, as though he couldn't get enough of the sight of her.

Fräulein von Losch looked at him and smiled. 'Why the public formality? Call me Lulu, as I invited you. Only my family call me Luise.' She held out her glass, and when Roland went off to get it refilled she said to Vanessa, 'You have not been married long to Mr Antrobus, I understand?'

'No, that's right. Just over a year, actually.'

'He is an interesting man.'

'Thank you for saying so.'

'He would enjoy Berlin, I think. It is interesting also.' Luise – Lulu – said this with a sly little laugh; and after Roland had returned with her drink she went on, 'Since the war, you know, Berlin has become very artistic, very exciting. Photography, film, theatre, painting, music – all is experiment, pushing back the frontiers of interpretation. It is a good time. You must come and visit . . . both of you.'

'Yes, we really must do that,' said Roland; and Vanessa wondered why he should sound so avidly eager all of a sudden. He had never expressed any interest in Berlin before.

Conversation moved on to a discussion about conditions in Germany since the Great War. Lulu made no bones about the fact that she was a Communist sympathiser, and paid little credit to the Weimar Constitution which had been introduced in 1919 following the Kaiser's abdication. Nor was she particularly optimistic of an improvement in her country's social and economic plight now that Field Marshal von Hindenburg was president.

Vanessa had read enough in the national papers to contribute a few intelligent comments of her own, but after ten minutes of listening to their guest's impassioned defence of Communism she tactfully withdrew and went over to join Kay Murray from the *Advertiser*. Kay had stayed on at the party after the rest of the Press, including Dulcie Fox, had left to cover other engagements, and Vanessa was interested to get her friend's reaction to Fräulein von Losch.

'Strictly between you and me,' said Kay, lowering her voice and turning away from those nearest, 'I think the woman's a bit of a freak, but by golly she certainly does have style! What a good job she's so skinny – half an ounce more and she'd look ridiculous in that get-up.'

Being small and plumply curvaceous herself, Kay had difficulty with the current breastless, hipless fashions, torturing her ample flesh by squeezing it into boned corsets. 'Does she ever *eat*, I ask myself,' she went on, rolling her eyes. 'I mean, if she swallowed a *pea* she'd look pregnant!'

Vanessa couldn't resist laughing. 'I trust you're not going to write bitchy comments like that in your column.'

'Of course not. I shall describe Fräulein von Losch as divinely elegant, excitingly avant garde, and burning with creative artistry. As for her work . . . well, I *could* say that photography has never reflected the wounded nature of man's soul more closely. That's pretentious enough, don't you think? Or shall I be more honest and report that the Antrobus Gallery's exhibition is a gloomy assortment of extremely depressing pictures?'

'Roland would fry you alive if you wrote that! He's wildly enthusiastic about his exhibition.'

'He's also wildly enthusiastic about his Fräulein,' Kay observed drily.

'Yes . . . I had rather reached that conclusion myself.' Vanessa threw a troubled glance over her shoulder to where her husband was still hovering attentively at Luise von Losch's side. 'But then she *is* the guest attraction, and I know he's pinning the Gallery's reputation on the success of her show. Don't forget, she's almost unknown in this country, apart from London, and Roland's anxious to earn all the credit for bringing her to wider notice in the provinces.'

'Oh, I'm not doubting his motive, Vanessa.' Kay Murray's bright black-button eyes followed the direction of her friend's glance. 'It's just that it strikes me as out of character for somebody as self-restrained as Roland to behave like—' She paused, finishing her sentence on a little shrug.

Vanessa looked at her. 'Like what?' she prompted.

'No, really, it doesn't matter. Forget it.'

'Like *what*, Kay? Tell me, I'm curious.'

'Well . . . to behave like a man who wonders whether he's dreaming.'

5

'There's a gentleman wishing to speak to you on the telephone, Madam.'

Ethel, the Antrobus's parlourmaid, tapped at the open door of the dining room, where Vanessa was occupied checking the coming week's menus with their cook, Mrs Prescott. 'He didn't give any name. He said it was a personal call.'

'Thank you, Ethel.' Vanessa put the list of menus aside, and excusing herself to Mrs Prescott, went out to the telephone in the entrance hall.

'Hello – Vanessa?' For a second she didn't recognise the voice on the other end of the line. 'Remember me? Larret Fitzgerald?'

'Larret—?' Her heart gave an almighty thump. She heard herself saying in a brightly artificial manner, 'Well, what a surprise – how nice to hear from you! How are you?'

'I'm fine – and you?'

'I'm very well.'

'Good. Hope you don't mind me ringing you out of the blue like this. As a matter of fact I'm here in Wolverhampton, and I was wondering whether we could meet perhaps for a drink or something.'

'A drink?' Her pulse began racing. 'Oh, I don't know . . . I'm not sure.'

51

'Does that mean your husband's at home?'

'No . . . no, Roland's away in Manchester.'

'Fine. Then I'll be over there in around twenty minutes to collect you.'

'But I'm not dressed for going out . . . I mean, no – please don't come to the house.' Vanessa's mind went into a spin and she couldn't think clearly.

'All right,' he said, refusing to be put off, 'I'll meet you somewhere in town. Shall we say by St Peter's in the square, about twelve o'clock? That'll give you an hour.'

'But Larret—'

'Sorry, Vanessa, I've no change left for the box. Have to ring off. See you there at twelve—'

There was a little click, and the line went dead.

Seated beside Larret in his nippy Triumph roadster as they roared into the country away from Wolverhampton, she felt terribly guilty. On the trolley-bus into town she'd kept wondering what on earth she thought she was doing, behaving as recklessly as this, stealing away to meet a man labelled with the reputation of a cad and a lady-killer, yet she hadn't been able to resist the curiosity of finding out why exactly Larret had bothered to call her.

He had had to exercise all his charm before she would agree to their driving somewhere out of town in case they were seen together and word of it got back. Foolish to stifle her objections perhaps, but somehow nothing else had seemed to matter but the smile in his eyes as he'd coaxed her into accepting. And now here they were on this heavenly summer's day, the car hood down and the warm wind buffeting their faces, the open road stretching ahead to take her away from dreary reality.

They stopped eventually at a country pub called The Horns out at Boningale, a pretty little spot with roses climbing the mellow brick walls and a view of the Clee Hills in the distance across the heat-hazed fields. Larret brought their drinks into the garden. So far they'd both avoided discussion of Sybil's broken engagement: Vanessa was reluctant to be the first to raise the subject, and Larret didn't refer to it. Instead he talked a lot about himself, explaining his silence these past three months by the fact that he'd been home to Ireland, visiting relatives at his boyhood home of Lugnagall near Sligo.

'Sligo has strong connections with William Butler Yeats,' he said. 'That's why I was intrigued to find you reading Yeats's poetry last time we met.' Between them rose a memory of that afternoon in March when Vanessa had joined him and Sybil for a cup of tea at Lyons' Corner House. 'But I suppose poetry must be something of an inherited passion for you. Read much of it, do you?'

'When I'm in the mood, yes. Do you?'

He laughed, and mocking his own soft, attractive brogue, replied, 'Ah, to be sure, I was raised on it, was I not.' Then more serious again – 'Only late at night, when I'm all alone and feeling blue and the wireless is playing something sentimental. Perhaps then.'

He raised his glass and took a drink, his eyes still holding Vanessa's.

'I wouldn't have put you down as being such a romantic,' she said lightly.

'Oh? Then how would you "put me down"?' he asked, with subtle, amused emphasis, leaning in his seat to take his cigarettes from his blazer pocket.

'That's not a fair question. I hardly know you well enough to say.'

'But well enough to trust me.'

'How do you mean?'

'You've complimented me with your charming company this afternoon.' He offered her a cigarette from the packet. She shook her head. 'But you don't think I'm much of a romantic. Fair enough. I suppose my character must have taken a bit of a knocking when I broke things off with Sybil.'

There, now it was out in the open at last.

Vanessa glanced away awkwardly. 'You didn't make yourself exactly popular, that's for sure. Sybil was terribly cut up about being jilted like that.'

'Well, she was bound to make a great song and dance about the whole thing. You know what she's like.'

'For heaven's sake, my sister was engaged to marry you, Larret! How did you expect she'd behave? It's the first time in her life someone's taken something away from her that she really wanted, and she's having a job coming to terms with the way you've hurt her.'

'But isn't it better to cause a little hurt in the short term than make the biggest mistake of both our lives? OK, Sybil was in love with me – or at any rate, in love with the idea of getting married. She enjoyed the excitement, the novelty, being the centre of attention, parading me about like some showcase dummy. But whatever we had going between us, believe me it was bound to fizzle out within a year or so.'

'Yet you still went ahead and got engaged to her.'

Instead of answering that directly, Larret lit his cigarette and drew on it heavily, then blew the smoke through his nose and said with a lop-sided smile, 'Maybe I drank more than was wise New Year's Eve.' And Vanessa remembered how triumphant Sybil had been about his proposal at some fancy-dress party, made in front of everyone as midnight chimed in 1927.

'Come on, don't look at me like that,' he protested a little ruefully, pulling a face. 'Can't you just imagine what married life would have been once the dazzle had faded? Two people with hardly anything in common, keeping up the stifling pretence of wedded bliss for the sake of appearances, living like a couple of strangers in private? God, it would have been hell.'

The description could almost as well apply to her own marriage, Vanessa thought, except living with Roland wasn't hell; it was simply rather disappointing.

'Besides,' Larret added, 'Sybil's too young yet. And too spoilt and too damn' demanding. I hoped getting engaged might alter that, but I was wrong. And to be frank, in the end I wasn't prepared to risk tying myself down to anything permanent.'

Vanessa waited while someone from the bar room finished clearing empty glasses from a neighbouring table, then she said, 'I think you behaved very badly.'

'Oh?'

'Though in fairness it was probably the wisest decision, even if Sybil doesn't see it that way.'

'Of course not.' Larret didn't appear to mind the criticism. 'As you said just now, she's had something taken from her that she wasn't quite ready to part with. Our engagement was a new, exciting game with me as favourite toy, only I stopped playing it before she'd had time to get bored.' He drew on his cigarette again. 'Does that sound terribly unkind?'

'A little. Though it's true Sybil is too spoilt and too

demanding, always wanting things her own way. She's got her father to blame for that.'

Vanessa made herself meet Larret's eyes. 'There's . . . something else we haven't mentioned yet,' she said.

'Something else—?'

'I know this sounds ridiculous, but according to my sister it's *me* who's been the cause of all the trouble. She's trying to make me the scapegoat for what's happened between the two of you, spreading it about that you threw her over because . . .' Here she drew an unsteady breath and swallowed. '. . . because you're in love with me instead of her.'

The suspicion of a frown flickered across Larret's face, but other than that he showed no reaction, nor did he say anything; and after a moment she plunged on awkwardly, 'It's typical of Sybil to seek to put the blame on someone else and I don't for a second believe what she says, of course I don't, she was hysterical when she said it . . . but she isn't a total liar, she must have had *some* grounds for the accusation, even if it was only petty jealousy. You can see how embarrassing this is for me, Larret . . .'

Again she paused waiting for him to speak, expecting he would deny Sybil's story, laugh it off as an invention; and when he still remained silent, she felt compelled to add, 'She claims you told her you needed to burn me out of your system, or something.'

'That's right. That's what I told her,' he said at last, quietly.

'Oh.'

For a moment Vanessa thought she couldn't have heard him properly; and then she said 'Oh' again, the colour rising in her face.

'I've been in love with you for months. Why do you

think I risked a phone call to your house this morning?'
Larret continued. 'It was because I couldn't bear to let
another day go by without trying to see you.'

Throwing the half-smoked cigarette away he reached
across to take Vanessa's hand, holding it imprisoned in
his own, his dark blue Irish eyes fixed on her face in a
look that was eagerly serious now, almost pleading.

'I didn't go back to Sligo just to visit relatives. I
went to get away from the pressure, away from Sybil's
tantrums and your stepfather threatening legal action for
breach of promise . . . and most of all, my darling, to
get away from the torture of wanting *you* and not being
able to do a damn' thing about it. No, let me finish—'
he went on urgently as she uttered a little cry, 'I know
there isn't chance in a million you could ever feel the
same about me, but I just can't help myself, don't you
see that? You're so incredibly, beautifully lovely. I'm in
a dream being here alone with you at last.'

'You mustn't talk like that—' She was more shocked
by her own rush of feelings than by the realisation that
Sybil had been telling the truth after all.

'You mustn't talk like that—' Even as she said it
she thought how ridiculously stuffy she was making
herself sound. 'It was wrong of me to meet you today.
I shouldn't have.'

'Why did you, in that case?'

'I – I – because I wanted to hear your side of the
story,' she said clumsily. 'About why you broke off your
engagement to my sister.'

'I see.' Slowly he released her hand and slumped back
in his seat, all the eager pleading dying away from his
face. 'There's no hope for me then?'

Vanessa bit her lip, knowing she ought to say no. And

57

when she didn't answer he asked her the same thing again, almost angrily this time – 'There's no hope for me then?'

'Larret, how can there be? I'm a married woman.'

'I could make you ten times as happy as Roland Antrobus. I dare you to say you feel nothing at all for me.'

'This is unfair—'

'Say it. *Say it!* You feel nothing whatsoever for me.'

'I can't. You know I can't,' she responded desperately. 'In any case what does it matter how I feel—'

'—you'd never leave him?'

'I would never *harm* him. Roland's my husband. I love him. I couldn't be unfaithful to him.'

'And *I* love *you*, Vanessa.' Larret took her hand again and bent his head to kiss its upturned palm, his dark hair falling forward and brushing her wrist. The touch of his mouth disarmed her. Hesitantly, she stroked the lock of hair away from his forehead, then let her fingers lightly trace the outline of his brow and cheek and blunt, square chin.

Wasn't this in its way being unfaithful to Roland, she asked herself? And hadn't she already betrayed him a dozen times or more in her imagination?

'I knew you cared something for me,' Larret said exultantly, smiling at her. 'No matter how hard you've tried to disguise it, I could read it in your eyes whenever we've met, so why pretend to yourself our relationship means nothing?'

Vanessa shook her head, glancing round the empty garden, striving for a measure of self-control. 'I like you . . . of course I do. I find your company very attractive. But that's as far as it goes. You mustn't think I want to

58

encourage you, because if I did it would be wrong as well as stupid and dangerous.'

Then getting from her seat and smoothing the creases from her knee-length frock – 'I think we should drive back into town now, please.'

Larret followed to his feet. 'OK. But you know I want to see you again, don't you?'

'I don't think that would be very wise.'

'The devil with whether it's wise or not. It's what I want – what *you* want.' He caught at her, swinging her round on the grass to face him. 'Vanessa – oh, my dearest – do you have to be so confoundedly sensible? We could be wonderfully, marvellously happy together—'

'Like you were with Sybil?' she couldn't resist throwing back. 'Why should I trust you, Larret – tell me? Why should I risk my marriage and security, everything I have, for some grubby little hole-and-corner affair with my sister's ex-fiancé? Even if I was tempted, I hope I'm not such a silly little fool as that.'

As if stung by the way she'd flung Sybil at him, he pulled her into his arms and kissed her suddenly and violently, not caring if anyone came out and saw them. The sensation of his mouth on hers took Vanessa's breath away. She struggled to release herself, striking at him with her fists; and then a feeling of such delicious weakness swept over her that she found she was clinging to him instead and surrendering her lips to that insistent kiss.

When Larret released her she was immediately so embarrassed by her momentary submission that she turned on him furiously – 'I hope you're satisfied now!'

'On the contrary. I want you more than ever. And

59

I believe that you want me as much, however you deny it.'

She could have cried with the humiliation, knowing that he spoke the truth.

He made no attempt to touch her again, but lit himself another cigarette and said through a mouthful of smoke, 'Come on, let's get in the car, I'll run you back and we'll talk about this.'

Vanessa refused to take any of Larret's telephone calls next day, telling the housemaids to inform Mr Fitzgerald she was unavailable. She wondered unhappily what he would think, whether he would be terribly hurt; and then in the next breath told herself she didn't care a hoot what he thought, he had the most colossal cheek to behave as he had and the wisest thing she could do was to forget about him.

Forgetting Larret Fitzgerald was simpler said than done, though. No matter how hard Vanessa tried to fill her thoughts with other things he was there all the time, his handsome face imprinted on her mind, his voice repeating over and over 'I love you, I want you', the remembered touch of his mouth still burning her lips.

If only Roland were home to give her moral strength, she thought despairingly, and not absent in Manchester fussing with his wretched photographic exhibition. It would be so much easier to despise Larret if she had her husband's presence to remind her of her proper loyalties, to exorcise the devils of temptation whispering their insidious encouragement.

But Roland Antrobus had devils of his own to wrestle with; and on the Sunday when he'd been expected back at 'Mayville' he telephoned to say his plans were changed and he was travelling instead to Leeds, returning later in the week.

Luise von Losch needed him to be with her up there. He was sure Vanessa would understand.

6

Vanessa said nothing about Larret Fitzgerald to her husband. There didn't seem much point in mentioning she'd seen him – it would only have invited complications – and besides, Roland had brought problems of his own back with him from Leeds. He seemed oddly preoccupied, throwing himself into his work at the Gallery for long hours at a stretch and retiring into brooding silences at home. Caught up as she was in her own private turmoil Vanessa read less into this than perhaps she might have done, and it was left to others to remark on his behaviour.

Her best chum at school had been a girl named Marjorie Lake. Marjorie was now married to a Frenchman and living in the Dordogne, but whenever she was home to visit her family she and Vanessa always made a point of seeing one another.

Roland's return from the north had coincided with one of her visits.

'Don't mind me asking, but the Gallery's doing all right is it, Vee?' Marjorie enquired, glancing away from the dressing-table where she was powdering her nose. The two young women had spent a day shopping together and Marjorie was staying for early dinner at 'Mayville' before Roland ran her back in the Morris Cowley to her parents' place.

Vanessa took up the honey-coloured georgette frock she was changing into for dinner. 'It's doing all right as far as I know. Roland's happy enough at any rate,' she answered, holding the frock against her and examining her reflection across Marjorie's shoulder in the mirror. 'Times might be a bit tight for everyone, but he hasn't lost any of his regular patrons. Why do you ask?'

'Oh, I wondered, that's all. I thought the Gallery might be running into trouble.' Marjorie touched a hand to her pretty hair, a rich deep auburn which she wore in a chignon, refusing to sacrifice her best feature to the prevailing cropped fashions. 'Only he's acting as if something's preying on his mind, hadn't you noticed?'

'To be honest . . . no, I can't say I had, really. He's seemed much the same as always. But then I suppose I've had rather a lot on my own mind lately,' Vanessa said frankly. Knowing Marjorie was to be trusted, she'd confided in her about Larret Fitzgerald and the attraction she felt for the young Irish architect, while prudently drawing a veil over the scene in the pub garden at Boningale. There were some things which couldn't be shared even with one's closest chum.

'Though now you come to mention it,' she added as an afterthought, kicking off her shoes to step out of her skirt, 'maybe he *has* been a little wrapped up in himself since coming back. Apart from bed, the only time we see each other is at the meal table, and it's difficult getting conversation out of someone with their head buried in a newspaper.'

Marjorie threw a glance towards the bedroom door and lowered her voice. 'You don't think he's being huffy about – well, you-know-who.' She silently mouthed the name Larret. 'Somebody could have seen the two of you together the other week and mentioned it.'

'In that case Roland would have said so. It's not the kind of thing he'd keep to himself, not with the low opinion he has of . . . certain parties. Probably he's just a bit over-tired, that's all. Feeling deflated now the von Losch exhibition's off his hands. You know how enthusiastic he gets about planning and organising these dos.'

Vanessa slipped the georgette frock over her head and pulled it down to cover the slender contours of her body.

'Be a dear and fasten me at the back, would you?' she said; and while Marjorie obliged her, after a few moments she went on again suddenly, 'Tell me honestly, Madge, am I being silly to think so fondly of – you know, *him*? He's telephoned again. He's desperate to see me. I said no . . . but would it be such a crime, I mean, just to meet for maybe half an hour? He's not *all* bad, Madge, whatever they say about him.'

'Are you asking my opinion or trying to talk yourself into something?' the other responded lightly, re-seating herself at the dressing-table. 'Because either way, it sounds to me as though you don't really know *what* you want.'

'I don't.'

'You'd be a chump to encourage him. And saying yes to any more meetings most certainly would be encouragement. On the other hand, if it's dangerous excitement you're looking for—' Marjorie shrugged into the mirror and left the end of the sentence dangling. She knew quite well how dull Vanessa's marriage to Roland Antrobus had become, compared with the romantic Gallic

65

happiness she herself enjoyed with her husband, Jean-Luc Tiersot; though she had no suspicion that the marriage was actually still unconsummated. That was another thing Vanessa chose not to divulge, in this case for different reasons.

'Sometimes I quite hate him for being so impossibly good-looking,' Vanessa said fretfully. 'It's so unfair. Why couldn't he have stayed safely out of reach engaged to Sybil instead of stirring up my life the way he has and causing all these beastly complications.'

'It's a unique type of flattery known as Irish blarney,' Marjorie told her. 'And more fool you for being taken in by it. OK, so he's Douglas Fairbanks in the flesh, and I agree it's hard to resist a man like that when he claims you're the love of his life – but if you don't want to get burnt, darling, take my advice and don't play with fire. Don't even open the box of matches.'

For a fleeting moment the expression on Vanessa's lovely face showed her ambivalent emotions. Marjorie was absolutely right: she *shouldn't* play with fire. The problem was, Larret's persistence was weakening her resolve, making it so very, very easy to give in to temptation.

'Anyway, it doesn't matter, I'll be out of reach in another few weeks, thank God,' she said, forcing a little laugh. 'I'm off on this trip to dig out my roots in Pembrokeshire, and with any luck my absence will put the kibosh on his attentions.'

'Don't bank on it,' Marjorie answered prosaically. 'There's only one way to throw charmers like him off the scent – saying NO, very loudly and often. And *meaning* it.'

* * *

The lorry was standing outside the coach-house doors when Vanessa came into the drive from the bus-stop. Its back was half-piled up with pieces of junk and scrap metal, and as she walked across to see what was going on two men in long khaki aprons emerged from behind the coach-house carrying between them an old bed, its springs sagging rustily on the frame and bindweed trailing from its mildewed headboard. The bed had been lying out there against the wall ever since she'd been at 'Mayville'. It used to be in Roland's parents' room; his mother had died in it.

One of the men, the younger and fatter of the pair, gave her a cheery grin and said, 'Afternoon, Missis,' as they went by. The other, taller, stronger-featured, merely glanced her up and down before swinging the bed on to the back of the lorry.

'Excuse me – has my husband told you to take that?' Vanessa asked him out of curiosity, since Roland hadn't mentioned anything.

Instead of responding, the man turned and walked away, ignoring her completely, leaving his mate to deal with the question. 'That's right, Missis. This an' all the other rubbish out the back there.'

'Your colleague appears to have trouble with his manners as well as his hearing,' she observed, a little put out by the incivility.

'Mr Brockhouse?' The younger chap grinned again, showing the gaps in his teeth. 'Oh, do' you mind him, Missis. He do' say much ever.'

She examined the trade name painted in red and gold lettering on the cab door. 'James Brockhouse. Scrap Metal Dealer. Sun Street, Wolverhampton.'

'Is this him – James Brockhouse?' she queried.

'Jim Brockhouse, he's the gaffer, aye.'

Vanessa made a mental note of the name and went inside the house, where she found one of the maids making the men a pot of tea in the kitchen.

'Don't use that china, Ethel,' she said, noticing the tray set ready. 'Some old crockery from the back of the cupboard will do. If it gets broken it won't matter too much.'

She went into the dining room, glancing through the leaded windows overlooking the terrace. Jim Brockhouse was across to the right by the rose bushes, dumping a broken lawn-cutter into the wheelbarrow. Before she could turn away again she saw him pause a moment and wipe his hands on the front of his work apron, then kneel down and take a lush pink rose between his cupped fingers and gently, almost reverently, press his face into its perfumed petals.

For some silly reason Vanessa felt embarrassed; and the image stayed with her the rest of the afternoon till Roland came home.

'To be honest, darling, it simply slipped my mind to tell you,' he said at dinner when she asked about the scrap lorry. 'There was so much useless old rubbish lying around, I decided it was high time to get rid of it. It needs to be cleared out anyway if—'

He stopped.

'If what?' Vanessa prompted.

'Oh . . . if I ever think of selling "Mayville".'

She put down her knife and fork. 'Selling "Mayville"? What an extraordinary idea. Whatever for?' The suggestion astonished her.

Roland shrugged and retreated behind the evening's *Express & Star*. 'Only a thought. It's as well to look ahead and consider all eventualities.'

His off-hand tone made it plain he didn't wish to take the matter further; but the disquiet he'd planted in Vanessa's mind refused to go away, and after dinner when he announced he'd be out for the rest of the evening, she responded awkwardly, 'Roland, before you go – can I ask you a question? Marjorie made the comment that you seem preoccupied, as though something's worrying you, and she wondered if it might be to do with the Gallery. You would tell me, wouldn't you, if there was anything I ought to know?'

Instead of answering, her husband looked at her in what struck her as a most peculiar way. Maybe it was only a trick of the light, but just for a moment Vanessa could have sworn she read a flash of hostility and something else – could it be guilt perhaps? – in his eyes.

'You *are* bothered about something, aren't you,' she persisted. 'You haven't been at all yourself these past few weeks.'

'Oh, for heaven's sake, Vanessa—' He went to open the door as if to put an end to the conversation; then paused and swung round again to face her. 'I suppose Marjorie has been and put some nonsense in your head and you're fool enough to give it credence.'

His aggressiveness took her aback. 'She simply made an observation about the way you've been behaving recently. It isn't nonsense to say you were less than forthcoming the night she had dinner here – in fact you practically ignored us both until it was time to take Madge home.'

'I had other things to think about.'

'Precisely. That's why I'm asking you now, is anything wrong at the Gallery?'

'There is nothing wrong *at the Gallery*.' Roland emphasised the last three words in a manner which suggested whatever the problem might be, it lay elsewhere.

'But you're out of the house all the hours God sends. Some nights I've hardly seen you. You're sleeping badly, too.' Vanessa put aside the little piece of embroidery she'd been working on. 'Don't you think I have a right to know if something's weighing on your mind?' she appealed. 'Please, Roland—'

'I don't want to talk about it.'

'Why not.'

'Because I'm going out.' He turned again towards the door.

'It hasn't anything to do with the remark you made at dinner about selling the house, has it?' she pressed, concerned by his hostile attitude, and reluctant to leave things up in the air between them like this.

His hand on the knob and keeping his face to the door, he said on a note of irritation, 'I wish you weren't always so ready to jump to conclusions! If you'd listened properly, I didn't *say* I was selling the house. I said if I were ever to think of doing so.'

'It's obvious you've already thought of doing so, or you wouldn't suddenly be having scrap dealers coming here,' Vanessa answered him back, getting to her feet. 'It's unlike you to act without good reason, darling. Which leads me to think perhaps you're not being totally fair with me. No, please don't go yet—' as her husband pulled open the door. 'This doesn't by chance concern Luise von Losch, does it?'

The young German woman's name found its target. Roland spun round in the doorway. His features were

70

working as though he'd developed some sort of nervous tic, his whole demeanour so markedly altered that Vanessa felt a little thrill of fear run through her.

'Why should it concern Fräulein von Losch,' he said, and again she was aware of the peculiar look in his light blue eyes as he stared at her.

'You tell me.'

'Answer the question. You must have a reason.'

She didn't need to cast about for one. 'The change in you . . . it's only since you've been back from touring with the exhibition. All these hours you're spending at the Gallery . . . your behaviour, your lack of conversation, your moodiness—'

'My God, you don't give up, do you!'

'Deny it, then. Tell me it's nothing to do with her.'

Roland took a few steps from the door and lowered his voice.

'Unless you wish to provoke me to extreme anger,' he said in a tone that made her want to cower from him, 'you'll mind your own wretched business, Vanessa. Especially about Luise. Now I am going to go out for the evening. What I do, and how long I choose to be away from this house, is my own affair. Do I make myself clear?'

He didn't wait to see the dismay in her face or hear her response, but turned and strode from the room, slamming the door shut behind him.

Roland Antrobus's problem was of an equivocal nature. In Luise von Losch he had met for the very first time a woman with whom he was able at last to fulfill himself in the twilight area of his sexual preferences, and the situation was creating an overwhelming distraction from his normal life.

He'd found himself being caught up in a vortex, and far from wishing to escape, was all too eager to plunge headlong into its spinning darkness.

Roland had taken Vanessa as his wife because he genuinely believed they could make a successful go of things together. He loved her for her beauty, her intelligence, for the comfortable home she'd created for him at 'Mayville', for every reason possible; except sexual enjoyment. Even before they were married he'd realised that he did not want her as his partner in the kind of aberrant behaviour which gave him satisfaction; nor did he ever try to make her so, not wishing to besmirch her pure, clean, shining loveliness with that dark side of his nature.

It had all started years ago at preparatory school, progressing from there to his Army service in the Great War when he'd served as a junior intelligence officer in Palestine and been introduced to certain practices in the musk-scented bordellos which catered especially for tastes like his.

The first time he and Luise von Losch encountered each other Roland had known instinctively that here was a woman able and willing to give him what he craved. He had not been disappointed. During the weeks spent together promoting her photographic collection, Luise had shown him a glimpse of paradise so marvellously, shamelessly, erotically decadent that she'd become the object of his sexual obsession and turned the principles and values of his life around.

Now she had returned to Berlin and he felt like a man deprived of his very existence. He longed to be with her, and couldn't be; and because of what he'd done against Vanessa, rejecting her physically, being unfaithful to her, Roland's unhappiness was further fuelled by a bad conscience which manifested itself not in the usual way – buying his wife gifts and showering attention – but in guilty resentment.

The exchange of words between them this particular evening had been the first sign of the cracks which were insidiously beginning to weaken the structure of their marriage.

'Give me just five minutes that's all, Vanessa, won't you?'

Larret Fitzgerald's voice on the other end of the phone line held a note of pleading urgency.

'I'm sorry, it isn't convenient,' she said again.

'Listen – if you dislike me because of what happened at Boningale, I've already told you I apologise. I can't bear to think anything I did upset you.'

'You didn't upset me. And I don't dislike you. I simply wish you'd stop telephoning.'

'So when may I see you again?'

'I don't think you should.'

'But darling, you can't imagine what this is doing to me. I *love* you, for God's sake! I've been in hell for weeks—'

'I really do have to go now.'

'No – don't hang up.'

Vanessa closed her eyes. She felt exhausted. Roland's moods had swung from bad to worse in the space of a few short days and she was almost at the end of her tether trying to make allowances for him.

'Hello, are you still there?'

'Yes,' she said wearily, 'I'm still here. Larret . . . don't you think it's rather pointless, all this ringing up wanting to see me?'

'What else can I do – I daren't come to your house. If I wrote to you I doubt if you'd reply. Oh Vanessa – darling – the situation we're in, it's breaking my heart. I can't sleep, I can't eat, I can't concentrate on my work—'

'Please stop this. It isn't doing any good. Try and forget me.' But her words had no conviction. The truth was, she didn't wish Larret to forget her. She was feeling so low at the moment, so unhappy, she would have given the earth to be held in his arms and loved, just to feel wanted for a while. 'In any case, I'm going away, so it's a waste of time telephoning again.'

'You're going away?' She heard his tone change. 'Where to?'

Ought she to tell him? 'Pembrokeshire.'

'Oh.' Silence. 'When?'

'Next weekend, I think. I'm not certain.'

Silence again.

'I *must* go now, Larret. Goodbye.' But she didn't hang up the receiver. She couldn't. In the gilt-framed mirror above the hall table her face looked back at her with reproach in its expression.

'Hello – hello – Vanessa! Listen – is your husband travelling with you?'

'No . . . no, he isn't. Now please let me go.'

'Just one more thing, darling. This trip, it's the one you mentioned, to look for your father's family? What was the name of the place – Roth something, wasn't it?'

She looked at the face in the mirror again. Why

not tell him, the eyes seemed to say? Where's the harm?

'Amroth. The place is called Amroth.'

7

It was a moment Vanessa knew she was going to remember always. The open windows let in the sound of the sea smacking against the breakwaters on Amroth beach, and the mewing of gulls, and the sun-warmed, salt-scented breeze which stirred the parlour curtains of the boarding-house.

'This here's your Dadda's likeness,' her aunt Gwladys repeated; and for the first time since she was a tiny baby Vanessa was looking at her father's face, the face of Owen James the Fisher Poet.

The sparkling sea and the sunlight, the cliffs and the gull-shadowed sands – the familiar sights and sounds which he had known, she herself was sharing with him now she thought as she stared at the sepia photograph on the wall.

The years had faded his image. The features smiling back at her were blurred a little, the figure in the fisherman's jersey and corduroys standing in a doorway had that unreal, almost dreamlike quality of summers long ago captured for ever in an instant of time by the camera-plate. But humour and intelligence were there, and the dark Welsh handsomeness which had stolen her mother's heart away all those years before.

'How old was my father when this was taken?'

'*Duw*, now you've asked me!' Gwladys Lloyd, Owen's

sister, had to think. A little dumpy grey-haired woman, she was landlady of 'Min-y-don', the family-run boarding-house at which Vanessa's parents had first met. Enquiries at the New Inn at the other end of Amroth, where Vanessa stayed last night, had found her. 'Now you've asked me! As far as I remember it was the year his book of poems was printed, and that was—' Gwladys wrinkled her forehead.

'Nineteen hundred and two,' Vanessa said. She couldn't tear her eyes away from the photograph. After all this time, her entire lifetime, living with a mental concept based on her mother's descriptions, actually to see her father's face had brought her very near to tears. 'He looks . . . much younger than I'd always imagined him. Do I resemble him in any way?'

'I can't see much of a resemblance. No, you're more like your Mam as I remember her.' Gwladys turned her attention to the generously-laden tea trolley by the table in the window. Other members of the family were expected any minute. 'There's a pity Florence couldn't come with you to look us up, like.'

Vanessa had very much wanted her mother to join her on this visit, but Florence Parrish had had to decline. She was too frightened of upsetting Ernest, was the excuse she made; but Vanessa guessed at an understandable reluctance to stir up the past again and revive bitter-sweet memories of the love and happiness Florence had known in her first marriage.

'She'll come another time perhaps, out of season when you're less busy and there's room to put us up here. She sends her loving regards, by the way, and insists that I take her back news of you all.'

*　　*　　*

It was a curious experience joining the relatives for tea, sitting in the parlour of 'Min-y-don' where her father must often have sat all those years gone by, part of the family to which she herself belonged by blood and yet was a stranger. There was Gwladys's sister Nesta, married to a local farmer; and two young women who were Vanessa's cousins, the daughters of her uncle Wynford James; and another cousin, Gwladys's own daughter, who lent a hand with the running of the boarding-house. The menfolk were at work, of course. Vanessa would be meeting them at a family meal planned for Saturday night at Tregethin, Nesta's husband's farm.

It struck her how alike these women were, with their comfortable round bodies and comfortable round pleasant faces, and their voices that chattered non-stop in an accent whose Welsh cadences were softened by a rural burr. She noticed, too, how often each of them seemed to be watching her – examining her – not openly but from the edges of their eyes; and it suddenly occurred to her what worlds apart they were, her life and theirs.

What excited most wonderment was that she should have come down to Pembrokeshire alone without her husband. The idea of a married woman behaving in such an independent fashion had them all looking askance at one another; and though Vanessa couldn't quite understand the astonishment, the thought did cross her mind that in coming here she had journeyed back across twenty years in time. The lifestyle and conventions of a small Welsh seaside village were not the style and conventions of a major Midlands industrial town keeping pace with the changes of the post-war decade. Compared with her own, these women lived narrow, socially prescribed existences whose boundaries were their husbands, homes and children. Their conversation revolved around the minutiae of domesticity and gossip.

'How long have you been married?' she was asked.

She told them.

'And no children still?' It was almost like a reproach, an accusation.

'What work does your husband do for a living, then?'

She explained he was proprietor of an art gallery.

'An art gallery! *Duw*, fancy that!' They examined her afresh, their eyes pitying her for having a man in such a lily-white-handed useless occupation.

Vanessa had wanted to talk about her father, ask them questions. But his death had occurred so long ago his sisters could only offer generalities for answers, and the younger ones had never properly known him. Scribble, scribble, that was all he ever seemed to do, said Nesta; and Vanessa had a picture of him sitting alone with only the sound of the sea, feverishly pouring out in words the burning beauty of his imagination.

'I do a lot of scribbling myself,' she said, diffidently, 'you know – poetry, short stories, feature articles.' And again she read their eyes. They had been proud of their brother the Fisher Poet, proud of seeing his photograph in the newspapers, and folk with fancy names writing him letters from faraway places; but she sensed they had never really understood him, because he was different, not like them; a prodigy touched with the magic of the bards.

Her own inheritance was that 'different' side of him. She was as much the fruit of his talent as of his blood. And because she was kindred and yet doubly alien, the family's welcoming reception was stiffened with an undertow of caution.

*   *   *

She felt it again, less markedly, on Saturday night at Tregethin.

The farm lay a mile or so inland from Amroth among wooded, gently-rounded hills running down towards the sea. It stood at one side of the lane, stone-built and sturdy under its grey slate roof and its deep-ledged windows reflecting the golden light of a westering sun. Like many of the farms in the area, Tregethin was old; two hundred years old, said Ivor Lewis, Nesta's husband, when Vanessa enquired. It had been in his family for generations, and she could hear the pride in his deep, strong voice when he said that.

There were fifteen people at table this evening, and the wonder of it was that they were all so comfortably accommodated in the homely flagstoned kitchen. Had the whole family been there, Nesta said, she would have been feeding twice as many. She would have managed too, her capable manner implied.

Vanessa was put to sit between aunt Gwladys and her uncle Wynford James, a stocky man of middle height who worked as a boat builder along the coast at Saundersfoot. She had been told that of the brothers and sisters Wynford was the one who most closely resembled her father (a third brother, Tom, had been killed in the Great War) and during the meal she caught herself studying his features with engrossed absorption, trying to find in those weatherbeaten looks the darkly handsome face of the faded photograph.

'You'll be wearing Dadda away with your eyes!' one of his daughters said across the table, laughing.

'You leave her get on with it, now,' Wynford joked, brushing up the ends of his moustache, 'I'm forgetting the last time it is a fine handsome woman paid my old face such attention.'

Vanessa ducked her head to hide her blush as everyone joined in his good humour. To tell the truth, she was feeling a little self-conscious about her appearance this evening. She'd put on a knee-length tubular frock in pale gold silk, belted at the hips, hardly the most suitable attire for a farmhouse supper but the only evening wear she'd packed to bring. The other women were dressed in sensible summer cottons with hemlines touching their ample calves and their plump arms straining at the sleeves of cardigans. Vanessa felt decidedly overdressed, like a hot-house bloom amongst a patch of country flowers.

The meal was typically generous of the family's hospitality: steaming dishes heaped with food passed back and forth across the table to be piled upon plates and forked into appreciative mouths which somehow never stopped talking. The beef was home-killed, the vegetables home-grown, the blackberries picked fresh that morning from the field hedgerows.

There was no alcohol. Everyone drank tea.

'Come on – *duw*, there's plenty more!' they kept urging her. 'Put some flesh on you, look.' It offended them to leave food on the plate; an insult to the house, almost.

Vanessa, who hadn't been eating well for some time now, declined further helpings with repeated apologies, wondering whether they felt she was letting them down. When supper finished at last and the women got up together to clear the table and see to the dishes, she was shooed away outside to take the air, as though her meagre appetite were an indication to them that her English blood had made her 'delicate'.

The day had been very warm for early September. The air outdoors felt balmy still, full of the clean sweet smell of new-mown meadow grass, overlying the resinous dusty green of the summer woods. The light had almost faded, and the sunset was only a crimson afterglow beyond the violet shadows of the western hills.

Standing out here, a sense of wonder at the land's enchanted beauty overwhelmed her, a sudden intense pride in the legacy bequeathed her by her father. She knew she could never properly belong to his family, and yet some part of her, her James part, had its roots here. It was as if her life had hitherto been like a book lacking its opening chapter: now she was able to read that chapter at last and understand rather better the story which followed.

Pipesmoke drifted past her. There was a footfall on the pebble path behind.

'They have pushed you out, have they, that old clack of hens,' said her uncle Wynford.

She turned with a little rueful smile. 'Do you think I should go back indoors and offer to give them a hand?'

'Talk sense, girl – how can they discuss you if you are potching about in the kitchen there under their feet?'

She acknowledged the logic of this, and turned back again to the dusk-dimmed vista of fields and woodland falling gently away southward to the straight dark horizon of the sea.

For a while the two of them stood together in silence; until Vanessa said on a sudden shivering sigh, 'How beautiful it is here. There's a certain wild and eerie loveliness about this place . . . something mystical and timeless. You can almost *feel* it, can't you.'

'You have your Dadda's soul in you,' Wynford observed, sucking on his pipe. 'He loved these old hills and woods, did my brother Owen. Hours he would

spend walking in them, and then he would come home
and write for hours more about—' he paused a moment –
'about "pictures of echoes that call in the darkness lonely
and lost under tall trees and towers",' quoting the line as
though it were a familiar favourite he'd often called to
mind throughout the years.

'Oh – which of the poems is that from?'

'Which one? There, I'm forgetting now. He wrote
so many.'

They fell silent again, before Wynford went on reflectively, 'Any bit of paper would do for his composing. He
would copy it out in a fair hand in an exercise book – you
know, ruled with lines, like children use for school – and
keep the book tucked safe under his mattress. Sometimes
he would let me see, and sometimes not. After he and
your Mam got married I remember he took with him
half a dozen of these books to Tenby – every one of
them filled with his poems they were, too. What became
of them when he died I cannot say.'

'I can,' Vanessa said. 'My stepfather destroyed them.'

'*Duw, duw.*' Her uncle drew in his breath. '*Duw, duw*,
what a waste. Did he know what was in them?'

'He knew. He destroyed everything. All the letters and
photographs as well. Even the marriage certificate.' She
had never told anyone before about the marriage certificate. That had been Ernest Parrish's ultimate desecration
of her father's existence.

Wynford removed his pipe and spat over the wall.

'*Twp,*' he said.

Vanessa didn't ask what it meant.

'Mother wanted to keep in touch with the family and
bring me on visits, but he refused to let her. He was
insanely determined on us breaking every tie, which is

why I've grown up knowing so little about you all. Didn't you – I mean, didn't it ever occur to you to wonder why she never brought me back again?'

'She was a young and marriageable woman. She had gone home to her own people. It was not our place to interfere.'

'But wasn't there anyone curious to find out what had become of me?'

Her uncle patted his waistcoat pocket in search of his matches.

'We knew what had become of you. Mr Parrish wrote to your grandmother at 'Min-y-don' – Gwladys has the letter somewhere. We were not to think of you again, it said. You had been given a new name and a new life, and you would be brought up knowing nothing of your real father. From that time on you were to be as dead to us as Owen was – I believe that was the wording of the letter, but Gwladys will correct me.'

'Even so, he couldn't keep me from learning the truth in the end,' Vanessa said bitterly. 'He wanted to wipe out my mother's past as though it had never existed, and when he found he couldn't kill her love and take away her happy memories, instead he tried his best to crush her with his criticising and his bullying. But Mother still told me. Despite all he could do, she still told me. I can't remember a time I didn't know my real name was Vanessa James and my father had been a celebrated poet . . . and that I should be very proud of him.'

She turned away her head to hide her expression; but the pain and contempt in her voice had said it all.

'It's good you are telling me this.' She heard the scrape of a match, the sputter of its flame as Wynford re-lit his pipe; and when he had it smoking again to his satisfaction, he went on, 'I was closer to Owen than any in our family. The day he drowned at sea . . . no, even now I cannot speak of that, it cuts too deep, but this I will say, that I lost my friend as well as my dear brother. He was the dreamer I could never be. He saw my visions for me and he set them down in words I had no gift to write. When his book of poetry was printed he sought me out and placed a copy in my hand and told me, "This is for you, Wyn *bach*, because you know what it is I am seeing, and you understand".'

In the deepening dusk Vanessa saw her uncle's profile lit for a second by the glow of his pipe as he stopped to draw on it again. Years of working outdoors in all weathers had engraved the lines on his face and his dark moustache was grizzled iron-grey; but there was still some trace of a younger and well-featured man not too unlike her father, and no doubt with her father's way of speaking.

This is as near as I shall ever come to being with Dadda, she thought.

Because she was so moved, and because she wanted to share her feelings with her uncle, she hugged his arm and laid her head against his shoulder.

He pressed her hand, giving it a long, warm squeeze.

'If your Dadda could have lived to see you grown, there's proud of you he'd be,' he said a little gruffly. And then after a pause, 'Nesta tells me you are a poet too.'

'I try to be, after a fashion.'

'Well then, there is something I have for you here—'

Releasing her, Wynford reached inside his jacket pocket and fetched out a flat, slim oblong wrapped in paper. 'It is something of mine very dear and precious that I want you to keep.'

No need to ask what it was. She knew instinctively. The copy of *The Sapphire Shell* which her father had given to his brother all those years ago.

The moon had fully risen by the time she left Tregethin, and its sheen silvered the wet sands on Amroth beach and edged the glittering waves of an outgoing tide. Before she retired to bed in her room at the New Inn, Vanessa stood for a little while by the sea wall watching the lights of Tenby twinkle prettily across the bay, reminding herself that tomorrow she must go back to the churchyard and take some flowers for her father's grave. Her aunts had shown her where it lay, but their busy company was a distraction from the peace and stillness which would have allowed her to be with him privately in her heart.

After the clean, salt freshness of the night air, the cigarette smoke and stale beer smell of the public bar caught at the back of her throat. As she went towards the stairs, she felt rather than saw someone come up behind her; and a voice she knew and recognised immediately said, 'You know how to keep a chap hanging about, don't you, darling.'

Her hand flew to her breast. She spun round.

Larret Fitzgerald laughed at her startled reaction. 'Surprised you, eh?'

'Larret –! Good God! What are *you* doing here?' she cried out.

'Oh, I fancied a bit of a holiday, don't you know.' He came forward and caught her round the waist, making it the most natural gesture in the world. 'And Amroth sounded such a charming spot.'

'But – how did you know where to find me?'

'Deduction, my angel. There are no hotels, the guest-houses are full, and only two inns cater for bed and breakfast.'

She tried to pull away, throwing a flustered glance towards the door of the bar. 'But didn't the landlord wonder who you were?'

'He did.' Larret gave her one of his heart-stopping grins. 'I informed him I was your husband.'

8

'You can't just *say* that! You can't just walk into a place and say you're my husband!'

Vanessa was mortified. Mortified as well as acutely embarrassed, because hadn't she told Larret she was coming to Amroth; half-hoping that perhaps he'd follow her? Last night at the New Inn she had refused to let him anywhere near her room – and then didn't get a wink of sleep all night for thinking about him.

Now, early Sunday morning, he was back again, behaving for all the world as though 'Wifey' was being a sulky little madam for not being better pleased to have him join her.

She picked up a piece of driftwood from the shingle and threw it as far as she could into the waves. Amroth beach was virtually deserted. Only a few people were out at this hour, strolling along with their dogs by the edge of the sea.

'You can't just *say* you're my husband,' she repeated angrily.

'Sure and why not?' Larret seemed to find the whole thing somehow amusing. 'I thought it a damn' good idea, myself. Saves a lot of awkward explanations.'

'Oh, that's what you thought, is it. You don't really believe I intend introducing you to everyone as Roland, do you?'

'How will they know the difference, darling, when they've never set eyes on the genuine article?'

'They're my relatives, Larret – my father's family – and I'm not going to tell a pack of lies and mislead them.'

'In that case why tell them anything?'

'I'll have to say *something*! They're not likely to ignore you. By tomorrow it'll be all over Amroth that my "husband" has arrived from the Midlands, then what do I say? "Sorry, aunt Gwladys, it's only a silly practical joke"? Let me tell you, they won't think much of me letting myself be pursued down here by a man I'm not married to – joke or no silly joke.'

Larret pulled a face. 'A pity the Welsh are so lacking in humour.'

'Don't mock. I'm half-Welsh myself, remember.'

'Which accounts for your powers of enchantment to ravish my heart,' he said suavely.

Vanessa turned on him. 'Oh, try to be serious for heaven's sake! Can't you appreciate the compromising position you've put me in, telling people we're married?'

'I *am* being perfectly serious, my darling. And far from compromising you, on the contrary I'm doing my best to protect your reputation – as I'll explain if only you'll shut up for a minute and listen.'

He caught her to him, kissing her on the mouth to silence her.

'I want to make love to you, Vanessa, you know I do. I want us to be together somewhere we don't have to keep an eye on the time or worry we're going to be recognised. I want to spend a whole night alone with you in my arms—'

'Protecting my reputation?' she broke in incredulously. 'Don't you think you're presuming rather a lot?'

'*Listen*, I said!' Larret gave her a shake and kissed her again. 'I've got the whole thing worked out for us. There's a place to let a couple of miles from here. I've rented it for the week, and told the farmer chappie who owns it we're on holiday. He won't ask questions. I paid him in advance. That's all he's interested in. As far as your relatives are concerned, I'm Roland Antrobus here to join his lovely young wife for some peace and privacy – so what reason could they have to be scandalised?'

'You don't know them,' said Vanessa; and all of a sudden her heart was skipping beats. 'They'll insist on entertaining you. They're frightfully hospitable.'

'And as nosey as the Irish, I don't doubt.' Larret smiled into her upturned face, brushing the wind-blown hair from her eyes. 'Just leave it all to me, Wifey dearest.'

'I wish you'd stop calling me that.'

'Oh, but we have to keep up appearances. Most important.'

She looked away across the beach. Then after a moment looked back at him and answered gravely, 'All right – but I'm jolly well not going to call you Hubby.'

And because 'Hubby' sounded such an absurdly smug little word the way she'd said it, Vanessa repeated it again, starting to laugh on a slightly hysterical note that betrayed the wrought-up state of her emotions.

If her mother and father had listened to the voice of reason they would not have married, and she herself would never have been born. But Florence and Owen had been in love, blind and deaf to everything but what their hearts had

91

prompted them to do; and except that she was someone's wife already, wasn't her own situation very similar to theirs, Vanessa thought.

Sitting beside her father's grave in the tranquil quietness of Amroth churchyard, she admitted to herself that she *was* in love with Larret Fitzgerald, in love with his arrogant charm and his movie-star looks, in love with the thrill of being held in his arms and knowing he wanted her.

He made her feel so special, so desirable, so beautiful – all the things her husband had denied her, more so since Luise von Losch had arrived on the scene. Her starved femininity was magnetised by Larret's sexuality.

She knew she was capable of enjoying physical passion, her sterile love-making with Roland told her that. She also knew that she wanted Larret so much nothing else mattered, not propriety or morals, not even the danger to her hollow-centred marriage. She would be *glad* to give him her virginity, even proud that she was able still to offer him her purity because there was no other man in the world she would rather lose it to than him, she thought.

Don't blame me, Dadda, she whispered to the grey slate headstone. Don't condemn me. I know you understand the way I'm feeling. Once upon a time you felt it too, this wonderful emotion, so it can't be wrong. I want him so badly, Dadda, please believe me. And even if we haven't got a future—

No, she wouldn't think of that.

'Sufficient unto the day thereof' the headstone told her, the words inscribed there almost like an answer.

She touched her father's name above the quotation, tracing its weathered lettering with her fingers. 'Owen

John James. Born 23rd June 1880. Drowned at sea 2nd January 1906, aged 25 years.'

Closing her eyes Vanessa tried to conjure up his image, a young man hardly older than herself with so much yet to give to life, and take from it. What a tragic waste, to die with all that talent lost, all that bright promise still unrealised. A tragic, tragic waste . . . like countless thousand others of his generation who less than a decade later would march away to Flanders and never return.

She looked at his grave again, at the flowers she'd picked from aunt Gwladys's garden after Larret had left her this morning. At least you were spared the war, Dadda. You didn't have to go through that terrible hell before you died. It was the sea – the sea you loved – that took you, not the bloody slaughter in the mud of Passchendaele.

It was some consolation.

The sun felt pleasantly warm on the nape of her neck and the stillness seemed to wrap itself around her, no sound except the twitter of birds in the thick green yews, and the distant drawn-out whisper of the sea. From where she was sitting Vanessa could see the dancing sparkle of the waves through a gap between the valley's wooded slopes; and if she raised her eyes, in the afternoon haze was the flat dark shape of Caldey Island crouching in the waters outside Tenby.

She had never cared for churchyards; but this one was so full of peaceful beauty and repose she felt the dead slept very gently here, and wished again her mother had come with her because a visit might have eased the wound of grief Florence still carried even after all these years in memory of her beloved Owen.

Maybe the way things happened had been fated,

though. Otherwise there would be no darling Larret coming to fetch her this evening from the New Inn, and no week alone together, just the two of them, in the house he'd rented for them at Llanteg.

The place had apparently once been a coaching inn, said Larret. You could still see the stables at the back, and the wheel ruts where the stage-coaches had turned into the lane. It had the most fascinating history – and a marvellous atmosphere – and amazing views of the countryside and coast.

He knew Vanessa was simply going to adore it.

She did; the moment she saw it.

The evening sun was beginning to sink into swathes of rose-flushed cloud low in an ivory sky, sending shadows from the trees creeping across the lawn to touch the front of the house. A wall-garden spilled over with vibrant summer colours, crimson and orange and gold against the white of the stonework, and the long sash windows framed by sun-bleached shutters gave the place an old-fashioned elegance which added to the charm of its appearance.

'Well, darling?' Larret asked, leaning over to open the door of his nippy little Triumph and let Vanessa out. 'What d'you think – you like it?'

'Oh, Larret, it's perfect!' She was like a child in her enthusiasm. 'Aren't you clever to find such a beautiful house – and *look* at those views!'

'Only the best for my special girl. Just wait till you see what it's like inside.'

He vaulted easily out of the car and came and caught her by the waist to kiss her; then lifted her into his arms and carried her, laughing, across to the porch, setting her lightly back on her feet to feel inside his jacket pocket after the key.

'You know you've got to say the password before I'm allowed to let you in?'

She returned his teasing smile. 'You'd better tell me what it is.'

Cupping her face between his hands Larret kissed her again, with a lingering gentleness. 'I love you,' he murmured against her lips. 'I love you, my darling.'

'That's . . . the password?'

As always at the touch of his mouth Vanessa experienced a thrill of pleasure. She was so happy at this moment, so sure of what she wanted, that when he nodded and said yes she answered without any hesitation, 'I love you . . . oh, Larret darling, I *do* love you.' And it was the first time she had ever admitted that to him.

He gave her a warm hug and unlocked the door, standing aside with a flourish to usher her within. 'The magic words are spoken. Open sesame!'

Someone had already lit the gaslamps in the entrance hall and left them burning low, and the pools of golden-yellow light made a cosy, welcoming atmosphere. Immediately in front, a broad flight of stairs led upward to a galleried landing, while downstairs doors opened into well-proportioned rooms which at one time must have been the public bar and dining room of the coaching inn.

'Look at this—' said Larret elatedly, catching Vanessa's hand and drawing her into the first of the rooms. 'Isn't it marvellous? Look at that fireplace – eighteenth century without a doubt. And the gesso frieze round the walls – see that moulding? Beautiful! D'you know, darling, it's most unusual to find a period property with so many original features. The Victorians had a habit of ripping out anything of character and ruining perfectly good interiors with their ghastly renovations—'

He started to laugh. 'Anyhow, that's my professional opinion. Seriously though, what do you think, Vanessa – isn't this house absolutely made for us?'

She nodded, gazing about her. Perhaps the furniture was a little shabby and the Turkey carpets worn in places, but it gave the room a comfortably lived-in feeling, an impression enhanced by the gleam of copper and polished surfaces reflecting the last rays of sun streaming in at the windows. There was a faint smell of beeswax and roses everywhere.

'I wonder whose home it's been,' she said, going across to examine a pair of pictures on the wall, original watercolours by the look of them. 'Not the farmer's surely. Didn't you mention his place lies further up the valley?'

'I think he said his sister used to live here.' Larret took out his cigarettes and lit one. 'Why don't you wander round and see over the rest of the house while I fetch in our stuff from the car?'

She was upstairs when Larret found her again, sitting in the window seat of one of the bedrooms, her shapely legs curled under her on the cushion, lost in contemplation as she stared out at the fading landscape. She was thinking about last evening at Tregethin, with that other dusk falling while she'd talked to uncle Wynford of her father. Only twenty-four hours ago, yet already it seemed like a lifetime; and if anyone had told her she'd be spending the following night with Larret Fitzgerald—

'Shall I light the gaslamp, darling?' he asked, interrupting.

'Oh – no, not just yet.' She looked at him across her shoulder, smiling. 'Come and sit with me here and watch the sunset.'

'You're a funny romantic little thing, aren't you,' he said, kissing the back of her neck and sparing only a fleeting glance for the view before he sat himself on the cushion behind and folded her into his arms. 'Adorably sweet, though. It's always baffled me how you and Sybil managed to be related, you're both so different.'

Her half-sister's name introduced an unpleasantly jarring note.

'I'd rather we didn't talk about Sybil. Not here.'

'Sorry. Stupid of me. Didn't think.'

Larret held Vanessa tighter and nuzzled her ear; but her mood of happiness was broken and after a moment or two she said awkwardly, 'Darling . . . can I ask something personal. Did you and she ever . . . I mean, while you were engaged, did you ever go to bed together?'

'What a question to ask a chap!'

He tried to make light of it; but she said again, more insistently, '*Did* you?'

'I thought you didn't want to talk about her.'

'I don't.'

'Then let's drop the subject, eh.' He started to nuzzle her ear again, his hand moving over the silken folds of her frock to caress the swell of her breast.

Vanessa closed her eyes. Of course he had taken Sybil to bed, and of course she minded just a little; but she wouldn't allow that to spoil the magic of what was going to happen this evening. The scene was set, the circumstances were right, everything was perfect – the time, the place, the atmosphere, the way she felt towards this man. She *wanted* to give herself to Larret as proof of how much she loved and trusted him, and that was all that really mattered. The rest was a distraction.

His fingers found the outline of her nipple and started playing with it gently while he teased the nape of her neck with his tongue, his breath warm against her skin. His practised touch set pulses of pleasure throbbing inside her, and when he cupped her other breast to stroke it, Vanessa felt a deliciously languorous excitement spreading slowly through her body as her senses began responding in a way she'd never known before, certainly never with Roland.

'Do you like me doing this, my darling?' he murmured. 'Does it make you feel good?'

She gave a little whimpering moan and turned in his arms to find his mouth, pressing herself against him and yielding her modesty to the growing abandonment of her desire.

'Slowly, my angel, slowly. There's no need to rush, we've got all night.' Larret drew her to her feet and held her away from him, a half-smile on his handsome face as he gazed into her eyes and read in them her trembling eagerness. 'I've waited so long for this moment . . . we mustn't be impatient. I want to savour you . . . every beautiful, wonderful inch of you.'

He kissed her, tasting the sweetness of her parted lips, feeling them quiver when his hands slipped down the curve of her hips and caressed her thighs.

'Oh Larret, I love you, I love you,' she sighed breathlessly.

Beyond the window, the dove-grey dusk muted the colours of the countryside and absorbed the last crimson flush from the western horizon. In a while the room had grown quite dark except for a soft reflection of light from the gaslamps downstairs in the hall.

He undressed her; and when she had nothing left on but lace suspender belt and stockings, he caught her in his arms and carried her into the room next door where a big double bed was already made up. Here Larret laid her down against the pillows and began to kiss her body slowly and sensuously, each touch of his lips and tongue rousing Vanessa to a state of almost unbearably exquisite anticipation; and when he was naked himself and lying beside her ready to take her, she buried her face against his shoulder and whispered, 'I've never done this before . . . you're the first one, my darling. Roland couldn't . . . he isn't able to.'

She felt him pause.

'You're still a virgin?'

'Yes.'

'Oh my beloved girl – oh God, this is perfection!'

He crushed her to him, his own sexual arousal suddenly heightened beyond control by her confession; and just before he took her, a moment before the honey-hearted pain of penetration, she heard him give a low, exultant laugh.

9

'Well – what do you think?'

Sybil Parrish struck a pose in the doorway, one hand behind her head, the other on her hip, showing her appearance off to her parents. 'Don't I look a knockout!'

'You look more like some cheap little tart with that muck all over your face,' her father said sourly, glancing across the top of his evening paper. 'You're wearing too much lip rouge, Sybil. Go and wash it off.'

She pouted at him; and when he continued to glare, she gave a shrug and walked past his armchair to the walnut-veneered sideboard in the window bay, deliberately moving her hips in an insolent swagger.

'And while you're at it, put some decent clothes on,' Ernest Parrish added. 'I'm not having you go out of this house showing everything you've got, you hear? There's not enough material in that thing to make a blasted dish-rag.'

'But it's her new frock, Ernest,' his wife came in with one of her appeasing, nervous smiles. 'You know, she told you all about it – didn't you, Sybil? Didn't you tell your father about getting that frock on discount from Beatties?'

Sybil hunted round in the sideboard drawer where her father kept his supply of cigarettes, and helped herself to a packet. Since starting work as a junior sales assistant in ladies' fashions at Beatties, the big department store in Victoria Street, she had added to the contents of her wardrobe with several new stylish outfits, none of which found favour with Mr Parrish. The one she'd put on to go dancing this evening, a tunic of oyster satin with a plunging backline, fitting her down to the knee like a slinky sheath, was just the sort of thing that most disgusted him. No respectable female would ever dream of showing herself in public without wearing corsets. And it was obvious their Sybil hadn't got a stitch on underneath except for what she called her 'scanties'.

The girl put a cigarette between the scarlet bow of her lips and lit a match to it, tilting her head back to blow out the smoke.

'Pour me a glass of sherry, Mother, will you,' she said, avoiding her father's eye. 'I've just about got time for one before Gloria's here.'

'And that's another thing,' said Mr Parrish. 'Who's this Gloria?'

'I've told you. Gloria Millington. I work with her.'

'I don't like the look of her.'

'What's wrong with her? We have a good laugh together, Gloria and me, she's a lot of fun.'

'She dyes her hair.'

'What if she does? Everybody dyes their hair these days.' Touching a hand to her own sleek bob, Sybil watched her mother open the sunburst-patterned door of the drinks cabinet and take out the sherry decanter.

'Shall I pour you a glass as well, Ernest?' Mrs Parrish asked him.

He ignored her. 'I don't hold with it,' he told Sybil, eyeing her strawberry blondness with a hard frown of suspicion, 'so don't let me catch *you* getting up to that otherwise there'll be something to say about it, you hear?'

'*I* don't need to, do I, Daddy.' She drew on her cigarette again, and accepted the drink from her mother. Behind her, the clock on the fawn-tiled mantelpiece chimed a quarter to eight and she checked her wrist-watch automatically before raising the glass to her lips.

'Yes – well, you mind what I've said to you.'

Folding his newspaper Mr Parrish put it aside and got to his feet; and seeing his wife still hovering anxiously, he added on a note of impatience, 'Don't stand there, Florence. Get me a sherry if you're going to!' before turning away to glance out of the window at the sound of the garden gate banging shut.

Sybil came and peered over his shoulder. In the half-light beyond the sitting room's reflection a young woman in a fox-fur scarf and felt cloche hat was coming up the path.

'Oh, here's Gloria now,' she exclaimed, knocking back her drink and shoving the empty glass aside. 'She's early – eight o'clock I said. Hang on though, I can see a car. Maybe she's cadged a lift off somebody – hope it's Jack Holroyd!'

The front door bell gave a sharp peal; and after a moment the Parrishes's maid could be heard in the hall answering it.

'Jack Holroyd's a friend of yours is he, dear?' Mrs Parrish enquired brightly, seeing to the sherry for her husband.

'Sort of.' Sybil stubbed out her half-smoked cigarette before crossing the room to the doorway.

'Come on in, Gloria, I'm almost ready. Give me a

103

couple of minutes, OK? D'you want to say hello while Myrtle goes and gets my coat?'

'Don't mind if I do.' Gloria gave her friend an approving look and a smile that showed off big, square teeth. 'Told you that frock 'ld fit you like a dream, din't I?' she went on, coming inside the sitting room. 'Hello, Mrs Parrish, Mr Parrish. How are you both? Keeping well then, eh?'

Ernest Parrish winced at the accent, Black Country overlaid with the exaggerated phoney 'poshness' of a fashion sales assistant.

'Hello, Gloria dear,' said Mrs Parrish. 'My, don't you look smart for going out this evening!'

'Oh, like it, do you?' Gloria preened herself, turning round to give them a full view of her orange-coloured taffeta two-piece, draping the fox-fur from her hand as she did when she occasionally modelled for customers. 'Twelve guineas this set me back, would you believe. The fashion buyer got it from London. Mind, it's worth the money, in't it, Sybil.'

'I'll say.' Sybil took her own coat from young Myrtle and shrugged it casually round her shoulders, not bothering to put it on. 'Here, is that Jack Holroyd's car parked at the gate?'

'Yes, we're in luck, he passed while I was waiting for the bus and said he'd give us a lift to the Palais.' Gloria treated Mr Parrish to a confiding smile. 'You don't know Jack, do you? Oh, he's ever such a nice chap – got his head screwed on, I always say. Smart as paint an' all, in't he, Sybil. Always looks as if he's just stepped out of Burton's window.'

Ernest Parrish lit himself a cigarette to get rid of the cloying smell of scent she exuded.

'And what does this Holroyd do for a living?' he asked
testily, throwing the spent match in the fireplace.

Gloria was about to tell him when Sybil came butting in
hastily, 'Look, we'd better cut along or he'll be wondering
what's happened to us,' taking her friend by the arm and
propelling her towards the door again.

'I thought I told you to wear something decent before
you went out,' her father called after her. 'Sybil—!'

She pretended she hadn't heard. 'I won't be late,
Mother. No need to wait up for me,' she said through
the closing door; then dropping her voice – 'God, that
was a near shave. He'd have gone up the ruddy wall if
you'd said how Jack makes his money.'

'It in't illegal,' Gloria hissed back.

'You kidding? An unlicensed bookie? Use your loaf!'

Ernest Parrish heard the front door slam and the
click-clack of their Louis-heeled shoes hurrying to the
gate. He drew hard on his cigarette.

'I've changed my mind,' he said. 'I'll have a whisky
instead of that sherry, Florence.'

She obeyed. Twenty years of marriage had conditioned
her never to argue.

'Our Sybil's getting herself into bad company,' he went
on, glowering through the window as Jack Holroyd's
engine revved into life to the noise of slamming doors.
'I don't know what she thinks she's playing at, mixing
with riff-raff. She wasn't brought up to associate with
girls of that Gloria's type.'

'Perhaps it's only a phase she's going through,' said
Mrs Parrish. 'Would you like soda water with your
whisky, dear?'

'I always have soda water with it, don't I? I blame
everything on that blasted Irishman, I do, jilting our Sybil

after they'd hardly been engaged above five minutes. The girl's never seemed right since, she hasn't – and you're no help to her either, Florence, encouraging her to go off dancing every weekend, coming home God knows what hour of the night. You think I'm asleep and don't hear her come in, but I do.'

'She has to have *some* recreation, dear,' replied Mrs Parrish, knowing full well her husband was always snoring his head off by the time Sybil crept in around midnight. 'And the Palais de Danse is very popular. She might find herself some nice young man there.'

'I seem to recall she met Fitzgerald dancing. She'd be better off joining a drama society or something if she wants to meet a decent class of person.'

Ernest Parrish accepted the drink his wife brought him, though it would not have occurred to him to thank her. Instead he continued belligerently, 'I never took to him from the start. He smiled too much for my liking. I might have guessed he'd turn out a bounder – and I don't care what you say, I'm still not convinced that that Vanessa didn't have a hand in what he went and did across our Sybil.' Referring to the two as 'that' Vanessa and 'our' Sybil had always been Mr Parrish's way of drawing a distinction between his child and his stepdaughter.

'I'm sure Vanessa had nothing whatever to do with it,' his wife said in a rare show of defiance.

He shot her a look of sour contempt through his cigarette smoke. 'Don't you contradict me, Florence. I know what our Sybil came and said to me the day the fellow jilted her. She's a trouble-monger, that Vanessa. Has been from the start. I mean look at her now – down in wherever it is, Pembrokeshire, grubbing into things she'd be better off leaving dead and forgotten. What's she doing it for, eh, if not to cause trouble.'

'But she's only gone for a bit of a holiday—'

'Then why not Scotland? Or the Lake District? After all I've done for her over the years I resent it very much that the girl hasn't the sense to leave blasted well alone. I notice her husband didn't bestir himself to accompany her.'

'I expect he's been too busy, dear. He couldn't find the time, that's what Vanessa said.'

Mr Parrish made a noise of disbelief and swallowed his whisky. After a moment's deliberation he said savagely, 'More likely didn't *choose* to find the time. I told Antrobus the very day he married he was making a mistake, and he's had eighteen months to realise the fact. That match is going to end in grief, you mark my words.'

Yes, you'd like it to, wouldn't you, if only to see Vanessa made unhappy, Florence Parrish thought. You've never forgiven her for the constant reproach to your pride that she's Owen's child. Aloud she said, 'Oh, while I remember, dear, if you'll excuse me I'll go and have a word with Cook about tomorrow's menu.'

Sybil had been totally devastated when Larret ditched her earlier this year, but her tough little personality and the natural resilience of youth had pulled her through. The wound was to her pride as much as anything; and it was pride that forced her to lift her chin and look the world in the eye again, pretending rotters like Larret Fitzgerald weren't worth a toss.

Only her parents had seen how deeply she'd been hurt by his rejection and how much her state of mind had been

107

affected. Not even Vanessa knew the truth, not all of it. To her friends – and she had quite a few – Sybil seemed to shrug off getting jilted as 'one of those things', a stupid mistake, and throw herself back into the social scene with reckless new gaiety. But it was all an act, of course; a brittle, artificial act to hide a broken heart.

She was the sexual type in whom men had always shown interest; and now she deliberately set out to capitalise on her attractions and get herself another decent catch, somebody as popular but richer, more exciting, and even better looking than Larret Fitzgerald. A salve, maybe. A substitute. It didn't matter.

Jack Holroyd seemed to fit the bill. Jack was actually Gloria's older sister's boyfriend; but Maisie (the sister) was a dancer in a chorus-line and off on tour a lot, which left the boyfriend free to play the field. He was coming up to thirty, with curly brown hair and eyelashes a girl could kill for, five feet eleven of muscular strength dressed in handmade silk shirts. What Sybil found most exciting about him was the frisson of danger his presence generated, not in his looks or behaviour so much as the illicit way he earned a living working from the backroom of a billiards hall, and the crowd he mixed with, flashy types who hung out in that grey area just beyond the boundaries of the law.

To a middle-class girl with a private education (she'd failed the scholarship for the High School), brought up in snobbish Tettenhall Green and with a father who practised as a solicitor, Jack Holroyd and his pals represented the forbidden fruit on the other side of the fence.

'Eh, Sybil—' Jack said casually, one arm draped across the back of her chair as they sat watching the couples on the floor, 'bet you don't know the reason you take long steps doing the Tango.'

She gave him an arch look from the corner of her eye. 'It's a joke, is it?'

'No joke. You've heard of Buenos Aires? Well, that's where the Tango started, in the brothels. An' the gauchos – the Argentine cowboys, like – couldn't be bothered taking off their spurs an' boots when they danced wi' the girls so they used to keep their legs well apart, save ripping the tarts' petticoats.'

'Go on – you're having us on, you!' Gloria Millington told him, accepting a Turkish cigarette from the packet he was offering round.

'Honest to God. I was told that by a bloke in the Merchant Navy who seen 'em doing it.'

'In a brothel.'

'In a brothel.' Jack sat up, and producing an expensive-looking petrol lighter from his pocket, leaned across the table.

'Now you've put me right off,' Gloria pouted, taking a light. 'I'll have a fit o' giggles keeping my legs apart next time I get up to do it.'

A third young woman sitting with them let out a coarse little laugh and remarked, 'I thought that was when you lay down to do it, Gloria,' before taking a light herself. This was Renée Smith, who'd been chummy with the other since their schooldays and worked as a chambermaid in a commercial hotel round the corner from the Palais in Snow Hill.

Sybil considered Renée ugly, in an attractive sort of way. She had gipsy-black hair and pale skin and thin eyebrows pencilled in above dark eyes that held a lazy, take-me-to-bed expression when she talked to men; and though she was little and skinny and almost boyishly breastless, something about the way she moved and held herself was so sinuously graceful she reminded Sybil of a small, sleek alley cat.

Gloria treated her friend's comment with a sniff and looked away, trying to think of a cutting response; then suddenly spotting a face she knew she said instead, 'Here, Jack – isn't that a pal of yours? Why don't you go and get him to join us, make up the number?'

The rest followed the direction she was pointing. In the rainbow shimmer of light reflected from the globe of twinkling mirrors below the ceiling, a figure could be seen standing alone on the far side of the floor watching the dancers swaying to the band in the final movements of the Tango.

'Bloody hell, it's Alan Slater,' Jack exclaimed. 'What's he doing here – I thought he was still down the Smoke!'

He rose to give a wave, and when the other chap failed to notice, he excused himself and left the table.

'Who's Alan Slater?' Sybil enquired.

Gloria patted a hand to her brassy blonde hair. 'Eyes off him, Sybil. It was me as saw him first.'

'He's in the same line o' business as Jack,' Renée told her, flicking the ash off her cigarette, not bothering to look round.

'He must be interesting.'

'Yes, you could say that.'

'I've heard he's got a bit of a reputation,' Gloria said avidly, watching Jack push through between the tables. 'He's been inside prison once for robbery.'

'If you're going to tell the story, get it right. He was nicked for handling stolen goods,' said Renée in an irritated tone.

'How would you know?'

'Eric told me.' Eric was Renée's current boyfriend and a pal of Jack's. He'd been supposed to meet her here at the Palais de Danse and hadn't shown up yet, which accounted for her sulky temper.

Sybil had never met anyone with a prison record and the idea added a sudden morbid thrill to her enjoyment of the evening. The band music had stopped now, the floor emptying as couples returned to their tables or popped out to use the lavatory and sneak a surreptitious tipple – the Palais wasn't licensed to sell alcohol so 'drinkies' had to be smuggled in inside overcoats and handbags.

She took out her vanity mirror to touch up her lipstick. The smoke-hazed warmth of the hall had made her nose shine, and the bottle of Empire port wine she and Renée and Gloria had been sharing between them in the Ladies gave a flush to her cheeks. She wasn't exactly looking her best, Sybil decided, but what the hell.

A shadow fell across the table, and she glanced up. For a second she couldn't see anything of the man standing in front of her because of the dazzle of lights from the revolving globe.

Then he moved, and the cupid bow of her red-rouged lips gaped open a little.

'You ain't met Sybil Parrish, have you, Alan,' Jack was telling him; but Sybil hardly heard the reply because of the sudden loud hammer of blood in her ears. She was looking at the most sexually attractive man she'd ever laid eyes on; though what it was that so instantly excited her she couldn't think. He wasn't conventionally handsome like Jack or Larret Fitzgerald, and he was older – in his forties, surely – with brilliantined hair and a pencil-thin moustache. Not her type at all.

She only knew at this moment of first meeting that she wanted Alan Slater, wanted him badly, and she intended doing everything she could to win his interest.

10

After that first wonderful night with Larret at Llanteg, the following days had brought a new awakening, a new discovery, a new exploration of sexual passion for Vanessa. Never till now had she realised how good making love would be, nor the intensity of pleasure her body was capable of feeling – as though her virginity had been a lock barring the door into the secret treasure-chamber of her womanhood.

She neglected her relatives at Amroth. Nothing mattered except being in Larret's arms. They went out to eat at Saundersfoot or Tenby, but her appetite fed more upon his kisses than on food, and the only hunger she knew was for his skilled, arousing hands, her only intoxication the sobbing heights of ecstasy he brought her to.

This surely was love, the real thing, this obsessional need to keep touching and holding him, begrudging every second he was away from her sight. Mornings seemed to come too quickly as the week slipped away, and Vanessa would watch each new dawn stealing in to trace the outline of his features as he slept beside her and long for Time to stand still, dreading the moment they must say goodbye.

Larret made her no promises for their future. Whenever she'd tried to discuss it he brushed it aside in light-hearted fashion, making a joke of it.

But then on their final night at the house something had changed, and he seemed of a sudden to be irritated by her need to be assured how much he loved her. Hadn't he proved it enough, for heaven's sake?

'You have, oh Larret, you have!' she cried. 'I've never been more happy – so happy I can't bear to think it's almost over.'

'My dear, all good things must come to an end, it's a rule of life,' he replied.

She thought he meant their week together. 'But there'll be lots of other chances – we'll make sure of that. It only needs a little careful planning. Roland's so seldom at home we can talk on the phone every day and we'll see one another as often as possible. I've been working out how best to arrange things—'

He had tried to interrupt; but she was too eager to share her dreams with him, rushing on, 'Larret, listen, what's to stop me coming over to Moseley now and again and spending a night with you? We could go out to dinner or maybe the theatre—'

'I don't think so. It wouldn't be a sensible idea. The lodgings I have aren't up to much and the landlady's a bit old-fashioned about that kind of thing. Apart from which we *must* be careful, darling. I could easily lose my job if my bosses suspect I'm messing around with a married woman. You know how it is.'

Messing around with a married woman. Put like that, it had sounded so grubbily sordid.

The hurt in Vanessa's eyes must have betrayed her, because Larret drew her into his arms and went on a little more gently, 'I'm only thinking of you, my angel. People can be so unpleasant about situations like ours. They judge by appearances. They'll remember I was engaged to Sybil and they'll start blaming everything on you, saying you deliberately set out to seduce me away from your sister, that you obviously couldn't give a damn how many hearts you break, whether it's hers, your husband's – or even your mother's.'

That had shaken her. She hadn't considered the effect their affair might have at home. She could imagine her mother's distress if it were known she had embarked on a relationship – Vanessa had to be honest, an *adulterous* relationship – with Sybil's ex-fiancé. And to make matters worse, her stepfather's reaction would be one of bitter anger which knowing him he'd take out in his usual bloody-minded fashion. Vanessa couldn't risk putting her mother through that, not even for Larret.

Yet how was she to survive being separated from him after the passionate closeness they had known together? How could she go back to living a life full of lies in the emptiness of her marriage to Roland?

'For God's sake don't say anything to Roland!' Larret urged her. 'He could turn extremely ugly and cause a lot of problems. Be patient, darling. Trust me. We'll just have to play things by ear for a bit. I'll never be further away than the end of the phone should you need me, and I'll try my best to see you whenever I can. Only *trust me* – OK?'

So many sad, reluctant farewells to make. To the lovely old house at Llanteg. To the family relatives in Amroth (with awkward apologies and a promise to return again next year). To her father's grave. To Larret.

Once back in Wolverhampton it felt as though the fortnight she had been away belonged already to another world, a beautiful golden dreamtime; and in the taxi-cab home from the station Vanessa had wondered again how on earth she was going to cope with keeping up the pretence of normality now that Larret had become her lover.

The moment she walked through the door of 'Mayville' however, she found her immediate problem had nothing to do with Larret Fitzgerald.

It was her husband Roland. Apparently he had disappeared.

None of the domestic staff knew what had happened. Roland had left them no instructions. He had simply closed the Gallery four days ago and gone – no one knew where. The only information Vanessa was able to glean from her worried phone calls was that he'd talked about business abroad. In Berlin.

When she went searching for his passport it wasn't in the bureau, nor was his leather suitcase where it should be; and the fact that his Morris Cowley had been left parked in a side-street by the station, where it was found the following morning, all pointed to the obvious: Roland had followed Luise von Losch to Germany.

Vanessa was placed in a difficult dilemma. Even so, her mother thought she should wait a further twenty-four hours before she took any action – which proved sound advice, because a telegram arrived at the house on Wednesday, saying 'Expect arrive home Saturday. Roland'.

'What did I tell you. He's been off doing some gallivanting of his own,' Larret told her on the telephone, laughing. 'Sure, and why not! You mustn't let a guilty conscience get you worked into such a tizz, my darling.'

She wished he wouldn't laugh about such things. She

had wanted his support not his amusement. And that dig about a guilty conscience hurt her just a little. It was true Larret had a habit of making light of serious matters; but at the same time Vanessa well remembered how deeply intense he had been about his love for her, and wondered whether it was because he was so sure of her now he'd made his conquest that he could afford the occasional carelessly wounding remark.

She had been nervous all day waiting for Roland, too nervous to concentrate on the half-dozen or so letters she'd tried to settle down to write. After several attempts to start one to her friend Marjorie Tiersot in France, Vanessa had abandoned the effort and instead killed time aimlessly flicking through magazines or staring out of the windows into the rain-sodden garden.

Evening had fallen and she'd already had to ask for dinner to be put back an hour when the crunch of Roland's car tyres on the gravel of the drive announced he'd arrived at last.

She came out into the hall as Iris went to open the front door, and the two of them heard the slam as he got from the car and then his footsteps, heavy, weary-sounding, coming towards them along the side of the house.

In the thin curtain of drizzle which slanted across the porch-light he looked utterly done in, his eyes so sunk and red-rimmed with fatigue that Vanessa thought immediately he must be ill and hastened down the steps to take him by the arm while Iris relieved him of his suitcase.

'Leave me, I can manage,' he said, shrugging Vanessa off and dragging himself ahead of her into the house. 'God, what a swine of a journey that's been—'

117

'You look awful, Roland. What's been going on? Are you all right?' she asked him, increasingly concerned. He seemed to be in a state of physical collapse, swaying on his feet, fumbling with the buttons of his overcoat so clumsily that Iris had to help him off with it. 'Nobody could tell me where you were – I haven't known *what* to think.'

'We'll talk about it later. At the moment all I'm interested in is a steaming hot bath and a very large brandy and soda.' Turning away, Roland blundered across the hall and started up the stairs, catching at the handrail to support himself.

Iris gave a discreet little cough. 'Beg pardon, madam, but what am I to tell Cook about serving dinner?'

'Oh, it'll have to be put back another half-hour, I suppose,' Vanessa replied distractedly. 'I'll go and speak to her myself, Iris, if you'll ask Ethel to draw the Master a bath and warm him some towels.'

Roland didn't want dinner, however. He had eaten already – he couldn't remember what or where, Euston station perhaps – and he was too exhausted to be hungry now. Instead he had another stiff brandy later by the drawing room fire while Vanessa ate alone.

When she joined him afterwards she found him in silk dressing-gown and cravat looking rather more relaxed and refreshed from his bath, though with a tell-tale flush of colour in his face.

'Let me get you a drink,' he said thickly, draining his own glass. 'I'm ready for another refill here.'

She had taken a small sherry before dinner, which was all she normally drank; but she was still so apprehensively on edge that she thought something a little stronger might help to settle her nerves and get her through the rest of this evening, and so she answered as she sat down, 'Thank you – I think I'll join you and have a brandy.'

'Good idea.'

She watched him go through the archway, none too steady on his feet still, and pour a generous amount of spirit from the decanter which young Ethel had left out for him on the Benares silver tray. Without looking round he said, 'Aren't you dying to ask where the blazes I've been these past ten days?'

There was a slight hesitation before Vanessa answered.

'I know where you've been . . . or at least I suppose I can guess. With Luise von Losch.'

'Perceptive of you.' Roland added a splash of soda to the glasses. 'And of course you're right. I've been at Lulu's apartment in Berlin. The two of us together.'

He didn't need to spell it out. She understood. It was what she had long suspected. He and his ice-blonde Fräulein had been up to much the same thing as she and Larret at Llanteg. The irony of the situation didn't escape her; but neither did it make her feel any more comfortable.

'You don't seem especially mortified,' he went on after a moment, still keeping his back turned. 'Aren't you going to make a scene about it?'

'Would you feel any better if I did?'

'I don't know. Let's face it, old girl, whatever stink you kicked up it would be no more than I damn' well deserve. I've been a lousy husband. No good to you in bed. Completely useless—'

Suddenly his voice cracked; and when he came back through the archway with their drinks Vanessa could see by his expression he was having to struggle to stay in control of himself.

'Roland—?'

'Hang on. Allow me to demonstrate what a hypocrite you've married. Suppose the boot were on the other foot, eh. Suppose I hadn't gone chasing off like a bloody fool to Berlin, that I'd stayed here, and you'd come home from your holiday in Wales and confessed to me that you'd spent that time with another man. D'you know what *I* would have done? I'll tell you. I think I'd have gone half out of my mind. I think I would want to kill you, Vanessa. Now what d'you say to that.'

She felt herself go cold.

'Come on – what d'you say?' he repeated, handing her her drink and going to stand in front of the fireplace. He was swaying slightly as he stared at her, and it occurred to Vanessa that he was more than just a little drunk.

She chose her answer carefully. '*If* I admitted such a thing, I hope you would have the decency to do what I am doing now. I hope you'd be prepared to listen to me first and at least give me a chance to explain my behaviour. Isn't that the only civilised way to deal with these situations?'

'Civilised—!' Roland made a sound that could have been a laugh, except it held such bitterness. 'Ah, but you see you've never been in my position, so the rules of civility don't apply. You can't understand how it feels can you, Vanessa, the degradation of being so totally possessed by someone they become your reason for living, your whole horizon, the only thing that really matters – that there's no hell on earth worse than the misery of losing them—'

His voice cracked again. Raising his glass he gulped its contents.

There was an awkward pause; and then Vanessa said

120

unsteadily, 'I didn't realise things had become quite so serious. That day the scrap dealer, Mr Brockhouse, was here and you and I argued, do you remember? – you reacted so angrily when I brought up Fräulein von Losch's name I suppose I must've guessed then that your regard for her went well beyond professional admiration. It was the photographic exhibition, wasn't it – all the excuses you made about helping to organise the tour. That was when it began.'

Roland nodded.

She looked down into her brandy. Its opaque amber surface trembled a little and she realised that her hand was shaking. If she was going to tell him about Larret this was the moment, one confession for another. And then what—? In the light of what her husband had half-threatened about killing her, and Larret's own insistence that their affair mustn't become known, what dangerous Pandora's Box might she not be opening?

'Have you decided yet what you're going to do?' she went on guiltily. 'I expect you'll need to think about arrangements, find somewhere you can live together. She – she wants you to do that, does she?'

Roland didn't answer; and when she glanced at his face his features were screwed up as though he were trying not to cry, his eyes tightly shut, his mouth compressed, the fleshy chin quivering into ugly dimples. It was awful to see a grown man, such a dignified and respectable figure, reduced by emotion to this sudden state of pitiable anguish.

Vanessa put her glass aside and got up from her chair, crossing the hearth to him to touch his arm.

'Perhaps you'd better tell me what's gone wrong. Obviously something's making you terribly unhappy.'

'Oh God—' Her husband averted his head from her. 'Oh God, what a bloody mess . . . what a bloody ghastly mess—'

For a moment he couldn't go on; and then he downed the rest of his brandy and let out a sobbing hiccup. 'What am I to do? She says she doesn't want me, she says I'm beginning to bore her. It's over, it's finished between us, she says. Go home to your wife, go home to England, that's all the answer I've had from her the past couple of days. God, I wish I knew what the devil I'm to do, Vanessa!'

He turned round to look at her again, his misery so raw he seemed oblivious of the tears wetting his cheeks. 'I wanted to put an end to myself, y'know . . . I tried, I really did try. I went to the Kurfürsten bridge to throw myself into the river, do it in style with a bottle of champagne to see me off. But I couldn't do it . . . I couldn't damn' well do it. D'you know why?'

Numbly Vanessa shook her head.

'I started to think about you. Yes, *you*. About our marriage. An' then I thought about this house, how empty it always used to be. An' I remembered how proud I was the day I married you, a lovely young girl, so beautiful, so innocent. Haven't I harmed her enough, I thought. What's she ever done t' deserve this – a man who's only half a husband, who betrays her trust an' deceives her with another woman . . . an' now when it's all gone wrong, instead of putting things right what's he do, he throws in the towel an' does himself in like the gutless, yellow coward he is—'

Roland gave another loud hiccup and passed a hand across his eyes. He had started slurring his words a little.

'I don't think you're in much of a state to talk about this now,' Vanessa said with something of an effort. 'Look – maybe after we've both slept on it we can discuss things more rationally tomorrow.'

In a way she felt desperately sad for her husband, sad that he was so unhappy. Because she was in love herself, she knew how much it must be hurting that Luise von Losch no longer wanted him; and her own guilt tempered any anger she might otherwise have felt about the situation.

'But I *have* t' talk about it now,' Roland said, taking her by the shoulders and supporting himself unsteadily against her. 'Don't you understand? I want you t' know how sorry I am . . . how terr'bly, terr'bly sorry. For God's sake don't leave me, Vanessa, will you . . . please, don't leave me.'

The tears ran down his face and dripped on to the paisley silk cravat, darkening it with patches that spread together like a second pattern.

'Roland, I'll need time to think before I decide what to do – that's not asking too much, is it?' Time as well to think about herself and Larret and the effect all this could have for the future.

'But I'm sorry, I'm *sorry*!' Her husband began to shake her in a frustrated effort to try and make her realise. 'I've jus' travelled halfway across Europe t' come back t' you. I *need* you, darling. Forgive me for what I've done . . . say you forgive me, please? We can start again can't we, if only you'll let me have another chance.'

He pulled her into his arms and gripped her, his face pressed into her hair, beginning to sob incoherently like a child; and because she pitied him Vanessa did her best to calm and soothe him.

123

They were quits, she thought, she and Roland. She couldn't give up Larret – but neither could she walk out on her husband, not as long as he needed her this much. The priorities of her life were rearranged maybe, yet nothing had really changed; and she was still the loser.

11

The thin net curtain hanging askew at the window let in the pale grey light of the December afternoon, etching the shabby contents of the hotel room with a depressing starkness. In a corner of the ceiling above the bed a dog-eared strip of wallpaper was peeling away with damp, and just now while Larret had been making love to her Vanessa had stared up at it, hating it, hating the room, the lumpy mattress and the creaking bedsprings, the smell of stale fried food which lingered on the stairs and in the corridor, hating everything about this cheap, rather seedy commercial hotel that Larret had brought her to.

For the first few weeks it had been difficult for them to meet, even to telephone, because Roland was at home so much, playing his role of the repentant husband and driving Vanessa to distraction with his limpet-like attentions. Thank God at least he left her alone in bed. Whatever sexual pleasure Luise von Losch had succeeded in arousing, it was something he hadn't attempted to force upon his wife, so in that respect their domestic life reverted to its previous pattern.

Not until November, a month ago now, when preparations for a Christmas exhibition at the Gallery began occupying more of Roland's time, was Vanessa occasionally able to get away to be with Larret for an afternoon, meeting midweek to make love in hotels in Birmingham or Dudley: not the romantic trysts of which she'd dreamed but furtive, hurried assignations which left her less than satisfied and feeling just a little sullied.

Why did they have to come to such places, she wondered. Each one he brought her to seemed more awful than the last, and his love-making more perfunctory as though it were something he had to perform to justify the few hours' rental of the room. And instead of being as tender as he had at Llanteg, holding her and whispering endearments, once he'd finished he would roll off her to light himself a cigarette and lie on his back – as he was doing now – saying nothing, just watching the smoke drifting upwards.

He made her feel so *anonymous*. She might as well be anyone, some woman he had paid to use, his indifference reflected by this nasty, squalid little room. All those adverse things about his reputation she'd once so foolishly dismissed were lately starting to come home to roost; and though Vanessa told herself she mustn't ask it (she'd asked it too often) she suddenly heard herself saying again:

'I bore you, don't I, Larret. You've stopped loving me.'

No answer. He didn't even move, but lay there with one arm cradling the flat, hard pillow underneath his head, cigarette between his lips, staring at the ceiling while the noise of Dudley marketplace outside intruded into the silence.

After a while Vanessa could bear it no longer. Pulling up the straps of her camisole she got off the bed. The mirror on top of the washstand flung her swollen-lipped reflection back at her, the face of some cheap little floozy, her make-up smeared and her hair a mess.

'Oh, you going already?' Larret said indifferently, speaking at last.

'There's no point in my staying.' She glanced at him through the mirror. 'Anyway I'm supposed to be doing some Christmas shopping. I might as well get on with it.'

Flicking the ash from his cigarette he propped himself on an elbow. 'If you're catching the train into Birmingham we'd better not travel together—'

'Don't worry, I didn't intend to. It would be disastrous if anybody saw us, you've made that absolutely clear.'

'I'm glad you're so discreet.' His tone was as cool as her own.

Vanessa took a comb from her handbag and started tidying her hair. After a moment she said cuttingly, 'Tell me something, Larret. Purely as a matter of interest, is this how you finish all your affairs? If so, it rather lacks the effort you put into starting them. I'd have thought saying adieu requires as much blarney as saying hello. At least it ensures you're fondly remembered.'

'You think so? You've had that experience have you, darling?'

His sarcasm annoyed her. 'If I had, no doubt I could have read the signs before this afternoon. I bore you now, don't I—'

'"I bore you now, don't I." Mother of God, not again!' Rolling back against the pillow Larret mimicked her. 'You want the truth, Vanessa? I've been hearing that so many times the last few weeks the answer is yes, actually you *do* bore me. What else can you expect – all I keep getting from you lately is the same old thing. You're no fun to be with any more, you know that? You've become depressingly predictable.'

Vanessa closed her eyes, as though shutting out his mirrored reflection would shield her against the hurt of his words. Beyond the window of this shabby room people were going about their lives shopping ready for Christmas, the broad, medieval-sounding Black Country dialect ringing out in the cries of market traders; while here inside, the love affair she dreamed would last for ever crumbled and withered away into regret.

Was this how Larret had treated her half-sister Sybil? Sybil had idolised him too; and been rejected. Vanessa remembered her coming to 'Mayville' after he'd broken off their engagement, how violently upset the girl had been, blaming Vanessa herself for poaching him off her, and wildly threatening all sorts of vengeance.

She understood it all too clearly now. Larret was an actor who enjoyed the drama of attention, the big emotional scene, playing centre stage to an adoring audience; and like an actor he was clever at feigning the part, slipping into the role . . . no real depth to him, no substance, just the ability to manipulate the affections of gullible women while hiding his true motives behind a charming facade.

She felt a sudden nauseous contempt – for herself as much as for him.

'So, I'm predictable am I,' she said. 'Like all the rest of us you've used, including Sybil. The moment we lose our hearts it's the end of the game and time to change partners – is that how it's played? No wonder you get bored so easily.'

She heard him draw on his cigarette.

'What a shallow person you are, Larret. Shallow and vain and self-centred. And to think I've been so much in love with you—'

128

'Oh for God's sake, Vanessa, do stop being a bloody fool,' he told her harshly through a mouthful of smoke. 'You're behaving like some twelve-year-old. Face up to facts – you and I fancied one another so we've had a fling, like your husband had with his glamorous Boche. OK. End of story. Now why not trot off home to Roland like a good little wifey. I've broken you in for him and shown you all the ropes – even half a man ought to be able to make it with you now if you give him a hand. Sure, but I've done the pair of you a favour and probably salvaged your miserable marriage.'

The cruelty was so gratuitously deliberate that Vanessa refused to let him have the pleasure of seeing her reduced to tears. Instead she saved her heartbreak for the train, sobbing alone in the first-class compartment that carried her away from Larret Fitzgerald and out of his life.

Christmas at 'Mayville' was a subdued affair that year. Vanessa made an effort, but her spirit wasn't in it and the festivities failed to jolly her out of herself. The ridiculous thing was, she felt such sympathy for Roland now, and several times had been on the point of risking the consequences by sharing her fellow-feelings with him. Something always stopped her: pride perhaps. She had allowed herself to be strung along by Larret, duping herself into fondly believing she was the woman who could change him, when all the time he had been using her to pander to his egotistical vanity.

The hideous part of the whole affair was the ease with which he'd done it. Oh yes, no doubt she'd meant a lot to him during the excitement of the chase while she was still beyond his reach. But once she'd been caught and had yielded herself in bed to him the interest was lost, because a man like Larret needed constant stimulation to keep his appetite whetted, and after a conquest nothing palled so much as the pursuer finding himself pursued in turn by a lover he'd already wearied of.

Depressed and disillusioned, Vanessa turned to poetry to try and exorcise her pain, pouring her emotions on to paper. Much of what she wrote was adolescent in its awfulness compared with the poems of her father, in whose beautifully moving sensitivity she'd discovered so much to console her, so much that said it all.

There was one poem in particular which seemed to encapsulate everything she felt just now, written the year before his elopement with her mother in the spring of 1904. It spoke of loss and longing, of 'wasted, wanton, wishful wanting', the emptiness of existence without love. And though her feelings towards Larret were now so disenchanted, Vanessa was still honest enough with herself to admit she missed the colour and excitement he'd injected into her rather boring life, and the physical release of sexual passion.

She hadn't realised how much she would miss *that*.

Well, their affair might be over but one good thing at least had come of it: she no longer felt so guilty about Sybil. Before, there had always been this shadow at the back of Vanessa's mind that she'd been partly to blame for wrecking her half-sister's happiness; but now that she knew she had simply been the next in line, one more diversion to add to Larret's tally, the guilt was absolved, replaced by a sort of relief that the girl had been spared the much worse distress of being married to a philandering cad.

* * *

Having said that though, Vanessa was still a little concerned on Sybil's account.

At the start of the New Year, she and Roland had gone into town one evening to a performance at the Grand Theatre. After the final curtain, waiting on the theatre steps while her husband fetched the car, she had suddenly recognised her half-sister among a small group leaving the Sir Tatton Sykes public house across the street. Sybil was laughing in a noisily drunken manner and hanging on to the arm of a man, much older than her, who was holding her up while trying to light a cigarette.

Vanessa had no idea who he was – who any of them were, apart from Sybil. The other two young women in the group seemed to be arguing with the couple of chaps who'd followed them out of the pub. There was a bit of an altercation on the pavement with some pulling and shoving, and then all six of them set off in the direction of Princes Square, the young women's loud shrill voices carrying above the sounds of passing traffic.

Vanessa said nothing to Roland; but next time she saw her mother she brought the conversation round to Sybil, mentioning she'd seen her recently (though not the circumstances) and asking whether her half-sister had got herself in with a fresh crowd since she'd changed her job.

'She's become very friendly with one of the girls she works with,' Mrs Parrish told her over a plate of fancy biscuits. The two of them were in The Copper Kettle tea-room after meeting in town to go round the January sales. 'Gloria, her name is. Gloria Millington. She's been to the house quite a number of times.'

'What's she like?'

Mrs Parrish helped herself to a custard cream. 'Your

stepfather doesn't care for her much, but I've always found her pleasant, always very smartly dressed – what you'd expect, working at Beatties. She and Sybil go out dancing a lot. Your stepfather doesn't approve – well, you know him – but I think it's nice to see them enjoying themselves at that age, I do. And Sybil's so much brighter lately. Quite cheered up, she has.'

A waitress in black taffeta uniform brought a pot of tea to their corner table; and after she'd gone again Vanessa remarked casually, 'I wonder Sybil hasn't found herself another young man yet.'

Her mother glanced round the busy tea-room, then leaned towards her. 'Between you and me, dear, I've got a suspicion there *could* be somebody, although Sybil's never said and I don't like to pry – I'd rather wait till she decides to mention it. Only she's been wearing some bits of jewellery I know she hasn't bought herself – nothing expensive, in fact a little too cheap for my taste, what a young man might buy as a present, that sort of thing.'

Vanessa thought about the character she'd seen with Sybil the other evening. In the streetlight she'd been able to get a fairly good view of him. With his brilliantined hair and pencil-thin moustache and weasel face he'd looked the type who'd buy a girl cheap jewellery.

'Oh – there, I *know* what I meant to tell you, dear!' Mrs Parrish exclaimed in sudden vexation as she went to pour the tea. 'And I've forgotten all about bringing it with me – that's the trouble having to hide things where your stepfather won't see them. You recall I wrote to Amroth back in the autumn thanking the Jameses for looking after you?'

She passed a cup across the table to her daughter.

'You've heard from them?'

'Yes, a letter at last from your auntie Gwladys. She'd mislaid our address, that's why she's taken such an age in answering. Dear me, I *wish* I'd remembered to put it in my handbag! Things slip my mind just lately.'

'Don't worry, Mother, I'll read the letter another time,' Vanessa reassured her. 'What did aunt Gwladys say, anything interesting?'

'She wants us both to go and stay at Min-y-don. Well, *I* can't of course, there'd be all sorts of ructions if I dared so much as mention anything to do with Amroth, but it was sweet of her to suggest it, don't you think, dear? I always did like Gwladys. She and Wynford were my favourites. Oh, and talking of your uncle Wynford, what an impression you've made on him! He hasn't stopped going on about you according to Gwladys. The only thing that upset them all, she says, was that they never got chance to meet Roland while he was down there.'

Vanessa forced herself to concentrate on stirring her tea. 'You must have misread that bit, Mother,' she said lightly. 'Roland wasn't down there. Don't you remember, he was far too busy. Aunt Gwladys probably means they were sorry he couldn't join me.'

She hated herself for that little deception. She would rather lie to anyone than to her mother.

'What else did she say?' she went on, steering away from the subject of Roland. 'How's aunt Nesta at Tregethin? I don't think you ever went to Tregethin, did you – Nesta couldn't have been married when you knew her. Wasn't she still living at home with Grandmother James?'

'That's right, dear, she'd only just left school as I recall—'

Sidetracked, Mrs Parrish started talking about the family as she remembered them from those halcyon rosy days of her first marriage. No more prompting was required. Although she was only forty-six, the advent of middle age into a life which had been largely dominated by monotony and self-effacement found Vanessa's mother happy to escape more and more into her early memories. There was a corner of her heart where she and her true-love Owen still walked together hand-in-hand in a dreamworld filled with sunshine, joy and laughter. Nobody could take that from her. Nobody could rob her of the past, not even Ernest Parrish.

Vanessa sat and listened, aware how much such memories meant – and if she'd heard them all before, what did it matter.

She had done herself no favour by changing the subject though, because if only she'd enquired what exactly the letter *had* said about Roland, she would have realised her aunt had rather dropped her in it:

'What a pity we weren't able to meet Vanessa's husband,' Gwladys had written, 'particularly as they were staying so near the week he came down. Wynford's daughter Margaret saw them in Tenby and told us what a nice young man he looked, very much more handsome than Vanessa described him—'

It was unfortunate that Sybil Parrish found that letter.

She'd come across it while searching in her mother's chest of drawers, and curiosity had made her open it. The reference to Roland Antrobus didn't register very much at first; and then a crooked smile had curled Sybil's cupid-bow lips into a sneer.

She'd been waiting all these months to get her own back on her half-sister, and here it was – the perfect ammunition.

12

A week or so later Vanessa was again in The Copper Kettle tea-room, this time with her friend Kay Murray from the *Weekly Advertiser*. The same waitress in the crisp black taffeta uniform took their order, serving them at a table in the window where the soft sheen of a lemon-coloured winter sun outlined their profiles beneath the fashionable cloche hats.

Kay was on a diet, trying to reduce some of the extra weight she'd put on over Christmas.

'Honestly,' she grumbled, 'I shall be jolly glad when the fuller figure's back in vogue. I'm sick of denying myself the pleasures of life just to squeeze into a smaller-sized corset, and for what – to risk fainting either from hunger or lack of oxygen. It's not fair, Vanessa. I mean, it's part of my job to keep myself fashionable, and yet somebody said the other day torturing my feminine curves 'll give me varicose veins when I'm older. What a price to have to pay! And there's no need to laugh, my dear, *you've* never had my problem.'

'I can think of worse things to worry about,' Vanessa told her.

'Yes, death from slow starvation on a diet of cabbage water.' Kay gave a little shudder of disgust. With a glance towards the next table where a couple were just getting up to go, she went on, 'Do you know what my doctor said? He advised me I ought to eat less and take more exercise. More exercise – I ask you! And there's me running round the office like a headless chicken trying to meet my deadlines, fix interviews, fend off lecherous sub-editors, sort out photographers – all this on top of writing some riveting new angle on dreary old Lady Whatsit for the society column. If exercise could lose me weight, believe me darling I'd be as matchstick-thin as you are.'

Vanessa admitted her friend wasn't far off the truth, calling her thin. The affair with Larret Fitzgerald had left its scars. She hadn't been sleeping well for some time, and even Roland was passing remarks about her poor appetite.

She made some jokey response, her attention distracted for a second by another couple, a man and a younger woman, arriving at the just-vacated table. Something about the man struck a vaguely familiar chord, and while Kay went chatting on Vanessa studied him with greater interest, trying to place him.

He was tall, his features strongly shaped rather than conventionally handsome, the frosting of iron-grey in the dark hair making him look older than he probably was. It was his eyes and mouth she noticed particularly though – so sad and yet somehow so angry that she found herself glancing at his companion, wondering if maybe there'd been an argument between them. But the smartly-dressed young woman was talking to him in a quiet, conversational manner, looking at him occasionally with a smile which seemed to hold sympathy.

'God, darling – is that the time!' Kay interrupted herself suddenly. 'Heavens, I'll have to scoot, I've got an editorial conference at four o'clock.' She glanced round for the waitress.

Vanessa insisted on seeing to their bill so that her friend could get away; and having paid it, she was putting her purse back in her bag as she got up to leave when she stubbed the toe of her shoe and tripped over herself. It was a clumsy thing to do, and wouldn't have happened if she'd been watching where she was going instead of staring so hard at the couple at the other table.

Vexed, she recovered herself quickly. And as she began picking up the spilled contents of her handbag, the man leaned down from his chair and retrieved her fountain pen, handing it back to her.

Because she'd just been paying him such covert interest his helpfulness somewhat embarrassed her. With a flustered smile of thanks she said, 'I feel terribly silly doing that.'

'Don't worry, nobody noticed.' He gave a bleak smile in return which failed to touch the sadness in his eyes, and turned away.

It wasn't until she was halfway down the stairs that Vanessa suddenly realised where she'd seen him before – in the garden at 'Mayville' one day last summer. He was the scrap dealer – what was his name. Brockhouse. Yes, James Brockhouse. The man whose behaviour she had found so disconcerting.

The Antrobus Gallery was about to shut when Sybil Parrish turned up looking for Roland. She'd used the pretext of a raging toothache to get off work early, and in case anybody should wonder why she was in Darlington Street she had told them at Beatties her brother-in-law was running her round to the dentist.

The bell on the Gallery's panelled door gave a little tinkle as she went inside. She'd only ever been here a couple of times before, but nothing had changed: the same soft slate-coloured carpet and matt white walls, the same resinous scent of turpentine and varnish, the same genteel hush. The place reminded Sybil of a church, or a museum.

'Sorry, Miss, the Gallery's just closing—'

A young chap appeared from behind a sort of scaffolding displaying terracotta.

'Actually it's Mr Antrobus I want, if he's about,' she said.

'Oh, I see. Well he's not here at the moment, but he shouldn't be very long if you'd like to wait.' The young man came over to her, brushing a wave of fair hair away from his eyes. Sybil wasn't in much of a mood to be friendly or she would have noticed he was rather good-looking. 'Unless I can be of some help maybe?'

'No thanks, it's personal.'

She stared past him, examining the nearest pictures without enthusiasm; and when he didn't look like taking the hint to push off again, she added in a bored voice, 'Mr Antrobus is my brother-in-law, OK?'

'Your brother-in-law?'

'Uh-huh.'

Not seeming in the least put out by her manner the young man gave a grin and offered his hand. 'Well – pleased to meet you! I'm Michael – Michael Wright. I've got the flat overhead.' He gestured towards a spiral staircase at the back of the gallery. 'I don't actually work here, I'm just keeping a general eye on things till Roland gets back.'

The handshake was ignored. Sybil made it plain she

wasn't interested. She hadn't come here to indulge in small talk with some chap in baggy grey flannels and an old tweed jacket.

'You don't look much like your sister,' Michael Wright went on, shoving his hands in his trouser pockets. 'Not that I see a lot of her, of course – I'm generally out when she's here. I teach at the School of Art and Design—'

'She's only my half-sister.'

'Sorry?'

'She's only my half-sister.' Sybil gave him one of her looks and deliberately moved away, as though she found the exhibits infinitely more fascinating than his conversation.

Michael let her go. He watched her for a moment or two, his eyes drawn to the shapely line of her legs in their rayon stockings, before he went across to the windows and drew the blinds, shutting out the murk of a January dusk smudged by the sulphurous reflection of electric streetlights.

Sybil could hear him whistling to himself as he pottered about in the background. After a while he said, raising his voice – 'Well, what d'you think?'

She turned round. 'What?'

'That set of etchings you're looking at. What d'you think of them?'

Sybil hadn't been looking at anything. 'Yes, very nice I'm sure,' she answered indifferently. Actually, now she came to notice them they *were* rather good, the kind of thing she liked—

The bell gave its discreet little tinkle.

'Sorry I've been so long,' said Roland Antrobus, closing the door as he came in and shooting the bolt. 'Damn' queue in the post office again.'

'You've got a caller,' Michael told him, giving a nod in Sybil's direction. He added drily, 'She's just been admiring my etchings.'

Roland reacted with a start as the young woman in the velvet-trimmed navy costume moved into view.

'Sybil—? Good Lord, this is unexpected – how are you? Nothing the matter I hope?'

'Hold on to something, Roland, you'll be falling over,' she said rudely. 'No, nothing's the matter. I thought it was time I paid you a visit, that's all.'

'Well, er—' Michael retreated tactfully towards the staircase. 'If I'm not needed for anything else I'll be running along. I've got a whole pile of schoolwork to look at. Nice to know you,' he called across to Sybil. 'We'll meet again some other time maybe.'

'Maybe.'

She waited till he'd gone, then said, 'Are those really *his* pictures?'

'They're his, yes. Michael's an excellent artist.'

Throwing his hat and camel-hair overcoat across a chair her brother-in-law turned to face her. 'But you're not here to look round the Gallery, I'm sure. So what's this about.'

'You're right, I haven't come to look round your stuffy old Gallery. I've got a more important reason. Vanessa.'

'Vanessa . . . I see.'

'No, I don't think you do, Roland.'

'I beg your pardon—?'

'I don't think you see anything, otherwise you'd know what's been going on, wouldn't you.'

'I haven't a clue what you're talking about.' He frowned at her. 'Vanessa isn't sick or anything, is she? Is that why you're here?'

Ignoring the sign by the door saying 'Please refrain from smoking' Sybil reached in her handbag after her Woodbines.

'She could be dead for all I care,' she said brutally. 'I'm here because of what she's been up to, that precious wife of yours. And since it involves you as well as me, I thought we ought to have a chat about it.'

'About what? For heaven's sake can't you make yourself clearer! What are you saying Vanessa's been doing?'

'I'll tell you what she's been doing—' Sybil put a cigarette between her carmine lips and lit it, savouring her moment of revenge. 'She's been having an affair with the man I was engaged to.'

There was an incredulous silence.

'Yes, that's right,' she went on, giving a nasty little smile. 'Larret Fitzgerald.'

A dull red spread over Roland's well-fleshed features. He looked for a second as though he was going to explode; and then he said thickly, 'You're lying. I don't believe it.'

'It's the truth. Ask her yourself. Ask her about Wales.'

'*Wales*—?'

'That holiday she took at Amroth. Larret was with her.'

'Now I know you're lying. She stayed as the guest of her late father's family while she was there.'

'Not at their house.' Sybil was getting into her stride now. 'Perhaps she didn't tell you that. How odd. But then she wouldn't, would she, Roland. I mean after all, she didn't tell you *you* were supposed to be in Amroth with her. Yet *somebody* was – and the Jameses thought it was you.' She drew heavily on her Woodbine before she added through a mouthful of smoke, 'Why should they choose to think that, I wonder.'

Roland reached over and snatched the cigarette away. Staring round for somewhere to crush it out, he said angrily, 'I know what your game is. If you imagine this preposterous tale carries any weight with me, you're wrong. Vanessa warned me a long time ago you'd been accusing her of God knows what with Fitzgerald, coming to the house and upsetting her, making threats—'

'I can prove what I'm saying,' Sybil retorted.

'Show me your proof!'

'It's there in a letter the Jameses sent my mother. Larry was seen with Vanessa in Tenby. They'd spent a week together somewhere – she'd been passing him off as you, pretending you'd gone there to join her. OK? Is that proof enough?'

The dark flush ebbed from Roland's face leaving it a dreadful mottled colour. He stared fixedly at his sister-in-law, and the expression in those light blue eyes unnerved her enough to take a step backward.

'Where is this letter. Where is it, I want to see it.'

'I didn't bring it along.'

'Of course not. It doesn't exist.'

'It exists all right—'

'In your imagination, maybe. Why spoil a good tale for the sake of the truth, Sybil! You've always resented Vanessa. You've always done your level best to spite her, you and your confounded father. She's been made to bear the blame for everything – *everything*. And you can shut up a moment and listen—' as Sybil made to cut in. 'It surprises me not in the least a spoilt bitch like you comes here spreading this sort of muck against my wife. You've got to have your scapegoat, haven't you

– eh? It sticks in your throat that Fitzgerald walked out on you.'

'He walked out on me because of *her*!'

'For God's sake, girl, grow up and learn some sense. He walked out on you because he caught cold feet – and if you weren't so damn' stupid you'd realise he did you Parrishes a favour. The man was a cad.'

Roland was losing control of his temper. He had never liked his sister-in-law. She was a nasty little piece of work, with all the vices of her father and none of the virtues of her mother. Now he liked her even less for causing this intolerable scene. His every instinct was to disbelieve her allegation, see it as a product of the soured relationship between Ernest Parrish, Sybil and Vanessa. He *trusted* Vanessa. Whatever offence against the vows of marriage he himself was guilty of, he'd never had any reason to doubt his wife's faithfulness.

'You pompous prig,' Sybil told him viciously. 'You think you're always in the bloody right—'

'Get out.' Roland strode to the door and unbolted it. 'Don't say any more – just get out.'

She paused for a moment; then gave a shrug. 'OK, I'm leaving. I might've guessed I'd be wasting my time coming here. You can't face the truth, that's your problem.'

Drawing herself up, her small chin tilted in defiance, she walked past him. As she stepped into the street she threw back across her shoulder – 'And if you want your bloody proof, ask my mother to show you the letter.'

Roland was still seething when he drove home. Vanessa was upstairs getting dressed for dinner, and her own state of mind was hardly the happiest, either. While she was out this afternoon to change her books at the local library there'd been a telephone call from Luise von Losch. Iris had taken it. The young German woman was phoning from London and had left a message for Roland to contact her urgently.

The moment her husband entered the bedroom Vanessa could tell by his face that something was wrong.

'You've spoken to Iris?' she asked him awkwardly, accepting his usual peck on the cheek as she went to the wardrobe.

'Iris? No, I haven't seen Iris.' He sounded livid, she thought. 'I've just received a most unpleasant visit from that half-sister of yours.'

'From Sybil—?'

'She's been to the Gallery with some cock-and-bull story about you and that character Fitzgerald. Either her father put her up to it or the girl's insane – she's accusing you of having an affair with him.'

Vanessa's heart turned a somersault. Through the sudden quick hammer of blood in her ears she heard herself answer, 'Oh . . . really?'

'Can you credit the gall of it! She even claims there's some letter the Jameses wrote your mother saying you'd been seen in Tenby or somewhere with the fellow.'

Taking off his Fair Isle pullover Roland threw it aside on the bed and unfastened his cufflinks. 'I've half a mind to ring up Ernest Parrish and tell him his daughter wants a damn' good talking to. This obsession she's got about you ruining her engagement is getting past a joke.'

He glanced at his wife. She was standing with her back to him still facing the wardrobe. In the full-length mirror casting her reflection he could see her lovely features had turned deathly pale.

146

'Come on now, darling, you're not to upset yourself,' he went on in a quieter manner. 'I'm on to Sybil's game. I told her the wretched story wouldn't wash. I think I know you rather better than she imagines.'

'Then you don't believe her?' Vanessa asked unsteadily.

'Good God, of course not! For one thing you're too intelligent a woman to fall for the charms of a loose fish like Fitzgerald, and for another—'

Roland paused.

'—well, I was going to say for another thing you're married to me, but perhaps that's not a consideration. I mean, in view of my own recent conduct.'

'With Luise von Losch.'

Vanessa looked up and met her husband's eyes through the glass. She took a deep breath. In her mind she said, Roland there's something I want to confess. But even as she opened her lips to repeat it out loud, her nerve failed her, and instead she said quickly – 'Roland, there's something you ought to be told. Luise – she phoned here today.'

For the rest of her life she would never forget the expression which crossed his face. Disbelief, astonishment, agitation – and then an emotion so naked she had to look away, she couldn't watch it.

'Lulu phoned *here*?' Even the eagerness of his voice betrayed him. 'When – when – what time was this?'

'Just after three, while I was out. Iris took the call.'

'And the message – was there a message?'

'She's in England.' Vanessa turned from the mirror. 'In London.'

'*London*—!'

'She left a number for you to call her back.'

'She's in London. Lulu's in London.' Flustered, Roland

looked round the bedroom, his glance skipping from object to object blindly, not really seeing. 'She's here – she wants me to call her. Oh God—!'

'Will you?' Vanessa asked him. Suddenly she herself was very composed, very calm. Since his return from Berlin last autumn they'd both been play-acting at normal life, keeping up a facade to fool the watching eyes of the world, and of each other. Luise von Losch's phone call was the catalyst – no, the catastasis, that part of the drama where the action had finally reached its highest point.

Her husband's response to the question of 'Will you?' was about to determine the fate of their marriage as well as the rest of their lives.

'I *must* call her back, Vanessa. Try to understand. I must, don't you see? God knows, I've wanted to forget her – but I can't, it's impossible – I *need* her.'

'More than you've ever needed me.' It was a statement.

He looked down at the floor. After a moment he nodded.

'In that case, Roland, there's something I want to confess to you.'

13

It hadn't always been an empty marriage. They had loved and respected one another. But after that terrible night in January 1928 any love and respect that remained was finally dead.

In view of his own admitted adultery there wasn't a lot Roland Antrobus could say about Vanessa's affair with Larret Fitzgerald without painting himself as a hypocrite – words like deceit and outrage and betrayal could hardly be flung about and not blow straight back in his face. Nor was he physically violent, as Vanessa had feared he might be. Instead he'd heard her out in a silence more unbearable than anger because it was so icy cold; and when she had finished he went downstairs to make his call to London, closing the bedroom door on her as though he were closing it on a concluded chapter of his life.

That night he had slept in the guest room. When Vanessa came down next morning she found the breakfast table empty and was told the Master had already left the house.

During the next week Roland was seldom at home, and when he was he barely addressed her. They continued sleeping apart. The following week, the first in February, she was tersely informed he was going to London – he couldn't say for how long. In the meantime the Antrobus Gallery would remain open under other management, and he had arranged facilities for Vanessa to draw upon his bank account as required.

Should she need to contact him for any urgent reason, Roland left a Hampstead number.

He refused to discuss the future of their marriage. He preferred leaving that decision till they'd both had time for sober reflection, he said, and until then would be obliged if his wife would keep the matter strictly private since it was nobody else's business but their own.

Those grey, wet weeks of February which dragged out the fag-end of winter would have been easier to endure if Vanessa could have shared her anxieties; but in deference to Roland's wishes she stayed silent, passing his absence off to friends as business, pretending nothing was wrong. It was a role she'd become adept at playing just lately.

What hurt her so much – no, not hurt her, more annoyed her – was the way her husband had reacted when she'd owned up to her own misconduct. For heaven's sake, he'd done the same himself – at least he could have said he understood, she thought; at least he could have shown more toleration. But wasn't that just like a man: his own adultery was a misdemeanour to be treated with indulgence and forgiven; but his wife's adultery must be punished as though it were the most heinous and unpardonable offence.

Her annoyance turned to temper, and temper to rebellion. What seemed especially unjust was that Roland should be in London cavorting about with Luise, while Vanessa herself was sentenced to solitary confinement stuck at 'Mayville', expected to twiddle her thumbs and do penance until he came back. And when – *if* – he came back, then what? Would he press for divorce, or would they stay married? They could hardly go on as if nothing had happened!

Life wasn't all gloom, though. The clouds produced a glimpse of silver lining when half-way through the month Marjorie Tiersot wrote from France to say she was expecting a baby in September. This would be Marjorie's first child, and her glowing happiness succeeded in cheering Vanessa somewhat. She replied at once, sending love and congratulations to her old schoolchum; and then found her letter expanding to a detailed ten-page confession of the past six months' events, and her present rather wretched situation.

Marjorie in turn wrote back immediately. Vanessa must come and stay with them at Le Palombier – and no argument. She needed to get away – needed a change of scene. They would *love* to see her – she could stay for as long as she wished. It would be springtime soon in the Dordogne, the most beautiful time of the year—

This early in the evening there were only a few chaps downstairs in the billiard hall; young ones, unmarried, out of work, standing about sharing a cigarette between them while they watched a game. It wouldn't be till later that the place filled up, about nine o'clock.

Somebody was whistling 'Tea for Two' – Sybil could hear the jaunty tune through the floorboards, somehow plaintive and forlorn-sounding as though the whistler hadn't really got his heart in it. She started humming the tune to herself, fiddling with the kiss curl on her cheek as she wiped the condensation from the window to peer down into the dingy rainswept street again for Alan Slater.

Ever since the night they'd met at the Palais de Danse

151

Alan Slater had fascinated Sybil; fascinated, and yet somehow repelled her. It was hard to decide whether she liked him or loathed him. Any other man, and she would have packed him in the first time they'd gone out together when he took her to some scruffy dive along Bilston Road and got her drunk on port and brandy. And while she was being sick on the sawdust-covered floor he'd gone off and left her 'to see about a bit o' business'. He was always 'seeing about a bit o' business'. Dodgy business. It was how he made his living.

Sybil hadn't packed him in though. Instead she'd become addicted to him, addicted to the feeling of revulsion/attraction that he roused in her. What in God's name did she see in him? She couldn't say. She didn't know. At home at night in her nice clean bed in nice clean middle-class Tettenhall Green she would lie awake and physically cringe at the thought of him touching her; yet when she was having sex with him (not making love: love was too decent a word) he could do what he liked with her, abuse her, degrade her, make her feel dirty, and still she stayed with him.

She had a name for this room above the billiard hall in Stafford Street – the Waiting Room. It was meant as a joke. Actually the place was used illegally as a bookie's office by that Jack Holroyd Sybil had once fancied so much. Which was another joke. She didn't fancy Jack one little bit these days, not since he'd called her a stupid slut and worse in front of them all at the Palais de Danse for throwing herself after Alan.

'Jealous?' she'd asked.

'Jealous—? Don't talk daft. I wouldn't touch you wi' a bloody barge pole, not now Slater's had you.'

She wondered why Jack had said that; but when she

repeated it afterwards to Alan Slater he'd just laughed at
her in that cruel sort of way of his.

'Tea for Two' had stopped now and the whistling
downstairs took up a new tune – one Sybil was lately
growing to like – called 'Only Make Believe'. She examined her reflection in the darkness of the rain-smeared
window, singing the words; then wearying of that, looked
at her wristwatch again.

Twenty-five past eight. She'd been stuck up here
almost an hour.

More damn' fool you, she told her reflection. Why
don't you go, eh? What is there stopping you?

The hall door's hinges creaked in unoiled protest as
somebody else came in from the street, and after a minute
she heard Slater's voice below on the stairs. She could
tell straight away it was him by the accent, Birmingham
rather than Black Country, one of the scars of his Balsall
Heath childhood.

Her heart beat a little quicker. She listened to him
climbing up, heard him stop outside the door, heard him
cough as he lit a cigarette.

'Hello, sweetheart.' He came inside, shutting the door
behind him and turning the key. In the sallow light of
the single electric bulb tiredness made him look all of
his forty-odd years, and Sybil wondered yet again what
his attraction for her was, this small-time crook with his
greased-back hair and hard, thin face.

'Hello, Alan,' she said, moving forward. 'I've been
waiting.'

He didn't apologise. He never did. 'I've 'ad a bit o'
business to see about.'

He took her chin in his hand and kissed her, sucking
at her lips, his mouth cool from the rain and tasting of

cigarette smoke; and as always whenever he touched her she felt an instant's revulsion followed at once by the swift spark of arousal.

'You'm looking a smasher,' he said, standing back to eye the silk sash blouse and narrow skirt approvingly. 'I ain't seen you in that before.'

Sybil gave a wheedling little pout. 'I thought perhaps we might go somewhere nice tonight. I'm fed up with this place.'

She tossed a look at the nicotine-yellowed walls and threadbare carpet, the ill-matched bits of furniture, Jack Holroyd's stuff. At one side was an ugly Victorian horsehair sofa, its leather cracked and split with age, spilling its innards; and opposite stood a gas stove with its door ajar and the burners lit to heat the room.

Slater glanced round him indifferently. 'What's wrong with the place? What you griping about? It's cosy enough.'

'But I want to go somewhere else for a change!'

'I'll take you out Friday, eh. The Hippodrome, then on to the Tatton Sykes for a drink. I don't feel like traipsing round town tonight, I've had an 'ard day of it.'

He produced a bottle of whisky from the pocket of his mackintosh, putting it down on Jack's desk as he went to warm himself in front of the stove.

Over his shoulder he said, 'What time was you 'ere, then?'

'The time we arranged, half past seven.'

'Anybody asking for me?'

Sybil shrugged. 'There was somebody downstairs when I came in. He didn't give a name. He said you'd know him.'

'If it was a fat bloke wearing an old-fashioned derby,

154

I know him all right.' Slater grinned at her wolfishly, showing his teeth, and with a drag at his cigarette he added, 'I bet these villains wonder what the 'ell's going on, you with your lah-di-dah talk and your posh-looking clothes. It ain't what they'm used to 'ere, I'm telling you! So what else did he say?'

'Nothing much. Seemed keen to find out who I was.'

'I bet. For starters you ain't Mary Pickford.' Still grinning, he took off the wet mackintosh and slung it over a chair, then came back to the desk and opened a drawer to bring out two glasses.

As he began pouring them a whisky Sybil said quickly, 'No, not for me, thanks. After what happened last time, Daddy's warned me he'll stop me from going out of a night if I do it again. And he means it as well! – he was livid!' On that occasion she'd been so drunk she couldn't stand upright, and the racket she'd made creeping into the house in the early hours had woken her father.

'Oh – Daddy was livid, was he,' Slater mimicked her. 'Daddy's little girl been naughty, Daddy 'as to smack her botty.'

'Knock it off, Alan.'

She hated him taking the mickey. It got on her nerves. When she'd first set her cap at him at the Palais she had deliberately played down her poshness (as he called it) because she thought he'd be more attracted to her if she made herself out to be common. That was a mistake. Although Alan Slater wasn't bothered by his own inferior background and street-corner education, what he wanted on his arm was Class, a nice young thing with a bit of swank, who sounded her aitches and knew how to dress smart; a girl who'd be good for his image.

He liked Sybil to exaggerate the airs and graces. He

liked to hear her talk about her 'Daddy' the solicitor. And if he ridiculed her for doing so, that too was part of his pleasure, because he was ridiculing 'Them', the nobs, the social caste she represented, the people he both envied and despised.

Helping himself to a stiff whisky he knocked it back in a single gulp; then wiping his slim moustache he said, 'Some'at tells me you'm not in a very cheerful mood tonight, sweetheart. Come on, let's 'ave a bit more sparkle, eh. I can't 'elp it if you've 'ad to 'ang around – I s'pose that's why you'm sulking.'

'I'm not sulking. I feel like going *out*, that's all.'

Sybil flounced over to perch herself beside him on the desk. Borrowing his cigarette to light up a Woodbine for herself, she added petulantly, 'Anyway, I could do with some fresh air, it's stuffy in here, it's giving me a headache.'

'Open one o' the windows.'

'I'll be cold—!'

'You'm a bloody fussy wench.' Draping his arm round her, Slater kissed her again and poured himself a refill. 'When I offered to take you somewhere last Sat'day you dain't want to go, you was all for us stopping up 'ere and 'aving a laugh an' that. So what's different tonight, then?'

The difference was she'd had something to laugh about last Saturday. It seemed her visit to the Antrobus Gallery hadn't been such a waste of time, because that fat bore Roland had gone and cleared off down to London 'on business'. Business her eye! Sybil knew better than believe that excuse, and if she'd got rip-roaring drunk last Saturday night it had been as much on the sweet taste of revenge as on the booze Alan Slater gave her.

She drew on her Woodbine and passed him his cigarette back. Down below the noise at the billiard tables was getting louder now, and a wireless was playing somewhere. After a moment she said, 'If you want the truth, Alan, I'm *bored*. I feel . . . oh, I don't know . . . flat, I suppose. Flat and fed up.'

'Fed up with me?'

'No, not you, you're not so bad. At least with you I can have a bit of fun. But then you're not like anybody else I've ever met – I mean, I do things with you I haven't done before, and you take me to places I've never been, and most of the time I enjoy myself – so that's OK.'

'But you say you'm feeling flat.'

She nodded. 'Tonight I am, yes.'

'Then we'll 'ave to do some'at about it, won't we, sweetheart.' Slater gave her his wolfish grin again, but his hard eyes had a speculative look. 'How would you fancy a little pick-me-up to put them bubbles back – not booze nor nothing, but some' at else, some' at a bit more exciting.'

'What kind of something?'

Stubbing out his cigarette butt he reached into the inside pocket of his cheap serge suit and brought out what looked to Sybil like a tin of snuff.

'This what's in 'ere 'll put you on top o' the world,' he said. 'A guaranteed promise.'

'But what is it?' She leaned her elbow on his shoulder, curious, her short-bobbed strawberry blonde hair brushing his ear as she craned to see inside the opened tin. If that was snuff it was odd-looking snuff – white, like icing sugar or cornflour, she thought.

Slater didn't answer her question. He produced from the same pocket a silver mustard spoon of all things, and

157

with exquisite care scooped out a small measure of the powder, tapping it lightly against the tin to level it down.

'Game to try it, am you?' he asked, as though double-checking.

'I'm game enough to try anything once.'

Sybil put out her half-smoked Woodbine and took the spoon from him. Sudden nervous excitement made her hand shake a little. She might not know what this white stuff was, but she knew what to do: she'd seen snuff-takers do it.

'Well – here goes!' Pressing a finger against one nostril, she held the bowl of the spoon to the other and took a good hard sniff. The powder felt cold inside her nose.

She waited a couple of seconds. Nothing. 'Now what happens?' she demanded, giving the spoon back.

Again he didn't answer; simply closed the tin with a deliberate click and replaced it safely inside his pocket, his eyes not leaving Sybil's face.

Just as she was wondering why he hadn't taken it himself, suddenly the most extraordinary sensation seemed to wash over her, flooding her mind with a rush of incredibly heightened awareness. She couldn't believe how quickly it happened – couldn't believe its effect. It came out of nowhere. In the space of another minute or two she'd started feeling really good – exhilarated, confident, bloody marvellous in fact—

'It's got a kick, eh,' Slater said, still watching her.

'A heck of a kick! God, I feel *fantastic*!' She wanted to leap in the air, dance round the room, sing, shout, laugh, act like a crazy thing. 'What *is* that stuff, Alan?'

'I told you. A pick-me-up for putting the bubbles back if you'm feeling flat.'

'But aren't you having any?'

He shook his head. 'Ta, I'll stick with this –' raising his glass of neat whisky.

Everything was becoming brilliantly defined. The light from the naked ceiling bulb was sharper, brighter to her eyes. The crummy room-cum-bookie's office seemed transformed, the colours in the carpet vivid. She could hear the patter of each separate raindrop on the dirt-filmed window, hear the voices of the players at the tables, the notes of music on the wireless.

She began to laugh, joyously, twirling round and clapping her hands, her head thrown back, like a child on Christmas morning.

Slater downed his whisky; and when she stretched out her arms in an invitation to dance he stood up from the desk and caught her by the waist, drawing her close to him.

'You look good,' he said.

She couldn't stop laughing. 'Wow – that stuff's amazing. It's magic! I feel bloody wonderful, Alan – come on, let's have some fun!'

Swaying against him in a couple of dance steps she began singing along to the distant wireless, looking into his eyes as though she were singing just for him. The lean, hard face with the pencil-thin moustache and slicked-down hair made her feel deliciously decadent. She was on cloud nine, wishing this sensation would go on for ever. It was so dangerous, yet so exciting being his woman, the girlfriend of a petty crook who'd served a prison sentence; and God, how she loved him, *loved* him!

Slater's hands moved from her waist and squeezed her breasts. He put his mouth against her ear. Glancing towards the horsehair sofa he said softly, 'Aye, let's 'ave some fun, my wench . . . some *real* fun.'

14

Although it was still only the beginning of March the weather had turned mild over the past few days, and this morning in the garden Vanessa had noticed the first hint of coming spring in the softness of the air and the timid warmth of the newly-risen sun.

Roland had returned late last night from his five-week absence in London. As a result she'd got very little sleep, and was up early hoping a walk out here before breakfast might freshen her before she had to face him.

The garden was always so peaceful at this hour. Birds were chirping in the still-bare branches of the trees, but otherwise there'd been only the occasional sound of traffic along Compton Road to disturb the stillness as she wandered the gravel paths, trying to calm her mind of the fears she'd been having to wrestle with for much of the night.

Whether it was a hangover from these foreboding thoughts, or whether some other presentiment, she couldn't say; but as she'd paused on the terrace steps to gaze back at the brightly-coloured crocus candle-flames just starting to show amid the green-white drifts of snowdrops, and the golden splash of daffodils against the old stone walls, Vanessa had found herself thinking she might never see this garden in springtime again.

It was after ten o'clock before Roland made his

appearance. She heard him put through a number of calls on the telephone; and then he came into the drawing room where she was waiting.

Not even giving her the courtesy of responding to her greeting he began at once, coldly, and without preamble – 'I've just been on the blower to Horace Pritchard.' Horace Pritchard was his solicitor. 'I've made an appointment to call at his office later today. There're a number of things I need to discuss with him.'

'And may I enquire if our marriage is a topic on the agenda?' Vanessa tried to match his coldness and keep the anxiety from her voice as she seated herself in one of the armchairs.

'I shall be seeking advice on that particular subject, yes.' Roland glanced at her briefly, then looked away again.

'I won't bother beating about the bush, Vanessa. I've decided the best course of action is a legal separation.'

'I see . . . Well, that makes sense of a sort, I suppose. You spend five weeks with Luise von Losch and come home to tell me you want a separation. Presumably it's never crossed your mind I might wish to discuss my own position in the matter?'

'In view of your admitted adultery with Fitzgerald I can hardly think what purpose that would serve. The marriage is dead. I'm not prepared to overlook your misconduct—'

'*My* misconduct, Roland – what about your own? There's equal fault on both sides, don't forget!'

'If you'll let me finish. I was going to say that since I am myself guilty of the same offence, it would appear to me that a separation between us is the only practical solution. I don't know how you feel, Vanessa – and frankly I don't care – but speaking personally I will be a lot happier once the whole thing's cleanly finished and we're living under separate roofs.'

Vanessa considered the import of this in silence. To be honest, now the chips were finally down, her husband's decision wasn't too much of a nasty shock: she had had adequate time to consider the probability that he might want her to leave and find somewhere else for herself. 'Mayville' was his, after all – his family home. Naturally if there were a legal separation, then *she* must be the one to go, not him.

She looked down at her hands, at the rose-cut diamond engagement ring partnering her wedding band. She never usually wore the ring unless for social engagements, but this morning after she'd come in from the garden, something had prompted her to put it on as a gesture, as though she'd had the feeling this was the last time she would have the moral right to wear it.

'Of course, with regard to money and that, I shall make the necessary arrangements,' Roland went on, going across to the window bay and standing with his back to her, looking out on to the sunlit drive. 'It depends what Horace Pritchard advises, but I'll probably open a bank account in your name and pay in a regular sum – then you can draw on it as you wish to support yourself.'

The way he said it made it sound like charity.

'As a matter of fact, I'm thinking of returning to work,' Vanessa informed him quietly. 'While you've been in London I've written a couple of pieces for Kay Murray at the *Advertiser* and the *Express & Star* want to commission another series of articles. So you see I haven't exactly been wasting my time . . . if this separation goes ahead, Roland, I'd prefer to be as independent of you as possible.'

'*When* the separation goes ahead you can do as you like,' he answered cuttingly. 'Meanwhile I think I'm being more than generous in continuing to maintain you.'

'And am I supposed to grovel?' Stung by the injustice of his attitude, she rose from the chair. 'Is that what you expect?'

This time she got no response.

After a moment she began again, more emotionally, 'I don't want us to part as enemies. Whatever's gone wrong between us recently, can't we at least remain on civil terms with one another? Ours hasn't been a bad marriage. Its only fault is that we're not compatible in the one area that probably matters the most—'

'Oh, for heaven's sake, spare me the post mortem!' her husband interrupted, turning from the window, his features working. 'What's the point of trotting out apologies. The truth is, I was always the wrong man for you, Vanessa, just as you were always the wrong woman for me. Now let's leave it there, shall we.'

As epitaphs went, that was perhaps as fitting a one as any on which to end two years of life together.

Telling her mother about the breakdown of her marriage and her imminent departure from 'Mayville' was a task Vanessa shirked for a couple more weeks.

She could guess with what satisfaction her stepfather would receive the news, and frankly didn't give a hoot whether it pleased him or not – her sole concern was for her mother, who had always been rather proud of having Roland for a son-in-law, not least because of the art gallery and the detached house in Compton Road. Roland's civic standing had reflected well on Mrs Parrish among her small circle of acquaintances: it seemed so unfair to deprive her of one of the few things in her life which had given her any happiness.

Ironically (even perhaps aptly) the occasion of Ernest Parrish's birthday part-way through March seemed as good a time as any for Vanessa's bombshell. Each year there was a special Sunday tea-party at the house in Tettenhall Green which Vanessa and her husband were expected to attend – though Roland had only ever been once, in those happy days just after their engagement.

When she arrived alone this afternoon there had been the usual snide comment from her stepfather and the usual little flutterings from her mother; from Sybil nothing, not a word, which was surprising. Sybil in fact didn't look at all well, Vanessa thought. The girl had lost some weight, which didn't suit her, and her pretty face had a sickly washed-out pallor making the shadows under her eyes like bruises.

Even more surprising, she showed none of her normal hostility when Vanessa wanted to know if she'd been ill.

'I've been off my food, that's all,' she answered in a subdued manner, picking at her plate. 'I expect I've been overdoing things a bit.'

'You can say that again—' put in her father through a mouthful of ham sandwich. 'I can't for the life of me understand why you're having to work so much extra time lately. I said to your mother only last night, I've half a mind to go into Beatties and ask them what they think they're playing at.'

'Oh Daddy, don't,' Sybil said listlessly. 'You'll only

165

lose me my job doing that. I told you – I'm working the overtime to save up for a holiday this summer.'

'You'll need a holiday this summer the way you're going on. A sanatorium is where you'll be spending it as well, my girl.'

'Another sandwich, Vanessa dear?' enquired Mrs Parrish. 'There's plenty of the bloater paste.'

'No thanks, Mother. I've eaten enough. I ought to leave a bit of room for the cake.'

'I'll have another one—' Ernest Parrish's false teeth clicked as he swallowed the half-chewed food in his mouth and handed his plate across the table. To Vanessa, seated opposite, he said, 'That husband of yours gone off on his travels again, has he? Only one of my clients was telling me somebody else is running his arty-tarty gallery for him these days.'

Just as she started to reply, Vanessa's eyes encountered her half-sister's. For a second she thought she read in Sybil's expression a flash of something more like the old antagonism before it died back again into dull indifference.

'As a matter of fact Roland's been in London,' she answered; and then on a quick little rush of breath – 'But I'm glad you've mentioned him because there's something I've got to tell you all, and I thought I might as well break the news today while we're gathered *en famille*, as it were.'

There was a surprised pause round the table. Then her stepfather let out a snort and said with unnecessary crudeness, 'Don't say the fellow's managed to get you pregnant at last.'

'On the contrary.'

Turning to her mother she saw Florence Parrish's

nervous, vacuous smile fade; and reaching to touch her across the starched white cloth, she said quietly, 'I'm sorry, Mother. I know this is going to upset you. But Roland and I . . . well, you see, Roland and I have decided not to live together any more. He wants a separation. So I'm afraid it looks as though our marriage is pretty well finished.'

Later, when she had digested the family's reaction after springing that shock on them, what really hurt Vanessa most wasn't Ernest Parrish's gloating pleasure and his comment, 'Don't think you're coming back here to live'; it was the pain in her mother's face – bewilderment chased by disbelief, and then a sad, hangdog reproachfulness. For the first time in her life Vanessa was made to feel she had disappointed her.

But at least the thing she'd been absolutely dreading hadn't happened. Nobody mentioned Larret Fitzgerald.

This should have been Sybil's golden opportunity – her moment of triumph, the chance she'd been waiting for. Instead, quite incredibly, the girl's only response to her half-sister's announcement was to say across the table, 'Serve you right – now you know how I felt', and even then there'd been no fire in the words, nothing spiteful or vengeful. It was almost as though she couldn't be bothered any longer, as though the harboured anger and resentment had been burnt away and replaced by apathy.

Sybil had always been an unpredictable girl. There was never any fathoming the whys and wherefores of her behaviour. But whatever her reason for keeping silent about Larret, Vanessa could only feel deeply grateful to her because it had made a ticklish situation very much easier.

As it was, the birthday tea still ended on an embarrassingly strained note and she had made her departure shortly afterwards.

From the moment she embarked on the night ferry for Calais Vanessa resolved she was going to enjoy this holiday. Watching the harbour lights of Dover disappearing into the darkness of the Channel waters she made herself a firm promise not to think about what she was leaving behind, but to store all those negative memories in some left luggage compartment of her mind until her return, and in the meanwhile live only for the relaxing weeks ahead in France.

The last – the only – occasion she'd been abroad, it had been with Roland on their honeymoon in Paris. That too was now relegated to the past, and this time Paris became a pleasure to relish for a couple of hours until she had to board her train at the Gare Austerlitz.

After that, the real adventure began; and as if paying compliment to her spirit of determined optimism the journey down to Bordeaux was quite the most beautiful Vanessa had ever experienced. The French countryside wore such a different look after the wet greens of the English spring she'd left behind: its colours were deeper and richer, an impression which increased the further south she travelled.

Beyond Tours the lush dairy pastures gave way to a landscape of vineyards, and white stone houses with fluted red-tiled roofs, and the occasional chateau standing in noble isolation beneath a turquoise sky. And then in the shining afterglow of early evening the rural scene in turn gave way to the built-up outskirts of Bordeaux and a more industrial perspective of factories and tenements cleft by the turgidly yellow waters of the Garonne.

Here Vanessa needed to change trains again for the last leg of her journey to the Dordogne. Arriving nine o'clock that night in Bergerac, she found Marjorie Tiersot and Marjorie's charming dark-haired husband Jean-Luc waiting for her at the platform barrier. It was wonderful seeing them both again; but once in their Citroën saloon, tired out with excitement and travel, she'd finally succumbed to fatigue and slept soundly all the way through Issigeac until Marjorie roused her a few kilometres from Le Palombier.

In the yellow beam of the headlamps Vanessa had a vague impression of tall wrought-iron gates in a stone wall, and then a narrow lane running beneath the shadowy branches of trees, and a turning, and then the pale reflection of the house, with the golden warmth of lights spilling into the darkness from its windows.

After a nightcap she was packed straight off to bed, too exhausted to do justice to late supper – and woke next morning refreshed and also very ready for the cooked breakfast Marjorie brought upstairs to her.

Jean-Luc had already left for Bergerac: he worked in one of the departments of the *hôtel-de-ville*, the town hall. Tomorrow, said Marjorie, they'd have luncheon with him there and then look round the shops; but today was going to be a quiet day all to themselves, just pottering about while Vanessa had a good rest and got comfortably settled into the house.

It really was a lovely place. It had been built originally as a farmhouse about three hundred years before and was part of the estate of a chateau – a very dilapidated chateau, said Marjorie – whose entrance gates they'd driven through last night. The farmland had been sold off long ago and Le Palombier now only had about an acre of ground of its own, bordered on the north by a little wood and on the south and east by vineyards. The wood was full of the soft throaty cooing of ring-doves, *les palombes*, from which the house derived its name – a romantic whim of Jean-Luc's mother, who had come to live here as a young bride in the 1880s.

This far south the early April sun already had a pleasant heat to it; and having finished her unpacking Vanessa was sent to sit outside on the terrace while Marjorie fixed them both a bite of lunch. Marjorie was now in the fourth month of her pregnancy and looking wonderfully well, Vanessa thought a little enviously: a contented marriage and forthcoming motherhood evidently agreed with her.

'I know. I'm very, very fortunate,' smiled Marjorie. 'In fact sometimes it scares me to be so happy just in case I'm tempting fate. I suppose that's why I love to share all this—'

She turned from the beautiful countryside view from the terrace to look at her friend. 'I hope you'll stay here at least a month, Vee, more if you can – I mean that.'

'What about Jean-Luc?'

'Jean-Luc's glad for you to be with us as long as you wish.'

'Then he's obviously forgotten the old Chinese proverb about guests, like fish, beginning to stink after three days,' Vanessa told her with a laugh, 'or don't they know that one in France?'

'Oh yes – a pithier version! Seriously though, darling, we'd like you to feel you can treat Le Palombier as home. If you want entertainment there's lots going on to keep you amused – quite a few British live round

170

here and they're always throwing parties. Or if you need to be alone to do your writing or whatever, you can have the use of Jean-Luc's den. It's nice and quiet there.' Marjorie's hazel-green eyes softened a little in concern. 'You *need* this holiday, Vee. You're looking awful. Absolutely washed out.'

'I feel it. This last couple of months has been a nightmare – I can't tell you. It's just a relief to escape from the whole wretched mess and get my life back into some kind of perspective. Oh Madge, aren't I lucky having a friend like you – you're a brick, do you know that? The number of times I've wished I'd had more sense and heeded your advice. About Larret, I mean.'

'Well, let's be honest, you *were* a bit of a prize chump diving into bed with that specimen. But I suppose the benefit of mistakes is that we learn from the experience. At least you won't be repeating the same again in any great hurry.'

'You can bet I won't. It was one of the stupidest things I've ever gone and done, and no excuse to say I was in love with him—'

'Now come on, don't be too hard on yourself, Vee,' Marjorie said quickly, squeezing her hand. 'Being in love is a little like being mentally unhinged – it does all sorts of funny things to the brain. For what my opinion's worth, every so often two wrongs *do* make a right. I mean – OK, you had your fling with Lothario, and old Roland's gone off with some arty fräulein – but look at it this way, instead of being trapped for life in a dead-end marriage, the pair of you are free to do whatever you want now. So a bit of good *has* come of it.'

Vanessa looked away. The light here had such a soft,

pure quality that the distant landscape was like some lovely painting.

'Yes, but so much hurt's been caused, Madge,' she said after a moment, reflectively. 'You don't know what things have been like since Roland got back from London. Oh, he's given me time to sort my affairs out and everything else, but it's like living with a complete stranger, one who never looks at you, never speaks.'

'I suppose he'll go ahead and sell the house?'

'Oh no – no, he intends keeping "Mayville". Though I expect he'll want to reduce the staff – which is another awkward thing, because they all know what's going on of course, and it's been horribly embarrassing trying to pretend in front of them that nothing's wrong.'

'Have the two of you discussed divorce at all?'

Vanessa shook her head. 'Only the legal separation. Divorce might be a bit tricky, don't you think – I mean, which one of us would sue? We're each as guilty as the other.' She pulled a face. Then with a sudden self-mocking smile – 'You know, Madge darling, I faithfully promised myself I'd put all this ghastly doom and gloom to the back of my mind while I was here. So let's make a deal, shall we. After today – *no more Roland*!'

15

'Your glass appears empty. Can I get you a refill?' a cultivated English voice enquired at Vanessa's elbow.

She glanced round. The voice belonged to a grey-haired man in evening dress, one of the guests at this rather boisterous party being thrown in her honour by a couple familiarly known to everyone as Binkie and Twinks. Binkie and Twinks (alias Mr and Mrs Bertram Snelle, late of Holland Park, London) were part of the 'Set' of ex-patriot residents here in the Dordogne. They had descended upon Vanessa like wasps after fresh jam within days of her arrival at Le Palombier, and had absolutely insisted on holding tonight's 'meet Vanessa' bash to get her acquainted with the other members of the Set – though as Marjorie remarked, any excuse for bringing out the gin was a good enough peg on which to hang a party at the Snelles.

'I'm not sure I want another drink just yet,' Vanessa said by way of thanks. 'Two's generally about my limit.'

'Wise of you. Binkie's gins are pretty lethal.' Her maturely debonair companion held out a hand. 'We haven't been introduced. My name's Douglas Webb-Davis.'

'How do you do.' She returned his smile. 'Vanessa Antrobus.'

'The belle of the occasion, I believe.' He held the

handshake a fraction longer than was necessary before releasing her to ask, 'This your first time here in the Dordogne?'

She nodded.

'So, what d'you make of it – or haven't you had chance to see a lot so far?'

'Not that much, no. Madge and her husband are taking me for a look round Monpazier on Sunday – it's terribly picturesque, they tell me.'

'Oh yes, Monpazier's well worth seeing. Supposed to be *the* outstanding example of a medieval bastide – you know, a fortified what-not. Still got the old walls and all that.'

Douglas Webb-Davis jerked his head in the direction of two young men standing outside the open French doors at the edge of what Twinks Snelle called her 'Palm Court', a terraced garden fringed by the shadows of palm trees in the night's luminous moonlight.

'You want to have a talk to those chappies there,' he said. 'Basil and Anthony. They'll give you a complete run-down on the cultural history of the area. And if you're *very* charming to them, m'dear, you might even be invited to take tea with Monsieur Guignol.'

'Who's Monsieur Guignol?' Vanessa asked him, examining the rather languid-looking pair.

'A vicious old brute, believe me. The one occasion I was introduced to him he took an immediate dislike to my sitting in his chair and sank his teeth into my ankle. I have the scars to prove it.'

There was a pause. 'Oh you mean it's a *dog*!'

'A dog? A pekinese, m'dear! A species specially bred for snuffling and snapping. Now m'self, I'd rather have spaniels—'

Just on this they were interrupted.

'Douglas – *darling*! Binkie told me you were some-where round the place.' Out of the crowded, noisy gaiety of the party their hostess wafted over on a billow of magenta silk and perfume. 'Naughty, *naughty* boy, why didn't you come and tell me you'd arrived? I've been absolutely frantic with anxiety!'

She rose on tiptoe to embrace him, kissing the air an inch from his cheeks with a 'mwah-mwah' sound; then tucking her arm affectionately into Vanessa's, she enthused, 'What do you think of her, Douglas – isn't she a poppet? Isn't she divine? Binkie's crazily in love already.'

'He always seems to have the best of taste,' Webb-Davis said, watching Vanessa's reaction with a certain sly amusement. 'But what's happened to the adorable Sylvia, isn't she coming this evening?'

Twinks's pertly pretty features hardened into a gri-mace. 'You *are* behind the times, Douglas darling. Just for that I'm going to take Vanessa from you and give her to Leo – you've hogged her to yourself quite long enough, you dreadful man.'

Rather like Alice in Wonderland arm-in-arm with the Duchess, Vanessa thought, she found herself borne away, replenished with a generous gin and It, and ushered into the presence of a bearded youth slumped across a chaise longue by the stone-built hearth.

This was Leo, introduced to her as an artist on the verge of being discovered. Unfortunately the future prodigy was too drunk to be other than an utter crashing bore, and after ten minutes Vanessa made her excuses and escaped outside to the Palm Court for a breath of air, where she got rid of her untasted gin into one of the plant tubs.

Here she fell into conversation with Basil and Anthony, owners of the snappy pekinese. It emerged that the pair lived in a converted granary, Le Patelin, a few kilometres from Monpazier, where Basil worked as an English language teacher. His friend Anthony was a poet.

'Oh – have you had much published?' Vanessa asked him.

'The odd ode has appeared in reviews now and again,' Anthony replied indifferently. He seemed to wear a permanently wearied expression and spoke in a Home Counties drawl as though everything was too, too much of an effort. 'Actually, I'm not terribly eager to be published at the moment. One has to be frightfully, tragically young to be successful as a poet and I, alas, am in my fallow years.'

'You think youth and tragedy are what sells poetry?'

'They help. Look at Rupert Brooke and Wilfred Owen – and poor, dear Edward Thomas. All young, all dead in the Great War. All selling.'

'My father died young,' Vanessa volunteered. '*His* work received a good deal of acclaim. You'll have heard of him, I'm sure – the Fisher Poet?'

'The Fisher Poet.' Anthony looked her up and down and pursed his lips as though sucking a lemon. 'The name strikes a chord.'

His horse-faced chum Basil, refilling their glasses from a wine bottle, said in the same bored tone, '*The Sapphire Shell*, dear heart. We have it on our bookshelf.'

'Why, so we have.'

In the silver wash of moonlight they glanced at one another, like conspirators.

'Are you writing anything special at the moment?' Vanessa began again when it was obvious the subject of her father was not to be pursued. 'The countryside round here must give you lots of inspiration.'

'Oh, my dear, I not a *nature* poet,' Anthony said, terribly offended by this suggestion. 'I don't gad about *looking* at things. I write on the metaphysical plane, my themes are abstract and illusory. Just now I am spending several hours each day in the contemplation of a wall. That to me is *thrillingly* inspiring.'

Vanessa resisted a strong desire to burst out laughing.

Keeping a straight face she said mischievously, 'I imagine the texture of the wall must be very important? I mean, a brick wall must influence your poems in a rather different way than – well – a stone one, don't you find? And I suppose its size and colour affects the spectrum of your work, to some extent.'

Anthony's languorous features permitted themselves a look of gratification.

'What a pleasure to have one's artistry understood,' he murmured, throwing his eyes towards Basil. And then with a pouting smile for Vanessa – 'My dear, you really must come to tea with us at Le Patelin. Ask Marjorie and her charming husband to bring you on Sunday and we'll pursue this fascinating subject further, mmm? *Such* fun. And of course, Basil will introduce you to Monsieur Guignol.'

'When he was going on about his fallow years I expected him to add, "I shall be published in the ripeness of my maturity and then, dear heart, you may claim the satisfaction of having once met me",' Vanessa laughed, taking off Anthony's affected drawl when she was recounting this conversation later on to Marjorie. 'Honestly, Madge,

I'm glad you weren't there to hear him or I'd never have been able to contain myself!'

'Well I hope you behave on Sunday,' Marjorie ribbed her, 'otherwise you'll be thrown to the ghastly dog.'

'But I thought we're going to Monpazier this Sunday?'

'Le Patelin's on our way. And Basil and 'Tony lay on the most *amazing* tea. Actually, once you get to know them well they're both real sweeties – a bit precious perhaps, but they'd do anything to be of help.'

'I gathered that. I just happened to mention the short stories I've started writing, and Basil straight away offered to look through the scripts for me in case they needed any editing. I hadn't the heart to tell him I'd worked as a newspaper reporter. It might've hurt his feelings.'

'Hmm, and talking of hurt feelings—' Marjorie leaned closer to her friend and cast a significant glance down the room. 'See the blonde there in the doorway, the one in pearls? That's Sylvia, Binkie Snelle's ladyfriend. The silly old fool's been having the most torrid affair with her for months now – and don't we all know it! Even Twinks, though she pretends not to care. They've been rowing half the evening, she and Binkie, because Sylvia's turned up. Still, that's one of the drawbacks to socialising as a Set – everybody hops in and out of bed with everybody else. It's positively incestuous.'

'Is that experience I hear talking?'

'Good grief, no! Me, I'm very much on the fringe. The benefit of marrying a Frenchman is integrating with local society, and not being stuck with the same old bores all the time. In any case Jean-Luc doesn't care a lot for this—'

With a tilt of the head Marjorie indicated the laughing, braying, shrieking couples throwing themselves about the room to a Charleston. And then clutching hold of Vanessa – 'Oh Lord, here's Douglas Webb-Davis making a beeline for us. I'm off, Vee. See you later!'

Kissing her fingertips to the figure weaving towards them, she exited in the opposite direction.

'My dear, wha's this—' exclaimed Webb-Davis thickly, 'still not got a drinkie? You'll never be asked t'join the club, y'know. Where's Marjorie runnin' off to in such hurry?'

'Oh . . . looking for her husband.'

'Not thinkin' of leavin' already, surely? The night's still young – and you are beautiful.' The effort at gallantry accompanied an unfocused leer and a clumsy grab at Vanessa's hand, which he tried to kiss.

She edged herself away. 'It's getting late,' she suggested tactfully.

'Nons'nse. Party's only just gettin' into full swing. Can't have the main attraction disappearin' on the stroke of midnight, what?' He pushed his gin-flushed face towards her and she caught a whiff of stale cigars and scent. 'Only Cind'rellas leave at midnight.'

Vanessa made a show of checking her wristwatch. 'Actually, it's a quarter to one,' she observed.

'Quarter to one? Damn' me, an' I haven't claimed a dance off you all evenin'—' Webb-Davis had to raise his voice above the sudden hullabaloo somewhere overhead. 'Come on, m'dear, let's shake a leg an' show 'em – shall we, eh?'

Someone was cranking up the gramophone again, filling the room with the tinny strains of a Foxtrot which partly drowned the racket upstairs. Before she could decline his offer, Vanessa found herself clamped in his arm, his hand clutching hers, and the next minute she was being bumped and bounced round the floor, lunging and slipping, tripping and sliding, doing her best to stay upright on her feet as they collided into half a dozen other couples.

In the midst of all this rowdy drunkenness somebody barged into the gramophone, sending the needle skidding wildly across the record. The noise tore through the dancers' shrieks like cloth ripping, and for a second everything fell suddenly quiet.

Then a voice – a woman's voice – screamed out, 'You *bastard* you – you *bastard*!' and Twinks Snelle appeared in the doorway from the stairs, her face contorted with crimson, ugly anger. 'Get your bloody woman out of my house, you bastard. Go and screw the bitch in the bloody hedge – you're not having her in my bed, you hear!'

For the next ten minutes the row between Twinks and the imprudent Binkie had degenerated into a ghastly slanging match; yet even at its most violent, when missiles were being hurled as hard as the obscenities, nobody had seemed to take it seriously, treating the fracas as all part of the evening's entertainment.

Next day Vanessa had been embarrassed to look Jean-Luc Tiersot in the face. When she'd tried to apologise for her compatriots' behaviour, he simply gave a Gallic shrug and said, '*N'importe. Chacun son goût*', which had sounded somehow rather funny coming from a Frenchman.

After that weekend she didn't see much of the Set. She wasn't their type. Not that this upset her: having other diversions as well as her writing, Vanessa was perfectly happy being moved to the social sidelines. It struck her there was something sad and even futile about such an artificial, brittle mode of existence, every week a roundabout of the same old places, same old faces, trying to blank out the boredom with drinking parties, bridge and adultery.

Why did these people bother living in France? She supposed it must be for the climate; certainly not for the ambience and lifestyle of their adopted country, of which they seemed almost arrogantly ignorant, preferring to stick together in their own little chummy, bitchy circle.

Vanessa herself was now totally in love with the Dordogne, captivated by its incredible beauty, often borrowing Marjorie's old bicycle and setting off at dawn to spend a day alone exploring. She loved the landscape's colours – the orangey stone of the cliffs above the silver rivers, the gnarled bare brown of vines against the paler brown of earth; weathered blue shutters, and sun-bleached pastel walls, and rust-red tiles. Above all she loved the light here, loved its clear, pure, luminous quality that made everything look soft and slightly out of focus, blurring the green freshness of the countryside.

If the day were too wet for expeditions she would sit in Jean-Luc's den and work on her short stories, or the series of articles the *Express & Star* had commissioned, distilling all these colours into her writing and polishing them until they glowed like jewels through the words. Released from the mental block of the past fraught months, inspiration flowed from her pen. She was writing more competently now than she had for ages, and the combination of this fluency, together with the stimulus of her surroundings and plenty of relaxation, was doing marvellous things for Vanessa's wellbeing.

A diet of fresh air and Marjorie's cooking soon put back the weight which worry had lost. After three weeks at Le Palombier she was not only feeling a hundred per cent better, she was looking it too, her blonde hair (which she'd started wearing in a longer bob) shining with health and her sun-warmed skin radiantly lovely.

Among the Tiersots' acquaintances who visited Le Palombier was one of Jean-Luc's colleagues, Victor Michelet. Victor was a bachelor, not blessed much in the way of looks but possessing a charming manner and good humour that made him very pleasant company. His open personality extended to his admiration of Vanessa, which he made no effort to disguise; and since his English was more fluent than her stumbling schoolgirl French, he always made a point of engaging her in conversation whenever he came to the house.

After a while it was suggested that maybe Madame would do him the honour of joining him for lunch one day? Madame saw no reason to refuse the invitation. The following week they met again, this time at a dinner hosted by another of the Tiersots' friends, at their lakeside home at Lougratte. Vanessa was looking particularly attractive that night, and Victor had been emboldened enough to tell her so as he kissed her hand, declaring he 'had only the glance for her' – which was all very flattering.

One of the nice things about Frenchmen, she decided, was their ability to pay a compliment with no motive other than making a woman feel the most desirable and beautiful in the world. The eyes helped, of course. And the accent. And the hand-kissing. And when Victor invited her out for a Sunday spin in his sports car she accepted.

The weather that weekend was perfect, the sunlight like honey, the cloudless sky a beautiful soft deep blue. Their destination was the medieval town of Cordes in the neighbouring department of the Tarn, and as they motored south along the quiet roads Victor related something of its history and the role the town had played as a centre of the heretical sect known as the Albigensians, or Cathars, which had been bloodily suppressed by the Catholic Church of the time. One of the worst atrocities happened at a place called Montségur, Victor said, glancing from the road to look at Vanessa with his dark, clever eyes: on that occasion some two hundred Cathars had been burnt to death in a single day by the Inquisition.

But whatever brutal deeds this area had witnessed in its past, the passage of centuries had long removed all trace and what remained now was a romantic landscape of vine-clad hills and lushly fertile valleys.

Cordes itself could be discerned long before they reached it, a cluster of shallow roofs and white plaster walls perched high on top of a hill looking over the countryside. After taking the winding road up to one of the medieval gateways, Victor manoeuvred his Salmson sports car into a labyrinth of narrow cobbled streets so hemmed in by buildings that the midday sun barely penetrated the deep violet shadows at their lower storeys. A lot of the architecture was of the thirteenth and fourteenth centuries, he explained, pointing out to Vanessa the decorated stonework fronts of many of the houses, one of the town's principal attractions.

'You seem to know an awful lot about the place,' she said.

He smiled and shrugged. 'But of course! I was born 'ere.'

Every little alleyway revealed a different treasure. In one they came across a bronze-smith's workshop and Victor insisted on buying her a souvenir, a brooch

183

patterned with a circle of clasped hands, very delicately made and very lovely.

'This will keep our friendship the – 'ow do you say – the always green,' he said as he'd pinned it on for her.

'Evergreen,' she corrected him, laughing.

'*Ah oui*, evergreen.'

Later, weary after walking up and down so many cobbled streets all afternoon, they drank coffee beneath the blue-and-green striped awning of a café in a little square by the church of St Michel at the top of the town.

'So – I 'ope you have liked this visit to Cordes?' Victor enquired eagerly, anxious for her approval. 'She is beautiful, no?'

'Very beautiful. And I've enjoyed myself tremendously.' With a sigh of contentment Vanessa leaned back in her seat and held her face up to the warmth of the sunshine. 'In fact this has been altogether one of the nicest days I can remember, thanks to you.'

'Do not thank me – it is my pleasure! You 'ave paid me the compliment of your company, so for me also it 'as been a good day. You are an enchanting lady, Madame Vanessa, *très belle, très charmante—*'

For a moment the ever-present smile faded away and he seemed to be looking at her somehow differently, she thought. 'I like very, very much to make you 'appy. There is somewhere a little sadness, I think? Forgive me, but sometimes when you are thoughtful it is there in your eyes, and I see it.'

'You're very perceptive, Victor. What else do you see, I wonder.'

'Oh – all those things which for a Frenchman are so interesting and so attractive.' Suddenly he was smiling again. 'I 'ope that you will permit for me to take you on another excursion like today? Is that all right?'

'Of course!'

She enjoyed being with him. He made her feel relaxed, unthreatened, totally carefree, and she liked the flattery of his attentions, the fun of his harmless flirtation. It was good to be admired; good to be able to trust a man again. To be herself.

16

My own sweet darling Sybil,

Though you only left my arms an hour ago I can't sleep until I've told you ten thousand times again how much I love you. Dearest angel, you looked so marvellous tonight – I felt the proudest, luckiest man in the place to have a girl like you at my side. You are everything that is beautiful – do you know that? I want to look at you and hold you and kiss you – just *be* with you – every minute of the rest of my life. Once we're married it's going to be such heaven. I'll spoil you to bits – you'll have the best hubby a girl could ever want, you'll see.

The bed feels awfully cold and empty now you're gone – I want to close my eyes and pretend you're here again, but it's no use. Oh darling, thank you for tonight, thank you for being so wondrously generous and giving. You're all the more precious to me now, my sweetest one. I love you, love you.

Now and for ever more yours,
Larry.

His letter, like the rest Larret Fitzgerald had written, was limp with constant folding. After their bust-up Sybil had meant to burn the lot together with her other mementoes of him, but she was glad now that she hadn't. She needed to remind herself what it felt like to be happy once . . . needed to remember the normal, decent things about her past.

Tears dripped from her chin. She wiped them away with the back of her hand. Outside her bedroom window the May sunshine was pouring its golden warmth into the Sunday calm of Tettenhall Green, bringing out children to play and couples to sit in their gardens; but the face in Sybil's mirror was contoured with shadows – a drawn grey face staring back at her with misery and self-loathing in its eyes.

What a mess she had made of her life. What a terrible, terrible mess. She folded the letter away inside its envelope, and laid it on her bedspread with the others. Her hands were shaking. She felt and looked like death.

There was a hesitant knock at the door, her mother's voice asking – 'Your father wants to know when you're coming downstairs, Sybil?'

'Later. Tell him I'm having a rest.'

Silence; then her mother going away again, obediently.

The girl longed to run to the door and call out after her, needing her mother's arms to comfort and hold her, love her, while she wept. She didn't move though; just sat on the bed staring at the stranger staring back at her.

Where had that other face gone – the pretty one, the one that used to know how to smile? The one that had pouted and teased and flirted so much with itself? Perhaps this face in the mirror was a mask which hid that other. This face wasn't Sybil's. It was ugly. It looked softly and prematurely tired beneath the eyes, and its mouth drooped with unhappiness.

What are you doing to yourself? this face seemed to say. Why don't you stop, you stupid idiotic fool, before it's too late?

She was trying to stop – she was, she was trying so hard. She hadn't seen Alan Slater for a week now, but she still had his filth in her body, in her blood, and in her mind. It was cocaine he'd been giving her. Cocaine; innocent and white as snow. Cocaine to dope her up till she was high as a kite in her head, then pitch her down into a hollow, hungry craving.

God, what she wouldn't give for one more fix . . .

She clenched her hands and pressed them between her knees, hunching her shoulders. Her whole body shook in a spasm of nausea. Slater had known what he was playing at, all right. He needed her doped, because no girl in her senses would agree to the things he'd wanted them to do in that tatty, sordid room above the billiard hall. Half of it Sybil couldn't remember. What half she did was so obscene and vile she felt befouled, dirty, rotten inside where he'd touched her; and though she'd scrubbed her flesh till it was raw she couldn't get rid of the taint of Slater's depravity.

'You think you can split wi' me now?' he'd said a week ago. 'Bloody try it, my wench. You can wriggle as much as you like but I've got you so well 'ooked you'll keep on crawling back to me.'

That was the rock-bottom moment she had realised she'd got to break away, or wreck her life. Her fascination for this horrible, repellent man had curdled into shuddering abhorrence. She was ruining her health, losing her friends, upsetting her parents, in danger of getting the sack from her job – and for what? Slater disgusted her; but not nearly as much as Sybil disgusted herself.

How to pick up the pieces of her life from here, though? Which way back to self-respect and wholesomeness? If she closed her eyes the pictures in her head were always the same – images of the wonderful, magical days she had known with Larret Fitzgerald. She even dreamed of Larret, dreamed she was as much in love with him as she'd ever been, and he with her. She longed so much for something strong and safe to cling to that her mind went skimming over the later painful memories, and hugged itself for comfort to the good times, recapturing the laughter and the fun they'd known together, the places they'd been, the plans they'd both made, the loving they'd shared.

I was happy with him, so happy, she said to the face in the mirror. Maybe . . . maybe if I went to see him, I could be happy again?

The face made no answer; just looked at her with its desperate, pleading eyes and quivering mouth.

Her parents thought she was spending the night at Gloria Millington's. Sybil had felt unusually guilty about lying to her mother and father, but she'd been giving them enough concern just lately and didn't want to add to their anxiety.

An early evening train took her into Birmingham. From there she caught a bus to Moseley where Larret had his diggings in one of the substantial Victorian houses at the top of Wake Green Road. Outside the house the pollarded lime trees which looked so ugly and dead in winter were in leaf now, their stunted crowns smudged with a pale greenness glowing in the soft light of a street lamp. Sybil stood in their shadows staring at the house. Lights were burning in its upper storey. She was feeling physically sick with nerves, panicky and yet excited, scared of what Larret's reaction would be when he saw her.

His little Triumph roadster was parked in its usual

place by the ivy-clad wall. She took this as a sign in her favour, and as she passed the car she ran her hand along its wing for luck, recalling all the golden times she'd once enjoyed in it – days out at Aberystwyth, picnics on Cannock Chase, never-ending crazy summer evenings in the Clent Hills.

There was a gate at the side; beyond it a gravel path half-choked with weeds, leading to a fire escape and then the garden, blurred with dusk between rectangles of yellow light spilt across the lawn from neighbouring windows. The fire escape ran up the wall to a landing, and doubled back on itself to go up again to a smaller landing and a doorway.

The door was standing ajar. Sybil could hear band music drifting out from Larret's wireless. Half way up her courage failed her for a moment and she turned to go back down; then pulled herself together again, willing her trembling legs to carry on climbing. Larret had been cooking something or other because the smell of burning toast lay on the air, an ordinary, homely sort of smell.

She knocked at the door. No answer. The music was too loud. After waiting a bit she knocked again harder.

'Hang on – be with you in a second,' he called out, and Sybil's heart leapt at the remembered Irish smoothness of his voice.

He must have only just finished shaving himself: he had a towel round his bare shoulders, and there was a little slick of soap beneath one ear where he'd hurriedly wiped his face before coming out of the bathroom.

She took a breath.

'Hello, Larry,' she said.

He stopped dead in his tracks when he saw who it was, his eyes and mouth dropping open in surprise before he recovered himself. She knew he was alone in his digs because he didn't give that involuntary glance behind him that would have betrayed he had other company.

'Sybil—!' he exclaimed with a disbelieving laugh. 'Good God, I hardly recognised you – what in hell's name are you doing here?'

'I – just wanted to see you. How are you keeping?'

'Fine, fine.' He thrust his hands into his flannel trouser pockets, amused but also clearly embarrassed. 'You'd better come in.'

His living room hadn't changed very much from how she remembered, and under the burnt-toast smell it still had its old aroma of stale cigarette smoke and eau de cologne. The same rather frightful curtains hung at the window, and the same two posters – a Toulouse Lautrec and a Beardsley – covered the wall behind the settee. The dried flowers Sybil had given him two Christmases ago had cobwebs on them now, but otherwise the place was no more untidy than before.

'Can I offer you a drink or something? You look as though you could do with one.'

'I wouldn't mind a gin.'

'I'll make that two.' Larret shut the outer door and went and turned down the wireless. 'It's a bit of a shock I must say, you showing up out of the blue like this.'

'I wanted to see you,' Sybil repeated, her hollowed eyes following him fixedly as he came past again. Now that he'd let her inside his digs she knew she had done the right thing coming here; she was feeling less jittery already, more certain of herself, reassured by the familiar surroundings. 'You don't mind, do you, Larry? I – I was in Birmingham anyway and I decided I'd look you up . . . for old times' sake.'

'Why should I mind,' he said from the kitchen doorway, 'just as long as we keep this a friendly visit and
it doesn't turn into another of those ghastly rows about
your sister or whatever. Or is that why you're here,' he
added a little uncomfortably.

She shook her head. 'It isn't, I promise. I thought –
well, I thought it would be nice if you and I could patch
things up, that's all.' Then she saw a sudden look of
wariness on Larret's face and quickly corrected herself.
'You know, get back on speaking terms and . . . sort of
be pals again.'

'Oh. Yes, sure. Fine by me.' He stared her up and
down and then gave a shrug and disappeared into the
kitchen, and she could hear him moving about over the
quiet background music of the wireless, a chink of glasses
as he poured their drinks.

Sybil got her Woodbines out and lit one. The darkened
silhouette of her reflection in the window followed her
movements and for a second, before she thrust it from
her mind, the image intruded of that stranger she kept
seeing in her bedroom mirror. She drew on the cigarette,
sucking the smoke down hard, and turned away.

'Here you are—' Larret said, bringing her out a large
gin and orange. 'Park yourself on the settee while
I go and put a shirt and tie on. I'm afraid you've
rather caught me on the hop, I was getting ready to
go out.'

'You're going out? Oh – does that mean I won't be
able to stay very long?'

'Were you intending to? I thought this was a social
call.' He looked at her as he strapped on his wristwatch.
'Anyway, you won't want to leave it too late if you're
travelling back tonight, what with buses and trains and

things to catch. I'd offer you a lift into town only I'm driving in the opposite direction.'

'But Larry – Larry, please, I've come all this far—' she began.

'Sorry old thing, no can do,' he overrode her firmly, heading towards the bedroom door with his own drink. 'Delighted as I am to see you again, I've got somebody rather special to meet and I wouldn't like to keep her waiting. I'm sure you understand.'

Sybil's fragile facade of self-control started to splinter. The gin slopped in the glass as she raised it to her lips and gulped it back. Of course there'd be someone else; the Larrys of this world were never short of female company. Hadn't she always known that, even if she fought against accepting it?

She pulled her slouch hat off and threw it aside, suddenly miserably let down. For days she'd been looking forward to this evening, pinning so many hopes on it to give her back her happiness and make things as they used to be for her and Larret. And now – now she felt the stranger in the mirror invading her once more, dragging with it the nightmare that she called her life.

She followed Larret into the bedroom, the same bedroom where two years ago he had helped himself to her virginity.

'Please, won't you stop and talk a bit?' she begged. 'I'll be honest, I told you a lie – I wasn't in Birmingham at all today, I came directly over here from work. I just *had* to see you, Larry – and it's nothing to do with our engagement or Vanessa or anything like that.'

Larret removed a freshly laundered shirt from its hanger in the wardrobe. Turning his back on her he put it on, and with an insulting indifference to her presence unbuttoned his trousers and dropped them round his buttocks while he tucked the shirt-tails in before adjusting himself.

'OK, now suppose you tell me what exactly this is all about,' he said with growing impatience, searching for his collar studs. 'From the state of you I'd say you were in trouble, you're looking bloody awful. What the hell have you been doing to yourself.'

I've been missing you, Sybil longed to cry at him. But would he care; would he even want to know.

Instead she made a little helpless gesture and said with pathetic bravado, 'What have I been doing? I've been living dangerously, that's what – getting into the wrong sort of company and trying to kid myself I was being so clever and sophisticated.'

There was a pause while Larret finished fixing on his collar; then taking up a silver-backed brush to attend to his thick dark hair, he remarked, 'You're not pregnant I hope.'

'No—'

'Because if you are it's no good running after me for help.'

'I'm not. Slater – I mean the bloke I went with, Alan Slater, he always made sure nothing like that would ever happen.'

'Well at least he was a gentleman.'

'*Gentleman*—!' Sybil drew heavily on her Woodbine and looked down at the glass she was clutching. 'He was the lowest, vilest form of life that ever crawled this earth. God knows what I thought I saw in him. I had to get stinking drunk before I could bear him coming anywhere near me, let alone touch me. He was disgusting—'

'Look, old thing, the problem is yours not mine, and in any case I'm not particularly interested,' Larret cut in, more concerned with getting a good knot in the red and cream silk tie he'd just selected from a row of others. 'In fact if you want the truth, it's not only embarrassing but a bit of a bloody nerve, you suddenly taking it into your head after, what – a year or more? – to show up on my doorstep and want to start discussing the rather sordid details of your private life.'

'You asked what had happened to me,' Sybil told him piteously. 'Don't you think I *know* how terrible I look? I can't eat, can't sleep properly, can't stop shaking, I feel so ill all the time—'

'Then see a doctor.'

She gave a laugh that quivered on the edge of tears. 'What could a doctor do. Here's the only medicine that's any good,' she answered, raising the glass and gulping off the rest of the gin.

Larret threw her a contemptuous look. 'Well, if you're not prepared to help yourself it's no business of mine that you're turning into a lushington. You always were pretty stupid about drinking for the sake of getting blotto.'

He made to push past her to return to the living room, but Sybil caught at his arm and he must have read the desperation in her pale, thin face because instead of shaking her off, he paused and added a little less cuttingly, 'Why not be a sensible girl and try and pull yourself together. You've had a bad experience – OK, it's knocked you about a bit, but you're a natural survivor and it's a pity to ruin those charming looks of yours.'

'Then help me to pick up the pieces, Larry?'

'Pick up the pieces—? What in God's name d'you expect me to do?' He jerked her hand away. 'I've got a life of my own to live. Whatever we had, you and me, it's over, it's finished – haven't you got that fact through your head yet? I don't know what you think you're playing at by coming here and expecting me to feel sorry for you, but let me tell you you've made a big mistake, because the only thing you're getting out of me is the suggestion that you leave again right now.'

'No – please, no—' Stubbing her cigarette into an ashtray Sybil went after him. 'I *need* you – believe me it's the truth – Larry, I need you, I can't go on without you!'

'You've managed it well enough so far.'

'But I haven't, I haven't – look at the mess I'm in.'

'Oh, come on – you're blaming me because you get in with the wrong crowd and you drink too much? Sure, that's hardly my fault, is it. You're old enough by now to know what you're doing.'

Larret tried to shove her aside but she clung to him tenaciously.

'All I'm asking is another chance for us to be together and be happy, the way we used to be,' she cried hopelessly. 'What's wrong with wanting that – tell me, Larry! Tell me what's wrong with wanting happiness again. Have you forgotten what wonderful times we always had? Don't you find yourself wishing they'd never ended?'

'I've things of better interest to occupy my mind,' he said, beginning to lose all patience. 'And at this particular moment the only thing I'm wishing is that the girl I've arranged to meet at half past eight will still be waiting. Now do me a favour, Sybil – get your hat and leave, OK? Go right away out of my life and just forget you ever knew me.'

Burying her face against his clean white shirt Sybil responded by bursting into a sudden desolate fit of weeping.

'Oh, for God's sake – mind what you're doing, I don't want bloody lip-rouge everywhere!' He grabbed her by the shoulders, holding her off at arm's length and giving her an angry shake. 'Silly little bitch, what the hell is the matter with you.'

For a moment, too choked by the thick knot of tears clogging her throat, she couldn't answer; and then, struggling for self-control, she whispered through her sobs, 'Why are you doing this to me, Larry . . . why? You swore you'd always love me, always and always . . . you wrote me so in all of your letters. You'd never leave me, you said, you'd love me till the end of time . . . and I thought you meant it.'

Larret gave a hard, derisive laugh. Releasing her he moved away.

'I've loved a lot of women, yes including your boringly virtuous sister. But it's only a word, it never meant anything – a bit of fun for a month or two, that's all. I'm the sort of chap who's easily distracted by a pretty face, and just as easily bored. If you were clever you'd have guessed that.'

'I know about Vanessa,' Sybil flung after him wretchedly. 'Her husband's left her because of the affair she had with you.'

'So –? And am I supposed to feel guilty?'

Picking up her hat Larret thrust it towards her, then

in a final act of rejection went across to open the outer door. And as she stared at him, blinded by her burning tears, Sybil felt the stranger in the mirror overwhelming her.

17

By the time Vanessa returned from the Dordogne at the beginning of June, her half-sister had been discharged from hospital and was convalescing in a nursing home somewhere out in the country. Vanessa's first thought on hearing the news was that Sybil must have been involved in some kind of accident; and she was therefore all the more shocked and horrified to learn the truth from her mother, that the girl had attempted to take her own life by slashing her wrists with her father's open razor.

It was a miracle she was discovered in time. Another five minutes and she could have bled to death, the doctor informed her distraught parents after Sybil had been rushed unconscious into the Royal Hospital. Then as if that wasn't enough, the Parrishes had received a visit from the police, asking all sorts of questions about possible motives and suicide notes and the like; and then of course, because Ernest Parrish was a solicitor, and a member of the Rotary Club and the South Staffordshire Golf Club, as well as being a noted Freemason, his daughter's regrettable 'accident' was reported in all the local newspapers.

'They even came here to the house wanting a photo-graph of Sybil,' Mrs Parrish said forlornly. 'The very nerve, as if I'd let them have one. Your stepfather's quite beside himself . . . it's making him ill, it is.'

'Never mind about him – what about you, that's more important,' Vanessa wanted to know, concerned by her mother's exhausted appearance. 'You're not blaming yourself for what happened I hope, are you? After all, you'd been doing your best for weeks and weeks to get Sybil to see her doctor, and it's no fault of yours if she refused to go.'

'Your stepfather thinks it is. He's saying I wasn't strict enough with her.'

'That's rich coming from him! If he'd been a bit stricter himself instead of indulging her so much, she mightn't have turned out to be such a self-willed little madam,' Vanessa said angrily, telling herself it was typical of Ernest Parrish to expect her poor mother to carry the guilt to relieve his own troubled conscience.

Mrs Parrish dabbed her eyes with a crumpled handkerchief. 'He's right though, dear. I've let our Sybil have her own way far too much. All that going off dancing and drinking . . . staying out till all hours, and telling lies about who she was with and what she's been up to.'

'Mother, you know as well as me Sybil's a law unto herself. No one's ever stopped her doing anything she's set her mind on. And in any case, why should you be held responsible – it was her father's job to put his foot down if he didn't like the way she was carrying on. I'm sick of him criticising you when he knows you're in no position to answer him back—'

Vanessa reached over for her mother's hand.

In a quieter tone she continued, 'At least thank God she's OK now, and that's all that counts. Let's just hope she's given herself a big enough fright to make her realise what a stupid thing she tried to do.'

'Oh, I think she realises that,' Mrs Parrish replied with a sad little smile. 'She seems a changed girl . . . keeps saying how sorry she is for the bother she's causing everybody. I don't know, dear . . . perhaps it's wicked to admit this, but in a funny sort of way I love her more dearly now than I've ever done. Isn't it strange . . . I see something of you in her, somehow.'

'What's so strange about it. Sybil's as much a part of you as I am.' Vanessa gave her mother's hand a squeeze before releasing it. 'She's been spoilt, that's all. Whatever made her so desperate she was driven to – well, to do what she did, maybe it was the lesson she needed to learn, wouldn't you say?'

'I don't know. She refuses to talk to us about it. The doctor in charge of the nursing home – such a nice, kind man he is – he told your stepfather we mustn't ask her questions. We've got to wait for her to tell us in her own good time, he said.'

Vanessa nodded. 'I'd like to go and visit her. The place is out at Codsall, isn't it?'

'That's right, dear. The Balmoral. It's supposed to be the best one in the area. Terribly expensive of course, but one of your stepfather's golfing partners recommended it.' Her mother seemed to brighten a little. 'I'm sure Sybil will be pleased to see you – visiting hours are in the afternoon. Oh, but how will you get there? You haven't got the use of Roland's car now, have you?'

It was the first actual reference either of them had made to Vanessa's separation from her husband.

'Don't worry, I expect I'll be able to borrow one from somewhere,' she answered. 'I'll ask Kay – you know, Kay Murray – she'll lend me hers. I've got to pop into her office anyway, I want to pick her brains about going back to work again for the *Advertiser*.'

*   *   *

Having returned from those blissful two months at Le Palombier feeling so much stronger and more positive about the reorganisation of her life, Vanessa wanted to get the distressing task of moving herself out of 'Mayville' over and done with as quickly as possible. She and Roland had already had a coolly polite and businesslike discussion about the arrangements, and he'd raised no objection to the list of belongings which she wished to take. The immediate priority now was to find herself somewhere else to live. After that she could think about employment.

It was her mother who found her the nice little flat in Paget Road, on the ground floor of a spacious terraced house. The property belonged to a distant cousin, a Mrs Brereton, and backed on to the playing fields of Vanessa's old school, so that from her rooms she had a view of the poplar trees bordering the hockey pitch where a different generation of High School girls now played. During the midsummer afternoons while she was moving in, she could often hear their eager young voices carrying through her opened windows, and a feeling of nostalgia would creep over her for those sunny, peaceful, pre-war schooldays left behind, like sepia memories in a photograph album.

Whoever had rented the place before her, they must have had artistic taste because the walls were lined with a lovely creamy-pink William Morris 'pomegranate' paper and they'd bequeathed her an Arts and Crafts style table which Vanessa adored the minute she saw it. Now that the break-up of her marriage was officially a fact, she intended reshaping her life into something more creatively individual and filling it with beautiful things to reflect her own identity – beginning with these pleasant, airy rooms which from now on were going to be her home.

Tasting freedom again was a strange experience initially, and one Vanessa found she would need to readjust to. For three years she'd been living as an extension to somebody else, first as a fiancée and then as a wife. Now she was – what? a half-wife; still Mrs Roland Antrobus in status and title, but in the eyes of society a woman slightly less than respectable because she happened to be living apart from her husband.

Well, the War had knocked a lot of such démodé attitudes for six. To be legally separated or divorced nowadays was even considered chic in some circles, and in any case Vanessa wasn't about to make herself socially invisible just because she was living alone again. Maybe at first she would miss not having a maid – there'd been tears and real sadness when she said goodbye to the staff at 'Mayville' – but she had cared for herself before and rather enjoyed it. She liked being alone. And she was looking forward to the challenge of being in control of her life in every way possible, even financially.

Having said that however, she was about to find full-time re-employment not quite as easy as she'd envisaged. Her hopes had been pinned on Kay Murray at the *Weekly Advertiser*; but Kay had pulled a very long face when Vanessa called by to enquire about coming back on the staff again as a general reporter.

'Nothing doing on the *Advertiser*, darling,' Kay apologised. 'You can go and have a word with old Jonesy the editor, but I think you'll be wasting your time. Work's a bit short everywhere just lately – we get hopefuls by the dozen for every vacancy we advertise. Freelancing's no problem, you know we'll always commission features from you, but if it's a job you want – well, the only thing I can suggest, darling, is trying the other papers in the area.'

At least Kay had come up trumps about loaning her little Austin Seven for an afternoon. Having learned to drive in Roland's Morris Cowley, Vanessa had no trouble at all getting used to the smaller 'Chummy': she had never been nervous of motor cars, and in France had even driven Victor Michelet's just for the fun of it.

Motoring over to the nursing home at Codsall, she'd found herself thinking about Victor and really rather missing him. He'd been such a perfect companion, attentive and courteous, flattering her in the most delicious way without ever taking liberties, yet at the same time doing marvels for her self-esteem. Every woman who had been hurt needed a Victor to make her better, Vanessa decided. A pity there wasn't someone like him for Sybil.

The Balmoral turned out to be one of those huge and very ugly redbrick piles built by some affluent Victorian industrialist as a vulgar means of showing off his wealth. During the War it had been used as a military hospital, a function far better suiting its endless marbled corridors and large, high-ceilinged rooms and spacious grounds.

Vanessa found her half-sister in a private room on the second floor, overlooking the lake. Sybil was reclining on a day-bed flicking through a magazine, and wearing a pretty summer frock; and at first glance it was impossible to guess there was anything wrong, until one saw the bandages round her wrists.

They greeted one another a little awkwardly. Vanessa had brought roses and Sybil's favourite chocolates and a selection of lightweight reading; but after they'd exchanged the usual banalities she found it difficult to know what else to talk about, and an embarrassed sort of restraint stifled the conversation until all of a sudden Sybil herself broke the ice by saying—

'Mother's been telling me about the flat you've gone to live in. I suppose you must be finding it a bit of a squash after "Mayville".'

'Well – different, perhaps,' Vanessa agreed. 'But the rooms are beautifully light and airy so I can't say I miss not having the space to move about. And anyway there's only me to fall over myself.' She gave a smile; and when she got a half-smile in response, risked a rebuff by adding, 'I hope you'll drop round for a visit when you're properly back on your feet again. Would you like to?'

Sybil turned her head and looked out towards the lake, glittering in the cloudless sunlight. A breeze was swaying the rushes round the margins of its further shore where someone – the original owner probably – had built a folly in the shape of a little ruined temple.

Without taking her eyes off the scene she said in a low voice, 'Thanks . . . yes, I'd like to come and see you. While I've been stuck in here I've had a chance to think about a lot of things. They encourage us to do that – the doctors, I mean. It's part of the treatment.'

Then glancing down at her bandaged wrists and biting her lip, she carried on, 'People who do what I did . . . what I tried to do . . . they're regarded as being not quite right in the head . . . a bit unbalanced. See, I'm not afraid to say it. Apparently I had some sort of breakdown. One of the doctors told me it's like breaking a leg, you have to put your mind in a mental plaster-cast to allow it time to heal itself.'

'And d'you feel you're healed yet?' Vanessa asked her gently.

'I don't know. I'm calmer I suppose, but that could be the pills and stuff they're giving me. At least I feel *myself* again. I really went off the rails towards the end . . . when I think about it now it's like looking at somebody else doing all those stupid, awful things.'

The girl picked at a loose thread. 'I can't talk about this to Mother and Daddy. They wouldn't understand, and anyway I've caused them enough trouble without upsetting them more. I feel so sorry for them . . . especially poor Mother. She always cries when she comes to visit me and I wish she wouldn't, it makes me see how much I must have hurt her.'

'If it's any comfort,' said Vanessa, 'I happen to know you're dearer to Mother than you've ever been and the only thing she wants is to have you home, happy and well again.'

'Happy—' Sybil made the word sound like a profanity. 'I don't think I'll ever be happy. I'm just not cut out for it. Shall I tell you something—' She looked up quickly. 'I can say this now because it doesn't matter any more . . . but all those years I hated you, Vanessa, I realise it's only myself I was hating really. Do you know why? It's because I was jealous . . . jealous of something you had and I wanted to share. Doesn't make sense, does it. I mean, *I* was the one given the clothes and toys and everything, *I* was the one Daddy spoiled – yet whatever I got it wasn't enough, I couldn't be happy. And you were, Vanessa. That's the reason I was jealous – of your happiness.'

The girl lay back against the day-bed and closed her eyes. After a long, painful moment she went on again,

'What a laugh, eh. Hating you because of that. I couldn't
work it out . . . you had no *right* to be happy, you with
your hand-me-down things, always getting pushed away
and treated second best by Daddy. I knew you weren't his
child and he didn't want you. And in a crazy way that's
why I used to resent you, you should have been jealous
of *me*, and you never were, never. A storybook's about
all I can remember you asking for.'

It was a confession revealing something of the catharsis
of the past traumatic weeks; and Vanessa appreciated
what an effort it must have taken. The old Sybil wouldn't
have had the humility or grace to speak so honestly.

She waited till her half-sister had finished, and then
said quietly, 'I wasn't happy that you hated me. Nor that
your father never wanted me. I suppose these were things
I had to teach myself to live with.'

'And then there was Larry,' the other continued as
though she hadn't heard her. 'Good old Larry, the love
of my life, my one big chance—'

'*Must* we talk about Larret Fitzgerald? Haven't we said
it all already?'

'Oh, but you haven't heard the best.' Sybil levered
herself up on an elbow and gave a lopsided smile which
didn't quite manage to hide the sudden quiver of her chin.
'See, I thought it'd be an idea if we got back together, me
and Larry, so I went along to visit him. God – I must have
been in a pretty desperate state! Anyway, I sang him my
little song about us kissing and making up and being pals
again . . . and guess what the bastard said.'

Vanessa looked down at her hands. 'I should think he
didn't want to know.'

'Right. He didn't want to know. He threw me out.'

The quiver spread to Sybil's lips, dimpling the corners

of her mouth and making the smile even more pathetically lopsided. 'Well I suppose I'd rather asked for it. I was daft enough to hope there was a chance he'd take me back . . . why should I complain if he wouldn't play along, he'd already broken my heart and trampled all over my feelings.'

'Larret Fitzgerald doesn't have feelings, except for himself,' Vanessa said bleakly. 'I discovered that to my own cost after . . . well, afterwards.'

'You mean after he'd had his little fling with you.'

She nodded. 'You'd guessed about that, hadn't you. But believe me, Sybil, you were wrong to put the blame on me for Larret walking out on you – what happened between him and me didn't start until a long time later.'

'I know that now. All those lies about him being in love with you, they were just his way of saying he was sick of me.' Sybil's eyes were looking suspiciously bright, and she was having a struggle to control herself. 'It's a bit of a joke, isn't it, Vanessa. One of the few things you and I have got in common is the fact we've both been to bed with Larry Fitzgerald. If it weren't so bloody funny I think I'd want to cry—'

Suddenly the hurt was too much, and turning away she buried her face in her arm.

'Don't – please don't,' her half-sister pleaded, getting up to go and kneel beside the day-bed. 'A man like that, he isn't worth it. Haven't you paid a big enough price already?'

'D'you know what he said . . . he said none of it ever meant anything . . . all that happiness I thought we had, it was just a sham,' Sybil whispered.

'Forget him. Try telling yourself there's far better fish in the sea than Larret Fitzgerald. Besides, he's more to be pitied than anything else,' Vanessa consoled her. 'One of these days he's going to end up on the scrapheap lonely and pathetic, with nothing but his fading looks and shallow charm to see him through. Now come on, Sybil, blow your nose—'

The girl sat up, wiping her eyes with her bandaged wrists, and took the handkerchief held out to her.

'I can't understand why you're being so nice to me,' she said through her tears, 'when I've been such a rotten, spiteful, sneaky little bitch—'

'So you have. But you know it honestly doesn't matter. Don't you think it's time we buried the hatchet and tried to be chums?' Vanessa asked her gently. 'We're both at a sort of crossroads in our lives, aren't we, Sybil.'

There was a sniff; then a hesitant nod.

They looked at one another. And for the first time since she could remember, Vanessa felt the genuine bond of sisterhood between them.

It was Dulcie Fox who suggested the idea. Vanessa had gone to see her at the *Express & Star* offices in Queen Street, hoping for more luck with finding herself a job, but only getting much the same answer she'd had from Kay Murray on the *Advertiser* – that the general economic outlook wasn't too bright just now, and newspaper employees were being laid off rather than taken on.

Why was she looking for full-time work anyway, Dulcie had wanted to know. Vanessa explained her reasons: she needed something to keep her occupied, as well as provide for herself, and her commissions as a freelance writer couldn't guarantee her a regular income. Besides, a job would help her to live more independently without having to depend for money solely on the goodwill of her estranged husband.

Dulcie, who was all in favour of women's independence both in and outside marriage, suggested she keep an eye on the 'Situations Vacant' columns. Vanessa had shorthand and typing skills: until something more suitable cropped up she could always do secretarial work for a while, and employment of that kind was still generally available.

Vanessa thought about it; and deciding the idea was worth a try she started looking through the weekly columns. Because she would have to rely on buses for transport she needed something fairly central, which whittled the choice down a bit; and the fact she'd had no previous experience as a secretary rather counted against her, as she was to discover.

However, she persevered.

Then one Friday evening at the start of August, an advert appeared in the *Express & Star* which had instantly attracted her attention.

'Wanted, reliable young lady of smart appearance for general office duties, shorthand and typing a requirement. Hours nine to six, Monday to Saturday, wages to be agreed. Apply with references to James Brockhouse, scrap dealer, Sun Street, Wolverhampton.'

It was the name which had caught Vanessa's eye. This was the third time she'd come across Jim Brockhouse, the first being at 'Mayville', the second in The Copper Kettle tea-room, and on both occasions she'd had reason to remember him.

Well, third times were supposed to be lucky, she reminded herself, and she suited his advertisement in every respect. So why not be a devil and apply . . . and see what happened.

18

Lying behind the Low Level railway station in a rundown district of Wolverhampton so far neglected by town planners, Sun Street retained under its grime and disrepair a good deal of its Victorian appearance. It was one of those streets where commercial enterprise had supplanted family life: for every couple of properties still occupied, a greater number had been converted to the use of businesses, one-man efforts which were continually closing down and re-opening again under some other name.

Jim Brockhouse's scrapyard was probably the most permanent feature, having been established here since the turn of the century. Originally it must have contained a block of stables, because to reach it one had to go through a wide archway into a cobbled courtyard where there were substantial outbuildings, and beyond that an area of waste ground now filled with rusting scrap of every description.

On a day like this, glaringly bright with August sunshine, the street wore a shabby look as though no one had taken a broom to the steps or a brush to the paintwork in years. Everything was slicked with a thin, fine coat of sooty dirt from the railway. A few children were playing marbles in the gutter, and as Vanessa came along they stopped to watch her;

but otherwise the place seemed to doze in the afternoon heat.

She found the address she was looking for, the house next to the archway. Like its neighbours it carried enamelled signs on its walls advertising Vinolia Soap and Mazawattee Tea and the like, which with the tub of red geraniums on its doorstep at least gave a bit of colour to the drabness.

Jim Brockhouse's office was in what had once been somebody's front parlour. While the very pregnant young woman who'd shown her inside went off in search of him, Vanessa took a critical look round, not terribly impressed with the place – if this was supposed to be an office, she thought, it was the untidiest one she'd ever been in. Papers were scattered all over the place, on the floor, round the walls, even dumped in the fireplace; not only papers either, but files and ledgers and order books, all left lying any old how with invoices and correspondence.

She moved a pile from a chair and sat down. Dust motes danced along shafts of sunlight streaming through the window, and on the opposite wall the outlines of pictures which had once hung there showed against the faded pattern of the paper like a ghostly memento of the house's previous occupants.

It seemed a long time before the pregnant young woman returned, and then only to poke her head round the door and inform Vanessa that 'he' was on his way, and did she fancy a cup of tea?

Vanessa declined.

Another five minutes dragged by.

Then there was a sound of voices, a man's footsteps approaching down the passage, and the door opened again and Jim Brockhouse came in. He was dressed as Vanessa had seen him at 'Mayville', in long canvas apron over trousers and collarless shirt, his sleeves rolled back to the elbow to show brown, well-muscled arms. Her immediate thought as he acknowledged her was how tired he looked.

Rather curtly, without apology for keeping her waiting, he said, 'Mrs Antrobus, is it? How d'you do – I'm Jim Brockhouse. I see you had no trouble finding us.'

'The directions in your letter were most helpful, thank you.'

'Good.' He shoved aside some of the papers on the mahogany roll-top desk and propped himself against it, folding his arms. 'Right – would you like to tell me some'at about yourself, then p'raps we can take things from there.'

It was obvious he hadn't remembered her.

Deciding she wouldn't mention they'd met before, Vanessa produced her references and gave him a brief outline of her previous employment. While she talked she was aware she was being examined very thoroughly, from her cream straw hat with blue silk ribbon-band matching the colour of her frock, to her slender calves and Louis-heeled shoes. She wondered whether she hadn't dressed 'up' too much for this interview: Jim Brockhouse didn't look impressed by what he saw. Instead the crease between his eyes grew deeper, and by the time she'd finished speaking he wore the same curiously angry expression she recalled from their encounter at The Copper Kettle.

'So you're applying for job o' secretary wi' no actual experience o' the work involved,' he said abruptly.

'I'm sure you'll find me competent enough. I can type and take shorthand dictation, and answer the telephone, and arrange appointments. I can also make a decent cup of tea. What more do secretaries do?' It was meant light-heartedly.

'*I'm* the one conducting the interview.'

His sharpness was so unnecessary that Vanessa was quite taken aback. 'Of course. I'm sorry.'

'Right. Now then, how are you at business letters?'

'Typing them, do you mean, or composing them?'

He considered the word 'composing' and rejected it. 'I mean writing the blessed things yourself,' he said, producing a packet of Players' Navy Cut cigarettes from his apron pocket.

'Yes, I can do that, Mr Brockhouse. I'd only require an outline of what you wanted saying.'

'Hmm.' He examined her again with that peculiar frowning look. 'Tell me some'at. What made you decide to apply to come and work for me? It's lowering yourself a bit, in't it, after being on the newspapers?'

There was no point beating about the bush with a man as blunt as this, so Vanessa answered candidly, 'There are no vacancies at the moment. And I want employment. I believe I'm capable of doing the job ably and efficiently, and Sun Street's not too far to have to travel. And no, I don't consider I'm lowering myself, Mr Brockhouse.'

'Fair enough.' He gave a cursory glance over her references. 'Where is it you live, you'll have to remind me.'

'Off Tettenhall Road. I said in my application—'

'I know you did, Mrs Antrobus. All the same, mebbe you'll refresh my memory.'

She obliged, omitting the fact that she was separated from her husband. That was personal business and she saw no reason to mention it here.

Jim Brockhouse went to take a cigarette from the packet, then changed his mind.

'D'you smoke these things—'

Vanessa shook her head.

'That's as well. I can't abide a woman smoking.' Putting the Players away, he added tersely, 'Any case, it'd be asking for trouble wi' paper scattered everywhere. Are you any use at setting things straight? I could do wi' a proper system in this place – the books 're in a right blessed muddle.'

'Perhaps you should get a filing cabinet? I don't imagine anyone can run a business efficiently with their office so disorganised.'

'You reckon. Well, when I want advice on running my business, Mrs Antrobus, I'll ask for it.'

'I beg your pardon! I was only trying to be helpful – I wasn't implying any criticism.' This time, provoked beyond herself by his manner, Vanessa stood up from her chair.

'Since you clearly don't consider me suitable to work here, Mr Brockhouse, there seems little point in continuing our interview. But thank you anyway for seeing me—'

'*I'll* be the judge o' whether you're suitable or not,' he interrupted. 'And if you adopt that haughty tone wi' some o' the blighters owing me money, you'll do very well, I'm telling you. Now sit yourself down again. Let's decide how much I'm going to pay you.'

She gave a glance towards the door. There was nothing preventing her from leaving this boorishly uncivil man to find himself some other secretary.

And then suddenly, completely out of nowhere, the image came into her mind of that little scene in the garden at 'Mayville' when she'd witnessed this same boorishly uncivil man kneeling in the grass to cup a rose between his hands; and for no reason that she could possibly explain, something forced Vanessa to resume her seat.

The wage he had offered was a few shillings more than she'd been expecting. And when she started work the following Monday morning she found a large filing cabinet already installed in what was now 'her' office.

The pregnant young woman, whose name was Dymphna but was known as Dimps, and whose job she was taking over, had volunteered to stay an extra day to show her the ropes.

'There in't much to it really,' Dimps explained brightly. 'I know the place looks a bit of a mess like, but that's only 'cos I got behind myself when I was under the doctor them few weeks wi' my legs. They all swelled up,' she added when Vanessa seemed a little mystified. 'Talk about elephantitis! I wasn't able to bend nor kneel nor even hardly walk. The doctor told me I'd got to stay off my feet like, till they went down.'

She helped herself to another sugared bun from the paper bag in her lap, and watched Vanessa fetch a heap of files and begin sorting through them.

'I do like that frock you'm wearing,' she said with her mouth full. 'I always think lemon's ever such a nice colour. Mind me asking where you got it?'

'D'you know, I've had it so long I can't remember,' Vanessa answered abstractedly. 'I've an idea it might've come from Beatties.'

'I wish I could afford Beatties. I always buy my things from The Red House.' Dimps pointed to something with the bun. 'That bottom file – see it? – that's all the accounts for this year. There's some more invoices at the back o' the desk drawer need entering, otherwise I think it's up to date. He's very particular about keeping the accounts, is Mr Brockhouse.'

'I can imagine.'

The way Vanessa raised her eyebrow sent Dimps into a fit of giggles. Glancing along the office passage, she leaned forward as much as her waistline permitted and said through another mouthful of bun, 'You don't want to be nervous o' the Gaffer. He doesn't like it. Oh, he can be sharp when he wants, all right, but he doesn't mean nothing by it really.'

'I think I prefer his bite to his bark, all the same.'

'Go on wi' you! He just takes a bit o' getting used to. You'll find he's a decent enough chap to work for − I mean, look how he was wi' my legs. "My word, Dimps," he says when I showed him, "they oughtn't be like that. I'll run you round the out-patients and get 'em seen to." He did an' all. Put me in the scrap lorry and drove me there hisself, he did.'

Much as Vanessa enjoyed the artless chatter, it was a relief when Dimps had finally departed and she could get on with the Herculean task of bringing some sort of order to the muddle she'd inherited. It took time, but by the end of that first week the place certainly looked a good deal better organised.

It was too much to hope that Jim Brockhouse would praise her efforts. As she'd already found, he was a man of few words and very little conversation. More often than not he communicated by means of notes left for her attention in his large, strong, sprawling hand, asking her to deal with this or that; though to do him justice, since he was out of the yard for many hours each day this was probably the most practical system, and at least showed he trusted his new secretary to carry out the jobs unsupervised.

He had a gang of three men working for him. One of them Vanessa half-remembered from the day at 'Mayville' as the gap-toothed, overweight young lad she'd spoken with on that occasion. The other two were brothers, both tall and swarthily good-looking in a gipsy sort of way, with eyes that followed her appreciatively when either came into the office. She was inclined to let them go on thinking there was a husband she went home to, because if they knew she lived alone they were the type who would probably try to get over-familiar and Vanessa wasn't at all anxious to encourage that.

She had been working at the yard about a fortnight when a young woman called in on the Friday afternoon. The weather had turned very humid, with a sultry, oppressive atmosphere threatening thunderstorms by evening, and it was so close inside the office that Vanessa had both doors open wide for a breath of air. Above the busy clatter of her Underwood typewriter the background noise of the town came drifting through the heat of Sun Street, broken at intervals by the hoot and rattle of trains leaving the station, and it wasn't until the woman spoke that Vanessa realised somebody had entered and was standing behind her.

Looking round, it took her a moment to recognise the caller as Jim Brockhouse's fashionably-dressed companion from The Copper Kettle.

'So sorry—' she said at once, getting up from her desk. 'I didn't hear anyone come in.'

'That's all right, I can see you're busy,' the other

222

answered pleasantly, taking off her straw cloche hat and glancing about. She had chestnut hair sculpted into Marcel waves, and pretty almond-shaped eyes framed by finely drawn brows. 'I must say, you've performed blinkin' miracles in here. Jim said the place was looking tidier – his usual understatement!' Her accent, like Jim Brockhouse's, was Black Country without being broad. 'I don't suppose he's got round to mentioning me at all, but I'm his sister-in-law, Mary Carter.'

'Vanessa Antrobus.' Vanessa held out a hand and smiled uncertainly.

'Pleased to meet you.' The smile was returned. 'You won't mind if I call you by your first name, will you? I hate formality, it makes me feel uncomfortable, and Mrs Antrobus *is* a bit of a mouthful, 'specially for a place like this.'

Perching herself on a chair, Mary Carter carefully crossed her silk-stockinged legs and smoothed down her skirt, which was in this season's fuller, longer length. In a chatty way she went on, 'How are you liking it here? Settling in, are you? I see now what our Jim was driving at when he said you looked like a lily stuck in a blinkin' muck-heap. You're an improvement on the last 'un he had working for him, any road.'

Vanessa wasn't certain whether to feel flattered or not by her employer's description. 'A lily stuck in a muck-heap' sounded Jim Brockhouse's style, though.

'I'm settling in very well, thanks,' she replied. 'The worst was shifting that mountain of paperwork and trying to make some sense of Dimps's ledger entries. Whatever system she used, it was erratic – putting it mildly!'

'Aye, she was a dozy effort, Dimps, an' no mistake.' Mary examined her carefully manicured fingernails. 'If it was up to me she wouldn't have stopped here a week, but she needed the money what wi' the babby, and her husband out o' work an' all, and Jim was feeling sorry for her. He can be like that, you know.'

'Yes, so she mentioned.'

It was on the tip of Vanessa's tongue to add that he seemed to keep that side of his nature very well hidden; but on second thoughts perhaps it wouldn't do to criticise, and besides, she had a feeling this visit of Mary Carter's was to give her the once-over to see what she was like.

'To be honest,' she went on, 'I see so little of Mr Brockhouse I haven't had much chance to get to know him yet. He seems – well, how can I put it – a rather private individual.'

'Oh, he's that all right,' Mary agreed with her.

'In fact I know even less about his family. Nobody here ever mentions them.' Which was true: since she'd been working at the yard Vanessa had learned absolutely nothing about her employer's home life, and she didn't like to appear inquisitive by asking questions.

'I suppose there in't a lot to tell, that's why.' The other gave a quick smile; and then adroitly changed the subject, asking, 'Your husband doesn't mind you working, then? I wish mine'ld let me – I could quite fancy a little job, just for some'at to pass the time, but Norman won't hear of it, he says my place is in the home. Your husband's employed local, is he?'

'Oh . . . yes and no. He travels a lot.'

'That's nice. What line o' business is he in?'

Reluctant to explain about the art gallery, Vanessa answered vaguely, 'You know, buying and selling, that kind of thing.'

'A commercial traveller, you mean? I wish Norman

was away from home more often. You can see too much of 'em sometimes, can't you?' Mary touched a hand to her hair. 'Your Mam looks after the kiddies, does she?'

'Sorry?'

'The kiddies. Or haven't you got any? No? I don't blame you. Norman keeps on about him and me starting a family, but I'm in two minds. I think I'd like to wait a bit before tying myself down. I mean, they're a bit of a bind aren't they?'

Vanessa made a noncommittal sound. Trying to show some interest she asked, 'Have you been married long?'

'Two years, that's all. How about you?'

'The same.'

'Course, it hasn't been that easy wi' my sister being so ill an' all,' said Mary. 'It's taken up a lot o' time, Norman understands that, but he's from a big family and they've all got little 'uns of their own, so I suppose he feels he's missing out—'

She glanced over her shoulder as a lorry rumbled past, leaving a cloud of brick-dust to settle over the geraniums on the doorstep.

'What's been the matter with your sister?' Vanessa enquired politely, thinking she ought to be getting on with her typing if she wanted to have it finished before she went home.

Without looking round the other answered, 'It was a growth o' some sort,' and the way she said it, slightly off-hand, sounded almost uncaring until she turned back again. Behind its made-up prettiness, the expression in her face betrayed her. 'She's only been dead a few months.'

'I'm so sorry, I didn't mean to—'

'It's all right, you weren't to know. You won't mention

225

anything to Jim though, will you. Only he's taken Peggy's death very hard and he can't bear to be reminded.'

Vanessa was at a loss to know what to say, and there was an awkward little pause before Mary got to her feet, shaking out the pleats in her skirt.

'Well, I suppose I'd better let you get on,' she said. 'It's been ever so nice having a chat wi' you.' And with another lingering glance all round the office – 'She used to work here, Peggy did, after her and Jim were married. Funny thing . . . for a minute when I came in the door just now, I felt as how I was seeing her again. Trick o' the light, I expect . . . apart from the way you wear your hair you're nothing much like her to look at. Not really.'

19

When they came out from the political meeting in the
bierkeller they could see the Brownshirts waiting for
them, half a dozen young thugs lurking in the shadows
at the bottom of the street – 'like hyenas,' Erich von
Losch said contemptuously.

Erich was Luise's brother, a student at Berlin's
Friedrich Wilhelm University. Except that he was the
younger by a couple of years, the boy and his sister could
almost be twins with their blond hair and Prussian-blue
eyes and fine, pale features. They shared the same tastes
too, as Roland Antrobus had already discovered; and
though those tastes might run to the bizarre, here in
the louche and liberal climate of the German capital
where decadence corroded the cynical, brittle gaiety of
the beau monde, no vice was so excessive that it could
not be pandered to.

'What's going on here?' Roland asked apprehensively
in German as the gang of SA youths, sporting the
red and black swastika emblem on their armbands,
spread out to block the narrow street. 'We're not giving
them any trouble, why do they want to stop us getting past?'

'If you ask them politely they might tell you,' Erich
said, 'though I would not advise it. They would say you
had provoked them.'

'But perhaps if they know I'm an Englishman, a visitor—'

His naivety caused some amusement.

'On which side were the English in the War?' somebody reminded him, one of the others who had left the meeting with them. 'These Nazi goons are stupid, but their memories are not so short. Why offer them excuses?'

'You think they need excuses, Fritzi?' Lulu von Losch glanced over her jacket shoulder at the man who'd spoken; and then with jaunty carelessness tucked her arm through Roland's as they carried on walking.

'It is our politics the SA do not like, *liebchen*,' she told him, 'so to them it does not matter if you are Japanese or Eskimo – you were with us in the *keller* and that brands you as a sympathiser. Fritzi is right, these Brownshirts are goons – but dangerous goons. So now we see them off, *ja*?'

They advanced towards the silent pack confronting them, Lulu, Roland and Erich in front, the rest on their heels. Roland could feel a little prickle of fear between his shoulder blades as the gap between the two groups narrowed. This was none of his quarrel, he told himself nervously. He'd only been at tonight's Marxist meeting because he'd wanted to impress his darling Lulu.

With maybe a dozen yards still to go, the Brownshirts suddenly sprang into attack and came charging up the street, yelling Nazi slogans, their jackboots thudding on the cobbles as they drove between the little party. Fists began to fly. With an answering yell Erich von Losch swung a punch at the nearest one, knocking him sideways, and as the young thug went down he gave him a kick in the head for good measure.

The scene disintegrated into mayhem. Lights came on. Faces appeared at windows.

Spotting one of the gang coming at him through the scrimmage, Roland raised an arm to defend Lulu and managed to grab the attacker by the shoulder-belt and butt him in the face, hearing the satisfying crunch of bone. Blood spurted everywhere. Behind him Lulu let out a scream of fury as a second one lunged for her, tearing the silk of her blouse, scoring the marks of his nails down her breast. Roland grappled with the Brownshirt, pulling him off her and driving a knee up hard between his legs.

Next moment something struck the back of his head – and the world exploded into spinning darkness.

Luckily his expensive Homburg saved his scalp from anything worse than a painful bruising. By the time he'd recovered consciousness the fight was over and the Brownshirts driven off, leaving their opponents bloodily victorious, with Roland acclaimed a hero in the cause of Marxist Communism.

Hoisted between Erich and Fritzi he was carted off for a drink through streets still jammed with traffic, even at this late hour. Berlin never slept. The clubs and red-light cabarets frequented by perfumed homosexual boys stayed open until dawn, when the swaying, clanking trams carried them home to the anonymous suburbs.

Bubi Rudi's, down one of the little alleys off the Kurfürstendamm, was a favourite haunt of Lulu and her brother. It was in a low basement room, all Bauhaus chrome and glass, and lit by smoke-wreathed spotlights that turned the faces round the tables into ghostly masks with black-rimmed eyes and painted mouths like crimson gashes. At a piano by the bar a transvestite in sequined gown and long blonde wig was crooning the new hit song, 'My Best Girl Friend'.

Nobody turned a hair at the rumpled state of Lulu's party.

'We've been canoodling with Adolf's *Scheisshemde*,' she paused on the stairs to announce to the room, and her gutter reference to the Brownshirts raised a cynical trickle of laughter.

Leaving Erich to order beer and schnapps, Roland went to clean up in the lavatory. There were smears of blood on his shirt and his white kid shoes. His head felt as if something had split it in two, and to add to the mess he sported a lump above his eyebrow already turning purple, and a swollen cheekbone where he'd struck himself in falling.

The sight of his battered features didn't displease him. In fact he was rather proud of the way he'd acquitted himself. Perhaps now he'd earned his battle stripes Lulu would be less reluctant to take him back as her 'official' lover: he'd been here in Berlin three weeks already, renting a room a few doors from her on the Tauentzienstrasse (which was in the artists' quarter, where she and her brother shared an apartment) and so far he had yet to spend more than a single night alone with her.

It was like throwing a scrap to a starving dog. Separation had only served to feed Roland's obsession for this woman since their last meeting all those months ago in London. Ever since he'd been like a soul in limbo, hating the life that was keeping him apart from her and yet having to endure it while he went through the mechanics of tying up the loose ends of his business and his marriage.

When he came back from the lavatory she was talking to the singer, showing off the angry weals disfiguring her breast as though they were trophies.

'Come – you must meet a friend of mine,' she said, taking hold of Roland's arm and hugging him. 'This is Mischa. Maybe you do not recognise him, no? He is one of my best models for the photographic studies for my new collection.'

Behind the mask of rouge and pan-stick Mischa smiled at Roland with the same inviting look of interest Roland noticed he'd often been getting lately. Homosexuality was rife here in Berlin. After the Great War the financial chaos of the times had driven thousands of young men as well as women into prostitution, and from that had sprouted the moral degeneracy which had turned Kaiser Wilhelm's cultural metropolis into a city steeped in dissipation.

Roland returned the smile, holding the other's eyes just long enough.

'No, I can't say I recognise him,' he answered Lulu, 'not with the clothes on.'

'You would prefer me with the clothes off, I think?' Mischa suggested, and his voice had all the hard smartness of the Berlin accent. '*Liebling*, you must come and see me pose, I promise you will find me irresistible.'

'Roland is not for you,' Lulu said reprovingly, giving him a tap on the cheek with her forefinger. 'He is mine, so you keep your eyes off him, *ja*? Besides, he is a married man.'

'So? A cat can look at a queen . . . or a queen at a cat.'

'Mischa, you are *ein frecher Dachs*. Now see, for that I will not invite you to our table.' But her words were softened by the tone of affection. 'You will sing for us another song instead, I hope.'

The transvestite pouted her a kiss. 'For you and your nice friend, *schatzi*, anything.'

As they were walking away to the alcove where Erich and the rest sat drinking, Roland asked her with pathetic eagerness, 'Did you mean that, what you said, my darling – do you really think of me as yours?'

'Of course.'

'Because I *am* yours, you know that, don't you.'

'*Natürlich.* You tell me things are finished with your wife—'

'I swear to you, they are!'

'—so then you are free to belong to me, if I wish.' Lulu paused a moment, turning to look into his eyes. 'If *I* wish,' she repeated. 'You understand?'

'I would do anything for you, my sweetest angel – only let me stay with you, don't send me away again, that's all I ask,' he said beseechingly.

She put out her hand, gently tracing the bruises on his face; and smiled.

'You have earned me for tonight, I think, my Englishman. And then . . . then we shall see, maybe.'

'No, sorry, I'm afraid I've no idea when my husband will be back,' Vanessa told the voice on the other end of the line. 'May I ask who's calling? Oh . . . I see. Well, can I suggest you try his home number? You have already? I see . . . and they couldn't tell you either. No. Oh dear. In that case I'm awfully sorry, I can't think how else I can help. No. Yes, of course . . . no, no, that's perfectly all right . . . not at all.'

She said goodbye and replaced the receiver.

'Roland's solicitor's office,' she said to Sybil when she came back from upstairs, where she'd taken the call on her landlady's telephone. 'They wanted to know when he'll be home from Germany – some papers he has to sign, or something.'

'Papers about what?' Her half-sister turned from the window. Framed in the golden summer light the thin, drawn features had a touch of colour. This was the first time Sybil had been to visit the little flat in Paget Road: after being discharged from the nursing home at Codsall several weeks ago, she'd only just returned from a holiday on the Isle of Wight with her parents.

'Probably something to do with the lease of the house, I expect,' said Vanessa. 'I haven't told you, have I – Roland's letting "Mayville" for a year?'

'Oh? Where's he going to live?' The girl came and joined her on the sofa, self-consciously pulling down the sleeves of her cardigan to hide the dull pink scars inside her wrists – an action that was lately becoming a bit of a habit. 'Or is he proposing to park himself on his ladyfriend in Germany?'

Vanessa shrugged. 'All I know is what he chooses to inform me. But apparently he's found tenants for the house, so it looks as though he's either planning on staying in Berlin, or maybe using the flat above the Gallery.'

'I thought there was somebody living above the Gallery already,' Sybil said. 'Fair-haired chap – can't recall his name off-hand – teaches at the School of Art and Design.'

'Oh, you mean Michael Wright. Yes, he's helping to run the place while Roland's abroad.' There was a pause; a look of interest. 'I didn't realise the two of you had met.'

Sybil dropped her eyes. Uncomfortably she answered,

233

'It was that time I went round to see your husband about
. . . well, you know what about.'

Larret Fitzgerald. Vanessa didn't need reminding. But
that unfortunate little incident belonged, like so much
else now, to the past. Sybil's confession in the nursing
home had gone a long way towards reconciling her to
her half-sister, and her only interest for the moment was
encouraging their cautious friendship, not to dwell on old
mistakes and memories.

'Well,' she said lightly, with a smile, 'I wonder, would
you like to meet Michael again? There's an exhibition of
his latest work at the Gallery next month – I've been
invited to the party he's throwing to launch it, and I so
hate attending these functions by myself. You'd do me
a favour by coming along with me, really you would.'

Sybil seemed to take her time about responding; then
she answered, still a little awkwardly, 'Thanks . . . all the
same, I think I'll have to decline. I doubt I'd get much of
a welcome.'

'For heaven's sake, why?'

'I was jolly rude to him, Vee.'

'So what if you were – I don't suppose Michael will
hold it against you!'

'How do you know.'

'Because I've met him myself a couple of times, and
I know what he's like. Honestly, Sybil, he's terribly
friendly. Oh, do say you'll come with me, please? We
can dress up in our glad rags – it'll be such fun.'

'But *look* at me—' The girl pulled at her sleeves again.
'I'm such a freak.'

'Who says so,' asked Vanessa gently.

'Daddy does.'

Trust Ernest Parrish to be thoughtless. 'He's just

concerned for you, that's all. It'll do you the world of good meeting lots of interesting new people.'

There was another pause.

'Actually—' Sybil said at last, in an odd little tone, 'actually, I wouldn't mind. I haven't been to a decent party in ages, not since . . . well, anyway, not for a long time.' And then quickly, with just a trace of her old petulant self – 'Of course, now I'm not working at Beatties any more I've lost most of my friends, so I don't get chance to go out partying and that. I envy you, Vee, honestly I do – oh, I don't mean in a nasty way – but there's me stuck in the house with Mother and Daddy fuss, fuss, fussing – and you, you've got your freedom, and this lovely flat to live and a job and everything. You seem so content,' she added with sudden, touching wistfulness.

'At the risk of sounding boringly noble,' said Vanessa, 'if I seem content it's only because I refuse to let things get on top of me and make me miserable. There's no special secret—'

'But you've got your *freedom*,' the other repeated.

'Yes, and at what price? I'm still a married woman. Life has its limitations. I'm only free in so far as I live by myself.'

'God, I wish *I* did!'

Vanessa had to laugh at her expression. 'Come on, don't be so impatient, you've only just turned twenty.'

'And how old were you when you left home? Eighteen, as I remember.'

'My circumstances were different, weren't they.' Vanessa leaned from the sofa to collect the cups and saucers they'd been using.

'I'll go and make us another pot of tea,' she said,

getting up; and then to change the subject – 'Mother's been telling me you're after a job with Rigby's in Worcester Street.'

'Mm. The interview's Monday morning.'

'What happened about Beatties, wouldn't they have you back at all?'

'No—' Sybil watched her half-sister go into the sun-filled little kitchen. 'No, I'd been taking too much time off work, they said. I didn't even get a reference out of them either, stingy beggars.'

Vanessa said something she couldn't quite catch because of the noise of the tap running.

'Anyway,' she added, raising her voice, 'how're things going with this new job of yours, Vee? Poor old Daddy, he thinks it's frightfully *infra dig* you're working at a scrapyard – he claims you're only doing it to embarrass him.'

Again, there was just a little flash of the old-style Sybil.

'One day he'll have something good to say of me!' Vanessa lit the gas-ring for the kettle. 'Actually, the job isn't too bad—'

Coming back again into the sitting room she continued, 'To be honest, I wasn't sure I hadn't bitten off more than I could chew, the amount of work there needed doing. It wasn't quite what I'd envisaged when I applied for the vacancy – I occasionally feel like pointing out to Mr Brockhouse he should have advertised for a head cook and bottle washer, not a secretary.'

'You're enjoying it, though?'

Vanessa considered the word 'enjoying'. 'Well, it's a challenge, let's put it that way. And the work varies so much – yes, I suppose I *do* enjoy it. There's only one fly in the ointment—' She hesitated again.

'What's that?' the other asked, inquisitive.

'Well . . . Jim Brockhouse himself. Or rather, his attitude. I mean – OK, he's only just recently lost his wife, and from what I can gather he must have been devoted to her . . . but that doesn't excuse his bloody-mindedness. He's so – oh, I don't know – so extraordinarily *rude* to me. As though somehow it's *my* fault.'

Sybil helped herself to a Woodbine. 'Losing his wife, you mean.'

A little nod. 'It's the way he speaks to me,' Vanessa said crossly. 'The other day he had the cheek to tell me I was posh because I said "pardon" not "eh". I felt like scratching my head and picking my teeth, just to annoy him.'

'Perhaps it's only his habit,' Sybil shrugged. 'We had one like that at Beatties – couldn't ask you to do a thing without he was criticising. None of us liked him.'

'I don't know. I wouldn't put it down to *habit* – not exactly. He seems all right with the men in the yard. And the secretary he had before spoke well of him. D'you know what I think—' There was another hesitation. 'Oh, I agree this might sound a little bit far-fetched, but his sister-in-law told me I reminded her in some ways of his wife. So maybe there's the answer – he doesn't care for the resemblance.'

'Then why the hell did he employ you,' Sybil said through a mouthful of smoke.

'Who's to say with a man like that.'

'If I were in your shoes, Vee, I'd hand him in my notice smartish – and tell him where he could bloomin' well stick it!'

'I've considered that.' Every night she rehearsed to herself in bed the pleasure it would give her describing to Jim Brockhouse precisely what she thought of him.

Next day at the office though, somehow something always held her back. Vanessa hadn't a clue what it was – certainly not pity for him; she only knew that in a strange kind of way – call it woman's intuition – she got the feeling his ill-tempered behaviour was all a put-on facade, and that he wore it for his own protection.

In the kitchen the kettle set up a reedy whistling. As she went back to attend to it she added a little defiantly, 'Except I'm not ready to concede defeat just yet. I'll give Mr Brockhouse another couple of weeks . . . there's something I'd like to prove to myself, to find out if I'm wrong.'

20

Even without turning her head, Vanessa knew which one of the Heron brothers had just walked into the office. She could generally tell Frank Heron by his smell, a pungently masculine odour of sweat and greasy metal and tobacco; whereas his younger brother Tony always reeked of the lemon-scented brilliantine varnishing his black curly hair.

This was Tony.

'Hi, babe,' he said cheekily, in an American accent he'd picked up from the new 'talkie' film *The Jazz Singer*. 'How's ya doin', good lookin'.'

'Very well – how's yourself?' Vanessa glanced briefly behind her.

'Kinda better for seein' my favourite li'l lady. An' my, you sure do look a knockout this mornin', cutie pie – you musta guessed I'd be around.'

Sauntering across, he parked himself in her typing chair, tilting it back and resting his boots on the desk. With his hands behind his head, he reverted to his ordinary accent. 'Gaffer on a job, is 'e? Only I've been lookin' for him up the yard.'

'No, he's still about somewhere—' She finished filing away the batch of receipts. 'I haven't heard the lorry. Do you want him?'

'Not particular. I've got all I want right 'ere, ta.' He

shifted slightly to admire her legs. She was wearing a smart little navy skirt this morning, beautifully tailored to emphasise her slender calves and small, neat ankles.

'So when am you free to come out wi' me, eh?' he asked casually. 'Tonight? Tomorrer? If you can't make Friday, 'ow about Sat'day?'

Vanessa shut the cabinet drawer. 'Sorry. Not this week, next week, nor even sometime, Tony,' she said, equally casual, playing his game. 'Excuse me—' She pushed his muddy boots off the desk. 'Do you think I might have my chair, please?'

Instead of moving himself Tony only grinned, a bold expression in his dark gipsy eyes. He and his brother Frank were well aware of their attractiveness to the opposite sex, and both knew how to make the most of it.

'Depends on what you'll offer me to budge,' he answered.

'I'm offering nothing, I'm asking you politely.'

'Ask me politely again, eh, chick – I love that posh voice o' yourn. It really does things to me. I even lie in bed imaginin' you an' your old man at 'ome, all lah-di-dah – "Oh I say dahling, would you care awf'lly for a spot of tiffin, what?"' He exaggerated Vanessa's slightly middle-class voice, still watching her face with that bold, hard smile. 'Cor, if I was 'im I'd 'ave a job controllin' meself, I'm tellin' you.'

'Yes – well we won't go into that,' Vanessa said smartly, taking him by the arm of his overall to move him out of the way.

Her closeness encouraged him. With a quick playful lunge he pulled her against him, catching her off balance so that she was forced to put her hands on his shoulders to steady herself.

It was at this moment Jim Brockhouse chose to walk into the office.

For a second the three of them froze. Then Mr Brockhouse said, angrily, 'What the hell's this about? Tony, why ain't you up the yard?'

'Just goin'—' Tony Heron scrambled to his feet, the smile suddenly sheepish. 'It ain't what it looks like – we was only 'avin' a bit o' fun, Mr Brock'ouse.'

'I don't pay you to have fun. Go on – clear off.'

'On me way.' Without even a glance for Vanessa the young man disappeared through the door as though something had kicked him.

'And you—' Jim Brockhouse turned on her, 'I expect better behaviour out o' you, you understand?'

The injustice of his accusation was so unfair that before she could stop herself Vanessa was giving him his answer in no uncertain manner. 'That's right—' she exclaimed indignantly, 'blame me! Don't trouble to enquire whose fault it is, will you. For heaven's sake, Tony was only fooling round – you know what he's like. He grabbed me, that's all. What else do you think he was doing!'

'Now there's no need to take that tone o' voice wi' me—'

'Begging your pardon, I'll take what tone of voice I like. Ever since I've worked here, Mr Brockhouse, you've done little else but snap and snarl – God knows I don't deserve it. I try to do my best, and much thanks I get! You're the most ill-tempered and cantankerous person I've ever come across. And what's more,' she added for good measure, 'if you're looking for excuses to get rid of me, don't bother, I'm very glad to go!'

Chin up, Vanessa glared at him. All the resentment and vexation bottled up inside for weeks had been vented in

241

that outburst – and even if the words weren't quite as she'd rehearsed them, at least they made her sentiments perfectly plain.

'You're not going anywhere,' Jim Brockhouse said in a curious tone. His face had gone very white; and as she continued staring at him she saw a change of expression in the deep-set eyes, from anger to something more ambiguous.

She didn't know why, but it made her feel suddenly uncomfortable.

In a quieter manner, she said after a minute, 'I'm sorry . . . I shouldn't have blown up like that, perhaps I was too hasty. But all the same—'

'Mebbe all the same it needed saying,' he finished for her, still in that curious tone. 'Aye, I know. No need to be sorry, it was me spoke out o' place, Vanessa.'

He turned for a second to close the office door. When he spoke again, he surprised her by sounding almost friendly. 'You mustn't encourage them Herons to get too fresh, they'll only take advantage. They're good lads, good workers—'

'But I *don't* encourage them,' Vanessa defended herself. 'What you saw when you came in was just harmless teasing, that was all.'

'Even so, I'm only warning you to watch 'em, Vanessa.' Again he used her name, something he'd seldom done before. And then, something he'd *never* done before – he actually smiled at her.

The difference that sudden touch of warmth made was remarkable. All the severity in his face disappeared, and for a moment Jim Brockhouse looked a different man – younger, kinder; even quite handsome.

Then he said something which astonished her just as

much. 'By the way, my sister-in-law tells me I've got to congratulate you. She's been reading your pieces in the *Express & Star*.'

'Oh—' She couldn't think what else to say. She sat down.

'Aye. Apparently she enjoyed 'em. I dain't realise we had so many famous women in Wolv'rampton.'

He made it sound as though the compliment was for herself, though Vanessa didn't doubt he was referring to the subject of her series, 'Leading Ladies', which she'd written while she was staying in the Dordogne.

Thrown by the turn of conversation, she hesitated before responding, 'Wolverhampton's rather under-rated . . . I mean, people seem to suppose because it's in the Black Country there's nothing here but factories and canals.'

'Mebbe they've got a point an' all.'

'Yes, but it's only one half of the picture. It puts us in a category. It implies we're unremarkable—'

'Most of us are. What's wrong wi' that?'

'I disagree.'

'You're doing a lot o' disagreeing with me this morning.' Again, he smiled.

His interest gave Vanessa confidence. 'Well, I like to think what I write puts the record straight a little . . . you know, shows Wulfrunians as characters, individuals, people of invention and imagination. I mean, we're no less gifted than any other area, it's just that we have to work harder to be recognised for *what* we are because of *where* we are.'

Then realising she was in danger of making a speech she coloured up, ending on an embarrassed laugh, 'Sorry, I'm quoting from one of my articles.'

'Quote away, I'm very impressed.'

Jim Brockhouse went over and seated himself by the window. The soft pewter sheen of the rain-washed day outside silhouetted the dark hair flecked with grey, and the strong, lean line of his jaw. All the frowning irascibility of his usual manner was gone, and for the first time since she'd been working for him Vanessa felt she was witnessing something of his other side – that side of his character she'd only heard about from people like Dimps and Mary Carter, but never till now had actually believed in.

As he was at the moment he was even quite likeable. Five minutes ago she'd been ready to hand in her notice; but then five minutes ago it wasn't *this* Jim Brockhouse she'd been angry with, it had been the other one – in fact she found it hard to credit they could be the same, until she reminded herself which of his two sides she had observed in the garden at 'Mayville'.

'I'll have to read these pieces o' yourn for myself, I reckon,' he said. 'Our Mary's kept 'em by to show her friends – you've made an impression there, I'm telling you. I got a right flea in the ear when I said I hadn't seen 'em, but then I'm the sort that only reads the headlines and the sports page.'

He continued looking at Vanessa.

'I meant it what I said,' he added, all of a sudden. 'I wouldn't like you to leave from here. You're too good a secretary.'

'Even with no experience?' she couldn't resist reminding him.

'Is that what I told you?'

'When you interviewed me for the job.'

'So I did. Well, put that down to me being – what did

you call me just now – ill-tempered, and what was the other word you used?'

'I believe the description was cantankerous,' she said awkwardly, 'for which, again, I apologise. It was rude of me. Even if I thought the criticism justified, you're still my employer, Mr Brockhouse.'

'It doesn't mean you can't have an opinion.'

'In future I'll be more careful to keep my opinion to myself.'

'And in future *I'll* try not to gi' you cause to speak your mind the way you did,' he answered. 'Believe me, however *cantankerous* I've been wi' you, it's nothing to how I've been wi' myself these past few months since . . . well, I expect you know . . .'

'Mrs Carter told me about your wife. I'm very sorry.'

Jim Brockhouse sat forward, elbows resting on his knees, head bowed, his fingers thrust through his dark hair.

'Aye . . . you don't realise how much you love 'em, till they're gone. I'd gi' the world to have Peg back wi' me. Count yourself fortunate you've got your husband still alive, Vanessa. You look after him . . . there's nothing worse than going home to memories, I'm telling you.'

And then with something more like his customary abruptness, as if he'd given away too much of himself, he rose to his feet. 'Well, come on, we've both of us got work to do – it won't tend to itself wi' us sitting talking.'

Jim Brockhouse had been dragged up the hard way. Born thirty-eight years ago in one of the poorest areas of Wolverhampton, he was the illegitimate son of a housemaid, the result of an evening's ignorant pleasure in the town's West Park. His birth certificate stated 'father unknown'; but in actual fact the young man who had begotten him was a senior pupil at the Grammar School, eighteen years old, the same age as the mother. His family being reluctant to recognise their son's responsibility, Jim's father was packed off to Durham University and the pregnant little housemaid was paid ten guineas for her silence.

After her baby was born, in 1890, she married a scrap dealer named Charlie Brockhouse, living with him at the house in Sun Street where he ran his business. There were no children from their union, and for this she had to suffer cruelly, enduring the black temper of a husband who blamed their lack of heirs on her solitary act of fornication, not on his own sterility.

Young Jim was seven when she was killed, crushed under the wheels of a runaway dray, taking the secret of his paternity to the grave. Within eighteen months Charlie Brockhouse had found himself another wife. This one was a flighty little piece, more concerned with spending his money enjoying herself than staying at home playing dutiful spouse. She had no interest in her husband's stepson. She fed him when she remembered and spoke to him if she felt inclined; otherwise the boy was treated no better or worse than one of the dogs that guarded the scrapyard.

When the War broke out she ran off with a sailor, and that was that.

Third time might have proved luckier, except Charlie Brockhouse had lost the heart for marriage. He'd got his stepson to help with the business, and if Jim was none of his own getting, well he'd have to make do with the beggar – at least the lad was bright, which was some consolation. The teachers at his National School (which he'd left at twelve) had even suggested he try for a scholarship. Charlie had laughed at them.

By the time Jim was sixteen he could have run the scrapyard single-handed. At twenty-one he'd not only got a sound, smart head on his shoulders – smart enough to be respected in a trade more generally noted for its brawn than its brain – but he was getting himself known about the town as a decent, likeable young chap. Not bad-looking either, according to the wenches who'd started setting their caps at him.

The adult Jim Brockhouse was a complex character, though. His stepfather may have boasted that he'd licked him into shape, but it was the lessons he'd been taught by life that had made him what he was – tough, a bit cussed; even a bit intolerant. No one could get really close to him. And despite his popularity no one could honestly say they knew him. The loss of his mother had robbed Jim of the only source of love he'd ever had in childhood, and the scars showed, because as a grown man he found it very hard to show affection except to his horses and dogs.

The Great War ended in 1918. A year later, boosted by the rusting detritus of tanks and guns now fallen silent, the market in scrap metal had expanded and the yard in Sun Street now had a lorry as well as its horses and carts. Business was looking up. Ironically, progress was the end of Charlie Brockhouse, because in 1923 he died of septicaemia after gashing himself on a smashed-up motor car.

Everything he owned was left to Jim.

Like most other young men of his class and his generation, Jim had been drafted into military service during the War and 'done his bit', serving with the Shropshire Light

Infantry rather than the South Staffordshire Regiment. He was one of the lucky ones. He came home. But the Somme left its scars, to add to those he'd got already.

The year following Charlie's death he found himself engaged to a girl who'd been chasing him to marry her, and at her father's insistence he decided he would better himself and buy a house in St John's Square for them to live. St John's Square was one of those areas that used to be considered middle-class until the middle-classes moved out to the suburbs; it had its own church and graveyard, and Georgian houses with brass plates on the front doors engraved with the names of doctors and solicitors. By 1924 its gentility had been dented enough to accept a scrap dealer without raising too much of an eyebrow.

The house in Sun Street was turned into an office and its upper floor – Jim's childhood – was left to collect the cobwebs of lumber and unhappy memories. When the engagement was called off by mutual agreement he decided he'd remain in St John's Square and live a bachelor life. And for twelve months he did.

By this time he'd educated himself enough to join one of the adult institutes offering advancement to those whose intelligence made them keen to learn more, and it was here he met Peggy Robinson, whom he married in the spring of 1926.

Peggy Robinson was the sort of soft little vulnerable creature that arouses a man's most protective instincts. She had meltingly brown velvet eyes and a sweet, curved mouth designed for kisses, and her nature was all tenderness and warmth. Jim couldn't help but love her. He adored looking after her. She awakened in him a longing for something entirely his own to cherish and spoil.

For the first few months he thought he was in heaven; and if Peggy didn't care too much for the physical side of marriage, well Jim didn't press her. His only experience of that kind of thing had been in the Army, and whores weren't the same as a wife. What Peggy *did* care for was helping with the business. She was good at that: before their marriage she'd been working as a clerical assistant and could turn her hand to anything like book-keeping and type-writing.

That summer they went away to Bournemouth where they'd spent their honeymoon, liking the place enough to want to go back again. Halfway through the week Peggy complained she wasn't feeling very well – so Jim cut short their holiday and brought her home to see the doctor. The doctor thought she had 'tired blood' and prescribed a course of iron tablets, which didn't seem to do a lot of good. She started losing weight. The pretty little pansy face grew peaky; the brown, adoring eyes took on a pitiable expression. Once the pains in her body became a feature of the illness she was taken into hospital.

All winter and the following spring Jim Brockhouse went to and fro, to and fro, between the scrapyard and that hospital ward. In the summer Peggy picked up enough to come home for a while. But they were living on false hopes. By October she was back inside the Royal again, and Jim's existence turned into a nightmare. If his sister-in-law Mary Carter hadn't seen he got his meals he could have starved for all he cared. Many a night he slept where he dropped, on the floor.

When Peggy was diagnosed as suffering from some disease he'd never heard of, myeloma, it was as if God had kicked him in the face for daring to think that life owed him some happiness. As she worsened, so did his bitterness. In the latter stages of her illness, when the bone tumours had spread and the doctors told Jim his wife was dying, he seemed to twist that bitterness in upon himself and let it fester, like an illness of its own, re-opening old scars, old hurts, old memories.

'After much suffering,' read the obituary in the *Express & Star*, 'Margaret (Peggy), dearly beloved wife of James Brockhouse, aged twenty-seven years . . .' The only living being apart from his mother who had ever shown him real true love. Now both of them were dead.

By the time Vanessa Antrobus arrived on the scene to work for him three months later, Jim was no more reconciled to the loss of his wife than he'd been that deceitful bright morning in May when Peggy had died. The only reason he'd engaged Vanessa was because she hadn't been frightened to stand up to him, and he respected her for that. And as the weeks turned into autumn and he got to know her better, she became somebody he found he could rely on.

21

Ernest Parrish wasn't exactly in the best of tempers this evening. For one thing he'd cut himself again shaving – ever since their Sybil's 'accident' (as he chose to think of it) he'd got rid of his open razor and was using a new-fangled safety contraption that nicked his face to pieces. And for another thing, which irked him just as much, Sybil was off to some fancy arty do with that half-sister of hers.

Mr Parrish didn't trust Vanessa. He felt sure she was up to something. Every time he'd seen her lately – and that was getting a sight too often – it was 'Sybil darling' this and 'Sybil darling' that, as if the pair had been the best of friends all their lives. And his wife was as bad; she encouraged it. Not a week went by without she and Sybil weren't over at that flat in Paget Road – *he'd* never been invited, naturally! – leaving him to spend the evening by himself; or they'd be meeting together for luncheon in town, the three of them.

Nobody told him anything these days. Sybil especially. He and she had always been so close, so like one another, he'd prided himself how much she took after him. But this sudden chumminess – he didn't approve of it, it made him feel excluded. He knew why as well: it was that Vanessa's doing, pushing herself between them, shoving him out.

Not for the first time, the analogy of the cuckoo in the nest had seemed appropriate to Mr Parrish.

He didn't approve either of Vanessa's separation from her husband. Very bad form, he thought. And she'd made matters worse getting herself a job as clerk or something in a scrapyard. A *scrapyard*—! There was no excuse for that. All said and done, she was still a member of the family, and it'd look well if his pals at his golf club got to hear about it. Imagine the comments in the clubhouse. 'I say, old man, what's this they're saying about your daughter?' Once word got round, he'd be a laughing stock, he'd probably have to resign.

Still, what could you expect from a girl like that Vanessa. He'd never liked her. He'd never liked her husband, but at least the chap was socially acceptable. When his pals at the club asked 'what does your son-in-law do for a living', he hadn't minded telling them Roland Antrobus ran an art gallery. Some of the best families in England had sons-in-law with art galleries.

But a *scrapyard*—!

There was a badness in that girl, bad blood; he'd always thought so. Look at her father, what had he been, just a common working chap with a lick of education, a fisherman who scribbled poetry stuff, a Welshman. Ernest Parrish had no time for the Welsh. If he'd had his way he would have sent Vanessa back to Amroth after he married her mother, and let the father's family have the trouble of raising her. Only Florence wouldn't part with her; so despite the bruise to his pride he'd brought the cuckoo up himself, clothed her, fed her, had her educated, given her his name.

And this was his reward. To feel ashamed of her.

Shame only compounded the grievances Mr Parrish

nursed already – dozens of them, little pinprick irritations feeding on his dislike and resentment that he'd always been made to feel second best to Owen James. Nor had he forgotten Vanessa's part in ruining their Sybil's engagement, which had led to his daughter taking up with the wrong crowd and going off the rails, which in turn had led to her health being affected, and then her 'accident'.

One way or another that wretched Vanessa was to blame for everything. So what was she playing at now, he'd like to know, behaving so friendly all of a sudden, if she wasn't intent on causing more mischief for Sybil.

Coming downstairs from the bathroom, where he'd been brooding on these things while taking his ritual once-a-week soak in the tub, Mr Parrish could hear the family laughing together in the sitting room. As he opened the door somebody shushed and the laughter was cut off abruptly, leaving him with a nasty feeling he himself had been the butt of their hilarity.

He went in. The fire had been lit against the chill of the October evening, and the three of them were sitting by it, Sybil and her mother on the sofa, Vanessa in the hearthside chair. His wife's cheeks looked flushed, and she avoided meeting his eye, he noticed; and his daughter was wearing the silly smirk of somebody trying to stop themselves from giggling.

'What's all the noise in here,' he asked suspiciously.

'Oh . . . just a little joke, dear,' said Mrs Parrish.

Sybil made a gasping noise, and clamping a hand to her mouth turned away from him, her shoulders shaking.

'A joke, eh. Well isn't anyone going to share it?'

Leaning back among the cushions of the chair, her legs elegantly crossed, a glass of sherry in her hand, Vanessa

returned his irritated glance with an eyebrow raised in
cool amusement.

'It wasn't very funny, actually,' she said; and then,
irritating him further, she added casually, 'Do you know
you've got little bits of paper all over your face?'

He caught sight of himself in the mantelpiece mirror.
He'd had to use some lavatory tissue on the cuts where
he'd nicked himself, and he'd been so preoccupied he'd
forgotten about it before he came down. With his bald
head, half-moon eyebrows and waxed moustache the
paper gave his face a foolish, clownlike appearance.

'Thank you, Vanessa, I am aware of the fact,' he
answered tersely, vexed he'd made himself look a figure of fun.

There was an outburst of unladylike snorts and Sybil
collapsed against her mother, clutching her stomach and
hooting in merriment.

Mr Parrish glared at her. He wasn't a tall man, and the
royal blue quilted dressing gown he was wearing bulged
unflatteringly over his shirt and trousers, robbing him of
his usual pin-striped solicitor's dignity.

Drawing himself up he said, 'Stop that silly row at
once, Sybil, you're making an exhibition of yourself.
What's the matter with you.' He looked at his wife.
'What's the matter with her, Florence. Has she been
drinking?'

'A little glass of sherry with Vanessa, that's all, dear.'
Mrs Parrish seemed to be having difficulty with her words
and he looked at her closer, wondering what she was
smiling about. He hadn't seen Florence smile properly
in years. It was unsettling.

Coughing and wiping tears from her eyes, Sybil
straightened herself on the sofa. 'Oh dear . . . bet that's

messed my make-up,' she said, still breathless from laughter. 'I suppose I'd better pop and fix my face again before the taxi cab's here—'

She stood up. Despite the ruin to her powder she was looking very attractive this evening; even her father privately had to admit as much. The gauntness hollowing her features had completely disappeared, replaced by a prettiness that showed little trace of the pouting, sulky expression of the old-style Sybil. Her strawberry blonde hair was growing into a long bob, like Vanessa's, which suited her very much better than the boyishly cropped cut with its affected kiss-curl that she'd had before. The short, tubular-shaped clothes had been replaced, as well. For tonight's party at the Gallery Sybil was wearing a below-the-knee sculptured jersey outfit in bronze, a colour which flattered her creamy skin and emphasised the blueness of her eyes.

When she'd gone upstairs Ernest Parrish said testily, 'Since everybody else is drinking, Florence, I'll ask you to get me a whisky,' and went over to the fireplace to rid himself of the bits of bloodied paper.

'Stay where you are, Mother, I'll see to it—' Vanessa uncrossed her legs to get up.

'I asked your mother, not you,' her stepfather retorted, glowering at her through the mirror.

'Mother's not a servant, and it's time you stopped treating her as one,' she observed, going behind him to the sun-burst cabinet where the drinks were kept.

Her remark flicked Mr Parrish's temper into anger. 'I'll treat your mother as I see fit! This is my house, may I remind you. You're only here under sufferance, young woman.'

'Of course. But then haven't I always been?' Vanessa

said equably. 'How would you like your whisky – water or soda?'

'Now you look here—'

'*Please*, Ernest, don't start another argument,' Mrs Parrish intervened, seeing the dark rush of colour to her husband's face. 'It'll only upset our Sybil if she comes down again and hears you shouting. You mustn't spoil the evening for her, dear. This is the first real night out she's had for ever so long – and you know how much she's been looking forward to it.'

'She wouldn't be going at all if I had my way,' he snapped, turning round. 'And I'll thank you not to interrupt me when I'm speaking, Florence. Remember who's master here.'

'Oh, do stop being such a bully,' Vanessa said calmly, fixing him a double scotch with a splash of soda. '"Remember who's master here" – do people really say things like that any more? I thought it went out of fashion with ham actors in Victorian melodramas. Here's your drink—'

There was a sound of a vehicle drawing in at the kerb outside, and Sybil calling down, 'The taxi cab's arrived, Vee.'

Putting the scotch on the mantelpiece, Vanessa collected her bag and evening wrap; but as she went to move away her stepfather grabbed her by the arm to stop her. Pop-eyed with indignation he spluttered, 'How *dare* you speak to me in such a manner! What gives you the right to question my authority, eh – eh? Who the devil d'you think you are, coming here with your scrapyard airs and graces, you insolent little madam – I won't stand for it, you hear me!'

She didn't trouble answering, just looked at him with

the same cool amusement which had annoyed him so much a few minutes earlier.

'Ernest, *please*—' repeated Mrs Parrish, getting up.

She was ignored. 'I'm on to your game, my girl,' he blustered at Vanessa. 'You think I don't know what you're up to – you're wrong. You can fool our Sybil and your mother with your blandishments, not me. Understand this, you cause our Sybil any more harm with your mischief-making, and you'll be biting off more than you bargained for, I'm warning you.'

'Oh, for heaven's sake, Ernest, that's enough!' Mrs Parrish said more sharply, pulling his hand from her daughter.

He thrust her away. 'You keep out of this, Florence—'

'I will not keep out of it. Vanessa's quite right – you *are* a bully. Lord only knows how I've put up with you for so long.'

The peal of the front bell cut through her words. It was answered by the squeak of the scullery door as Myrtle, the housemaid, went to see to it, and Sybil's footsteps clattering downstairs.

Ernest Parrish's face had gone the colour of mottled putty. Not since the earliest days of their marriage had his wife ever dared to address him thus. Shaken, he stared at her.

'Hurry up, Vee, the driver's waiting—' Sybil popped her head round the door, too keen to get going to notice anything amiss. ''Bye for now, Daddy, 'bye, Mother.'

Her mother turned, brightly forcing a smile in response. 'Enjoy yourself, dear. Have a nice time.'

'I'll try. Vee, come *on*—!' She disappeared again to take her coat from Myrtle.

Keeping her voice down, Vanessa said with a dismissive glance at her stepfather, 'Will you be all right now, Mother?'

'Of course, dear.'

'Of course she'll be all right,' Ernest Parrish echoed sourly, lighting himself a Woodbine. All the posturing and bombast seemed to have shrivelled out of him suddenly, like hot air from a pricked balloon, leaving him in a tetchy humour.

His small eyes narrowed against the cigarette smoke; and when Vanessa had kissed her mother and gone from the room, he took his glass of scotch and sat down beside the fire in silence, to indulge himself in the punishment of ignoring his wife for the rest of the evening.

Michael Wright's party was already in full swing when the two sisters arrived at the Gallery. Not knowing quite what to expect, Sybil had imagined there'd be quite a lot of arty old fogies present, and was agreeably surprised to find more than half the guests were young and interesting looking. A waitress was going round serving canapés and glasses of wine, and somewhere in the background drifted the soft, relaxing music of a gramophone playing 'Loving that Man'.

There was a moment's pause in the buzz of conversation as heads turned to see who'd just come in, and several people smiled and waved as they recognised Vanessa. A tall, fair-haired chap, engagingly debonair in evening dress and black bow tie, excused himself to his female companion and came across.

'Vanessa – delighted you could make it!' he greeted her warmly. And to Sybil – 'So, Miss Parrish, my hopes have come true that we'd meet again. Now the evening's complete.' It was only by his smile that Sybil remembered the rather untidy young man in tweed jacket and flannels whom she'd been so unpleasantly rude to the last time she'd encountered him.

A little awkwardly she said hello. The transformation in Michael Wright's appearance impressed her almost as much as his apparent pleasure to have her as one of his guests at this launch.

'How are you both?' he continued once they'd got rid of their coats, taking the sisters on either arm to usher them in. 'Vanessa, you're looking utterly ravishing – or should that be ravishable?' There was a glance of masculine approval for her black crêpe frock with coloured bugle beads catching the light in a fan-shaped design.

Sybil would have liked a similar compliment for herself, and felt a bit piqued when Michael added instead, 'Let's fix you up with drinks and then I'll do some introducing—' before going off in search of the waitress.

Somebody wandered over and started talking to Vanessa about Roland, wanting to know when her husband would be back in England. Avoiding getting involved Sybil moved away to look at a group of drawings mounted under spot-lights nearby, charcoal studies of nude torsos done in a bold, aggressive style which rather appealed to her.

She was still examining them when Michael returned with their glasses of wine. He was accompanied by the same young woman she'd seen chatting with him earlier, and whom he introduced to her now as Delia something.

'D'you mind awfully if I leave you to get to know each other?' he apologised. 'I'm wanted all over the place—' waving to another couple of guests just arriving. 'I'll rejoin you both as soon as I'm free, OK?'

When he'd gone, Delia asked in a languid sort of way, 'Have you known Michael long?' She had striking features, the kind of face that was ugly enough to be beautiful, with a wide mouth and almost oriental eyes, and was dressed in a pair of heavy silk 'lounging pyjamas' – very daring, Sybil thought – which made the most of her superb long legs.

'To be honest, I don't actually know him at all,' Sybil confessed. 'He's a friend of my sister—' She indicated Vanessa, still being talked at by the chap behind. 'I've only met him once before, and that was briefly.'

'Count yourself lucky,' Delia said. Her sleepy, husky voice had a fascinating quality. 'I'm not sure dear Michael improves with acquaintance. He's always so annoyingly charming. And when one's not in a mood to be charmed, believe me it's quite maddening.'

'You sound as though you know him rather well.'

'Mm . . . *rather* well.'

Delia glanced aside as somebody in the crush spoke to her. After a brief exchange and a lazy little laugh she turned back again, changing the subject. 'By the way, I noticed your interest in the charcoal studies. What d'you think? Not bad, are they. I'm wondering whether to buy one.'

'Really?' Sybil took a long sip of her wine. 'I'm afraid I don't know much about art,' she said cautiously.

'My dear, you don't have to *know* about art to like what you see. Trust your instincts. Ask yourself if you can *live* with it. It's rather like choosing a lover.' The slanting eyes held an inscrutable little smile. 'Actually, these were done by a friend of mine, but that's not the reason I'm thinking of buying. You should get one as well.'

'A lover?'

'A lover, a drawing . . . whichever.'

'Maybe I will.' Sybil longed to ask this exotic creature if she was Michael Wright's girlfriend. The way she'd seen the two touching and smiling suggested as much. She couldn't decide whether to like her. Delia exuded that certain something known as 'it' – confidence, style, sexual assurance, attractiveness – the things Sybil used to think she had herself, before Alan Slater had befouled it all.

Slater.

She pushed the name from her mind and finished her wine.

For the next ten minutes they pursued the desultory party chit-chat of people with little in common, until Delia said suddenly, glancing past her, 'Sorry – you won't mind excusing me just for a second? I must have a word, it's my Head of Department—'

She fluttered her fingers at somebody, and started languorously edging her way through the guests towards them.

Left by herself, Sybil glanced round the room in search of Vanessa. Her half-sister had moved, and was across the other side talking now to a plump, bubbly young woman whom Sybil recognised as Kay Murray, from the *Advertiser* – they'd been introduced at Vanessa's wedding.

'What's this, all on your lonesome?' Michael exclaimed, reappearing unexpectedly at her elbow. 'Where's Delia swanned off to? I left her here to take good care of you.'

Sybil jerked her chin.

He followed its direction. 'Oh – vamping Archie Nicholson,' he said, in a tone that wasn't quite joking.

'Is that her boss?'

'Kind of. Archie's a head of department at the School. Jolly nice chap. Look, I say – can I get you another glass of wine, Miss Parrish? I must be making a poor sort of impression the way I'm neglecting you!'

He pushed a wave of fair hair out of his eyes and gave her such a rueful smile that Sybil felt a queer little twist of the heart. She said quickly, 'Please call me Sybil, won't you. "Miss Parrish" makes me sound about ninety. And before you go dashing off again—' she hid her glass behind her back so he couldn't take it, 'I want to apologise for the beastly way I behaved last time we met. I was pretty obnoxious, wasn't I.'

'Pretty obnoxious?' Michael pulled a face. '*Totally* obnoxious as I remember, but it didn't put me off. I admire a girl with a bit of spark, especially one as attractive as you.'

'Oh . . . you think I'm attractive?' She tried not to sound pleased.

'I'll say! I thought so the very first moment I saw you.' He smiled again, this time with a look that went all over her face, the sort of look she hadn't had from a man in ages and ages. 'Shall I let you into a secret, Sybil? I asked your brother-in-law for your telephone number, intending to call you.'

'Uh-huh?' She wanted so much to believe him. 'You didn't, though.'

'No, but that was Roland's fault. And I'm not going to tell you why, so don't ask me.'

'Oh, I can guess.'

From somewhere Michael produced a pencil and a scrap of paper. 'Right, now I've the chance again – what *is* your number?'

'Supposing I give it you, what do you want it for?'

Sybil asked, knowing the answer full well yet not wishing to seem too readily eager.

'What do you think? Invite you out with me for an evening, of course!' he answered her, laughing. 'And I'm not taking no for an answer, I'm warning you.'

'But what about Delia?'

'What *about* Delia—?'

'Well, isn't she . . .'

'She's a friend,' he said, guessing the problem. 'A friend, and that's all. Now let's get you that drink, and do stop asking questions.'

22

Just before Christmas Vanessa received the best present she could have wished for, a letter from a London publishing house accepting her collection of short stories, *Masks and Faces*.

Having tried more than half a dozen other publishers, she'd grown so resigned to having the stories rejected she'd virtually given up hope of ever seeing them in print, and Merryman & Co. had hung on to them so long she was beginning to think they'd forgotten to return the manuscript.

Her first reaction on reading their letter was astonished disbelief – disbelief instantly followed by elation so jubilant she went dancing round the flat whooping and clapping her hands like a child before dashing off to telephone her mother on her way to work.

Mrs Parrish was delighted.

Jim Brockhouse received the news rather less enthusiastically.

'So you'll be handing in your notice now, I suppose,' he said gloomily.

Vanessa didn't have time to wonder why he seemed so put out, she was too excited. Somebody signing themselves Jonathan Connell wanted her to go down to London to discuss *Masks and Faces*, and if that meant taking a day off work, surely *one* day wouldn't bankrupt the business?

'Do you know London?'

'I've been there a few times.'

'You be careful then,' Jim warned her. 'It's a big place to get yourself lost in.'

She arrived at Euston station in a snowstorm that muffled the morning and whitened the grimy face of the capital, clogging its streets with banks of slushy drifts through which her taxi cab made slow progress to the offices of Merryman & Co., in one of the less fashionable squares of Marylebone.

Number thirty-four was a relic of Dickensian London. Its warren of book-lined rooms and narrow gas-lit staircases exuded a musty, dusty atmosphere like the library of a gentlemen's club. Jonathan Connell himself proved not quite as old-fashioned as his surroundings. He was a small, neat man with a small, neat moustache and pomaded hair, rather dandified in mustard waistcoat and paisley silk bow tie, and wearing shoes of white buckskin with brown toe-caps, a style more generally associated with the type of person cited in divorce cases.

Offering Vanessa a brisk handshake and a glass of excellent dry sherry, Mr Connell seated her in an armchair and proceeded to business. He'd been much impressed by her stories, he told her. Liked the freshness of their themes, the way she'd linked one story to another. Good balance. Well-crafted. She handled her descriptions nicely. He would have preferred to publish a full-length novel first to get her name established, but Merryman were prepared to take a gamble with a small edition, see how it sold.

He was interested to learn about her father (Vanessa had mentioned that and her freelance work in her covering letter). Inherited the pater's talent, eh. Another glass of sherry? Now then, as to editing, there were some changes he'd like to suggest, a little fine-tuning, nothing too drastic. Would she be agreeable.

She would.

She came away from the meeting in a dream. On a sudden impulse born of euphoria she telephoned Jim Brockhouse at the scrapyard. His voice at the other end of the line sounded terse, but he was glad to know her interview had gone so well, he said, and what time train was she catching back, she'd got to work in the morning.

Vanessa treated herself to a celebratory luncheon at a chic little French restaurant where the waiter reminded her of Victor Michelet – surely a lucky omen, because she'd been sharing Victor's company while writing *Masks and Faces* at Le Palombier. They still kept in touch with the occasional letter; and she was looking forward to hearing of him from Marjorie Tiersot, who'd be over here next month with the baby to visit her parents.

There was just time enough after luncheon for Vanessa to brave the slush of Oxford Street for a look round the big department stores, and then it was back in a taxi cab to Euston with the misty grey winter dusk blurring the skyline.

The train was slightly delayed on the homeward journey and it had gone half past nine when she arrived in Wolverhampton. Hurrying through a miserable drizzle to catch her bus to Paget Road, she heard somebody pip their motor horn, and looking round she was surprised to see Jim Brockhouse's lorry parked across the street from the station.

He opened his cab door and jumped down to come over to her.

'You dain't say on the phone if your husband might be meeting you,' he announced. 'What wi' the train being late I thought I'd best hang about in case he'd missed you.'

He still didn't know about her separation from Roland.

'Nobody's meeting me,' Vanessa responded, touched by his concern for her.

'That's all right then. If you hop in the lorry I'll run you home—'

She hesitated before accepting; and mistaking it for reluctance, he said a little tersely, 'O' course, if you'd prefer to get the bus. Mebbe a lorry's a bit of a come down after hob-nobbing wi' publishers.'

'Don't be silly. I'd be very glad of a lift – if it's no trouble?'

'If it was I wouldn't be offering.'

He held her firmly by the arm, waiting for a car to pass, then took her across and helped her into his vehicle. Out of the thin drizzle the cab was warm and smelled of diesel and cigarette smoke.

'Anyway, how did it go today?' he enquired when he'd cranked the engine and climbed in beside her. 'Got everything sorted out wi' them, did you?'

'More or less.' She told him about her meeting with Jonathan Connell. 'They'd like me to make a few alterations to the manuscript, that's all. It won't take me long. A couple of evenings.'

'And then you'll be rich and famous, I suppose.'

'Well, I wish I could say so, but I'll need to be successful first.' Vanessa couldn't disguise the thrill in her voice. 'The main thing is I'm actually being *published*. It's – oh, it's so much like a dream come true, I still can't believe it!'

Jim changed gear to negotiate the traffic in Queen Square.

'Your gain, my loss . . . though I don't begrudge you your slice o' luck, Vanessa. Tell you the truth I never expected you'd stay long wi' us,' he said in a strained tone. 'I recall you telling me when you come about the job, as how you'd only applied as a sort o' stop-gap. I should think the newspapers'll be falling over theirselves chasing after you now.'

Vanessa took her gaze off the rain-smeared windscreen to look at him. In the yellow wash of streetlights his profile was expressionless until he briefly returned the look, and then she read the despondency in his eyes.

'I don't know where you've got this idea I'm leaving you,' she reassured him. 'The only time I ever considered it was when you were being so impossibly difficult . . . but you've improved no end just lately.'

A couple of months ago she wouldn't have dared to speak to him so, but then a couple of months ago she didn't know him. Since their conversation in the office when he'd actually sat down and talked a bit about himself, the relationship between Vanessa and Jim Brockhouse had shifted to an easier footing and nowadays he was being friendlier and certainly a lot more tolerant.

'Well there's hope for me yet if you think I'm improving,' he said, drily, sounding relieved she thought. 'I know you never say aught about your husband, but I'd somehow got the notion he wasn't too struck on you working for me. What wi' that and your book getting published, I thought to myself I was bound to be losing you sooner or later.'

'My husband's got nothing to do with it,' Vanessa said quickly. 'It's *my* decision, Mr Brockhouse. And I'm staying.'

'Fair enough. And I'd prefer you to call me Jim when we're not in the office – OK?'

As they came out of Darlington Street into Chapel Ash he had to halt the lorry in a line of traffic, and while they were sitting there he suddenly went on, 'Tell me some'at. I know it's none o' my business this, but . . . everything's all right between you and Mr Antrobus, is it?'

She'd been wondering how long it would be before he got round to asking. Naturally he was bound to be curious about the circumstances of her home life.

'What makes you think it isn't all right,' she said levelly.

'Just a feeling. How long have you been wi' me now – four months, in't it – and I don't even know what he does, or his name, let alone ever seen him.'

'His name's Roland.'

'Roland.' Jim digested the information while he put the lorry into gear again. 'Sounds a bit posh, Roland Antrobus. Is the family a local 'un?'

'I believe so. His parents were dead before we married . . . I don't know their history.'

'My sister-in-law has the idea he spends a lot o' time away from home. Some'at or other to do wi' his job, is it?'

'Something like that.'

Vanessa was beginning to feel uncomfortable with this questioning; and as though he guessed so Jim said, going slightly off the subject, 'It's funny how you can adjust to living by yourself, in't it. When Peggy was alive I used to save up little things to tell her in the evening –

y'know, things we could share and have a laugh about. I've missed that like hell, I have. I used to wonder how I was ever going to cope wi' not having her to talk to. But you find you get used to it after a bit. Not the grief o' course, not the coming home to an empty house and not having somebody there to share your thoughts with . . . but the getting used to your own company, doing things different.'

He paused for a moment, watching his driving; then added, 'D'you find that an' all, Vanessa?'

'Getting used to being alone? Yes,' she said, 'yes, I do.'

'Aye, I thought you'd understand.'

She wondered if it wasn't something about the warm intimacy of this cab, their closeness together, almost touching in the darkness, that had suddenly prompted him to share his feelings.

She stole another look at his profile. Since he'd started being more relaxed with her at the office she had occasionally caught herself thinking what an interesting face he had; not handsome, like Larret Fitzgerald had been – though they were both dark-haired and blue-eyed – but good-looking in a stronger, more mature kind of way. When he wasn't wearing his brooding expression there was something open and honest about Jim's features that appealed to her; and when he smiled (admittedly not often) she liked how the smile curled the corners of his mouth and warmed his eyes.

Neither of them spoke again for a while, and it wasn't until they were approaching The Half Way House Inn that Vanessa broke the companionable silence by saying, 'You can drop me off anywhere round here. Paget Road's just on the left.'

'I'll see you to your door,' he said briefly.

'But it's a cul-de-sac—'

Paying no heed to that, he slowed the lorry to turn at the junction and drove into the narrow road, pulling up where she directed him. Here and there the glow of windows brightened for a minute as her neighbours peered between their curtains, disturbed from their reading or their wirelesses by the racket of the engine.

There was a lamp-post outside Vanessa's flat. The soft gleam of its gaslight filled the cab and reflected the pale ovals of their faces as she and Jim Brockhouse looked at one another.

'Well,' she said with an awkward smile, 'thanks for the lift . . . Jim.' She wondered whether to invite him in for a cup of tea, but immediately thought better of it at this hour. 'I'm really most grateful,' she added instead.

'You look tired,' he told her. 'It's been a long day for you, Vanessa. You go and get some sleep, and I'll see you again in the morning . . . not too early, eh.'

When he'd helped her down she walked up the path to her doorway and stood in the shadows listening to his lorry reversing back along Paget Road. Only when the sound of it had completely died away did she get her key out and go inside.

Marjorie Tiersot's parents lived in a pretty Victorian villa in Ormes Lane, at the top of a steep hill known as The Holloway overlooking the countryside at Tettenhall Wood. The house contained some of Vanessa's happiest memories, of those endless summer days of childhood when she was allowed to spend weekends here with Marjorie and the numerous Lake cousins. They'd been halcyon times, and she remembered them as always full of love and laughter and fun, the gramophone playing, dogs barking, lemonade on the lawn, the grown-ups in tennis dress, and Madge's brother Neville tearing up the gravel on his motor bicycle.

Neville went away to war and was wounded at Vimy Ridge. He came home minus both his legs; and though he clung on to his young life for another fifteen months before he died, the sunshine had already gone behind a cloud and the house was somehow never quite the same after that.

Until Suzanne. Madge's little baby daughter had brought the laughter alive again just by the magic of her presence. Vanessa could sense the difference the moment she'd walked in ... a kind of echo in the atmosphere awakening the golden ghosts of childhood. She'd been to morning service at Christ Church with all the family before spending the rest of the day with them, like old times; and sitting up here in the nursery with the January sunlight touching the room with the faded colours of long-ago summers, she felt a wave of nostalgia overwhelming her.

These four walls evoked so many memories. The rocking horse in the corner with its threadbare mane and tail; the Kate Greenaway frieze; the dolls' house; Neville's cricket bat. Even the linoleum and curtains were the same; nothing had changed.

Except Time.

At twenty-three Vanessa was now the same age Neville Lake had been at his death. He was the first young man she had ever properly noticed, the first she'd loved, and she'd idolised him with all the innocent clumsy passion of a schoolgirl, tongue-tied one day and ragging him the next, confused about her own emotions. Somewhere among her treasures she still kept a photograph of them both, Neville in his uniform and herself in pigtails, arm-in-arm on the steps with one of the cousins.

'You're very quiet, Vee,' Madge remarked, lifting Suzanne against her shoulder to be winded now the baby had finished feeding. 'Penny for them—?'

'Oh . . . daydreams, that's all. Here, let me do that—' Vanessa held out her arms. 'I was thinking about the times I used to come here in the hols, all those plans we were forever making . . . you remember? We'd stay awake for hours discussing the things we wanted to do and what we were going to be when we grew up.'

'I'd set my mind on joining a circus, as I recall,' Madge said laughing, buttoning the front of her blouse. 'It was either the circus or running away with the gipsies to live in a caravan.'

'That was before you had a pash on that spotty friend of Neville's – what was his name—'

'Gregory Ratcliffe. God, I'd forgotten him. D'you remember the ghastly moustache he kept trying to grow—'

'And the monocle.'

'Oh yes, and the *monocle*.' Madge laughed again and shook her head. 'And what about you, you wanted to be a poetess and marry Neville and have umpteen children.'

Vanessa laid her cheek against little Suzanne's downy chestnut curls. 'Well, I'm about to have my first book published,' she said, 'so I suppose that's one ambition realised. The other two I can't do much about, regrettably.'

'You can still have the umpteen children.'

'With an absentee husband?'

'Mm . . . difficult.'

From downstairs came a sudden burst of conversation as Jean-Luc Tiersot and Mr Lake, Madge's father, returned from their stroll round the garden to rejoin Mrs Lake in the drawing room before luncheon.

'Darling, what *are* you going to do about Roland?' Madge asked, more seriously. 'It's such a hideously unfair situation . . . will you divorce him?'

'I don't know. What grounds do I have.'

'Desertion. Adultery.'

'Roland pays me maintenance, that's not desertion. And he can cross-petition for adultery. Anyway, Madge, I prefer to leave well alone for the moment. I'm happy enough with my work and my writing, and getting the book in print.'

Vanessa glanced at her friend across the baby's head. She was going to add that if she felt like company she had Sybil to go out with these days; but Sybil had been seeing a lot of Michael Wright just lately, and it was awkward playing gooseberry in a threesome.

'You might kid yourself you're happy, but you're not exactly enjoying yourself,' Madge retorted. 'I mean, this dead-end job – almost every letter from you, you've been complaining about your dreary old boss and how fed up you are with his grousing and grumbling. I said to Jean-Luc, I can't understand why you feel you have to put up with it.'

'Oh, that was last autumn. Things have improved since,' Vanessa said hurriedly. 'The problem was, Jim and I had got off on the wrong foot with each other.'

There was a quizzical look. 'So now it's *Jim*, eh? You're a dark horse, Vee. How long's this been going on?'

'You can stop twitching your whiskers, there's nothing "going on". My employer and I have a perfectly respectable working relationship confined purely to office hours.'

'Uh-huh? Not that he sounds your type – he must be pretty ancient even if he *is* available. But then widowers can be attractive when they're worth a bob or two . . . so I've heard.'

'He's thirty-eight, and yes he is rather attractive, even without the bob or two. Now that's all you're getting out of me, so may we change the subject, Madge dear, please?'

Pulling a droll face Madge got up from beside the fire. Taking her daughter gently back into her arms she laid Suzanne down to sleep in the satin-draped mahogany cradle which had already done service for three previous generations of the Lake family.

'By the way, Victor Michelet still talks about you a lot,' she said, casually, over her shoulder.

'Victor—? Oh . . . really?'

'Mm. I do believe he's smitten, Vee. I've noticed he's been terribly spoony ever since the end of your holiday. Keeps dropping hints to Jean-Luc about asking you back again.'

'But his letters are always so – well, so polite and proper. What kind of things does he say?' Vanessa asked keenly.

Madge straightened from the cradle with one of her enigmatic grins.

'Darling, I'm not sure I should tell you in case my husband accused me of trying to influence you. You see, we've decided – Jean-Luc and I – that you really ought to come and live by us in the Dordogne. And before you answer—' she said, seeing her friend's face change expression, 'just consider what you'd be gaining. You could afford to rent a dear little property on the money Roland's giving you, and you'd have all the time in the world for lazing about in the sun with an ice-cold Chablis writing your books and things. Doesn't that sound heaven? And there'd be Victor taking you out and dancing attendance, and Binkie and Twinks and the rest of the Set if you needed amusing. Vee, you've absolutely nothing to lose. So what d'you say . . . will you give it some thought?'

23

Vanessa would have been a fool not to be strongly tempted by Marjorie's suggestion. She had fallen in love with the Dordogne, with its colours and its history and the seductive allure of its atmosphere; but she was realistic enough not to confuse the glow of memory with the facts of practicality.

It was one thing to spend an enjoyable holiday there; quite another to make it her permanent home. Things were different for Madge. Madge had followed her heart, she had adopted her husband's culture and integrated herself into local French society. The rosy picture she'd painted took no account of the problems of existence for an unattached young woman living off her own resources.

Oh yes, Vanessa was certainly tempted. Under the cheerless leaden skies of an English winter, it was pleasant to imagine herself basking on a sun-warmed terrace in the golden shade of palm trees, listening to the cicadas, a glass of wine in her hand and Victor by her side . . . and then how long before she became simply another ex-patriot, one of the Set, sucked into the parasitic lifestyle of people like Binkie and Twinks?

The Dordogne was heaven on earth. But heaven on earth had its price.

Besides, exile was impossible while the emotional anchors of pride and loyalty still tied her to her roots, to the gritty strength of the Midlands and the sea-girt hills of Pembrokeshire. It was here she wanted to make her future, not among the gin-and-tonic friendships of a coterie of bores.

She discussed all this with Jim Brockhouse one memorable day in February a week or so after Madge and her husband had returned to France. Jim was having to go over to Bridgnorth to see about some business, and he'd asked Vanessa if she'd care to keep him company and they'd make a day of it.

He arrived to collect her from the flat driving a motor car, a handsome gleaming black Humber. Expecting the lorry, Vanessa was caught on the hop and had to keep him waiting in the hallway while she ran and changed into something a little smarter, her camel-hair overcoat with the Liberty silk scarf she'd bought in London.

If the car was a surprise, so was its driver. She had never seen her employer in anything other than an old and rather shiny navy suit which he wore at the yard, yet here he was turned out in tweeds that wouldn't have disgraced the Prince of Wales, with polished Oxford shoes, a white soft-collared shirt, and his dark hair neatly trimmed and brushed.

Vanessa wondered what sort of business it was in Bridgnorth that could have dictated such a transformation.

Apparently the Humber was his own, not borrowed; and no, he said, he hadn't had the vehicle long. Did her husband run a motor car? Since the night of the lift from the station she'd found him often slipping in questions like this about Roland; and as usual she answered him, then changed the subject.

Their journey took them through Tettenhall westward

across the county boundary into the Shropshire countryside. Overnight the rain had cleared away and there was
a mist lying on the fields, reflecting the silvery light of
the February sky. It was one of those mornings when
everything had a still and silent quality: they passed little
traffic on the roads, and away from the scattered villages
nothing moved in the landscape except ragged flocks of
birds following the line of ploughs on upland pastures.

Jim didn't talk much. He was never terribly sociable
in the morning, Vanessa had noticed. Not until they were
almost in Bridgnorth did he explain where he was going,
to somewhere called Fort Pendlestone on the other side
of the Severn. Reckoning his business there should take
no more than a couple of hours, he arranged to meet
Vanessa again about one o'clock at The Cross Keys Inn,
pointing the place out to her before setting her down in
the high street.

A log fire was blazing on the hearth when she went
into the lounge bar. Its flames competed with several
old-fashioned oil lamps to send shadows across the
black-beamed ceiling and give the room a cosy warmth
that dispelled the bleary daylight from the window.

The Cross Keys had evidently been a venue for
cock-fights at one time, to judge from the number of
handbills on the walls, yellowing behind Victorian frames
alongside prints of strutting game-cocks with names like
the Staffordshire Dun and the Cheshire Pile.

Vanessa bought herself a drink while she was waiting
and took it across to the fire. When Jim Brockhouse
came in she was chatting to an elderly couple; and for
a moment or two he stood and watched her, the way she
smiled, the way the firelight rimmed her beautiful young

face and burnished the silken lustre of her hair. He could have looked at her for ever.

Then she glanced up and saw him and waved, and excusing herself came over to join him.

'Well that was a blinkin' waste o' time,' he said when he'd ordered a pint for himself. 'I come all this way to sign a contract, and some other blighter's jumped in ahead o' me. You think they'd have the courtesy to let me know.'

'So you've lost the business—?'

'Aye.' He didn't sound much put out about it though, Vanessa thought. 'Still, that's the way it goes. Any case, the contract wasn't really worth the money I was putting up, so mebbe I'm best off out of it. Let the other beggar be the loser.'

Jim paid for his beer and a refill for Vanessa, and went and sat with her at a table by the window.

'D'you fancy some'at to eat? They do a very good pork pie and pickle here, as I recall.'

'Thanks, I wouldn't mind,' she said. 'I must admit I'm rather hungry. I've been walking down by the river, it's given me an appetite.'

'I wish I could've been wi' you.' His eyes lingered on her face again as he got up to go and order; and when he came back he added, 'Tell you what – I'll take us for a bit of a spin as far as Bewdley before we go home, would you like that? Or will your husband be expecting his meal on the table?'

Vanessa looked down at her glass. 'Roland's away,' she said. And then, looking up again brightly, 'Bewdley sounds fun. I've only been there once – oh, years and years ago. I spent a day with a chum and her parents—'

She started telling him all about Marjorie; and by the

time their food had been served she'd moved on to Le
Palombier and her holiday, and the people she'd met,
and then Madge's effort to persuade her to join her out
there, talking in an animated, amusing way that was as
captivating to watch as it was to listen to.

When finally she'd finished, Jim commented, 'I can see
I'm going to have to put a ball and chain on you, Vanessa,'
but the wryness of his smile somehow failed to reach his
eyes, she noticed. 'You're intent on running from me,
aren't you. What's your husband got to say about this
Dordogne caper?' He pronounced it 'D'dorn'.

She evaded the question. 'But I've told you – I've
decided I'm not going.'

'I hope he's as glad as me to hear it.'

He left things at that.

Later though, after they'd driven downriver to Bewdley
and had parked the car to take a stroll across the bridge,
the subject had obviously been nagging him, because
half-way through talking about something unrelated, he
suddenly said, 'Don't think I'm sticking my nose in where
it in't wanted, but I'd like you to tell me some'at straight.
I don't mean to be offensive. You needn't answer if you
don't want to.'

'I suppose I can guess what it's about.'

Vanessa leaned against the stone parapet, coat collar
turned up, her gloved hands thrust for warmth inside her
pockets. The afternoon light was beginning to fade a little,
and a misty sunset turned the surface of the Severn into a
shivering pewter ribbon.

'You're curious about Roland, aren't you. You wonder
why I won't be drawn into talking about him. Well . . . I
do have a reason.'

'If you've got a reason, fair enough. I won't say any more.' Jim went to turn and walk on.

'No, Jim, I think you *ought* to know—' She stayed where she was, her head bowed; and he thought for a minute that was all she was going to say, until she glanced at him from beneath the rim of her brown felt hat and continued, hesitantly, 'You see, it's one of those situations that's difficult to talk about, and if I've never told you it's because . . . well, because it's my private life and nothing to do with anyone else. But if you want the truth . . . if you want it straight . . . the fact is my husband and I are legally separated.'

She saw the line between his brows deepen into a frown, but a frown of concern, not censure. 'You're *separated*—?'

'Yes.'

'Good God. How long has this happened, then?'

'We started living apart twelve months ago.'

Jim shook his head; and then with a laugh of disbelief he said, 'I thought he was a commercial traveller, some'at that took him round the country.'

'That's what I hoped you'd think. I'm sorry for the deception, but it seemed the best way of killing curiosity . . . I mean, young women no longer living with their husbands arouse a certain amount of opprobrium, and not everybody might understand my position.'

'By "everybody" I suppose that includes me an' all,' he said, as though that had hurt him. 'Surely to God, Vanessa, you know me well enough by now to know I'd never pass judgement wi'out cause. What d' you think I'd do – turf you out your job because you'd been deserted?'

She made a helpless gesture. 'No—'

'Why dain't you tell me, then?' he persisted.

She looked away across the river. On the opposite bank a young couple were walking among the naked willows, their heads together, arms entwined, engrossed in each other; and watching them she said after a moment, 'There didn't seem much point. Besides, if Frank or Tony Heron knew I was living alone—'

'And you think I'd run blabbing your business to a pair like that – some'at told me in confidence? God above, you ain't got much opinion o' me, have you.' The hurt in his voice hardened to an edge of anger. 'Don't you *trust* me at all?'

Vanessa met his eyes. She wished she could say yes; but would it be the truth, she asked herself. Larret Fitzgerald had taught her the folly of trusting a man, and emotional scars took a long while to heal.

'Trust has to be earned, Jim,' she said finally, 'and sadly I've got reason *not* to trust.'

'The reason being your husband.'

She didn't answer that.

The anger faded again, and his expression became more sombre. 'There's rotten apples in every barrel, Vanessa . . . the only trouble is, picking 'em out. You mustn't think just because you chose a bad 'un, the rest of us are all the same. We ain't.'

'I'm sure you're right.' She tried to sound as though it didn't matter, except the words somehow caught in her throat and came out husky.

Jim's gaze moved over her face, from her eyes to her mouth.

'Why is it always the best as gets the worse luck, eh,' he said quietly. 'I'll tell you some'at, I reckon Roland Antrobus needs his blasted head examined, chucking away a wench as wonderful as you.'

285

It was one of those seemingly unimportant statements that had the power to betray far more than was actually said, and it marked a shift in the balance of their relationship. This was not an employer talking to his secretary, but a man talking to a woman he admired, and Vanessa acknowledged the fact even as she felt herself redden at the compliment.

'But I'm not wonderful—' she began awkwardly, turning her head away so that he wouldn't see her quick confusion.

'Ah, but you are. As wonderful to be with as you are to look at. And there's not a man as wouldn't feel proud to be seen in your company.'

He went to say something else, hesitated, then added clumsily, 'Why d'you think I'm wearing a decent suit today – why d'you think I went and bought the Humber.'

Her confusion grew; and for a moment she didn't know how to respond. Then finding her tongue, she said in astonishment, 'You bought the car on *my* account—?'

'As good as. You made my mind up, any rate.'

'But I thought – I *presumed* – it was all in aid of your business in Bridgnorth.'

He managed a bleak smile. 'Now come on, would I get myself togged up to go traipsing round a barn full o' rusty machinery?'

Resting his elbows on the parapet beside her, he fixed his brooding gaze on the river.

'I in't much use at talking about things like feelings, Vanessa,' he went on again suddenly, 'but there's some'at personal I want to say, and I'm sorry if it makes you feel uncomfortable. That night I met you at the station, I . . . well, I felt so damned ashamed o' myself. There was me in my dirty old working clothes, and you the lady authoress just off the train from London, looking so – oh, I don't know, so lovely and smart. Tell the truth, I hivered wi' myself whether to stop in the lorry and let you go on. But I couldn't. It was raining, and you were all on your own, wi' nobody meeting you—'

'I was glad you were there,' Vanessa said softly; and she wanted to touch his arm, as if to reassure him. 'I couldn't give a hoot about your clothes or what you were driving. The only thing that mattered that night was your kindness.'

'Aye, well—' He glanced at her across his shoulder, the soft blue-grey light reflected off the water shadowing his eyes beneath the motoring cap. 'It riled me to think I'd let you down so bad. I promised myself, next chance I had to take you anywhere I was going to do things properly.'

She held his gaze. After a moment she said, 'You're a strange man, do you know that, Jim. You can be so arrogant, and yet so humble. I wonder if I'll ever understand you.'

'You'd have some fun trying. Peggy always reckons—' He corrected himself quickly. 'Peggy used to reckon she never understood me, either. She always said I chopped and changed too much.'

Whenever he spoke about his dead wife Vanessa sensed how deeply he must have loved her. She wondered whether this conversation they were having didn't perhaps spring from his loneliness. It wasn't unusual for someone recently bereaved to try and staunch their grief with other company, nor was it unnatural. Love didn't die at death. The closer two people had been in life, the greater the need to fill the void when one had gone, and the more necessary for that left-over love to find some other means of expressing itself.

Jim was attracted to her, that much seemed obvious. And he clearly admired her. The fact that he felt he didn't measure up to her own standards was touching rather than embarrassing. Why then, Vanessa asked herself, did she feel a reluctance to step into the role of the palliative stop-gap, acting as a pain-killer to help him through his grief?

As though he felt he had said too much too openly, he was quiet afterwards. They wandered together across the bridge to the further bank, where the windows of riverside houses were showing a cheerful glow of warmth against the gathering dusk; and then after a stroll they wandered back again to the car.

On the journey home Vanessa kept the conversation casual, chatting about Pembrokeshire and her father's family and her holiday at Amroth the year before last – without mentioning Larret, of course – and how she was planning on taking her mother there later this summer.

Jim seemed surprisingly interested to hear about her father's poetry. He admitted he enjoyed poetry himself – Housman's *A Shropshire Lad* was his favourite – and when Vanessa asked him if he'd read Yeats at all and he said yes, but not much, she insisted he must borrow her copy of *The Lake Isle of Innisfree* which she'd purchased in London. This gentler, more romantically sensitive side of his nature came as a pleasant revelation (he'd previously told her he didn't read a lot; she wondered why) until, yet again, she remembered the scene in the garden at 'Mayville'. Discovering the real Jim Brockhouse was a little like peeling away the layers of an onion.

It was dark by the time they reached Paget Road. This

time she invited him in. She'd already laid the fire, and while it was burning through and she made them a pot of tea, Jim roamed round the sitting room examining her books and pictures, picking ornaments up and putting them back, almost as though he needed to establish physical contact with the things surrounding her.

She brought in the tray and placed it on the sofa table.

'Decent little place you've got,' he commented approvingly, sitting down. 'What I call comfy. You'll have to pop over and see my house one day . . . one Sunday mebbe, when Mary and her husband are visiting.'

'I'd like to.' Vanessa kicked off her shoes and curled herself up on the hearth rug in front of the fire.

They hadn't mentioned Roland since Bewdley; but Jim was obviously still a little curious because he asked, leaning forward for his cup, 'Did you live here wi' your husband?'

She shook her head. 'We had a house along Compton Road. As a matter of fact you know it. You were there on one occasion.'

'I was—?' He gave her a look of startled surprise.

'Mm, the first time I ever saw you. You'd come to take away some odds and ends for us.'

'Good God. When was this, then?'

She had to think. 'About eighteen months ago. Billy was with you.'

'And you actually spoke to me?'

'Yes. You were awfully rude, you completely ignored me.'

'I was probably half-dead on my feet, what wi' running the business and living at the hospital. But – surely then, you must've recognised me the day you come to the yard about the job?'

'Oh, I knew it was you,' Vanessa said, answering his confusion with a little smile. 'We'd already met again. The second time was The Copper Kettle tea-room – you were sitting with Mary at a neighbouring table and you helped me pick my things up when I knocked my handbag over. Don't you remember that?'

Jim creased his forehead, looking aimlessly about the room. 'Tell the truth, I don't,' he admitted after a moment. 'It must've been around the time Peggy was – Peggy was worsening.'

'Well, I guessed you'd forgotten all about me, so I never mentioned it. Besides, as I recall, your manner when you interviewed me wasn't – how shall I say – conducive to such reminders?' Her voice held just a hint of teasing. 'In fact I had every intention of telling you what to do with your job, except—'

She paused; no, better not say it, she thought. Some things were too private. Jim might be embarrassed.

'Except what—?' he prompted.

'Oh, nothing. But I must confess, I'm pleased I changed my mind.'

'I'm pleased an' all.'

He finished his tea and got up reluctantly, with another glance about as though imprinting on his mind this place and everything in it. When she went to follow, he put out a hand and helped her to her feet; and standing like that face to face in the firelight they looked at one another, her hand still held in his.

At that instant Vanessa had the strongest feeling he wanted to kiss her. The impression was so vivid that when he released her, she immediately felt a sense of regret that he hadn't found the courage. If he'd done so, she knew she would have responded.

'I'd best go,' he said quietly.

'OK. And Jim . . . thanks for today.'

'It was my pleasure.'

He turned to get his cap. After an awkward moment he went on, not looking at her, 'Mebbe we can do the same another time, if you'd fancy it. I thought . . . I thought you might care to go to the theatre wi' me, some'at like that. Just for a change. We're both on our own, and . . . and to be honest, I'd welcome a bit o' company, Vanessa.'

Was that his loneliness talking again, she asked herself. Was it *her* company he wanted; or just any woman's. And why did it matter so much she should suddenly care . . .

24

There was a lozenge-shaped mirror hanging on a chrome frame over the fireplace in the Parrishes' sitting room, and reflected in it, one of those old-fashioned oleographs depicting a coach-and-horses inn scene. It was what Michael Wright always thought of as the Chocolate Box school of art – pretty, but banal.

Seeing their guest examine it, Ernest Parrish said in a patronising sort of way, 'Been in the family for years, that painting has. Worth a bob or two, young man, I'm telling you. It's an original, of course.'

'Oh, it's original certainly,' Michael tactfully agreed. He caught Sybil's eye. She had warned him of her father's fondness for this particular picture, and he was loth to cause offence by pointing out it was only a print got up in imitation of an oil painting. 'After the style of Morland, I'd say, sir.'

His deference went some way towards disarming Mr Parrish. When his wife announced last week (announced, not asked, mind) that Sybil's new friend was being invited to tea with them this Saturday, he'd jibbed a bit. The fellow was an artist; and Mr Parrish didn't approve of artists, not altogether. Not when they drew disgusting things like that naked whatever it was Sybil had hung in her bedroom.

'Morland, eh.' He'd never heard of Morland, but he

would remember the name for future. 'Yes – well spotted, young man. Just thought I'd test you out, that's all.'

He glanced at his wife. He didn't know what had come over Florence lately, she was looking a good ten years younger. The nervous little mannerisms which used to annoy him so much were less in evidence, and these days she was ready to put a point of view even if it disagreed with his own; which discomfited him.

She returned his glance, smiling as though she knew very well he was bluffing. Then patting the newly-permed waves of her silver-gilt hair, she turned to their guest and said, 'I was reading an article recently about paintings – something called Surrealism, is it? It sounded very interesting.'

That was another thing he found discomfiting, she'd started coming out with these extraordinary statements. Only last month they'd had the captain of the golf club here to dinner and Florence had monopolised the conversation prattling about toby jugs – toby jugs! – just because he'd mentioned the captain had an interest in collecting the damned things.

'Charming lady wife of yours,' the captain remarked next time they'd met. 'You want to try and persuade her to join the golf club, old chap.'

And now she was at it again, talking a lot of arty-tarty twaddle on a subject of which she knew nothing except what she'd read about.

Mr Parrish excused himself and went up to the bathroom.

When he came back down again they were discussing Vanessa.

'Yes, the book's entitled *Masks and Faces*. It's being published in July,' Mrs Parrish was saying, and her husband had to grit his teeth at the pride in her voice. She was for ever going on and on about that blasted book. Next thing, she'd be telling everybody about Vanessa's father being some cloth-cap upstart who scribbled poetry.

'Any sign of Roland Antrobus, d'you know?' he interrupted her truculently to ask Michael. 'I hear through the grapevine he could be selling the Gallery.'

'As a matter of fact, the sale's about to go through, I believe, sir,' Michael answered, with a civility pointing up the other's ill manner. 'I spoke to Roland – to Mr Antrobus I mean, a couple of weeks ago—'

'So the fellow's back in the country, is he.'

'Just briefly. He's had to return to his job in Berlin—'

'What job in Berlin?'

'I . . . gather he's working in a film studio, sir.'

Mr Parrish's face darkened. 'It's about damn' time he stopped this German nonsense and knuckled down to his responsibilities. All said and done, he's still married to my stepdaughter—'

'Ernest, dear – please?' his wife came in. 'I'm sure our guest isn't interested in hearing the family's business.'

'Yes, Daddy, do shut up,' Sybil added sweetly. 'If Roland wants to live abroad that's up to him. Vanessa couldn't care less what he does.'

'She couldn't care less about anything, that one!'

Grumbling, Mr Parrish gave the fire a poke and sat down. It was Vanessa's pernicious meddling that had undermined his own authority, he thought bitterly. 'Wretched girl, she's for ever causing trouble for people. I hope you've told this young man how she ruined your engagement?'

The room went suddenly silent.

Sybil turned red and shot him an upset, angry look before glancing at Michael, who'd found something interesting to study on the ceiling.

Sensing he might have said the wrong thing, Ernest Parrish began to bluster.

'Well—? You *have* told the young man, haven't you, our Sybil? You're both seeing so much of one another I'd have thought it was only natural he'd need to know you'd been engaged—'

'Oh for heaven's sake, Ernest, be quiet!' his wife said sharply. 'If wits were leather you wouldn't have enough to make a pair of spats for a gnat!'

She offered Michael a little gesture of apology. 'Yes, Sybil *was* engaged,' she told him, 'but it was only for a very short time, and I'm sure she'll prefer to explain the details to you herself. Won't you, dear?'

Sybil compressed her lips and glared at her father, not trusting herself to respond.

Michael came to the rescue.

'Sybil's so beautiful, I'm surprised she hasn't been engaged dozens of times,' he said gallantly, passing off his host's indiscretion with admirable tact. 'It's a ripping stroke of luck for me she's still unspoken for, or I'd probably never have met her.'

His chivalry saved the moment. Mrs Parrish could have hugged him.

'But darling, why get so upset about it – we've all got a few hidden skeletons,' he comforted Sybil later that evening. 'I'm sure your father didn't intend to embarrass you like that.'

'Well he did, horribly,' she said, snuffling miserably into her handkerchief. 'And I'll never forgive him, not as long as I live. He thinks he can say whatever he likes . . .'

'Now come on, sweetie—' Michael took her quivering chin in his hand and tilted her face, kissing the tears away. Round them the crowded bar of a pub on a Saturday night blared with conversation, and nobody took much notice of two young lovers kissing in a corner. 'He knows jolly well he's in the doghouse. And anyway, what does it matter? You surely can't think I'd get a sudden attack of cold feet about us, just because some idiot fiancé threw you over?'

Sybil gave a tremulous sniff. 'I hope not.'

'You'd better be sure of it!' He slipped his arm round her waist and kissed her again, on the tip of the nose. 'Let me tell you, I know what it feels like. The same thing happened to me, very nearly.'

'What—? *You've* been engaged too?' The jealousy was as swift and sharp as a physical pain. Sybil had fallen in love with Michael very quickly, and her emotions were still at the vulnerable stage. Any mention of attachment to another girl was bound to be wounding. 'What happened? Who was she? Do I know her?' The questions fell over themselves.

'What happened—?' He shrugged. 'It didn't work, is what happened. The lady in question found somebody less callow to amuse her. And yes, my darling, as a matter of fact you do know her.'

She ran through a list of all his friends. Michael was a popular young man with lots of acquaintances, the sort of acquaintances always throwing dizzy parties, and in the four months she'd known him she'd met quite a number of them.

Only one she'd never felt easy about; and that was

Delia, the languidly exotic beauty from that first night at the Gallery.

'Delia . . . it must have been Delia,' she said after a moment in a toneless voice. 'The way the two of you behave when you're together . . . it could only be her.'

'Oh, but I never actually sank to my knees and *proposed*,' he answered lightly, trying to jolly her along with one of his lopsided smiles. 'I had a bit of a thing about her, that's all. Like you had with your Larry Fitzwhatsit.'

Sybil pressed her hand to her mouth and gave a convulsive little sob. 'I think you've still got a thing about her . . . you're always hanging round each other, don't you think I haven't noticed?'

The grin slipped a fraction. 'Darling, we happen to work together, we share the same friends, I can hardly ignore her. OK, I may not be in love any more, but I haven't stopped liking her—'

'That's pretty obvious!'

'—as a person, as a colleague, and yes I admit it, a very attractive woman,' Michael persisted doggedly. 'I was hurt at the time, after she gave me the old heave-ho, but broken hearts don't bleed for ever. Anyway, I don't believe in broken hearts, only bruised pride. And that doesn't last for ever either, because if one's lucky, someone else comes along who's a million times more marvellous – like you.'

He tried to give Sybil a reassuring hug and take the handkerchief to dab her eyes; but she shoved him away, saying wretchedly, 'You make me feel so . . . so second best. I wish you'd told me right at the start about you and Delia.'

'Why? You didn't tell me about you and Larry.'

'That's different. I don't see him. I'm not with him every day, like you and her. Besides, I *hate* him.'

'No, sweetie, you don't really. You hate the shabby way he treated you, perhaps, and the pain and distress he caused, but the chap himself – he's much too worthless to waste anything as strong as hatred on.'

Michael drew her into his arms and held her until the hiccuping sobs had gradually quietened. He was sensitive enough to guess how badly Sybil had been made to suffer. The first time he'd met her she had been unnecessarily aggressive, as though on the defensive. And since he'd come to know her, and feel deeply about her, there'd often been times when he'd read between the lines of something she said, or some allusion she'd made.

She was sweet and lovely and amusing and intelligent. Whatever had happened in her past, he vowed he'd make it up to her for all that heartache.

'Feeling better now, angel?' he murmured after a while, his mouth against the smooth wing of her hair. Her head was bowed on its slender neck, her face averted in case people in the pub started staring at her before she'd composed herself. 'Can I get you another drink – a small brandy or something?'

There was a nod. She took her Woodbines from her handbag, cupping his hand with her own for a light; then she said with a little shivery smile, 'Thanks . . . a brandy 'ld be nice.'

While he was at the counter, she went outside to the Ladies to powder her nose and repair her lipstick. In the dimness of the single bulb, her face in the black-specked mirror stared at her heavy-eyed and pale through the cigarette smoke; and for an instant, like some ghost returning to haunt her, it became a memory of that other mirror-face Sybil used to see before her breakdown.

She thrust the image away, exorcising its horror, and settling her fox-fur round her shoulders went back into the bar.

What she could do with was cheering up, she thought. Something to get her out of herself. Something to make her sparkle. Today had been such a catastrophe so far . . . and men liked girls who were fun.

So when Michael asked her later, 'What would you like to do for the rest of the evening?' she'd responded a little more brightly, 'Why don't we go to the Palais de Danse? I promised I'd teach you to tango.'

Michael had learned the rudiments of dancing from his sister and her friends. His sister Eunice was seven years older than he was, a gap which had never particularly endeared them to one another, and like most little brothers he'd been a bit of an obnoxious pest. But Eunice and her chums had got their own back. Each time he'd jeered at them practising the shoulder-shaking Shimmy in the drawing room at home at Codsall, his punishment was the humiliation (for a twelve-year-old) of partnering these fragrant-smelling Misses in something equally ridiculous like the Turkey Trot or Bunny Hug.

By the time he'd grown up enough to appreciate the social advantages of dancing, Eunice was married, and he'd had to wait until his student days at art college before he managed to become proficient.

Michael had been to the Palais, in Temple Street, a few times before with Sybil but the spot wasn't one of their regular venues. Despite her love of what was known as 'crush dancing', he thought she always seemed a little apprehensive whenever they came here. Tonight there was a crowd on the floor when they arrived just after half past nine, and waiting for the band to stop so they could get inside, he noticed her again, nervously scanning the faces as if she were looking for someone.

'Anything wrong, darling?'

'No.' She gave him a dazzling smile. 'Nothing wrong.'

After the freshness of the night, the atmosphere in here was like an oven. Cigarette smoke hung in layers below the ceiling, undulating slowly with the movement of the rainbow-ball whose lights slid over the swaying couples in kaleidoscope patterns of shimmering colour. The air held a close, almost intimate smell of warm bodies and scent.

Having missed one dance while they found themselves a table, Michael and Sybil took to the floor for the following, a Hesitation Waltz. They made a stunningly attractive couple, he with his fair-haired English film-star looks, she so alluringly slender and pretty, and moved so well together they were soon creating attention.

The next dance was a Tango – the one Michael wasn't too sure of – so there was much fun sliding and lunging and swooping while Sybil taught him the steps on the edge of the floor – an exercise so energetic that, breathless with laughter, they had to sit out to recover before getting up again for an 'Excuse Me', where everyone changed partners.

Dancing with her cheek against his shoulder, she didn't see who had asked for the first exchange until Michael released her into the arms of a man with brilliantined hair and a narrow, wolfish face.

The instant she recognised that face Sybil felt her heart freeze to ice inside her. With a little cry of revulsion she struggled to push him away, calling out after Michael; but Michael had already been swallowed by the crush, and the band music drowned her.

'Well, well, what a surprise, eh.' Alan Slater read the shock in her eyes and smirked unpleasantly. 'Who's the new playmate, Sybil? I ain't seen 'im round 'ere before.'

This was the stuff of her nightmares. She'd heard Slater had left Wolverhampton; but the fear of him still clung to her mind, like dirt to a blanket. She had never been able to shake off its taint.

'I want a little talk wi' you—' His fingers dug into her flesh. Gripping her against him he guided her forcefully backwards across the floor, his hateful sinewy body glued to her breasts and hips in a parody of dancing. 'You went and walked out on me. Nobody treats me like that. Thought you'd wipe me off your shoes, did you?'

'Let go – you're hurting me—!' Sybil squirmed to try and free herself, searching frantically about for Michael.

'Here, watch where you'm sticking your elbow,' somebody protested. 'This ain't a ruddy Charleston.'

'Sorry, mate, her's 'ad too much to drink,' Slater flung back across his shoulder, changing direction through the press of bodies; and she realised with mounting panic he was steering her towards the door.

'For God's sake let me *go*, will you – get away from me!' She twisted her wrist out of his hand and started hitting him. 'I've got nothing to say to you – just leave me alone!'

'You'm coming outside wi' me. I reckon you owe me some explanations.' His mouth was against her ear, his strength controlling her, bruising her. He was enjoying this; she could tell as much from his voice and the look in his eyes, and the fact that her dismay was giving him pleasure deepened her fear.

Incredibly, the couples surrounding them ignored her behaviour. Lovers often quarrelled on dance floors. Girls sometimes got a little bit drunk. Nobody seemed to realise there was anything wrong here.

Then she saw Michael. For a moment a gap opened and she saw him, just a few yards away, dancing with a dark-haired woman. She shouted his name, waving desperately; and not understanding, he grinned and waved back at her.

'Cut that out,' Alan Slater said savagely. 'What's the matter, ain't I good enough any more? You weren't so bloody choosy last time I touched you.'

'Don't flatter yourself – I was scraping the gutter to let *you* touch me,' she threw in his face. 'Now get away from me, you bastard, before I scream the roof down—'

'You do that, Sybil, and you'll be meeting me again, I warn you. And next time it wo' be somewhere nice and public neither.' The threat in his words was explicit, suggesting something dark and stealthy and obscenely violent. She felt her flesh crawl.

They were off the floor now. Behind them, a swing-door led into the dance hall's vestibule. She'd be all right, Sybil told herself. The band would stop in a minute. Slater couldn't hurt her. There was always someone out here – the manager, people leaving their coats, people taking a breather. Slater couldn't hurt her . . .

But then what. After tonight – then what. He'd still be in the town, biding his chance, watching her; waiting. He'd always promised she couldn't get rid of him, and the spectre of that promise had never gone away however many nursing homes and doctors with their pills had tried to make it so.

Out of the noise of the hall, the vestibule seemed cool and quiet. The moment they were through the door she cried out for help and started pummelling him with her defenceless fists – and in the same moment somebody behind them said angrily, 'What's going on? What the blazes d'you think you're doing?' and it was Michael.

Thank God – it was Michael.

'You bloody stay out o' this,' snarled Slater. 'It ain't none o' your business.'

'It's very much my business.' Michael glanced from him to the manager, standing in evening dress keeping an eye on what was happening. He raised a hand for assistance; and as the manager began moving towards them Slater made a sudden snatch at Sybil, grabbing her back again.

She let out a scream.

'That's enough o' that – now break it up!' The manager broke into a run. Two more men appeared from the office behind him. Michael caught Sybil's arm and she felt the seam of her sleeve rip as Slater fought to hang on to her.

She screamed again, a little hysterically.

'Let go of her, you drunken idiot, what the hell's the matter with you?' Michael shouted furiously.

'Her's coming wi' me—'

'She's not.'

'Her's my — woman.'

'Here you lot, sort this out somewhere else,' interjected the manager. 'Any more trouble, I'm calling the police. Bert – Harry—' He motioned his head to the other two with him. 'Give 'em their coats and get bloody shot of 'em.'

'What d'you mean, she's *your* woman?' Michael demanded, ignoring this. 'Sybil's been with me the last couple of months – what the devil are you insinuating?'

'Her's mine,' Slater said again, in a sinister tone, 'and her's coming wi' me, so get your 'ands off her afore I smash your — face in.'

While this was going on Sybil had been struggling and crying at Slater to release her. Now she began striking at him, her aim hampered by Michael, still holding on tight to her. As the manager made to intervene, Slater suddenly lashed out with his fist and caught Michael a blow which knocked him off balance.

'Right – that's it. I've warned you. Now I'm getting the police. Harry – take care o' things here.' The manager hauled Sybil away and pushed her towards the swing-door before running down the stairs into the street. The man named Harry, a beefy young chap, grabbed Slater by the collar, but got an elbow in the stomach for his trouble as the other fought him off and lunged for Michael again.

They closed together in a wrestling hold, then broke apart, exchanging a flurry of punches.

'Stop him – oh, somebody stop him!' Sybil cried out, terrified that Michael was going to get injured. 'Oh God, he'll kill him!'

'I'll bloody kill 'im all right—' Slater side-stepped Michael's knuckles. Ducking into him he caught him round the waist, sending both of them crashing backwards through the swing-door on to the dance floor.

The 'Excuse Me' was just ending, its final bars of music drowned by the squeals of women as couples nearest the door scattered out of the way.

Michael was fighting to defend himself. He'd done some boxing at school, but this wasn't a clean scrap, it was the sort of vicious scrimmage Slater had learned on the backstreets of Balsall Heath.

They closed together again.

Then somebody shouted, 'Watch out, he's got a knife—!' and a moment later Michael was staggering back, a hand clutched to his shoulder, the blood already beginning to seep between his fingers.

The squeals turned into frightened screams.

Pandemonium broke out.

Slater confronted him, crouching like some beast about to spring, the narrow blade of the knife held forward, the rainbow shimmer of lights painting his face.

'Come on—' he sneered, beckoning, 'can't keep Sybil waiting. Come on, let's 'ave this finished.'

There was a movement behind. Slater half-turned, but not fast enough, as the man named Harry swung up a chair and cracked him across the side of the head – and as he went reeling Michael was after him, wresting the knife away.

The sight of her darling, bruised and bleeding, grappling on the floor with Slater was the last thing Sybil saw before she fainted.

25

'Sybil – a sense of guilt is about the most useless emotion anyone can have,' Vanessa said firmly. The two of them had just come away from the Royal Hospital, where Michael had been kept in overnight for observation – his shoulder wound was more serious than had first been thought, and he'd needed quite a number of stitches. 'For heaven's sake, you didn't ask to be assaulted. What was Michael supposed to do – stand by and watch that ghastly man shanghai you off the dance floor?'

'But if we hadn't have gone to the Palais it wouldn't have happened,' repeated Sybil mournfully.

'You *were* there. It *did* happen. From what we've heard, Slater was waiting for you. And now he's safely where he deserves to be, locked away inside a police cell.'

Vanessa held on to her hat. They were taking a short cut through St George's churchyard and the March wind gusting between the tombstones sent little eddies of dead leaves swirling into the air.

'Look—' she began again more patiently, tucking her arm through her half-sister's, 'you weren't to know he'd be at the Palais. You thought he'd moved to Birmingham – that's what you said in your statement.'

'Jack Holroyd told Gloria he had.' And Gloria had passed it on to Sybil when they'd bumped into each other one day outside Rigby's in Worcester Street, where Sybil was working now. 'Otherwise I'd have been too blinkin' scared to go *anywhere*. You don't know what Slater was like, Vee. He was . . . oh, he was loathsome. I must've been out of my senses ever to get involved with him.'

He certainly sounded a pretty nasty type, Vanessa thought. Just the sort who would prey on vulnerable, giddy young girls; a wolf in lounge lizard's clothing. When she and her mother had gone with Sybil to the station this morning, they'd been told the police were after him in any case for working as a 'fence' for stolen property, a crime for which he'd apparently served a sentence in prison already.

'Well let's jolly well hope you've heard the last of him,' she said. 'And darling, do try and remember, it's pointless dwelling on something that's too late to alter. I know I sound like a Dutch aunt, but remorse is good for one thing only, making sure you don't repeat the same error twice. I've learned that lesson myself. So just do as Michael says and stop blaming yourself. It wasn't your fault – OK?'

Sybil caught her half-sister's eye and managed a feeble 'OK.' Since last night she must have died a thousand deaths, terrified of losing Michael's respect once she admitted she'd been involved with Alan Slater. What decent chap would want to associate himself with a girl who'd shared her favours with a piece of dross like that? There were some things she could never reveal to anyone, some things so revolting she still refused to let herself remember them; but what she *had* confessed at the hospital just now was near enough the truth, so far as it went.

And because Michael was so wonderfully loyal and

understanding, he'd gone straight to the heart of the truth when he'd said, 'Poor little angel, you must have been hideously unhappy. You'd been hurt and you wanted distraction, that's all it was – Slater hooked you on the rebound.'

Everything was for a purpose . . . that's what Vanessa believed. If things didn't happen in the way they did, for the reason they did, and at the time they did, the outcome would be a different story altogether. Nothing was random. If Sybil had never met Larret Fitzgerald, he wouldn't have jilted her. And if he hadn't, she wouldn't have got herself involved with Slater. And if *that* hadn't happened, then perhaps . . . only perhaps . . . she would never have met Michael.

It was all part of a sequence; all part of a chain of cause and effect.

'Maybe you're right, Vee,' she said after a moment. 'Maybe I shouldn't blame myself too much. It *is* a waste of time having regrets, and anyway I burned my bridges when I . . . well, you know. When I got a bit desperate and tried to end it all.'

Distracted by a child's sudden cry, Sybil loosed her half-sister's arm in time to stop a hoop which was bowling along in the wind towards them, pursued by a little boy in a blue and white sailor-suit.

Returning his toy to him, she watched him run back along the churchyard path to his parents; and then changing the subject she continued in a more forcedly cheerful manner, 'I say, wasn't it an absolute fluke, Mother already knowing Michael's mother – fancy them being at school together!'

It seemed Florence Parrish and Evelyn Wright had both attended All Saints Girls' School years before. The two had grown up in the same neighbourhood – Florence in Gordon Street and Evelyn in Steelhouse Lane; and despite a difference in age they'd belonged to the same group of chums. When Evelyn left All Saints and went away to train as a teacher, the friendship was broken; though later on they'd occasionally run into one another at the central lending library, where Florence had worked until her first marriage.

After that, they had lost contact.

Neither could have foreseen they would meet again in quite such dramatic circumstances. The fact that both had been at the hospital today seemed one of those coincidences which Fate had intended should happen; and their pleasure on recognising each other in the waiting room was nothing compared to their astonishment when they discovered both of them were there to visit the very same patient.

'It certainly broke the ice,' agreed Vanessa. 'And let's face it, you won't feel half so nervous about meeting Michael's family now Mother's been invited as well.'

She took Sybil's arm again; and as they went out of the churchyard into St George's Parade she added affectionately, 'You really do love him an awful lot, don't you, darling.'

Sybil bit her lip. 'Am I that transparent?'

'You couldn't hide it if you tried. Everything about you lights up when you're together. Anyway, it's high time you had some happiness. After the last experience . . . well, I hope it all turns out a dream.'

'So do I. God, you don't know!'

'I rather think I do. And I'm positive it will – Michael's your Mr Right.' It wasn't a very original pun but it made Sybil laugh.

'Oh Vee, you're such a brick,' she said with a little hug. 'If there's one thing I wish just as much, it's that you'll find somebody, too . . . somebody handsome and really romantic who'll come and sweep you off your feet, because you deserve a second chance far more than I do. It seems so beastly unfair you've been left all by yourself.'

Unfair? Well, perhaps. Vanessa had never wanted her marriage to Roland to fail; but it had. And now she was caught up in a sort of limbo-life between the devil of moral convention and the deep blue sea of her innermost desires.

She longed to be loved again; longed for the companionship and commitment of love as well as its physical expression. No man had really kissed her since Larret Fitzgerald, no man had held her in his arms and made her feel desirable and needed. Larret had roused her sexually from the Sleeping Beauty prison of her virginity, tuned her responses to a quivering pitch of pleasure every time they came together; and starved of its fulfilment, her healthy young body was now betraying itself with the honey-sweet ache of frustration which only another man could satisfy.

She dreamed of him, this man. He came to her at night; and in the most secret, locked and guarded part of her unconscious mind Vanessa recognised him. She knew the taste of his mouth and the smell of his skin. She knew the brooding intensity of his gaze as he made love to her. And each time, just as she surrendered herself to his urgent possession, the sound of her own soft moaning wakened her and she would lie, sightless, seeing his face still imprinted on the anonymous darkness.

She was falling in love with this man of her dreams. She didn't want to, but she couldn't stop herself. It wasn't the same kind of falling in love she'd known with Larret: this was like the deep, dark undertow of a river drawing her down into the fathomless depths of her own emotions, and she was drowning in it.

He had a name, of course.

It was Jim Brockhouse.

Bewildered by the sudden dichotomy of her feelings for her employer, Vanessa tried to suppress them. The Jim Brockhouse she worked for by day wasn't the powerful sexual image which had started possessing her dreamself at night. Yet often when they were together she'd realise she was staring at him, and find herself longing for him to look at her with the same hungry intensity her sleeping mind had fabricated.

Why—?

What was just as bewildering was the change in Jim himself. Since their visit to Bridgnorth five weeks ago, he had reverted to what Vanessa thought of as his 'Mr Hyde' persona. The friendly little chats and interest in her writing which had marked his cautious thawing, these had stopped. She could sense an awkwardness now whenever he talked to her, a wary reluctance to appear too familiar, as though he'd regretted lowering his guard that day in Bridgnorth and were trying to distance himself.

And yet he asked her out – that was the paradox. They had been twice to the Grand Theatre and once to the Hippodrome; and each time he had been very proper and polite with her, not cold, not unfriendly, a model escort. But impersonal.

He'd never entered her flat in Paget Road again. The invitation was there, but his answer was always some

312

tactful excuse which she read as refusal. That one brief moment of unguarded intimacy they'd shared, which had seemed to tremble on the edge of something more tenderly physical, was clearly not to be repeated.

Vanessa wondered how much this ambivalence in his attitude was to do with the fact that she was still a married woman. Jim Brockhouse had a good many old-fashioned values. It was one of the things for which she respected him. He was also perceptive. He was lonely enough in his own life to understand her predicament, and to offer her the kind of social companionship which didn't breach conventions.

But it was a sterile kindness. Someone to sit near. Someone to talk to. Someone to pass a few hours' entertainment with. There was no real warmth or contact. If she brushed against him, he moved away. If she smiled, he didn't seem to notice. He made her feel what, doubtless, she was to him, just a substitute for his dead young wife.

And that hurt.

She knew how much he missed his wife. The anniversary of Peggy's death was only a few weeks away – one of those sad dates together with wedding days and birthdays and Christmases that were painful reminders in a year of bereavement. Jim had mastered his heartbreak; but the wounds of memory stayed raw, and if he had turned to Vanessa to assuage some of the hurt, why should she feel aggrieved about it? Didn't it explain why he wanted her company, yet seemed so withdrawn from her?

The logical answer was yes.

Ah, but logic was a cold fish. It didn't allow of emotion; it had no easy answers to explain the power of his invasion into her dark, erotic dreams.

*　　*　　*

313

'Hello – Vanessa, is that you?'

The voice at the end of the telephone was distorted by a noisy crackle somewhere on the line.

'Hello? Hello, can you hear me? It's Roland—'

Roland. Good heavens. 'Yes, I can just about hear you,' Vanessa called back. 'Where are you?'

He said something.

'Sorry, didn't catch that. You'll have to shout a bit, it's a terrible connection.'

'Birmingham,' he repeated. 'The station. Oh, blast it – hang on a second, there's a train announcement going on—'

A tinny echo of noise joined the crackle; and then he suddenly came through again in the middle of a sentence, '—the house tomorrow. Will that be convenient?'

'Sorry, will what be—?'

'Will it be convenient to meet me at the house tomorrow?'

'Yes, but which—'

There was a sputter of interference. The line miraculously cleared. Vanessa could hear the frustration in her husband's voice as he said again, as though speaking to an idiot, 'I will be at "Mayville". In the afternoon. I want to talk to you. Can you meet me there.'

The maid who answered the bell was young and pert, the sort of pretty little thing who enjoyed a flirtation with doorstep salesmen. Vanessa wondered what had happened to Iris. She had liked Iris.

'Mrs Antrobus, is it, ma'am?' A pair of disarming blue eyes looked her up and down, missing nothing. 'Will you please to come inside, ma'am. Mr Antrobus is in the drawing room.'

314

There had been changes here at 'Mayville' in the months since Vanessa had moved from the house. The walls in the entrance hall had been papered in a heavy mustard-brown pattern which she thought very ugly, and the period cupboard inlaid with pewter and tortoiseshell which had belonged to Roland's parents had been replaced by an unpleasant cheap-looking cabinet.

She found Roland helping himself to a drink – not the first of the day, to judge from his slight unsteadiness as he turned to acknowledge her. She hadn't seen him for – how long, almost a year, was it? – and the change in him was immediately noticeable. He had always been on the fleshy side; now he was running to fat, his belly straining against his trouser-band, and his features puffy. With his cropped fair hair and pale eyes he could pass for a well-fed Prussian *Bürger*, an impression increased by the foreign cut of the olive-green suit he was wearing.

'So – here you are,' he said with forced joviality as the maid closed the door behind Vanessa.

'Yes, here I am, Roland.' She glanced round the drawing room. Whoever had papered the hall had been busy in here, too. 'How are you?'

'Fine . . . fine. Jus' a bit tired after the journey, that's all.' He raised his glass. 'Care t' join me in a little drinkie?'

'I won't, thanks.'

There was a pause.

Then both spoke together, Roland saying, 'You're lookin' extr'mely well, old girl', and Vanessa – 'You've put more weight on.'

And then another pause.

She tried again. 'I thought you were letting the house to tenants?' she said, noticing several more rather tasteless changes about the room.

'Had to get rid of 'em. 's one of the reasons I'm home, get things sorted out with the agent chappie.' Roland grimaced. 'Have you seen the ghastly mess they've made of the decoratin' – place looks like a tarts' palace. 's all got t' come off again, of course.'

'And what's happened to the furniture – your lovely antique pieces?'

'Sold 'em,' he said promptly.

'Oh, Roland, you haven't.'

'Uh-huh.'

'What – even your mother's satinwood writing table?'

At least he had the grace to look discomfited. Avoiding her eye he gulped at his drink before he answered, 'Wasn't much use t' me, old thing. Better it went t' auction with the rest of the stuff. Any case . . . I rather needed the money, don't y'know.'

'But *I* would have bought the table from you.' Vanessa had always loved that dainty little Regency piece. When she moved into Paget Road she'd wanted to take it with her, but Roland said no, it had too much personal sentimental value. 'You might at least have offered me first refusal.'

'And how would you 've paid for it, eh. Out of your allowance? Cock-eyed sort of a bargain that 'ld have been, expectin' me to stump up for somethin' I was damn' well sellin'.'

The spiteful way he stressed the word 'allowance' seemed to answer the question of why he'd wanted to see her in such a hurry. She went and sat down, leaning back in the chair and crossing her legs, and said, 'Is this what this summons to your presence is about, Roland – money?'

'No.'

'No?'

'Well . . . ind'rectly,' he agreed after a moment, looking into his glass. 'I thought we ought t' have a little talk, y'know, sort of mull things over.'

'Yes. Well – I'd like a divorce,' Vanessa told him candidly. 'I don't see the point of a separation if we're never likely to live together again, so we might as well go the whole hog and do things properly, wouldn't you agree?'

He made to answer; then stopped and blew out his cheeks as though her frankness had rather caught him on the hop.

'Look—' she went on in a not unfriendly way, trying to be reasonable, 'I can just about manage to support myself on what I'm earning. If we divorced I wouldn't expect you to pay me so much allowance – I mean, we'd have to agree on an amount through our solicitors, but I'm sure we could come to a mutually fair arrangement. And divorce would mean a clean break, Roland. You'd be free to marry Fräulein von Losch—'

'Always supposin' she *wants* to marry me,' he interrupted, 'which she doesn't.'

'She doesn't—?'

'No.'

He tilted his glass to his lips and emptied it. Wandering back to the cabinet he added, 'Tell you the truth, old girl, things aren't exac'ly workin' out the way I'd hoped for me and Lulu.'

'But I thought, after last time – well, I thought you'd managed to sort out all your problems.' Vanessa watched him take the decanter and help himself to another malt whisky. 'I know it's none of my business, but isn't that the reason why you've sold the Gallery – so you can settle down in Berlin together?'

'That was the gen'ral idea. Trouble is, Lulu refuses t' see eye t' eye about it. She's a Marxist, d'you know. Different way of thinkin'. Reckons what I'm tryin' t' do is saddle her with bourgeois respec'bil—' Roland paused, steadying himself against the cabinet before carefully trying the word again. '—Respectability. That's it. That's what she reckons I'm doin'. And she calls me a capit'list. Says 's a crime t' have money and not share it. Says if I really loved her I'd give it all t' the Movement. So I've given it all t' the Movement, every last penny-piece, and still she isn't satisfied.'

He made a drunkenly exaggerated gesture. He looked so foolish, so pathetic, that Vanessa couldn't help but feel a little sorry for him.

'You've still got the proceeds from the sale of the Gallery,' she said.

He shook his head.

'But Roland – for heaven's sake, you can't possibly have gone through the whole lot already!'

There was a shrug. 'Pretty well. Why d'you think I'm strapped for cash, old girl.'

'And – my allowance?'

'Ah, well that's what I want t' talk t' you about. Y'see . . . the way things are just now . . . the money situation, and the job – I had a job, y'know, in a film studio, 'til the blasted Brownshirts burned the place – and then Lulu . . . Lulu . . .'

Roland's self-control suddenly started to crumple. He looked away towards the window; then after a couple of seconds turned back again, his pudgy chin dimpling as he struggled to suppress his maudlin tears.

He gulped a mouthful of whisky.

In a voice clogged with emotion he went on, 'I don't know what t' do. Sometimes I think I'm goin' mad. God, I'm so tired . . . so tired of bein' unhappy . . . tired of feelin' homesick. I need t' find some peace. Oh, Van'ssa, Van'ssa . . . please, can't we patch things up, old girl?'

26

The midsummer sun poured down between the shifting leaves like thick, warm honey and lay across Vanessa's shoulders with the comforting touch of a lover's arm.

She closed her eyes.

The air was drenched with the gentle, healing peace which haunts all country churchyards, its tranquillity disturbed by no more than the murmurous song of birds and the sough of the soft breeze carried inland from the sea, bringing a tang of salt to the fragrance of thyme between the lichened headstones.

She emptied her mind; made it quiet to absorb this moment. Behind her lids the diffused light flooded her with golden stillness, like a blessing. She and her mother had come to Amroth two days ago on this pilgrimage of reconciliation. For Vanessa it was the fulfilment of a promise. For Florence Parrish, it was a journey back to the past which had been a long time in the making, a journey in search of the ghosts of her youth and the love which belonged to those long-ago summers.

It had taken courage to return. For over twenty years all Florence had had to cling to were a few treasured memories, as yellowed and faded as an old collodion photograph. She'd been afraid that if she came back she would find nothing left to remember.

But a miracle had happened. From the moment she'd

arrived in the pretty seaside village, Amroth restored her memories to her as bright and fresh as though the years had never touched them; and when she came to the house, to 'Min-y-don', something had been waiting, some loving presence in the place which gathered her to itself as if it said, 'welcome home, *cariad*'.

It was here too, in the churchyard. The same feeling . . . like a joy at the heart of the quietness, like a glowing serenity.

Vanessa opened her eyes. Against the sun-shadowed greens of trees and grass she could see the splash of colour of her mother's silk frock and the flowers on her father's grave. Getting from the wall where she'd been sitting, she wandered over to rejoin her.

Mrs Parrish looked up with a smile as her daughter approached.

'Do you suppose, dear—' she wondered, 'do you suppose the family would object very much if I suggested replacing your father's headstone? This one doesn't do his memory any justice.'

Vanessa glanced at the smooth slab, weathered by the seasons and sea winds to the soft pale grey of pewter.

'You think it's too plain?' she said.

'He deserves something better . . . a little bit different. After all, he was the Fisher Poet, and Amroth gets a lot of visitors these days, your Aunt Gwladys was telling me. People will want to come and see where he's buried.'

'Mm. I don't know. I like this stone. It's nice and simple.' In keeping with the churchyard; sturdy and somehow rather homely.

She put her hand against the warmth of the slate and knelt to face her mother. The flowers they'd brought half-hid the brief inscription below the date of her father's death.

'Why not suggest adding just another line or so here—' she ventured. 'It might be more tactful. You know how prickly the aunts are about family pride, we don't want to upset them.' She could guess the sort of thing her mother had in mind: an ornately middle-class white marble angel which would look grotesquely out of place among these unadorned Welsh graves.

Mrs Parrish wasn't sure about extra inscriptions. She'd wanted to make some gesture of love for her dead husband; an act of atonement for the years of separation. This little plot of earth was all she had until her own death laid her here beside him, and a new memorial had seemed the most obvious and fitting tribute.

She was still thinking about it when the sonorous chimes of St Elidyr's clock reminded them of the time.

'Come on, we're going to be late—' Jumping up, Vanessa helped her mother to her feet. 'We'll talk it over this evening, shall we. See what Uncle Wynford thinks. I suppose really it ought to be his decision since he's head of the family.'

They walked back to 'Min-y-don' along the steep little lane winding downward to the sea between high-hedged banks full of campion and foxgloves and a few late-flowering bluebells. A group of holidaymakers passed them, straggling up the hill pushing a wailing infant in a perambulator. The infant reminded Mrs Parrish of the time, years gone by, when she and Owen used to walk this way each Sunday with their newborn baby daughter; and once the group had passed, she remarked with a touch of sad nostalgia how proud Owen would have been had he lived to see

Vanessa follow in his footsteps to become a published writer.

'Though something here in my heart tells me he's proud of you wherever he is,' she added on reflection. And then with one of her sudden jumps of thought – 'What a shame *you* didn't have a baby, dear. D'you know, I agree with Aunt Gwladys, it would have stopped Roland from gadding off and leaving you if he'd had the responsibility of a family to think about.'

Roland's gadding off wasn't a subject Vanessa wished to be drawn on. The only thing her husband's behaviour had resolved was the awkwardness of being seen with Larret Fitzgerald in Tenby on her previous visit. Now that she'd become (in the eyes of her aunts and female cousins) that most hapless of creatures, a wife who had been deceived and abandoned, none of them at 'Min-y-don' had a good word to say for Roland.

His recent half-hearted effort at reconciliation, prompted by one of his periodic attacks of self-pity, had lasted only as long as it took him to raise the loan of five hundred pounds against the sale of their former married home. In any case, Vanessa wouldn't have had him back again. The union was dead; and ought decently to be buried, because as long as it still existed – even if only in name – she and Roland would be stuck in this push-me pull-you position of never being free of each other.

Now he'd gone slinking back to his Lulu; and with 'Mayville' on the market, the time had come to end things cleanly, she felt . . . except that for some perversely stubborn reason, Roland was refusing to co-operate. A letter had arrived this last month from his solicitors. It repeated what she'd half-expected, that in the event of her bringing an action for divorce, their client would seek to cross-petition on the grounds of her own admitted adultery.

As evening fell, the beach had started to empty. In the neat, clean boarding houses of Amroth children with sun-bleached hair and sun-browned limbs were going to bed, leaving their deserted sandcastles to the slow invasion of the rising tide. It was that time of day when the summer's light was just beginning to fade. The hills of the Gower peninsula already lay in purple shadows on the far side of Carmarthen Bay, even while the western skies still blazed with the fiery embers of sunset, staining the sand and the glittering sea the colour of wine.

The air was warm, and made pleasant for walking by a gentle breeze. People were out with their dogs; couples strolled along the front to the New Inn or the Amroth Arms. And Vanessa – Vanessa sat alone in the shadow of a breakwater thinking of Jim Brockhouse with a wistful sort of yearning, wishing he were here to share the beauty of the evening with her.

She missed him. There was no point denying the fact. She *missed* him. Since she'd come away on holiday he'd seldom been out of her thoughts, as though their separation had brought him that much closer. Absence really did make feelings fonder: try as she might, she couldn't stop liking Jim more than was wise. He was the strong male presence she wanted in her life, and she was being honest enough with herself to admit it.

This wasn't the quick flutter of the heart she'd felt for Larret, or the staid security of affection for an older man she'd known with Roland; no, this was the steady growth of a special bond, something deep and bewilderingly powerful . . . and unreciprocated.

Her eyes filled suddenly with tears. She wiped them angrily away. It's no use crying, Vee, she told herself. No use eating your heart out for a man who won't compromise his principles. You've got a choice, my dear: either you lump the situation, or you find yourself another job. It's as simple as that.

There was a footfall on the shingle behind her; the familiar smell of pipe tobacco. She forced herself to brighten, to hide her misery with a smile of welcome as she got up to greet her Uncle Wynford, for whom she'd been waiting.

'Well now—' her uncle said, giving her a hard look as she took his arm, 'what shall it be, a walk for our health, is it? Or did you invite my company so you can tell me what's troubling you.'

'Why should there be anything troubling me?' she replied, with the sort of chin-up cheerfulness that fooled nobody.

'That's for you to answer.' But his tone was sympathetic, and as they went down the shingle on to the sand he added, 'You're like your Dadda, you wear your heart in your face. It's nothing you have to be ashamed of, girl.'

Vanessa debated whether to confide in him. She needed somebody impartial she could talk to, and maybe her uncle's advice would help her to decide what to do for the best. Although they were near enough strangers, she had this sixth sense about him, that they shared the same bond of intuition, the same way of looking at life, that must have been inherited through the blood-ties of their Welshness.

And yet what could she say—? Uncle Wynford was like Jim, both were men of integrity, bound by the rules of an old-fashioned code of conduct moulded by their

326

background; and both were made of the same strong moral fibre that wouldn't be stretched to accommodate behaviour which flouted the rules of custom or propriety.

On reflection, Vanessa decided, it might be wiser if she kept her own counsel – as well as her uncle's good opinion of her.

'Uncle Wyn, I'm not going to waste a lovely evening boring you with my woes,' she said lightly. 'I'm sure you've heard enough from the aunts to know what a mess things are in with my marriage. Anyway . . . that's a problem for my husband to resolve.' She didn't mention the word divorce. 'No, the reason I wanted your company all to myself was because I've got something here for you—'

She loosed his arm to reach inside the pocket of her linen jacket.

'This is a return gift by way of saying thank you for giving me your copy of Dadda's poems,' she went on, taking out a book and holding it against her breast a moment before offering it to him. 'I wanted you to be the very first—'

Her uncle took the book from her and turned it over in his square, strong, shipwright's hands to read the spine. The gold-leaf of the title's lettering was edged in crimson where the gleam of sunset caught it.

'*Duw* . . .' he exclaimed, with a kind of awe mixed with his pleasure, '*Duw*, it's your book, is it . . . *Masks and Faces*!'

'An advance copy. I brought it down with me. Look – see, I've inscribed it specially—'

Vanessa opened the title page to show him. There in her generously rounded script she'd written, 'For Uncle

Wynford James, with grateful affection from his niece,
Vanessa Antrobus'.

For a second he was too overcome to speak. His eyes,
exactly the same shade of slate grey as her own, were
suspiciously bright as he read the inscription for himself
before closing the book again carefully, as though it were
something infinitely precious.

'That's for you and Dadda,' she said.

He looked at her, his weatherbeaten features with the
heavy dark moustache – so like her father's features –
working with emotion. Behind him the incoming tide
swirled round the ends of the breakwaters with a sigh
like the sound of memory.

'There's a thing now,' he said at last, gruffly, clearing
his throat. '*Duw*, there's proud you have made us, girl.'

And she knew he was speaking for them both, himself
and Dadda.

They had been to a film at one of the Berlin picture-houses
earlier in the evening. Lulu had wanted to see its leading
actress, Marlene Dietrich, whom she and her brother
Erich knew from the Schwanneke Artists' Club near
the Kurfürstendamm. Marlene had become the toast of
Berlin after appearing in the 'hit' review *It's In The Air*
last year, and now Lulu was following her career with
fascinated interest.

After watching the film tonight Roland understood
why. The actress had portrayed a beautiful but ruth-
less young woman treating her lover with cynical contempt, deliberately arousing him for her own amusement before spurning his approaches. He could see
why Lulu had hung on the role so avidly: it was one
which she herself played to perfection, even to the

distinctly bisexual appearance of the Dietrich character.

The film's peculiar aura of evil glamour seemed to have affected her, throwing her into one of her perverse moods. This afternoon she'd been so different, so wonderfully generous, when they'd driven out to the Wannsee to do some lakeside photography for an art calendar she was working on. She had permitted Roland to make love to her for the first time in months. She'd even suggested he stay the night at her apartment and they make love again – properly, the way he enjoyed it, the way they always used to.

He'd been so grateful he had wept.

It was things like this, her casual acts of kindness chucked like scraps to a famished dog, that made his unhappiness just about bearable. Lulu had become his hell on earth; and yet he was as besotted with her now as he'd been at the beginning. For love of this woman he had sacrificed his marriage, his home and business, his country, his friends, his self-respect; he was virtually bankrupt, not only financially but emotionally as well. The one fragile anchor of hope in his existence was that she might still agree to marry him, or at least make some commitment not to go with other men. But that was whistling for the moon, and Roland knew it.

Between his bouts of wretchedness and maudlin drunken anger, sometimes he tried to remember the kind of life he'd led before they'd met – and it was like looking down a long black tunnel towards a pinprick of sunlight. If he gave his wife Vanessa the divorce she was asking for (and he considered it often) what terrified Roland was that everything would vanish and leave him all alone in darkness, no road back and no road forward.

God . . . what a choice.

He raised his glass of schnapps and tossed it down. On the way home from the picture-house they'd dropped in at this nightclub, called the Pearl Kite. It was a place used by some of Lulu's friends, where beautiful homosexual boys danced with elegant older men and the waiters were White Russian émigrés, refugees from the Revolution, who sold icons as a side-line to champagne and cocaine.

Lulu had been flirting shamelessly with every man in sight from the minute they'd arrived. Now she was sitting on the lap of a fat, bald man who looked like a Heinrich Zille caricature of a typical Berliner, stroking his glistening head and smiling at Roland. Roland knew that smile. There was a hint of sadistic enjoyment in the way it curled her lips; it gave her eyes the slyness of a cat's watching the protracted suffering of something it was slowly killing.

'Roland, you drink too much,' she said when he gestured to the waiter for another schnapps. 'You will be no good for me tonight.' But even as she said it she was letting the fat man slide his hand inside her blouse and kiss her neck.

'What the hell does it matter how much I drink. You don't damn' well want me anyway,' he answered wretchedly in English.

She gave a cruel little shrug and whispered something that made the fat man laugh and look at Roland with the same sly look.

'Take no notice, she is only teasing,' her brother Erich came in, lolling back in his seat with an arm draped round the perfumed youth beside him. 'She does it to annoy you, my friend.'

'She does it because I love her and she bloody well likes to make me suffer,' Roland said.

330

'But *schatzi*, there can be no real love without suffering,' protested Lulu, 'otherwise what is the point—'

'No pain, no pleasure,' the perfumed youth said, casting his eyes up at Erich and giggling.

Lulu ignored him. 'When a man tells me that he loves me, how do I know it is true unless I break his heart? Any fool can be happy. Like *this* fool is happy—' She twisted the fat man's nose with sudden contempt, making him loose her breast. 'But you, Roland, your love it is like a martyrdom, you endure it because you hope perhaps your reward will be . . . in heaven, *nein*?'

Uncrossing her legs and getting to her feet, she smoothed her hands over her thighs in a way that was unmistakably suggestive.

'Like it was this afternoon?' Roland replied bitterly. 'Or does it amuse you, watching me having to grovel on my knees in front of you?'

'Something like that, *schatz*.'

As the waiter returned with Roland's order, she took the glass from the tray; and raising it to him, still with the same little smile curling her lips, she said in English, 'Here's to rewards in heaven—' and swallowed the schnapps in one long fluid movement.

'May its gates open for us all,' Erich added with a laugh, stroking the cheek of his perfumed companion, 'especially tonight, eh *hübschi*?'

Lulu laughed with him, a brittle sound, as artificial as the over-painted couples twined together in the smoky heat of the dance floor.

'Come—' Draping her jacket over her shoulder and blowing a kiss to the fat man, she took Roland by the hand.

'Have fun, Erich,' she told her brother. 'Don't be home too early—'

The fat man's pale, pig-like eyes followed her with Roland as they made their way across the floor. When they got to the stairs he glanced round and gave a discreet little nod to a youth dressed in the too-big lilac sack suit of a pimp, who'd been leaning against the wall watching their table.

The other acknowledged his signal. With his hands thrust in his pockets, he slipped away in the same direction.

The fat man's name was Bönisch. He worked as an agent for the N.S.D.A.P., the Nazi Party, and his particular speciality was sniffing out anyone whom the Party regarded as its enemy. These enemies included all those believed to be associated in any way with the parasitic conspiracy of Jewish capitalists and Marxists who were sucking the life-blood from the beloved Fatherland.

Bönisch had been watching Lulu and her brother for a long time. He had infiltrated himself into their company. He knew where they lived, and how they lived. He knew the clubs they went to, and the cafés they ate at, the names and addresses of their friends. He knew how much money they had; and he knew how much of that money went to fund their Communist activities. He was like a man making a study of a nest of rats: it was only a matter of time before he destroyed them all, but first he wanted to acquaint himself with their individual characteristics and habits.

He likewise knew about Roland of course. He had a dossier on Roland. Roland himself would have been surprised to learn that in that dossier he was marked down as 'probably of Jewish origin' because he'd owned an art gallery, and because he'd worked at a Berlin film studio whose pictures were directed and produced and often acted in by Jews, and because his surname looked Jewish to a man like Bönisch, even though it was actually more Aryan than Bönisch's own.

And as though all this were not enough, Roland Antrobus was doubly damned because he contributed money to the cause of Marxist Communism.

From the moment he'd returned to Berlin three months ago, he was a dead man. His name, and Lulu's, and Erich's and their friends', were already marked down in Bönisch's book for 'attention'.

But at least the Party allowed him his last few hours in Lulu's arms before they came to the apartment in the Tauentzienstrasse at two o'clock next morning, the youth in the lilac sack suit and his little gang of Brownshirts.

27

Under its front-page headline 'Tragic Death of Local Arts Patron' the *Express & Star* had reproduced a photograph of Roland Antrobus and Luise von Losch taken at the opening of Lulu's exhibition at the Gallery two years ago in 1927.

The couple were standing together smiling into the camera, both dressed in black tie and tails, Roland looking smugly pleased with himself, Lulu with an enigmatic lift of the eyebrow that gave a touch of hardness to her androgynous features.

Further down the page was another photo, this one of Vanessa. It had been taken more recently, to accompany an article Dulcie Fox had written on the July publication of *Masks and Faces*, and showed Vanessa with a copy of her book looking luminously young and beautiful.

There was nothing in either picture to hint at the drama detailed in the news account of Roland's death. Nothing to suggest the morbidly bizarre events which had brought the three of them again to public notice.

The initial findings of the Berlin police had seemed to indicate that Roland had shot his lover in a fit of jealous passion before turning the pistol on himself – a scenario deliberately stage-managed by the killers. However, the inquest produced enough evidence to prove that both had been shot and killed by 'person or persons unknown', a verdict which suited the Nazi Party almost as well, and while it deceived no one, at least cleared Roland's name of murder.

Vanessa had been given the terrible news a day or so after the event. In her shock and distress it was only natural that the person to whom she'd turned for help should be Jim Brockhouse; that it was Jim who went with her to the Hook of Holland to receive her husband's body; and Jim who dealt with all the necessary forms and documents and funeral arrangements.

Ernest Parrish wouldn't have done it. Ernest Parrish was too busy trying to distance himself from the whole ghastly business.

Without the strength of Jim's support and sympathy, and the consolation of her mother and Sybil, Vanessa didn't know how on earth she would have managed. The fact that she was separated from Roland did nothing to lessen her grief that he was dead, nor her illogical guilt that he'd died in such a horrible manner. For all his faults he hadn't been a bad man, only a weak one; and maybe if they'd both tried a little harder in the beginning their marriage might not have gone off the rails.

Regrets like these were very painful. She needed to mourn; needed to come to terms with the sudden jolt into widowhood and its implications for her future. That September she went back to the Dordogne for a couple of weeks to stay with the Tiersots. At Madge's insistence everyone respected her wishes to be alone; even Victor Michelet, who called at Le Palombier to pay his condolences and went sadly away without seeing her again.

There was something to be said for solitude. Perhaps it was the healing quality of the peace and beauty of the

Dordogne landscape, but when Vanessa returned home she felt she had just completed some kind of rite of passage between one life and another.

The house in St John's Square which Jim Brockhouse had bought in 1924 was one of an elegant terrace of Georgian properties on the south side, each approached by steps leading from the street to a porticoed doorway framed between tall sash windows.

It was a large place for a man to live alone, but Jim liked a lot of room to move about in. He employed a woman to come in a couple of times a week to clean and do, but other than that he fended for himself quite capably. Most of the furniture was good solid quality mahogany, stuff he'd purchased when it was out of style with dealers, and pictures he'd picked up at auctions and suchlike – mostly watercolours reflecting his love of nature and the countryside.

Since his wife's death he'd kept very much to himself. His few visitors generally included his sister-in-law, Mary Carter, who on this particular Sunday had been invited with her husband Norman to make up a foursome at lunch with Vanessa.

The meal being over, Mary was now leaning back on the sofa in her brother-in-law's comfortable sitting room, exchanging significant glances with her husband.

Addressing herself to Jim's back, she said, 'Just who d'you think you're kidding, Jim? You can't tell us you're feeling *sorry* for her. If you want my opinion there's more to it than feeling bloomin' sorry – in't there, Norman.'

Norman Carter, a dapper young man with a short-sighted peering expression behind round-rimmed spectacles, nodded vigorously.

'I mean to say,' continued Mary, 'she's attractive and smart, and ever so easy to get on with, so we wouldn't blame you if you – well, y'know – if you like, *fancied* her. Would we, Norman.'

Norman shook his head equally vigorously.

Jim Brockhouse carried on gazing through the window into the walled garden behind the house, his eyes fixed on Vanessa standing out there in the soft October sunshine.

'I'm glad to hear you say that, Mary,' he answered sombrely, not turning round. 'I mean no disrespect to Peggy's memory, God knows . . . but I've still got a life o' my own ahead o' me. I can't spend it living like some blasted hermit.'

''Course you can't, mate.' Norman exchanged another quick glance with his wife. ''T in't natural, bloke your age. It's just that we thought, Mary and me – well, there in't smoke wi'out fire and we could see the way the wind's been blowing since Mrs Antrobus come back from France. You don't have to pretend wi' us, mate. We'm on your side. We only hope it all works out for you, like – in't that right, Mary.'

The young woman put down her teacup, wiping the corner of her mouth with a well-manicured finger. She was fond of Vanessa. Slightly in awe of her maybe, but there was nothing like being on first name terms with a real live authoress to enhance one's social lustre.

'I guessed there was some'at up when I catched you reading poems,' she observed slyly, watching her brother-in-law's face as he moved from the window. 'Football results is one thing. But poetry – I ask you!'

'There's nothing wrong wi' self-improvement,' Jim said tersely.

He hadn't told lies when he'd confessed to enjoying

Housman, that day spent with Vanessa in Bridgnorth last February. True, he had wanted very much to impress her, to smooth some of the roughness from his working class image in the hope she'd think a bit more highly of him; but his fondness for the beauty of language was something he'd acquired in the adult institutes which had given him the education his background had denied him.

'Not that it makes a ha'porth o' difference,' he added after a second, thrusting the dark lick of hair from his eyes. 'I could try and improve myself till the cows come home, but I know I'll never be good enough for Vanessa.' The way his voice lingered on her name was like an act of worship.

'Has *she* said as much?' queried Mary.

'No, o' course she ain't.'

'Then how d'you know, Jim, eh? Have you even asked her?'

'Am I likely to ask her some'at like that?'

'If you don't you'm never going to get anywhere, mate,' Norman chipped in again. 'If I was you I'd take the bull by the horns and come straight out wi' it, no beating round the bush, like. Honesty's your best policy, I'd say.' He had an unconscious habit of talking in clichés.

'Aye . . . mebbe.' Jim glanced again towards the window. 'Any road I don't want to keep Vanessa waiting. She's been left on her own long enough—' a statement with a subtle ambiguity. 'D'you mind if I go and keep her company?'

'You carry on. It's time we was off home anyway,' Mary responded at once, tactfully, looking round for her handbag. 'You ready to make a move, Norman?'

Norman got to his feet; and on a sudden impulse,

holding out a hand to Jim, he said warmly, 'Well, here's good luck to you, mate. You blinkin' well deserve it an' all. Just remember, faint heart never won fair lady, eh.'

When they'd left, having said their goodbyes and see you soons to Vanessa, Jim went out to join her in the garden. It was very peaceful here. The mellow golden light of afternoon spilled over the old brick walls bathing everything in a glow of autumn colour, and the air was full of the scent of the last of summer's roses still in bloom. The sound of somebody playing an oboe drifted from an open window nearby, lending the scene a haunting sweetness; and further off, beyond St John's Square, the occasional noise of Sunday motor traffic carried from Snow Hill.

Vanessa had wandered to the bottom of the garden where an old-fashioned rose bush grew against the wall, its blowsy velvet petals swooning open in the warmth.

As Jim approached she turned to smile at him, and said, 'We had this one at "Mayville". It's always been my favourite.'

'Aye, and mine.'

'I know.' She didn't say why. 'You've made a beautiful garden here,' she added instead, looking round her.

'Well, it's some'at as gives me a lot o' pleasure. And it gets me away from the scrapyard.' He followed her glance briefly. 'Peggy always liked that rose an' all.'

Vanessa cupped one of the deep pink blooms between her hands and bent her head to smell its fragrance, just as Jim himself had done that time, so long ago.

'You do miss her still, don't you,' she said quietly.

'Miss her, aye . . . aye, I suppose I do. Funny thing though, I don't seem to pine for her any more, Vanessa.

It's almost as if she's let me go at last, if you can understand.'

She looked up and found he was watching her. The expression in his eyes held the same disturbing intensity she had so often seen in her dreams, and she had to look down again quickly before her own eyes should betray her.

'Yes, I can understand that, I think.'

They turned and began walking back a little way towards a latticed arch smothered in sweetbriar framing the path. As they passed beneath it their hands touched accidentally; the merest contact of skin against skin, but it was enough.

Jim stopped.

'Vanessa, there's some'at I want to say to you—'

Now the moment had come he wasn't too sure how he ought to express himself. So much hung on what he was going to tell her, he was afraid of putting things badly and risking upsetting her.

He took the plunge. 'I'm not much good wi' words, but this is some'at as won't keep . . . and when you've heard me out mebbe it'll put the kibosh on our acquaintance, I don't know, it's up to you.'

Her heart gave a lurch. All day his manner towards her had been so strained and awkward even the Carters must have noticed. She waited apprehensively; and as though embarrassed by her silence he hurried on,

'You might think it's too soon after your husband's . . . well, after all you've been through, and I'm sorry if what I'm going to say sounds forward or unwelcome. But then I've always been a clumsy fool where you're concerned, my love.'

'No, that's not so—' she protested warmly. It was the

341

first time he'd called her by an endearment, and she clung in hope to the words, hugging them to her. 'I've never met a man as considerate and kind as you, Jim. God knows where I'd have been without you these last months.'

'I was glad to share some o' the burden. There's nothing I wouldn't do for you, you know that.' He paused. 'I suppose . . . I suppose while you were in France you dain't think about me ever . . . mebbe fondly?'

Vanessa sensed what it was costing him to ask her this. She raised her face, the sunlight tracing her cheek with the shadows of rose leaves. After a moment she said softly, 'I thought about you all the time.'

He gave a laugh of disbelief. 'You did?'

'Yes. I wondered whether I was being ridiculous to care so much for a man who could offer me nothing but friendship. I hope I was wrong.'

'*Friendship*—?' Jim stared at her. 'D'you imagine friendship's all it is? Dear God, don't you know how I feel about you?'

'I don't know anything. You've never said.'

'I'm saying now.'

She tried to read the change in his expression, praying that what she saw there was what she desperately longed it to be. 'You've always been so careful to keep your distance,' she said uncertainly. 'I thought you didn't want to get involved. You've never done anything that led me to suppose your feelings were more than . . . sympathetic.'

'Then I've put on a damn' good act. Shall I tell you the truth, my darling? The fact o' the matter is . . . I'm heart and soul in love wi' you. It was that day we spent at Bridgnorth, that's when I realised how much I was starting to love you – and I've been scared stiff ever since that I was going to do some'at to frighten you off me.'

Vanessa put her hand to her throat. Her heart was pounding so much she could feel herself trembling.

'You love me—?' It was incredible. She hardly dared to believe it.

'Aye. You're the only thing I live for.' He pulled her into his arms, holding her tightly, not knowing what else to say, overwhelmed by the sudden intensity of his need for her.

'Oh, my dearest,' she said on a little catch of breath, 'my dearest . . .'

Raising her head she looked into his face, seeing the honest decency of character in his features, the strength of his mouth, the warmth of his eyes, the way his hair fell forward on his brow. She knew every inch and line of that face and would never grow tired of it.

'D'you think I'm good enough for you,' he said thickly, 'an ordinary working bloke like me?'

She gave a quivering smile, and nodded; and just before he found her lips she whispered, 'I love you too . . .' words she'd spoken in the lonely darkness of her nights, words she'd murmured to his dream-self.

There was so much to talk about, so much to explain, so much laughter now the barriers were down at last. All the silly, stupid doubts were cleared away, all the anxieties each had entertained, the uncertainties and misunderstandings which for so many months had clogged their relationship.

That was the happiest autumn Vanessa could ever remember. She and Jim went out and about together everywhere, getting to know one another as people in love, not people apart. They spent Christmas Day as guests of the Parrishes at Tettenhall Green, Ernest Parrish putting a good face on things for the sake of the season; and on New Year's Eve they were invited as a couple to celebrate the engagement of Sybil to Michael Wright at a dinner dance at the Star & Garter Hotel.

It was the end of a decade. A time to bid farewell to the old ghosts of the past and begin again, the slate wiped clean, for a brighter and more promising tomorrow.